THE
FINAL
TRADE

ALSO BY JOE HART

NOVELS

Lineage
Singularity
EverFall
The River Is Dark
The Waiting
Widow Town
Cruel World
The Last Girl
The Night Is Deep

NOVELLAS

Leave the Living
The Exorcism of Sara May

SHORT STORY COLLECTIONS

Midnight Paths: A Collection of Dark Horror

SHORT STORIES

"The Line Unseen"
"The Edge of Life"
"Outpost"
"And The Sea Called Her Name"

THE FINAL TRADE

BOOK TWO
THE DOMINION TRILOGY

JOE HART

THOMAS & MERCER

Published by Thomas & Mercer, Seattle

www.apub.com

Amazon, the Amazon logo, and Thomas & Mercer are trademarks of Amazon.com, Inc., or its affiliates.

ISBN-13: 9781503936799
ISBN-10: 1503936791

Cover design by M.S. Corley

Printed in the United States of America

To my son, who reminds me daily to never give up.

Righteous fire burns both the wicked and the innocent.

—Anonymous

BEFORE . . .

She ran with the newborn pressed tightly against her chest as another explosion roared somewhere behind her.

The ground, muddy from days of rain, yielded to each of her steps, slowing her, holding her back as she struggled to distance herself from the onslaught of whining bullets and the screams of the dying. A plane streaked overhead close enough to make her eardrums flutter, and she ducked involuntarily, shielding the child with her body.

Her feet slipped in the mud and she began to fall, but a strong hand caught her. She looked into the face of the man beside her, eyes steady and unwavering as his grip.

"Come on!" he shouted over another blast of explosives. "We have to get over the hill!"

They ran.

A stray bullet zipped past, tugging up a spray of mud and water only feet to their left.

The baby began to cry.

The sound of a helicopter carried over the tumult but she couldn't make out from which direction it came. Hard to think. Impossible to decide what to do. There was only the baby along with the fear and weakness invading her body.

They reached the crest of the hill and paused, the man glancing back the way they'd come. He'd lost his gun somewhere during their flight, and now he had only the knife on his hip for protection. Not enough if they were cornered. Through the rolling smoke, the outline of a building emerged.

He gripped her arm harder and turned toward the structure. "Inside."

The building's south wall was partially blown away, an errant bomb having carved steel and concrete so that the fighting was clearly visible from this higher vantage point. They moved past a twisted mass of smoldering iron that might've once been a truck and found an alcove of reinforced concrete block.

She slid down against the wall, legs finally giving out. The baby let out another stuttering cry as heavy artillery pounded out a cadence of death across the plain. The man stood watching at the gap in the wall, his back heaving.

"We can't stay here," he said.

"I know, but I have to rest," she said, rocking from side to side. The infant's cries became more muted, less frequent. "You're okay," she whispered. "You're safe."

The man came away from the hole in the wall and sat beside them, his callused hand brushing so gently at the top of the baby's head.

"They'll try to take her if they find us," she said, looking into his sweat- and soot-smeared face.

"They won't find us. We're going to be okay."

The woman looked down at the child, still rocking her. She was nearly asleep, tiny eyelids halfway closed.

"We'll never let you go, Zoey. Never," she whispered, as the fighting raged on outside their sanctuary.

AFTER . . .

1

Run.

Zoey's feet dig hard into the loose silt and rock of the rising embankment a hundred feet above the highway. The sun is a bright disc behind a voluminous cloudbank coasting across the sky, shoved by a wind that tastes of dust as she sprints upward.

Run.

The man above her throws a look over his shoulder, eyes going wide at seeing that she's gained on him. He's dressed in dingy work pants and a faded red vest that flaps behind him like bloody wings. His hair is shaggy and dark, hanging down nearly to his shoulders. Zoey can smell him, smell the panic in his sweat, and she knows he's out of ammunition and time.

He reaches the summit of the sloping canyon wall and doesn't look back again as he disappears over the ridge of red, shattered rock. Zoey is barely winded as she scrambles up the last dozen feet and leaps onto the shelf. Merrill yells something from far below, but she doesn't stop to listen. She knows he's telling her to wait.

She grits her teeth. It would be easy to kill the spy, so simple to pull the trigger, but he might be able to tell them something useful. So instead she chases, waiting for the right time to strike.

The man scrambles up and over the top of the rise, layered in wide steps of blasted rock, as Zoey climbs into view.

Their eyes meet and then he is running again, parallel to the slope now.

Zoey zigs to the side, holstering the nine-millimeter Heckler & Koch handgun. She's so familiar with the weapon now, she doesn't need to look at the pressure holster to know it's secure. Her legs burn but feel strong. They're no longer weak and wasted as they were four months ago when she took her first unassisted steps. Weeks upon weeks of rehabilitation and strength training have brought them back to a lean and muscular state, and the rest of her body has followed suit.

She has never been this powerful. Never this fast.

The man eyes her again as she comes even with him on the lower stepped level. Without slowing he bends, snags a fist-sized rock and spins, hurling it at her head.

Zoey ducks, the rock snagging a tuft of hair from her ponytail before it falls out of sight.

He dodges left behind a monolithic boulder that's eroding at a ninety-degree angle. She takes the opportunity to leap up, thrusting herself with one hand, onto the next step.

Whipping the gun out of its holster, she covers the rock, moving around its opposite side. He isn't waiting for her as she'd hoped. A shadow flows across the rock beside her and she flinches, thinking somehow he's flanked her. But it is only a buzzard coasting high overhead, ragged wings motionless, riding the air currents.

Rocks clack together beyond the boulder and she moves forward, feet finding solid footholds as she descends.

The opposite side of the bluff is as sheer as its front is sloped. Here is the evidence of violent change done by millennia of ice that once moved through the area. The rock drops away in a dizzying openness for hundreds of feet before rolling out to a sandy floor strewn with fallen chunks of stone.

Her quarry runs along the edge toward a gap between their bluff and the next. Beyond that the upthrust stone gradually slants back into the desert like a spine into malnourished flesh. She follows, wind tearing at her like an enemy.

The man doesn't slow as he reaches the gap.

Zoey can see it's too wide. He'll never make it. She curses and skids to a stop, raising the gun.

Takes a second to breathe.

Kill him.

She starts to squeeze the trigger.

Her aim comes up. Centers on his back. *No.*

The gunshot shocks her and for a moment she thinks she's fired, that she's given in to the impulse to simply end him. But in that split second, she realizes she's taken her finger off the trigger.

One of the others.

The bullet hits his right hamstring as he begins his leap.

He pitches headfirst into the gully, a scream trailing up through the dry air for a moment before silence rushes back in. She curses and hurries to the edge.

The NOA spy lies on his back twenty feet below in a narrow ravine of broken slate. He stares up at her, blood coating his lips and staining the rock around his leg. Zoey glances around the drop, calculating quickly. Holsters the gun, then jumps.

She hits the first outcropping eight feet down on the opposite side of the gap and springs from it immediately, landing on another jutting lip of stone that breaks off. She falls the last ten feet to where the man lies.

When she meets the ground all feeling goes out of her legs.

Her knees fold and she crumples to all fours, gravel biting through her pants. Dust puffs into her face, blinding, choking. She gasps. *Stupid, stupid, stupid. All that work and now you've ruined yourself again.* She tries to rotate her ankles and after a terrifying moment of zero response, her feet begin to move.

Slowly the feeling returns, first in her lower back, then in her thighs, and finally her toes. It seeps in like warm water in a cold bath, and she grits her teeth, wobbling upright.

The man coughs out a mouthful of crimson, and she stumbles to his side, ripping the belt from around her waist. Arterial blood jets from a ragged exit wound on the front of his thigh. He coughs again except this time she realizes he's laughing.

"Was it worth it, bitch?" he breathes. "Hope so."

"You're going to make it worth it," Zoey says, snugging the belt around his thigh above the wound. She cinches it tight and the man grunts with pain, eyes going blank for a beat before his breath wheezes out. The flow diminishes.

"Where were you coming from?" she asks. When he only smiles at her, she picks up a long, thin piece of slate, and before she can stop herself, jams it into his wound. The man bellows.

"Town called Hellings," he sputters, and she pulls the rock out of his leg. He blinks rapidly and she knows there isn't much time.

"What were you doing there?"

"Looking for you. Looking for more women."

"Did you find any?"

"No. Between NOA and the Fae Trade they're pretty scarce."

Zoey clenches her teeth and resists stabbing him with the slate again. *Fae Trade.* The name never ceases to make her stomach turn. A traveling auction dealing in slaves, both women and men. Somewhere on the other side of the V between the two bluffs, Merrill is yelling her name, coming closer. "Records of the women that were held at the ARC, they have all of their history, right?"

"Yes."

"Like family, where NOA took them from, where they lived before that?"

"Yes."

"Where are the records?"

"Secure. In the ARC." He smiles again and she does stab him this time. His scream is choked, as though he's gargling glass.

"Are there copies anywhere else?"

He closes his eyes for a long time until Zoey slaps him awake. There is a soft gurgle in his chest and above it comes the sound of footsteps approaching the gap in the rock nearby. "Copies," Zoey says again. "Are there any outside of the ARC?"

"Yes."

"Where?"

"Zoey," Merrill says, climbing through the space between the two bluffs. Behind him are Tia and Eli, guns drawn and ready.

"Where are they?" she asks the man again.

He sputters, blood foaming on his lips. "Riverbend. Missile," he manages before his eyelids flutter and close. Zoey tries to shake him awake but he's out.

"What the hell were you thinking?" Merrill asks, stopping on the opposite side of the spy's body. Merrill's right pant leg is hiked up, caught on the head of a small bolt protruding from the shiny aluminum of the prosthetic leg that extends from his knee.

"He was going to get away."

"We could have headed him off. The four of us. It's a good thing Eli hit him. You could've gotten yourself killed."

"I didn't."

"But he's dead. And that does us zero good," Tia says, spitting beside the man's head.

"No he's not. Not yet."

She looks up at them. Tia meets her gaze and frowns, while Eli stares down at the bloody ground.

Merrill sighs and shifts on the slate. "Did you get anything out of him?"

"They're looking for me. When I asked him if copies of the women's information were stored anywhere else he said 'riverbend missile.' Does that mean anything to you guys?"

Eli and Tia shake their heads, but Merrill's gaze is steady on her. "Riverbend was a government missile installation in southern Idaho. Friends of mine did some training there when we were in the army."

Zoey stands. The records are what she's longed for, some link to her past, something to tether her to who she really is. And she's wanted it not only for herself, but for Rita and Sherell and all the girls she couldn't save. "You know where it is?"

"Yes. But that doesn't mean he's telling the truth."

"He wasn't lying."

"Regardless," Eli says, "we should get going. We're only sixty miles south of the ARC and they have at least one helicopter up and running. They could be here in a few minutes if that truck he and his friends were driving had a tracking device on it."

The man groans quietly as his eyes come half open. One arm rakes the ground weakly.

"We can't take him with us," Tia says.

"No, we can't." Merrill seems to grapple with something, then glances at Zoey. "Go ahead out to the road." He draws his handgun. "I'll be there in a second."

Zoey puts a hand on his arm recalling the lack of remorse in the man's eyes. "You don't have to." She crouches beside the spy. "Can you hear me?" After a long moment he nods. "You're bleeding internally and it looks like your leg's broken. When you're ready, take that tourniquet off."

She stands and walks with the rest of the group in the direction of the vehicle, and she doesn't look back when the man's pleading voice echoes out of the canyon.

2

It takes them the rest of the day and into the evening to reach the turn-off in the foothills of the Cascades.

When the mountains appear in the late afternoon, the sight has the effect of balm to a wound. Their gray outlines mean safety and home, something Zoey never had prior to six months ago.

Before that she knew nothing but the inside of the National Obstetric Alliance's Advance Research Compound. The nightmares reliving her flight from the facility are always in slow motion. The Director aiming his gun at Terra's head; her friend's last words—that she hadn't held her son before they'd discarded him like some piece of medical waste from the tank he was grown in; the gunshot, deafening in the cold space of the infirmary.

She and Terra and the other women had been stripped from their families, held captive, told that the virus that caused the dearth of female infants had turned deadly and killed nearly all of the world's population.

When in truth the American government had wiped out many of its own citizens in a massive civil war.

She can't help the derisive sigh that escapes her. Merrill glances over from the driver's seat of the Suburban, its yellowed headlights staining the narrow dirt road that leads to the undergrowth where they hide the vehicle. No one has spoken much on the ride back, and she knows it's because of her actions. She was irresponsible, dangerous, reckless. She should've waited for backup. A lance of shame runs through her, then dulls: *Riverbend. Missile.* It was information they needed.

As if reading her thoughts, Merrill says, "Riverbend's a long ways."

"You don't have to go. You just have to tell me how to get there."

The words come out sharper than intended, and she winces. She owes the entire group Rita's and Sherell's lives as well as her own. Her newfound friends had rallied around her, helping her rehabilitate not only her body, but her soul as well. All of them have been wonderful.

Except for Lee.

In the days following his departure from Ian's home, she tried to think about him as little as possible, since his absence hurt nearly as much as the therapy she endured each day. But as hard as she tried to forget him, he's remained an immovable fixture in her mind. Growing up in the ARC, he was her cleric's son and, early in her life, her occasional playmate. Later he became the one person who stirred a bright passion deep within her. Now his memory brings sadness riddled with spikes of anger.

Zoey gazes out the window into the blanketing night that covers the side of the mountain. She knows it's foolish to linger on memories. She has to focus on moving forward, and she can't deny today was a breakthrough.

"You know I wouldn't let you go alone," Merrill says.

"You'll stop me?" She looks in his direction as he drifts the Suburban over to a hidden path below the leaning pines on the side of the road.

"It's obvious now that I can't stop you from doing anything," he says, bringing the vehicle to a halt under the canopy of branches. Eli and Tia climb out, grabbing gear and making every effort not to get involved in the conversation. "I want you to think long and hard about what you're going to do, because like it or not, it affects everyone."

"That's exactly what they pounded into us in the ARC. If one of us broke the rules the next closest woman was punished as well. They kept us bound to each other." Lily's smiling face comes back to her then, the excitement radiating off her after pronouncing a word correctly. She sees Lily raising her arms up and down in the light of the flames from the downed helicopter, pretending to be a bird. One of Zoey's hands strays to her stomach and touches the healed bullet wound. Amidst the memory her anger rises even as she tries to quell the emotion.

"You know what I mean. All I'm asking is you not make a snap decision. Things aren't the same as they were before. Chelsea and Tia have been hunted for a long time. They still are. Now there's you, Sherell, and Rita to think about. If any of you were taken or hurt, I . . ." He stops himself, and she knows he's thinking about his daughter Meeka, her best friend and one of the women she failed to save.

"What?"

Merrill's voice softens. "I get that you want to know your heritage, find out what your last name is, see the place where you and your parents lived before all this. And I know you want that for Rita and Sherell too." She says nothing. The pines whisper and creak in the late autumn air. "I'm not asking you to give that up. But always remember you already have a family you'll never have to go looking for."

The darkness hides most of his features, and as she looks at him something bends, nearly breaking, inside of her before coming back into place. She swallows the knot in her throat and is about to reply when he climbs out of the vehicle.

"Let's get this old pig covered up," he says.

◆　◆　◆

After concealing the Suburban with camouflage netting, they begin the hike to Ian's cabin. They move single file through the forest that covers the side of the mountain like a maze. There is little ambient light from the cloud-smothered moon to see by, but Zoey could find the cabin with her eyes shut.

Here is the rock that looks like a dog lying on its back. Here is the broken tree that fell in a storm two months ago. Here is the scent of food drifting down through the forest. Here is the only true home she's ever known.

Dancing firelight appears in the dark, and after they wind through a section of crumbling rock and bramble, the cabin appears.

Built into the side of the mountain, its original structure is hidden almost completely from sight. The addition that's been constructed over the last four months looks native to the surrounding forest, with its supports of unfinished pine and steel roof thatched over with needles and boughs. In front of the dwelling a small fire burns in a pit and four grouse cook above it on a spit. A low growl comes from their right and a large, black dog appears, eyes reflecting the firelight.

"Seamus! Come here!" Zoey says, setting her bag down and kneeling. The dog's growling ceases and he bounds over, nearly knocking her flat as he runs into her. "Fat dog. You gained weight since we left," she says, scratching him behind the ears.

"He'd eat all our food if we let him," Eli says as he passes. "Big bastard needs to go on a diet."

"You're just pissed that he's in better shape than you are," Tia says.

"I'm a specimen of fitness. Look at this," he says, flexing both biceps so that they bulge in his shirtsleeves.

"That really does nothing for me."

"Admit it, I'm wearing you down."

"I'll turn straight the day you're not black anymore."

"Workin' on it, baby. I haven't tanned in nearly a month."

Their banter pulls laughter from Zoey as she gives Seamus one last pet and grabs her bag. A tall form stands beside the fire as they approach. Ian's smile lights up his entire face and even with his smashed and crooked nose, the old man is handsome.

"The wanderers return," he says, gathering Zoey into a hug. He is the only person unabashed about doing this. Everyone else in the group is always hesitant to touch her. For the longest time she assumed it was out of respect for her ordeal and paralysis, but now she's not so sure.

Ian holds her shoulders, studying her. "You're all safe?"

"Safe and sound."

"So good to have you back. Was the trip worth it?"

She glances at Merrill, who gives her a sidelong look. "I think so."

"Excellent, even better having risked and gained," Ian says. "Come sit by the fire; the birds are almost done."

As she's settling onto a wooden chair next to the fire pit, the cabin's front door bangs open, accompanied by a short squeal of happiness. Chelsea sprints down the stairs and leaps into Merrill's arms, kissing him hard on the mouth.

"You were gone so long," Chelsea says when she's separated herself from him.

"It was only ten days," Merrill says.

"That's long enough."

"Tell me about it," Eli says, settling into a chair opposite Zoey. "My ass is flat as a pancake from sleeping on the damn ground." He gives her a wink.

"That thing'll never flatten out," Tia says, pouring herself a glass of whiskey before handing the bottle to Eli. Three shadows detach from the addition that's still being constructed, and a second later Newton's and Sherell's faces appear in the dark, followed by Rita. Zoey notices with some amusement how close Sherell walks beside Newton. Rita and Sherell draw two more chairs to either side of her and immediately begin asking questions.

"Did you find any?"

"How about the chopper, did you see it? We heard it two days ago."

"How far did you go?"

Zoey grins. It had been all she could do to convince Rita and Sherell to stay behind. Both women are fully capable of taking care of themselves, but there is no denying she has an edge on them when it comes to fighting and shooting. She made it her sole purpose during and after her rehabilitation to learn everything Merrill could teach her about weapons and the ground fighting he calls jiujitsu, even with Chelsea's constant chiding about re-injuring her bruised spinal cord.

"We never saw a chopper, but we found a reconnaissance group." The low chatter around the fire stops. Zoey looks at Merrill for approval and he tips his head. "We caught wind of them southeast of here near the edge of the desert. Merrill and Eli heard people talking about three armed strangers asking about recent births and younger women. When we caught up to them and saw they were heading in the direction of the ARC, we set up an ambush to disable their vehicle, but it didn't work exactly how we planned."

She pauses, takes a sip of water, then finishes the story about chasing and interrogating the surviving spy. When she's done there is only the crackling of flames and the constant whisper of wind in the pines.

"So are we going there?" Sherell asks. "Do you think there's a chance we'll find out who our families are?" Zoey realizes the question is directed at her, not at Merrill or Ian or the rest of the group. She glances at Merrill.

"Everyone's agreed," Merrill says. "This is important enough to you three that we'll help you any way we can. No one in the group was given an ultimatum. Each person decided for themselves. If Meeka had escaped I would've wanted someone to help her find me."

Zoey looks at the people ringing the fire and the same choking sensation returns. Chelsea, the doctor and mother to them all. Eli, always there to make her smile. Ian, never without a kind word or encouragement. Newton, mute but so gentle and intelligent. Tia, gruff but insightful. And Merrill, another name for him she can't quite get herself to say yet.

They all gaze back. Her family.

Forcing away the tears that threaten to spill out, she says to Sherell and Rita, "If they're all in agreement then we should probably have our own meeting."

"I'm going," Rita says. "There's nothing—"

"After dinner," Ian interrupts, standing to retrieve the dripping birds from over the fire. "First we eat."

◆　◆　◆

The grouse is perfectly done and Zoey has to restrain herself from eating more than her share. After ten days of subsisting on cold meals out of cans, dried jerky, and water, the warm dinner is luxurious. When they're finished, the rest of the group begins to clean up while Zoey leads Sherell and Rita into the addition that consists of four new rooms, three of which are theirs. The bedrooms are simple and not entirely finished. There is still insulating to do, locks to be installed, more camouflage to be added, but each is a space of their own that reflects their personas: Sherell's walls plastered with her drawings, Rita's table stacked with books, her appetite for reading almost as voracious as Zoey's. But her own room is less adorned than those of the other women, a little bleaker, and she realizes that it mirrors her better than she thought. Regardless, the rooms are so much different than the cold, impersonal quarters they lived in at the ARC.

Prison cells, Zoey thinks as they enter her room. *Call them what they were.* Sherell and Rita take positions on the modest bed that Ian constructed out of scrap lumber while Zoey sits on a chair in the corner of the room.

For a second they are silent, merely looking at one another before Zoey says, "I know I don't have to ask either of you what you want to do because you feel the same as I do. But there's something to think about before we make a decision. This really is no longer their fight. They've taken us in, fed us, protected us, and now we're asking them to put themselves in danger again. It isn't fair, especially to Tia and Chelsea. They'd be hunted the same as us the moment someone saw them."

The other women seem to digest this before Sherell says, "I don't want them to have to go, but we need them if we're going to get there." She adjusts her dark hair behind her ear. "It's funny. I shouldn't care about people I've never really known before. I don't remember my parents at all. Can't bring up their faces or the sound of their voices, nothing. By all rights they're probably dead, but . . ." She shrugs. "I can't get away from that feeling. That need to know. It's there every day like a bruise that doesn't heal."

The room grows quiet again except for the slight hiss of wind that sneaks into and out of the rooms through the cracks in the walls. There is so much work to do here. There is life in this place. Potential. They could stay here, forget the past completely and forge ahead. *Always remember you already have a family you'll never have to go looking for.*

But Sherell's words are still there, hovering in Zoey's mind like a fog.

"My mother has a scar over her right eyebrow," Rita says, jolting Zoey from her thoughts. Rita stares at the floor between her feet. "I remember touching it once, tracing the line. It was like an L laid on its side. I asked her where she'd gotten it and she told me to be quiet. I think maybe my father had hit her. She wasn't pretty. She had big hands and a wide forehead like mine. But I thought she was beautiful and that the scar only added to it." Rita looks up and Zoey is surprised to see a shine to her eyes. "I think that's maybe why I was so angry all the time before. Because I envied everyone who couldn't remember anything. If you've never had it, how can you miss it, right?" She looks down at her hands. "Halie and Grace were like that. No memories of where they came from, so they were in no hurry for their induction. I'm not sure if they even minded being at the ARC. Halie asked me to walk around the promenade with her one day, a year before her ceremony, and I spit on her. She was just trying to be nice, but I was so angry at everyone because each day that passed was a day I couldn't get back to the only person I knew who truly loved me." She wipes at her nose and blinks rapidly. "I'm going no matter what."

Zoey feels the ghostly slide of soft hair through her fingers, the only memory she has, and the ache is there.

The bruise that never heals.

"We'll leave in two days," she says.

3

I am a comet, Wen thinks.

She sits up in her cot, early morning air creeping in through the broken zipper of the tent. More than cool, it is cold. *Always moving, never stopping.* She hears the sounds of the trade breaking down. The rev of an engine, tent poles rattling, men cussing at one another, at everything, at nothing. She's never gotten used to how early they leave. It isn't yet dawn.

She rises and pulls on her dusty cargo pants and stained blouse, fingering the tear near the collar. A man grabbed her as she was moving between two of the game stands last night, even though it's expressly forbidden to touch her. Before she could stick the sharpened crochet hook she typically carries into his stomach, he'd torn her only decent blouse. She'd left him lying and moaning in a spreading pool of blood while the fluting calliope music played obscenely on the midway. And she hadn't cried this time after closing her tent for the night.

She undoes the tent's flaps and peers outside.

The flatness of the Nevada desert is still startling to her even after seeing it dozens of times on the trade's routes. The scrub that stretches for miles is a muted purple, glimmering with frost, in the predawn light. The dry, packed dirt, cracked and veined beneath the low brush, fades into obscurity outside the borders of the town they camped near. To the west is the smudge of the Sierra Nevadas, their grandeur struck down by distance.

She sees this all past the jutting outlines of the carnival tents and fifteen-foot chain-link fence that acts as the trade's border. Even now the fence sags as it's deconstructed, poles being pulled by the dark shapes of men, a hauling truck trundling before them.

Wen breathes the air, the cold burning her lungs. They'll want their food soon. There isn't much time.

She dons her heaviest coat and heads toward one of the few buildings that is solid wood, instead of fraying canvas, keeping the image of a comet in her mind. The trade only pauses, never stops for good, and she is no different. What was the book she read in school? The one with the two boys who go to the carnival that arrives in the middle of the night? She can't recall the name but it was eerie and haunting, as were the forces that ran the carnival itself. That parallel isn't lost on her.

She passes a dozen men, all armed and huddled around a pot of coffee steaming over a fire. They give her looks but don't say anything. They've learned how far they can go and where exactly the lines are. It's the only thing she's grateful for in this place.

The mess building sits in the northern part of the camp near the fence line. To the right is the coliseum, a construction of wooden bleachers that circles what most of the men refer to as "the dance floor." The smell of blood is strong even outside the structure, but her gorge has ceased to react to the scent. *Desensitization*, she thinks the word is. Too much of anything causes it to lose its meaning.

Beyond the coliseum is the square shape of the nest, two stories, its upper windows lit no matter what time of day or night. A generator hums beside the building and a dozen guards stand near its base, talking quietly, several embers of hand-rolled cigarettes flaring in the gloom.

Wen walks through the open front of the mess area, its rows of seating empty at this hour. In the back she passes through a flimsy door and leaves the serving window's awning shut.

Two fluorescent tubes buzz to life in the ceiling when she flips a switch, and by their glow she begins to work.

She loses herself in the preparation of food. Lighting the stove, pans warming, oil out on the counter, refrigerator open, ingredients gathered. She does this without thinking, only moving, always moving. She's about to stir everything together when the kitchen door flies open and bangs against the wall.

Vidri stands in the doorway, his hunched, muscular shoulders giving away his identity even though she can't see his face. And even if she couldn't see him at all, she would be able to smell him. His body odor is the worst she's ever encountered, and that's saying something since showers and baths are rotated biweekly.

"Morning, sunshine," Vidri says. He motions with his head and an unfamiliar figure appears beside him, much thinner. "Tristan, this is Wen. She cooks and makes the sweets."

Tristan stares, dissecting her from across the kitchen. "Where'd she get a name like Wen? She don't look Chinese."

"It's short for wench," Vidri says, stepping through the door. Tristan follows behind him. When he stops beneath the fluorescent light she sees he's been drinking already. Without a word she turns to the fridge and retrieves a covered container, spooning a dollop of chocolate pudding into a bowl before sliding it to Vidri. He doesn't look at the dessert but continues to stare at her.

"It's more than last time," Wen says. "It's as much as I can spare without someone noticing."

Vidri places a dirty index finger into the chocolate and dips some out. He looks at it for a moment and licks the chocolate away before sauntering around the counter.

"Here, let me thank you," he says.

Wen shakes her head. "No."

"Come on, it's rude not to say thanks." He corners her and she leans away, the cabinet behind her pressing into her back. Vidri moves closer, his odor overpowering. It coats the back of her throat and nasal passages. If she weren't so used to it she would vomit all over him.

Vidri leans in and presses his mouth against hers. The touch of his lips along with his stench makes her want to shudder.

Vidri's lips part as he pushes his tongue against her teeth. After what seems like hours he steps back. "That's my love," he whispers. "You know I've been talking to them about us. Think I'm wearing them down. Soon I'll get permission and you'll stay in my tent at night." He brushes her cheek with one finger, rubbing it against her lower lip. The urge to bite him is almost too much. She can imagine the satisfaction of her teeth coming together, skin parting, bone cracking, Vidri screaming and dropping to his knees.

He withdraws his finger, looking at it before putting it in his mouth, sucking on it obscenely.

Without another word he turns and moves past the counter, grabbing the little bowl and spoon as Tristan follows. Vidri throws a last wink over his shoulder before they exit the kitchen, letting the door bang shut behind them.

Tears start to come to her eyes as she turns toward the sink, but she blinks them away, bending over before turning on the tap and filling her mouth with cold water. She swishes it around, spits, and does it again and again until she can't taste Vidri anymore.

Wen sets about heating a smaller pan on the stove, opening a window as she does to let the desert air usher out Vidri's smell. In less than ten minutes she has the two egg-white omelets made, just the right amount of cheese dripping out of the side, a garnishing of chives on the top of each one.

A little trill of fear goes through her as she resumes stirring the contents of a bowl she'd been working on when Vidri had interrupted her. This isn't even the dangerous part. If she were caught now there would be some excuses she could offer. If she were caught after this there are none. Even being a woman she might be brought to the guillotine at high noon wherever they stopped, forced to kneel before the entire trade, and the last sound she'd hear would be the rasping slide of death as the weighted blade fell toward the back of her neck.

The thought nauseates her but she's nearly beyond caring now. So many years passed, so many opportunities missed, and the one person who keeps her moving is probably decaying in the ground somewhere.

Wen stops herself. No more of that. She shouldn't have even gone down that lane of thinking. Just move, keep moving. Here and now, as Robbie always says, there's nothing else.

The fried cakes come out of the pan a golden brown, their scent making her stomach growl. With deft strokes of her largest knife she cuts them into sections, doing the math in her head. Five for the men's container, three for the women's. She wraps the two piles of cakes in pieces of worn cloth and tucks in her blouse, making it poof out around her waist a bit, before sliding the two bundles holding the cakes through a gap between the buttons. The warmth hasn't fully left the cakes and it seeps onto the skin of her stomach. After making sure the bulge doesn't look strange or obvious, she covers the omelets, sets the plates on a serving tray, and leaves the kitchen.

Outside the sun brightens the eastern horizon and the sound of work has increased. Wen glances both ways before scooting across the gap between the kitchen and the towering coliseum. A man passes her carrying a bundle of rope but he doesn't even pause to look at her. She's become a fixture of everyday life for most of them. Something to gawk at but never touch. Except for Vidri. He's getting bolder.

She spits on the ground thinking of the taste of his mouth again. Ahead, the midway is coming apart at the mercy of deft hands who've done this hundreds and hundreds of times. The stands decay in steady progress as more and more men appear to help deconstruct. Wen waits until she's sure no one is looking in her direction and flits to the far side of the wide alley, slinking behind one of the sideshow tents.

Ahead are the two shipping containers, their oblong shapes mere shadows in the early light. At their fronts three guards lean against the steel, talking. Their weapons are slung low from straps around their shoulders. Cigarette smoke drifts to her and she remembers another life where she puffed ten or more of the cancer sticks down to their filters every day. She shakes herself free of the past and moves.

Across the gap between the tent and the first container. She strides quickly and evenly, making sure not to trip. The silverware rattles on the tray and she watches the guards but they are deep in conversation. Moving day is always exciting, and it's the only day she can pass everyone relatively unseen.

The hole in the rear of the first container is round and about the size of a large man's fist. Wen pauses only a second, expertly drawing out the first cloth of cakes. She reaches up and dumps the cakes free through the hole. They don't hit the floor on the other side.

"Thank you," a whispered voice says, but she's already walking away, crossing to the women's container. The hole there is lower and she repeats the process. The women aren't ready and Wen hears the cakes strike the floor with dull thumps. She waits only a moment, listening, silently praying for movement.

After a teetering second she hears it.

A short scuffling sound and a muttered word she can't make out. It's enough.

She walks away from the back of the container, holding the tray with both hands now, the two cloths tucked away in her pants pocket.

4

When she reaches the nest, the guards look her over.

She had to retrace her steps to appear like she was coming from the mess building. She hopes the omelets haven't grown too cold.

The guard closest to the door approaches her, smiling as she stops before him. He pats her down, his hands lingering near her groin and on her chest, his breath smelling of smoke. She bears it without a word. They take turns frisking her, even gamble for the chance to do it more than once a rotation.

When he steps away and opens the door for her, she walks through it holding the tray near her stomach, head high. Before her the narrow stairway rises to the second floor while to the right the first level stretches out in a sprawl of chairs, couches, and a long mahogany bar that will be disassembled within the hour. Wen stops at the top landing. Another guard waits at the doorway to the second floor. He knocks once on the hardwood behind him and a muffled reply comes from within. Stepping aside, he opens the door, letting her pass.

Even though she's been in the upstairs room countless times, it never ceases to surprise her when compared to the bland surroundings.

The walls are a comfortable beige, but most of them are hidden behind lavishly draped bolts of red velvet suspended from the high ceiling. Portraits hang from the three windowless walls, their abstract subjects always looking like something different to her. The floor is polished tile the color of desert soil. A pool table with bright purple felt rests before the two windows that look out over the camp, and a ring of overstuffed leather chairs surrounds a small bar of polished wood. At the rear of the room a doorway leads to the bedroom. Not that she's ever been inside it, only seen glimpses of it as they pass into and out of it. And as she watches, the door opens.

Elliot and Sasha Preston stroll into the main room like royalty.

Elliot comes first, his strange, sweeping saunter eerie in a way that nearly raises goose bumps on Wen's flesh even after all these years. The ringmaster's brown eyes find her and move on almost at once. His gray hair is almost white and has been trimmed since the night before, the precise edge of his crew cut sharp and defined. He wears, as always, a loose, long-sleeved shirt that billows around him, concealing the small pistol strapped to his right forearm. She once saw Elliot shoot a man in the throat who had been caught hoarding food. He'd simply brought up his arm and a gun had been in his hand, like magic. She supposes that's why he likes the contraption so much.

Sasha glides behind him in a white, full-length gown complete with satin collars and cuffs as well as sparkling stones Wen knows are real diamonds. Her blond hair, piled high on top of her head, doesn't have so much as a hint of gray. The cruel lines of her face jut against taut skin, plastic surgery from years before that looks demonic now without the proper upkeep.

"Good morning," Wen says after Sasha shuts the bedroom door tightly.

"Good morning to you, dear," Elliot says, coming forward. "I believe you're several minutes late."

"Apologies. The stove heated slower than usual this morning." Elliot seems to accept this but Sasha continues to stare holes through her, the wall beyond, the world. Wen walks to the table between two of the largest chairs and sets the tray down. With a flourish, she draws the covers off the plates and the delicious smell of herbs fills the room.

"I never get tired of that," Elliot says, smiling. It is a showman's grin full of trickery and, at the same time, contempt. A snake's smile. His teeth are gray behind pallid lips. He motions to the tray and Wen bends forward, picking up an extra fork.

She cuts a small piece of one omelet off before doing the same to the other. She stabs both pieces and places them in her mouth, chewing quietly and swallowing.

"Very good, dear. Now step over by Hemming if you will."

Wen's head snaps around in spite of herself. The albino is so thin and wiry, she's sure if he stepped into the sun it would shine through him. Hemming smiles, the white skin of his face crinkling like crumpled paper, bald head polished and smooth. He wears a black T-shirt, black jeans, and shining black boots, the whole ensemble clashing marvelously with his pigmentless skin. What unnerves her the most is how he can move without being seen or heard. She's sure she was alone when she entered the room.

Wen steps to the bodyguard's right and stops near the wall. She can smell Hemming, a faint metallic odor, like an unfired gun. The Prestons seat themselves at the table but don't touch the food.

"Moving day. Always so much to do," Elliot says. "I assume you have something prepared to eat on the road today?"

"Leftover stew from last night. It'll be cold though," Wen says.

"Of course, of course. Just as long as you keep the troops fed, that's all I ask." He glances out one of the windows, fingering a button on the front of his shirt. "Has the supply run returned yet?"

"No. Not that I know of."

"Hmm." Elliot pauses before looking at her once again. "I need to speak to you about Vidri." Wen's jaw clenches. "He's been requesting your quarters be moved to his tent for some time now. I told him that you weren't part of . . . the other group, that your job is indispensable. In fact, in all my years with the different troupes, I'd have to say food was one of the most important aspects. A deal breaker so to speak. Starve a man's stomach and it feeds his anger. Regardless, Vidri's been quite persistent. What do you think of him?"

"I try not to." She thinks she sees a flicker of amusement in Sasha's eyes.

"You don't approve of his leadership of the guards?" Elliot says.

"It doesn't matter what I approve or disapprove of."

"Now that's not true. We value your opinion." Wen nearly sneers but holds it at bay. Says nothing. "Vidri has been honorable and one of our most trusted men for a long time. There could be worse vying for your attention."

Elliot waits for her to respond before frowning at her silence. "You're stubborn, you know. Sometimes you remind me so much of Sondra it's—" He stops, glancing at his wife as she stiffens in her seat. "I'm sorry, dear . . ."

"I think sufficient time has passed," Sasha says tonelessly. "I'm hungry." She draws herself closer to the table and begins to eat. Elliot appears about to say something more but stops and picks up his own fork.

And just like that Wen knows she's been dismissed. She turns from Hemming, who hasn't taken his eyes from her since she spotted him, and moves out the door, past the guard, and down the stairs, all the while continuing to count in her mind. She reaches three hundred as she walks away from the nest toward the mess building.

Five minutes since she took a bite of their food. Tested it for them.

The wait is getting less.

In the mess building Wen revels in the warmth of the kitchen. She would die for a cup of coffee right now. Real coffee. Not the instant shit she serves the men. Not the dried beans that are so stale they've nearly lost all flavor. A cup of freshly roasted and ground beans. Her mouth waters and when she closes her eyes she remembers the little apartment on the third floor overlooking Sandford Street. The light in the afternoon good, warm and gentle. She smells the candle that she used to burn no matter the time of year. Pumpkin spice. She'd cleaned the store out of them, had kept them in the pantry on the top shelf. She lets the memory consume her and feels the rough wood of her old kitchen table and then the rounded curve of her belly.

The door to the mess area creaks open and her eyes flash wide.

Robbie stands there, hunched and thin, in a jacket that's a size too big for him. He is hollow-eyed and pale.

"I'd absolutely murder someone for a cup of coffee," he says. Wen can't help it. She laughs. So strange their connection for they couldn't be more different.

"I was just thinking the same thing. Except I'd die for one," she says.

Robbie's face constricts. "I'd rather kill someone else."

She moves to him and they embrace. He smells of the open road, windswept fields and dirt. "So glad you're back," she says before releasing him.

"Me too."

"Take a cup of instant?"

"If I have to."

She goes about making their drinks, holding back the question so he won't think that's the only reason she's happy to see him. But when she sets the steaming mug of dark liquid before him, he's already shaking his head, reading her mind.

"Didn't find any."

Her heart sinks. "Really? None? You were gone for two days. I thought . . ."

"Some d-Con, but you said not to get that."

"No. It won't work."

He sips his coffee and grimaces. "Boiled ass."

"You know what that tastes like?"

He flips her the middle finger casually while taking another drink, their banter like a comfortable blanket. "I'm sorry I couldn't find any," he says, his tone more sober. "We only passed by one farm that I was able to convince Darner to stop at, and then it took Fitz and me the better part of twenty minutes to separate ourselves from the rest of the party."

"Do you think Fitz suspects anything?"

"He knows we're going to leave here soon."

"And he's ready?"

"He's terrified," Robbie says, shooting her a look. "Just like I am."

"It will work."

"You always say that, but you've never told me why it has to be ten-eighty. Why that specific type?"

Wen sighs, looking down at her hands. She waits for them to shake but they don't. "My father grew up on a sheep ranch in southern Idaho. When he was a boy he had a dog named Dusty. He told me he named him that because when he was just a puppy he would run so fast down their dirt road that he'd nearly disappear in the cloud of dust that flew up behind him. Coyotes and wolves were a problem back then and there was no way for the farmers to keep watch over all of the flock, especially on a ranch the size that he lived on, so my grandfather took to poisoning the carcasses of rabbits he shot. He'd leave them around the perimeter of the fences and most of the time there'd be a dead coyote or wolf lying not far away the day after." Wen stands and moves to the sink, dumping the last half of her coffee down the drain. She doesn't turn around, only stares at the wall. "My father said he was always really mindful of where Dusty roamed. Wherever he went, the dog followed and vice versa. But one day Dusty caught wind of something and didn't turn back when my dad called him."

"Ah shit," Robbie says.

"He found him chewing the last of a rabbit down on the far side of their property. It didn't take long. Right away Dusty started snapping and biting at the air. Then he ran in circles as fast as he could, but the worst thing, my dad told me, was the sound he kept making. It was a cross between a howl and a moan, and Dusty made it until he collapsed and quit breathing an hour later."

Wen turns and looks at Robbie whose face is even more bloodless than before. "He told me he'd never forget the numbers on the side of the jugs he helped his father empty into a hole later that day. Ten-eighty. He said he saw those numbers in his dreams for nearly a year after Dusty died."

"Damn, you really know how to welcome someone home. Why the fuck would your dad tell you that?"

Wen shrugs. "He was a drinker. Not sure he even remembered telling me afterward. When he'd get really liquored up he'd try to imitate how Dusty sounded before he died." Robbie shifts on his seat, fidgets with his cup. When he doesn't look up at her she moves closer, putting a hand on his shoulder. "Are you having second thoughts?"

"No. Not really. See, you . . . you could run and they'd just scoop you up and bring you back. Maybe put you in one of the containers for a night. But me? I know what would happen if everyone found out about me and Fitz." He makes a chopping gesture toward the back of his neck. "Can't have any queers running around in this brave new world." He laughs humorlessly. "I was a contributor to an e-zine for two years before everything went to shit. Those were the happiest times of my life. And now look at me, sitting in a kitchen in the middle of a wasteland discussing poisons."

Wen smiles sadly. "We're going to be all right."

"Yeah?"

"Yeah. And we're taking Fitz with us when we go."

"Well we can't very well leave him behind; he's the damn gate guard, you know."

"I know."

"What if I would've fallen in love with a tightrope walker?"

"I would've gently steered you away. Performers are always heartbreakers."

"Damn fine asses on those guys though."

She shoves him and turns to the stove and the dishes lining the counter. "Let's finish packing up. They'll be tearing down soon."

They work together without speaking, their movements those of practiced dance partners, never getting in the other's way. *Always moving. Like a comet*, she thinks, sealing off a huge container of flour.

But the question that sometimes keeps her awake at night is what happens when a comet collides with something?

5

Zoey watches the mule deer through the scope, centering the crosshairs behind its front shoulder.

"Distance is slightly less than five hundred yards," Ian whispers beside her. They lie prone with only inches between them, Ian's rifle resting on a rock, its stock tucked tightly into Zoey's shoulder. "Two minutes of angle up."

Zoey makes the adjustment on the scope. "Wind?"

"Negligible."

"You should be doing this. You're the better shot."

"The best way to learn is to do."

"It's kind of critical. We're almost out of food."

"Then you better not miss."

She hears the smile in his voice and silently curses him, tucking the stock tighter to her cheek. Even at five hundred yards the deer nearly fills up the scope's circle. She can make out a tuft of uneven hair on the back of its neck, possibly an old injury. *We all have scars*, she thinks before beginning to breathe slower.

The deer takes a step, pausing in its grazing on the plain below the outcropping. It turns its head in their direction, antlers catching a glint of sun.

Zoey's eye begins to water. She blinks.

The deer drops its head to feed again.

She breathes out. Holds it.

Two heartbeats pass as she squeezes the trigger.

The rifle nudges her shoulder as the shot resounds across the plain. There were fourteen deer in the small herd they followed to the rocky perch. As the shot echoes and rebounds off the closest canyon walls, thirteen run away.

"Beautiful shot," Ian says, getting to his feet and stowing the range-finder in a pocket. "Clean. He didn't know what hit him."

"How long will it keep us fed?"

"Depends on what weight he dresses out at. But we've been traveling for three days and this should definitely last us for at least two more."

Zoey stands, crossing the rifle's sling over her chest so the weapon rests against her back. Her hair has escaped her hat and flutters on the back of her neck in the breeze. Behind their perch the land drops away, coasting out over two small foothills dotted with evergreens. Past the trees the indefinite line of road curves in and out of sight, winding through the mountains ahead. And somewhere on the other side: Riverbend.

"I'll radio Merrill and have him bring the Suburban. We can camp in the trees for the night," Ian says, beginning to make his way down the side of the outcropping. He speaks into the small radio he carries. After several minutes they reach the gradual curve of the plain, passing over loose and broken shale that's sheared from the side of the hill over the years.

"I never said thank you for teaching me how to shoot," Zoey says after they've walked for a while.

"You already knew how to shoot when I met you. You just needed some adjustments."

"A lot of adjustments."

"Not so many. I've taught dozens with much worse aim than you."

"Thank you anyway."

"You're welcome."

They come to a stop a dozen paces from the fallen mule deer. Zoey examines Ian, the late afternoon sun making him look even older than he is. "Thanks for coming. I know what I've asked for you to be here. I know it hurts you to shoot someone."

"I'm glad I'm here, despite the guilt of what I know I might have to do."

She frowns. "I'm sorry it's like this."

"I know you are. But I didn't mention the guilt simply to make you understand how I feel." His lined face grows dark. "I've killed twenty-one men in my life that I know of. I did it for my country. I did it to protect myself or someone I loved. But the regret is always there. I can only remember the first man's face because I made myself forget after that. They all became the first because I couldn't bear to recall each and every one of them individually. I thought it would be easier that way, but it's not. The weight is still there."

Zoey stares at the deer. "I understand."

"Do you ever think about those who've fallen before you?"

A tapestry of faces scrolls past her mind's eye. She forces it to dissolve into a cold blankness. "Every day."

Ian appraises her and finally nods. "Let's get him dressed out." He hands her a knife and she moves to the rear of the animal. Ian's radio crackles and Merrill's voice comes through somewhat broken.

"Ian, you there?"

"Go ahead."

"The Suburban's stuck at the entrance of the plain. It got high-centered on a rock we didn't see."

"Do you need help?"

"It wouldn't hurt."

Ian gives her a look and she nods. "Go help them. I'll finish this up."

The old man starts off at a trot in the direction of the lowest point of rock in the western sky. She breathes for a long moment, simply tasting the air. The sparse prairie grass mingles with the dull brown of scrub the higher the plain rises toward the looming mountain range. The sun is nearly touching the land behind her, warming her back as another gust of wind tosses her hair against her neck.

She is still in awe of the world, struck silent at times by its openness, the vast beauty always stirring something inside her. She recalls the thought she had when they were preparing to attack the ARC a lifetime ago. She imagined being able to run free across a field without the fear of capture or death. A field kind of like this one.

The urge to do just that, to sprint across the open plain, is so tempting she nearly stands up, but something on the eastern canyon side stops her.

There it is again. A flash of light.

A reflection.

Binoculars or a scope.

Zoey's heart does a stutter step in her chest. As nonchalantly as she can, she reaches to the side, finding the rifle's stock where it lies behind the animal.

In one movement she yanks it from the ground and brings the scope to her eye. It takes several seconds to pinpoint the spot again; when she does she sees a flap of a fabric disappearing behind a rock.

She adjusts herself, lying down so the rifle barrel rests on the deer's carcass. Through the scope she finds the flash of movement again. It's a man, young by all appearances, a gun strapped to his side. He runs in a straight line, climbing the rocky hill several hundred yards away. Runs with purpose.

Her heart knocks against her rib cage, counting out split seconds.

The choice presses down on her like a thousand pounds.

Let him go or stop him?

He could be another NOA spy. Shoot him.

Or he could be innocent.

Innocent people don't run. Shoot. Shoot. Shoot.

The man climbs, hops behind a boulder, skips off another rock, and silhouettes himself against the sky at the top of the canyon.

Zoey fires.

The rifle kicks and she doesn't wait to see if he's fallen or not. She leaps up and sprints toward the rise, feet crushing small clumps of sage. The canyon wall looms above her and she slows, hearing the rumble of the Suburban's engine in the distance. She considers waiting for them to arrive but pushes the thought aside. She could've missed. If she did, and he is a threat, she might only have one more chance to stop him.

Zoey cuts diagonally up the incline, throwing glances at the summit every other step. She reverses directions, keeping the largest rocks between her and where the man disappeared. Her back begins to ache and a tingling shoots down her left leg.

Not now. Don't have time for this.

Ahead there are dollops of wet blood covering the ground, their round shapes glinting in the sun. She advances, rifle out before her, aiming purely by instinct. She reaches the top of the rise and pauses, gazing down.

The man lies on his back several yards away. The scuffs in the dirt say that he fell hard, his legs cut out from under him. His eyes are open and staring at her, chest rising and falling quickly. His hand scrabbles at something near his side.

"Stop moving," she says, coming forward. The rifle is steady in her hands. He freezes, eyes focusing on her face. She places the rifle barrel beneath his chin and forces his head back before stripping the handgun from a makeshift holster at his side. She steps back, keeping the rifle trained on him. "Who are you?"

The man grimaces as he tries to sit up. There is a small amount of blood pooling at his side. From the looks of it she barely hit him.

"What's your name?" she asks.

"Benny."

"Get up, Benny."

"I can't. You shot me."

"Yes you can. I only nicked you."

Benny stands and she examines him for a moment. Dark, straggly haircut done most likely by his own hand. Narrow features, pointed chin. Starved look about him. "Walk up over the hill and if you try to run, I'll shoot you."

"You already did that, bitch."

She lets the comment go unanswered. She herds him up over the rise and back down into the valley. The tingling is now in both legs and she has to concentrate to keep from limping. The Suburban is there below, Merrill, Eli, and Ian all heading in her direction. When they spot the man walking in front of her, Merrill and Eli draw their handguns, muzzles pointed at the ground.

"What the hell is this?" Eli says as Zoey brings Benny to a stop before them.

"He was watching us from the canyon wall. His name's Benny."

"Where you from, Benny?" Merrill asks as he pats the other man down, drawing a chipped knife from a sheath as well as a radio from one pocket. When Benny doesn't respond, Merrill holds the radio up before his face. "Who are you keeping in contact with?"

"They're going to be here soon," Benny says, looking up at the sky almost casually. "Then all of you are deader than dead."

Merrill glances at Zoey. "Did you see anyone else?"

"No."

"Vehicle?"

"Not out in the open."

Merrill returns his attention to Benny. "We don't want to hurt you."

Benny begins laughing but winces, holding his side. "You got a real funny way of showing it."

"Why were you watching us?" Zoey asks. Benny gives her a side-long glance before returning his gaze to the sky. With a quick movement she jabs the rifle barrel into his wound and he staggers to the side with a short cry.

"Zoey! That's enough," Merrill says. "We're not going to hurt him. We're going to bring him back to camp, give him something to eat, and talk like civilized people."

She feels her jaw tighten, but she only stares at Merrill before shifting her focus to Ian, who gives her a small shake of his head.

"Let's go, you in front—" Merrill says, but is cut off by a crackle of static from Benny's radio.

"Benny. Where you at?" a low voice says through the radio.

Everyone freezes.

"Benny. You read me?"

Merrill holds the radio up toward Benny. "Tell them you're fine or we'll shoot you in the head."

The other man stares at him for a long second before leaning forward. "No." Benny smiles. Zoey nearly brings up the rifle then, but pauses, something snagging her attention. There is a frayed area on the grimy jacket the man wears, stitching torn loose beneath the layers of dirt. It looks as if a patch was once sewn there. A second look at the coat itself brings her a sense of recognition. It's militaristic in style and very similar to the jackets the guards at the ARC wore in the fall and spring.

"You're from Riverbend, aren't you?" she asks. Benny can't hide his reaction. His head snaps around, eyes widening slightly.

"If he's from Riverbend, whoever's calling is close. There's no way the signal would reach over the mountains," Merrill says, eyeing the canyon wall.

"Let's get him back to camp, we'll figure things out there," Zoey says. The discomfort at being out in the open is akin to nakedness. She scans their surroundings as they make their way to the Suburban. Eli sits in the rearmost seat, holding his weapon on Benny while Merrill drives. They pick up the mule deer, draping the animal across the hood, before returning to the gap in the valley wall.

The ride is short, and after a bumpy trek back down the opposite side of the rise, the route empties out into the pine-dotted foothills above the highway. The other women and Newton are waiting in a small clearing beneath the pines a hundred yards from the road, the position giving them a clear view of the highway in each direction. When Ian and Merrill unload Benny from the backseat, there is a collective silence as they usher the man through the camp and past the small fire where Tia strips a pole for spitting a portion of the deer. Benny eyes the women as they walk, his gaze lingering longest on Sherell and Rita. Zoey's stomach turns when he smiles at them.

"Sit down against that tree," she says, motioning to a large pine. Benny does, grimacing as he settles onto the ground.

"Who is he?" Chelsea asks, coming to stand between Zoey and Merrill.

"His name is Benny. He's from Riverbend," Zoey says.

"Never heard of the place," Benny says.

"He's injured?" Chelsea asks.

"I shot him," Zoey says, ignoring the look that passes between Chelsea and Merrill.

"Newton, come here," Merrill says, drawing his handgun.

The tingling in Zoey's legs is slowly dissipating, but a knifing pain takes its place. She grimaces and shifts from foot to foot. Chelsea glances down and back up to her face.

"I'm fine," Zoey says.

"You're pushing yourself too hard. That bruising was serious and your spine's still healing. Do you want to undo all the hard work you've done?"

"No."

"Do you want to undo all the hard work *I've* done?"

"No."

"Because I'll just amputate your legs if you paralyze yourself again. Don't push me." Chelsea tilts her head forward and looks as stern as she can manage, which makes Zoey smile.

"I'm sorry, Doc. I'll be more careful."

"You better be. You nearly killed yourself rehabilitating."

"I'll be fine."

Newton approaches, stopping beside Merrill who hands his weapon to the younger man. "You watch him for a minute. Shoot him if he moves. Okay?" Newton gives a brief nod and aims the gun in Benny's direction. Merrill walks several strides away before stopping and waiting for the group to gather.

"We think he's from Riverbend," he begins. "He got a call on this while we were asking him questions." Merrill holds out the radio. "If he is from the installation then there's bound to be at least a few more with him, some of them possibly close by so we need to make a decision fast about what to do."

"If he doesn't respond soon they'll come looking for him. Won't they?" Rita asks.

"Probably. The problem is he won't cooperate."

"Threaten to shoot him," Tia says.

"We tried that. Called our bluff," Merrill says.

"So just go ahead and shoot him."

Merrill gives her a withering look. "If we do that then it still doesn't solve our problem. His friends will come looking for him anyway."

Zoey glances in Benny's direction. He's sneering, saying something to Newton who stares back at him, gun aimed toward the seated man's feet. "The problem is he's not afraid," she says. "He needs to be."

"Torture isn't what we do," Merrill says. They lock eyes for a moment before Zoey shakes her head.

"I'm not talking about torture. Fear doesn't always come from pain."

Merrill continues to gaze at her and finally nods. "That's exactly what I was thinking." He chews on his lower lip, studying Benny. "Okay. Chelsea, this is what I want you to do."

◆ ◆ ◆

Zoey and Chelsea approach Benny, who sits against the tree, his hands laced together in his lap. He grins at them.

Zoey touches Newton on the arm. "You can go see Merrill now." Newton turns away and hurries toward the rest of the group who are cutting up the mule deer.

"He doesn't talk. He retarded or something?" Benny asks.

"No, he's a genius," Zoey says. "This is Chelsea, she's a doctor and she's going to look at your wound."

"Bullshit. You're too young to be a doctor."

"You're right," Chelsea says. "I don't have a paper saying I'm a doctor, but I've treated over six hundred gunshot wounds and almost every one of them were worse than this."

"They're going to be here soon, you know that, right?" Benny says, ignoring her response. "They won't even believe their eyes when they come rolling in here. Five women? Three of them under thirty? Couple of them aren't too great looking, but the other—"

"Shut up and listen to me," Zoey says, and something in her tone wipes the grin from his face. "You have two options. One is you're going to let Chelsea look at your wound and then we'll talk about letting you go."

"Let me go?"

"Yes. We'll send you in the direction you were running, minus your radio. By the time your friends get here we'll be long gone."

"What's the other option?"

Zoey draws out the Heckler & Koch, points it at his forehead. "The other option is I shoot you between the eyes."

"You know, shooting people isn't always the answer," he says before slowly lifting his shirt and exposing the wound a few inches above his right hip. It's a ragged hole torn through fat and a little muscle, but it's already quit bleeding.

Chelsea examines the wound. When she stands up, her face is pinched. "That's not good."

"What?" Zoey asks.

"It's infected."

"Infected? How can you tell so soon?" Benny says, the slight sneer still tugging at his lips.

"There's already a little pus leaking on the entry side. It's a classic sign of infection."

Benny struggles away from the tree and tries in vain to see where the bullet entered. Slowly he settles back into place and stares up at them. "You're lying."

"I'm afraid not," Chelsea says in a tired way. "But you'll find out the truth pretty quickly."

"What do you mean?"

"Well, untreated infection only leads to one thing. Sepsis."

"What's that?"

"It's an immune response that causes inflammation nearly everywhere. First you get a fever and chills. Then your heart rate picks up until it's racing. Your breathing increases and you'll feel like you're drowning. Then the really bad stuff starts."

A look of horror crosses Benny's features. "Bad stuff?"

"Yeah. Your skin starts peeling off in different places and your vision fails along with bladder and bowel control. You hallucinate and it feels like you've swallowed a burning lump of coal. That lasts for around forty-eight hours, but I can tell you that it will seem like an eternity. Eventually your organs will shut down one by one and you'll die."

Benny's eyes flit between them. "They're gonna, they're gonna be here soon. And . . ."

Zoey kneels down so that she's on his level. "But I'm guessing there's not a doctor in your group or you wouldn't be so upset right now." She pauses, gaze unflinching. "You're going to do exactly what I tell you to or you'll die the most painful death imaginable. You won't remember your life or who you are while it's happening. It will just be pain and fear. Nothing else."

Benny's mouth works for a second before any words come out. "You can fix it?"

Chelsea nods, digging into her medical bag by her side. She draws out a syringe filled with a clear liquid. "If you do exactly what we say, I'll give you this and it will stop the infection."

"How do I know that's not poison?"

"You don't," Zoey says, still staring at him. "But I don't think you want to experience the alternative."

Benny swallows, sweat beginning to bead on his forehead even though the temperature has dropped in the last hour. "Okay, what do you want me to do?"

Zoey draws out the radio and holds it up to his mouth. "Tell them you're okay and that you found a small group of travelers. Tell them they aren't armed but have quite a bit of food. Say you're bringing them to the installation. Tell them one of the group is a doctor."

Benny blinks and licks his lips, which are cracked and dry as paper. "Okay." Zoey holds out the radio and triggers the button. "Greg, you there?"

There is a long pause before the same voice from earlier comes from the device.

"Benny? You okay?"

"Yeah, yeah everything's fine. I found a group of . . . guys. They aren't armed but they've got some good supplies, some of the shit we're running low on."

Static. "Really?"

"Yeah."

47

"Where you at? You need backup?"

Zoey shakes her head and Benny says, "No, no. I've got them convinced we can give them shelter. You head back to base and I'll bring them in."

Only silence answers his words and Zoey feels sweat run down the length of her spine.

"That last part almost sounded like an order, Benny," Greg finally says.

"No, definitely not. Just thought it made the most sense."

"Yeah. Well I don't take orders from you."

"I know, Greg, I know."

Zoey waves a hand at Benny and mouths the word *doctor* to him. He nods and she depresses the button again.

"Oh, and Greg? One of them's a doctor."

There is a blast of static, then silence before Greg's voice returns. "That's great. She's not doing so hot and if she dies, Ken's going to be beyond pissed."

Zoey stares at the radio, not believing the words she just heard. *She's not doing so hot? There's a woman at Riverbend?* She comes back to herself and draws a cutting motion across her throat.

"Yeah, I hear you. Hey, one of them's coming, gotta go. Be ready for us tomorrow. We'll party when everything's done."

Crackle of static. "Ten four."

Benny slumps back against the tree as Zoey tucks the radio away. "Okay, now give me the shot like you said. I did everything you wanted."

Chelsea uncaps the syringe, inserts the needle beside the bullet wound, and depresses the liquid as Benny hisses a breath between his teeth.

"There. The antibiotic will take care of any infection. You'll heal up nicely," Chelsea says, rising. She glances back at Merrill, who is waiting beside another tree, and nods. He approaches carrying a long rope, which he lashes around Benny, tying him tight to the tree trunk.

"We'll bring you some food as soon as it's ready," Zoey says, and she and Chelsea leave Merrill to his work. They make it a dozen steps before Zoey throws a look at Chelsea, who is fighting not to smile.

"You were excellent," Zoey says.

"I just followed Merrill's plan. But I have to admit, it was kind of fun."

"How much of that did you make up about the sepsis?"

"Some."

"Well I'm sure that water you injected him with will do wonders," Zoey says. She leans against Chelsea and a giggle escapes her as Chelsea throws an arm over her shoulders and begins to laugh too.

"Ouch! Damn it!"

They both glance in the direction of the fire to see Tia holding one hand in the other.

"What happened?" Chelsea asks as they near the other woman.

"Slipped and cut myself."

"Let me see."

"I'm fine."

"Let me see." Tia rolls her eyes but holds out her hand, exposing a cut that's not long but fairly deep. Chelsea tuts, and they settle on a nearby log, where she begins to clean the wound.

"My father used to be a dockworker and cleaned fish for a few fishermen in his spare time. He always said you cut yourself more often with a dull knife than a sharp one," Tia says. "Guess mine needs sharpening." She frowns at Chelsea's bag. "You're not going to use that eucalyptus shit, are you? I hate that smell."

"Well it'll keep this from getting infected," Chelsea says, dabbing some oil onto the cut.

"Guess I'll trust you. Kept me from losing my eye that one time after I ran a stick into it. Remember?"

"How could I forget? I thought for sure you weren't ever going to see out of it again."

"Gets blurry once in a while in the cold, but other than that it's fine."

Zoey watches Chelsea's careful and deft movements before saying, "I didn't know you don't have an actual degree."

She smiles, pulling a small band of gauze from the bag. "I always wanted to be a doctor. My mother was a trauma nurse. I suppose that's where it started. Six months after my sister was taken, I got caught too. I was held at a Marine outpost that doubled as a field hospital and NOA facility. A doctor there let me work with him since they were understaffed and there were so many casualties coming in. At that time the scientists were only studying my eggs so I was allowed to assist him. For nearly four years I helped in surgery every day. He let me read some of his medical textbooks at night and I ate it up. The war was basically over when a group of marauders broke through the outpost's defenses. He hid me under the floor in the operating room and I had to listen to him beg for his life."

She pauses, winding the last of the gauze around Tia's hand. "He taught me everything I know and I've used it to save people. To me that's what a doctor is."

"Well you're definitely my doctor," Tia says, flexing her hand. "But I'd be damn glad to know you even if you weren't."

Zoey smiles, pulling Tia to her feet. "Good as new?"

"Good as new."

"Is dinner ready?" Chelsea asks. "I'm starving."

Zoey glances to the right then and sees Benny staring at her. She looks away.

"Getting close. Mmm, venison again. Haven't had that in, well, at least six hours."

Chelsea and Tia laugh, turning toward the fire, but Zoey doesn't join in. She can still feel Benny's gaze heavy upon her, and in that moment she wonders if they've made a terrible mistake coming here.

6

They drive into the morning in a rumble of engines and swarms of dust kicked up by their tires.

The sun hasn't broken past the mountain range in the east and the shadows are long and cold, reminding Zoey that winter will come all too soon. She watches the boulder-strewn walls out the passenger window of the Suburban, the wind sawing past the top of the vehicle in a constant howl.

Merrill sits at the wheel beside her while Ian, Rita, Sherell, Newton, and Seamus ride in the seats behind them. Merrill's eyes are focused ahead on Benny's Jeep, which Eli drives, leading them through the pass. The prisoner himself is just an outline in the backseat beside Tia while Chelsea rides shotgun.

Benny had remained sullen for the rest of the evening, eating only a small portion of the food they offered before falling asleep against the tree he was tied to. They'd left at the first suggestion of dawn, and found the Jeep he'd been driving at the top of an access road connected to an adjacent highway.

The Suburban climbs higher through the pass, walls of stone growing to a neck-craning height on either side topped by flourishes of pine trees that perfume the air with their scent. The smell triggers the memory of chewing pine needles and the hollow ache when she was starving after escaping the ARC.

"Are you still sure about this?"

Merrill's words snap her back to the present and she glances at him before looking off to the side once again. "Riverbend's our only option. I don't want to give up because someone else is already there."

"I just want to make sure you've considered everything. There's a lot of risk."

"I know." She shifts in her seat. "But turning away knowing there's a chance feels wrong. I don't think Rita or Sherell would want to either."

"Okay."

"Besides, we can't ignore the fact that there's a woman being held there. If you don't want to risk it, we can go on from the other side of the pass alone."

"I didn't say that, Zoey. And I'm not fighting you, so quit acting like it."

She frowns, tugging a loose stitch on her pants. "I'm sorry."

"It's okay. You know I want to help you. If I didn't I would've left the first night I met you, after I knew that Meeka was . . ." His voice trails off and the image of Meeka smiling at her from across the lunch table is so clear and poignant that her throat closes. "Being a leader is never simple. I know the rest of them look to me for answers and I have to make the best decision for everyone."

"I know."

"No you don't. But you'll have to learn."

"What do you mean?"

He looks at her before returning his gaze to the cracked and crumbling road ahead of them. "If you don't know already, you will soon enough."

Zoey is about to question him further when they crest a rise in the highway and begin to descend, crimson light filling the land below them like a bowl splashed with blood. The pines become thicker as they wind down through the opposite side of the range, their trunks growing closer and closer together until a forest fills the sides of the roadway, their heights overtaking the receding rock walls. The beauty of the moment dispels the muddled thoughts surrounding Merrill's words, and she's unable to do anything other than soak in the experience.

So much beauty in the world alongside unlimited sorrow.

It is a bitter mixture that she still finds hard to accept. She wonders again where Lee is. What he's doing at that moment. Is he thinking about her? She can see the letter he left before abandoning her, can see every word like she's reading it now, even though she burned it months ago.

Goodbye, Zoey. Maybe someday we'll see each other again. Until then, know that I love you with all my heart and that there won't be a day that goes by I won't think of you.

She returns to the moment, knowing it is the only way she's gotten through the recent months. There is less pain by living from one second to the next, so she refuses to exist anywhere else besides the present.

They follow the road into a sprawling valley that rises and falls over foothills that seem to go on forever. Near noon the road begins to incline again, the forest thickening slightly as a junction in the road appears, and both vehicles slow slightly before speeding up again. To the left another stretch of abandoned pavement disappears into the green swaths of pine. A large cirque of sheer rock rises in the distance, its top razored against the skyline.

"Wonder what's that way?" Zoey asks as they cruise past the turnoff and continue through the valley.

"Place called Wayward Pines. Nothing there now. Just a ghost town," Merrill says.

"Ghost town," she says. The term sends a wash of goose bumps down her arms. "That's a pretty good description of everywhere."

"There's some places where people still live."

"Live or survive?"

"There's not much difference nowadays."

"There's a difference," she says, not meeting his gaze. "You called Seattle the last city. Why?"

"Because they attempt more than just surviving there. There's some efforts at industry, production of goods. That's where the other towns get their gas, a lot of their food, different supplies. The port is still open but ships don't move in or out as much anymore."

"The ocean. How big is it?"

This elicits a small smile from Merrill. "Big."

"I'd like to see it. The city, the ocean."

He sobers. "No you wouldn't. It was beautiful before. But now . . ."

"You've been there?"

"Once, since everything went to hell."

"And?"

"And I'd never go back again."

She waits for him to elaborate but he says nothing more. The sun continues its course across the sky. Both vehicles stop to refuel from the gas cans they brought as the afternoon shade creeps out from the western mountains. The air has grown drier the farther they've come, the constant moisture in the Cascades only a memory. How anything can grow here is a mystery. Such desolate and harsh conditions.

A clearing appears on the right and in its center is a small grouping of tall reed grass surrounded by a fan of ferns beginning to brown and wilt. A single, drooping flower with white petals grows beneath the closest fern. It appears out of place among the dryness, so fragile and unique in this arid country.

"Do you think we're really the last?" Zoey asks quietly so only Merrill can hear. It takes him a long time to answer though she knows he understands what she meant.

"No. There's others. You're not the last."

"Do you think Vivian was telling the truth? That they don't know what caused the Dearth?"

"I don't know. Obviously they lied to you all about the plague, but I think if NOA would have come up with a solution, things would be different by now."

She mulls this over. He's right. If NOA had discovered the cause and a way to fix the Dearth there would have been no reason to lie. Even now, if there were a way to reverse everything, maybe it wouldn't be too late for the remainder of humankind. Maybe.

After another hour of driving, the Jeep glides to the left side of the road and turns onto a narrow dirt strip that cuts across a plain dotted with sage and long grass that's beginning to brown with the cool fall nights. Eli stops the Jeep and they pull in behind it, Zoey and Merrill climbing out of the Suburban.

"This look about right to you?" Eli asks as he gestures to the dirt road running into the wilds.

"Yeah, this is it. He's not trying to run us around," Merrill says. "You get anything more out of him?"

"He says there's seven of them and one woman. Won't say anything more about her though. When I asked him about security he said they have a fence and an observation tower."

"Does he know the repercussions if he tries to squeal?"

"Oh yeah. Made sure of that."

"Good."

"We could let Ian out before we come into sight of the installation. Let him get set up where he needs to be to cover us."

Merrill nods. "There's some higher bluffs surrounding it: he could use one for a vantage point."

"How far down this road?" Zoey asks.

"Maybe two miles. It's after a sharp bend if my memory serves me, but it's been a long time."

"You need to start doing those mind exercises, old man. Even Ian doesn't forget as much as you do," Eli says.

Merrill ignores the jab. "Everyone ready?"

"Locked and loaded."

"We move when I give the signal. Not before."

"You got it, boss."

"We do this quick and clean, no one gets hurt. Especially our people." Merrill glances at Zoey as he says this. "Everyone good?"

"Good," Eli says.

"Good," Zoey replies.

They climb back in the vehicles and Merrill outlines the plan once again, adding the particulars about what Ian must do. The old man merely begins to uncase his rifle, face solemn, eyes focused on his task.

The vehicles pull out again and Zoey quells her nerves that are beginning to tighten by checking her handgun's load. It's ready. She surveys the landscape as they trundle on, making sure all of her hair is tucked beneath her hat. Rita hands her a bulky jacket and she dons it, making her form shapeless enough that a man wouldn't notice. The other women do the same.

After another minute of driving, a bend in the road appears beside a small hill. In the distance a curve of cliffs juts into the sky. Merrill pulls to a stop and Ian gets out, not saying a word as he moves up the rise and is lost almost at once in the gathered sage. In the Jeep, Eli switches to the passenger seat and Benny climbs behind the wheel.

"I don't like that he's driving," Zoey says.

"Can't do it any other way. They'll know something's up if he's not," Merrill says.

They wait for nearly ten minutes before continuing on, Merrill signaling Eli with a short blip of the horn. They creep around the bend and Zoey's stomach tenses at the sight that meets them.

Riverbend lies at the end of a dirt road on the other side of what was once a river, the dry bed only a groove in the land that runs beneath a heavy steel bridge. Beyond the bridge is a tall chain-link fence, its top looped with razor wire. A gate sits directly beside an empty guardhouse that has been partially torn open. Inside the fence are dark domes set evenly apart before several squat buildings, the missile caps Merrill described before they left so much larger in real life. A narrow two-story tower dominates the center of the installation's clearing; a figure mans the open space at the top.

"Here we go," Merrill says.

The two vehicles cross the bridge, tires rattling on reinforced grating. Zoey glances into the backseat of the Suburban. Calm faces meet her. Even Rita and Sherell appear collected. She gives them a small smile that they return.

Eight months ago we would've been at each other's throats, she thinks, readjusting herself in the seat. Now she would gladly die for either one of them.

The Jeep pulls even with the guard shack, stopping before the gate. She tenses, wondering if this is a trap. But her apprehension bleeds away as the gate snaps into motion, rumbling to one side with a growl.

They have electricity here. It's a good sign. She allows a fraction of hope to slip through the armor she's worn since learning of the missile facility. The information she's craved, since before she can remember, might be inside at this second: where her home was, what her parents' names were, what her name is.

Who she is.

Zoey swallows and regrips the H&K, keeping the weapon low and out of sight beside her seat.

They pull through the gate and it shuts behind them, the sound of it locking loud even with the rumbling engines. The tower looms beside them and she can't help but glance up. The guard's rifle follows their progress.

The Jeep comes to a stop and Merrill parks a car length behind it. Zoey's heart quickens, adrenaline beginning to stretch its legs in her veins.

A door in the largest building ahead of them opens, and several figures pour out. She counts them.

One, two, three, four, five.

All of them are heavily armed. Submachine guns hanging from slings. A confident swagger to their walk. They are dressed in military fatigues and button-up shirts. Combat boots puff the dry soil with each step.

The man at the front of the group wears dark sunglasses below a straw hat, the brim curled up on either side. His shirt is open to his navel, revealing a chiseled physique. Dog tags jingle against his chest. He eyes Benny behind the wheel of the Jeep before peering directly through the windshield of the Suburban.

"Steady," Merrill says. "Be ready to move if anything looks wrong."

The man in the hat says something to Benny through the open window of the Jeep. Shakes his head and motions to the largest building. The other four men span out in a loose half circle around the cars. She can see Eli nodding in the front seat. The man in the hat tips his head back and laughs. He fingers his rifle and begins walking toward the Suburban.

"Steady," Merrill says again.

The man comes even with the driver's side and stops. He's taller than Zoey originally thought, more powerfully built. Two deep lines engrave either side of his mouth, either from laughing or scowling. Wispy blond hair hangs down to his shoulders from beneath the hat. Zoey dips her head enough to obscure her face.

"Evening," he says. "Name's Ken."

"Merrill. Nice to meet you, Ken."

"Where you guys coming in from?"

"Washington. Our camp ran out of food about a week ago, so we headed east hoping to find something better," Merrill says.

"Benny says you're unarmed. That right?"

"Yes sir. Well, we do have one rifle for hunting. Actually had some luck yesterday and shot a mulie. Plenty of it left and we'd be happy to share it."

"I understand one of you is a doctor?" Ken asks.

"That's right."

"Which one is he?"

"Up in the Jeep there, in the back. His name's Terry."

"We could really use a doctor's expertise, to be honest."

"Well then maybe we can strike a deal. Terry helps you and we rest up for a while here. Get our bearings."

"That sounds good to me. Just one more thing. You in the passenger seat there, you're making me awful nervous the way I can't see your other hand. Like you to show it to me," Ken says.

Zoey blinks, keeping her face averted.

Her fingers tighten on the gun.

She turns her head in Merrill's direction.

"Oh, he's a little shy. It's okay, Steve, show him your hand," Merrill says. His closest hand points to her, index finger out, thumb up.

Like a gun.

Zoey brings the H&K up, pointing it directly into Ken's face. The skin around his sunglasses goes slack as Merrill whips up his own weapon, shoving it beneath Ken's jaw.

The men surrounding the vehicles begin yelling but no shots are fired. Out of the corner of her eye she sees barrels appearing in the Jeep's windows.

"Don't move," Merrill says.

"Sonofabitch," Ken says. "Not you, Merrill, if that's your real name. I'm speaking about my good friend Benny up there. I knew I should've put a bullet behind his ear the first time I saw him. Well, regardless, I guess we have some things to talk about here."

"Yes, we do," Merrill says. "Unclip your rifle and drop it on the ground. Tell your men to do the same."

"Can't do that, amigo. I said we'll talk and see where it gets us." Merrill pushes his handgun farther into Ken's neck. "Okay, I'll start. You—" But Ken pauses as he looks directly at Zoey, really seeing her for the first time. She stares back at him over the sights of her gun. Ken smiles. "You're in a bad position here. See, you may have gotten the drop on us with old Benny's help but I have a guardian angel in the nest behind me, and right now he has his crosshairs dialed in directly on your face. Wouldn't be a problem for him to put a bullet through your eye."

"I'm sure it wouldn't, but then you die at the same time."

"Let's be honest, in all likelihood we'd all die or, at the very least, get wounded. So how about we start over. You hand us your guns and we'll get you something to eat and we can speak in a civilized manner over some dinner."

"We both know that won't happen."

"No. No it probably won't," Ken says, sighing. "I knew today was going to be complete shit. It's a Monday. Did you know that?"

"Should we waste them, Ken?" the closest man yells. Zoey glances around the clearing, wondering who to fire at first. She glances up at the tower.

The man there has his rifle trained directly on Merrill.

"Not yet," Ken replies. "Me and Merrill here are having a little discussion."

"Drop your guns," Merrill says. "I'm not going to tell you again."

"Got one word for you, cousin. Stalemate."

The wind coasts across the installation, tossing dust into the air.

One of the men readjusts his grip on his machine gun.

A hawk cries mournfully in the distance.

There is swift whining and a sharp crack that breaks the tensioned silence.

Someone yells a curse and Zoey sees pieces of something fly out of the tower before the man's rifle tumbles to the ground. A split second later the sound of a shot rebounds off the nearest hills and rolls away like thunder.

Ken's men are screaming, shouting for orders.

Zoey spots the man in the tower, partially bent over, cradling his hand to his chest.

"Lost your angel," Merrill says. "Now drop your weapons."

Ken's lips peel back from his teeth in a snarl, their yellowness shocking. "Disarm!" he yells after a moment.

"Ken, I—" one of the men says.

"I said, disarm!"

Slowly the men do as he says. They place the weapons on the ground and step away reluctantly.

"Now you," Merrill says. Ken hesitates then unsnaps the sling from his shoulder and drops the gun to the ground.

"You just made the biggest mistake of your lives," Ken says, teeth still bared.

"Oh I doubt it," Merrill says. "I'm sure we'll make worse ones than this. Now let's have that talk you wanted."

7

As she steps inside the largest building, stale heated air rushes past Zoey, a warm exhale.

She glances around the space, gathering her bearings.

The building's entry used to be partitioned in what looks like a holding cell. The empty door and window frames are solid steel, their glass absent. Through the entry is a wide hall with multiple doors branching from it, most of them open. To the right is an area she assumes used to house another guard station. A long desk covered with strewn papers is flanked by a row of computer monitors, all of them tilted downward at head height.

Her footsteps echo in the empty corridor, a mournful sound. Lonely.

She keeps her finger outside the H&K's trigger guard but holds the gun tightly at her side, ready to bring it up at a moment's notice.

"Place is creepy," Tia says. The other woman steps to her left holding a sawed-off shotgun she's taken to carrying. They move forward in tandem, weapons covering either side of the hall. Zoey moves into the first open doorway, scans the room. It's a white box without windows, twenty feet square. The walls are barren except for holes that might've been made by screws or bullets. They check all of the rooms on the first floor. Some of them are occupied by old mattresses and body odor, but most are empty. They find a kitchen area at the rear of the building beside a stairwell that leads both up and down, and another short hallway ending in a steel door.

They stop to listen to the silence for a moment. Nothing breaks it.

"Benny said there were seven of them here and a woman," Zoey says. "We got six plus the guy in the tower. Should be empty except for her."

"Place is big. We'll need to split up."

"We go in twos," Merrill says, striding up to them. Behind him, Eli, Chelsea, and Rita are ushering the men into the building at gunpoint. Ken is at the front of the group. His sunglasses are gone and his eyes are a deep brown that pin Zoey to the floor. Eli checks one of the first rooms and guides the men inside. Several minutes later he appears, jiggles the doorknob, and comes toward them, holding out a ring of keys.

"Their fearless leader was carrying this. Looks like it'll open any door in here."

"Is Ian back yet?" Zoey asks.

"No, but I saw him coming down out of the hills and left the gate open," Eli says. "That was a hell of a shot. I bet it was almost a thousand yards and he blasted the guy's rifle right out of his hands. Shrapnel tore his fingers up pretty good."

"We'll have Chelsea look at him later," Merrill says. "First we find the woman they mentioned."

"Place seems empty. I'd say they were telling the truth about how many they were," Tia says.

"Regardless, we move carefully. Newton will stay and watch the door—"

Bang!

The entire group tenses. Zoey brings up her handgun, pointing it down the short hall at the steel door. There is a pause and then another quiet clanging of metal on metal.

She glances at Merrill, who nods in the direction the noise came from.

They move down the hall together, Eli searching through the keys as they reach the door. Zoey reaches out and tries the knob. It turns easily.

Eli rolls his eyes and puts the keys away, then counts down silently, his fingers closing into a fist.

Three.

Two.

One.

Zoey yanks the door open. Eli and Tia stream through followed by Merrill. Zoey goes last, covering the area inside the doorway.

They spill out into a massive garage smelling of wet cement and oil. The ceiling is high, patched with flickering fluorescent panels. Dirty light streams in through two long windows cut into dual overhead doors that she's sure a helicopter could fly through. In the center of the space is a huge vehicle the likes of which she's never seen before: oblong and armor plated, sitting high on four large wheels. Dark glass is set in reinforced squares along its front and sides and its bulk is the color of dark sand. Around the machine is a gathering of red boxes, their tops open to reveal glinting tools within.

And beneath the vehicle a short pair of legs pokes out, scuffed boots at their ends.

Eli and Tia cross the space swiftly, taking up positions on either side of the hulking machine. Merrill walks forward, handgun pointed at the figure, who grunts something. Another clang is followed by a quiet curse.

"Come out from under there," Merrill says. The figure freezes, the sound of work stopping immediately. Slowly the man scoots free from beneath the truck.

He is older than Zoey expected judging by the ages of the other men, his hair streaked with gray, face round and flushed red from his work. He wears a pair of glasses, frames so thin they're almost invisible. He sits up, grease-stained hands rising to shoulder level. His eyes flick around to all of them, hovering longest on Zoey.

"Who are you people?" he asks.

"Visitors," Merrill says. "Stand up and turn around slowly." The man does as he's told, knees popping as he rises. After shuffling in a circle he drops his hands to his sides where they open and close spastically.

"Are you going to kill me?"

"That depends. What's your name?" Merrill asks.

"Lyle. Lyle Partridge."

"Are you alone in here, Lyle?"

"Yes."

"How many people live at this installation?"

"Nine."

"One of the others said there were seven of them and a woman. Why did they leave you out?"

"Because they don't count me as part of the group. I'm not with them."

"You said nine counting the woman?" Zoey asks.

Lyle's gaze, watery and timid, flicks to her. "Yes, counting her."

"Where is she?" Zoey steps forward and brings up the handgun so it's level with Lyle's head.

He cringes. "Don't shoot me. I didn't do anything to her."

"Where?"

"The second floor. Third door on the right."

"Eli, give me the keys," Zoey says.

"Zoey, wait. We—" Merrill begins.

"Give me the keys," she repeats, holding out her hand.

Eli glances at Merrill and sighs, handing her the jangling ring. "I'm coming with you."

Merrill calls to her, but she doesn't stop. A sinking sensation is growing in her center. She pushes through the doorway into the hall, not stopping when Chelsea yells to her from the front of the building, the words meaningless amidst the sound of blood thudding in her ears.

She swings right and climbs the stairway, taking the treads two at a time, Eli close behind. She covers her path with the handgun, hurrying, being reckless, she knows, but the inflection in Lyle's voice set off an alarm inside her.

Zoey turns at the first landing and leaps up the next set of stairs, which empties out in a hallway much like the one below. To the left an open doorway reveals a tiled shower room, complete with a large, free-standing tub. The windows in the bathroom are clouded and covered with reinforced mesh.

She hurries forward, counting the doors.

One.

Two.

Three. She slides to a stop, tries the knob.

Locked. Brings the ring up and gazes at the multitude of shining keys.

Flipping through them, she takes only a split second to study each one. The sixth one she examines is brighter than the others, its serrated teeth polished from use. She slides it into the door's lock, feeling no surprise when it turns easily.

The smell is the first thing that hits her. The pungency of unwashed skin is so strong it almost makes her eyes water. The mingling of sweat and blood in the air turns her stomach, but it doesn't make her nearly as sick as the sight.

A woman lies facing the wall on a ragged mattress stained brown and black in places. She is thin, her bones prodding beneath translucent skin veined blue. Blonde hair, scraggly and unwashed, forms a dirty halo around her head. Her shirt may have once been white but is now a dingy shade of yellow, its hem barely covering her waist. A steel cable fastened to the wall with a large bolt runs down and disappears near her shoulder.

Zoey swallows bile and holsters her gun. She walks forward, feeling as if she is in another fever dream. Sounds come from the hallway, voices and footsteps echoing up the stairs. They're muted, unimportant. She kneels, the smell rising from the mattress and its occupant almost too much to bear.

Gently she reaches out and clasps the woman's shoulder, which is cool, almost cold, rolling her partially onto her back.

A heavy manacle is attached to one delicate wrist and it is this that the cable from the wall is bound to, allowing only limited movement. As the woman settles into her new position, some of her hair shifts, revealing her face.

Time stops.

Disbelief rockets through her.

A hand touches her shoulder and she jerks, turning to look into Chelsea's stricken features. Zoey shifts her gaze to the woman again, barely conscious of her words as more people fill the room.

"I know her. This is Halie."

8

Zoey holds the cup, letting the heat sink into her hands, not drinking the tea within. She sits on a worn chair in a room on the second floor, two doors down from where—

From where Halie was lying. Lying in her own filth, barely alive.

Closing her eyes, she turns the cup around and around. Wind scatters a handful of grit against the window and she gazes out through the steel mesh. How long? How long was Halie in that room? What had she endured? The thoughts make her stomach seize with nausea, and for a brief second she thinks she's going to be sick. She breathes deeply, trying to cleanse herself of the smell in the room, but it doesn't want to go away. It clings to her like a parasite.

A murmur of conversation fills the hallway and a moment later Merrill, Chelsea, and Ian appear in the doorway.

"Can we come in?" Merrill asks.

She nods.

They take positions in a half circle around her.

"How is she?" Zoey asks.

"Alive," Chelsea says. "Beyond that I can't say. She's still unconscious, malnourished, dehydrated among other things."

"Other things. She's been raped."

Chelsea's lips form a bloodless line. "Yes."

"Beaten?"

"It looks that way. We bathed her, moved her to a clean bed, tried getting some fluids in her. Eli and Tia are looking for medical supplies in the lower levels. If we can find an IV it would really help."

"Have Rita and Sherell seen her yet?"

"Yes," Merrill says. "After we got her situated they went in and visited her." He moves closer, kneeling down so that she is slightly above him. "What can you tell us?"

She releases a shaky breath. "Halie's a little over a year older than me. She was always kind and considerate. Her best friend at the ARC was Grace. They were inducted a few months apart." A numbness like the kind that used to inhabit her legs tries to seep into her mind. She almost welcomes it.

"I thought Terra told you that when NOA was done with the women they were killed," Chelsea says.

"She did." Zoey gazes down into the cup she holds. "Maybe they said that to frighten her. Maybe she assumed it, I don't know. The fact is, Halie's here, which can only mean one of two things."

"Either she escaped . . ." Merrill says.

"Or NOA let her out," Zoey finishes.

"Why would they let her out? What purpose would that serve?" Chelsea asks.

"You're right. What purpose?" Zoey says, mind warring against the invading paralysis. "They always have an agenda, some reason for what they do. How would they benefit by setting her free?"

The room falls quiet for a time, before Ian shifts from where he stands against the wall. "When she recovers, perhaps she'll be able to tell us."

"What if she doesn't recover?" Zoey asks. "What if . . ."

"We're going to take good care of her," Chelsea says. "She's safe now. You should get some rest too."

"I can't sleep." She chews on her lower lip. "Halie had a breakdown before she was inducted. She attacked a guard and they put her in the box. I wonder if she was afraid to leave the ARC. If they'd institutionalized her so much the thought of freedom sent her over the edge. And now look what they've done to her." Zoey takes a shuddering breath. "I want to talk to them."

"Who? Ken and the others? That's not a good idea," Merrill says.

"I need to know."

"And we'll find out, but first let's think about the best—"

"That's my friend in there, and it could've been me," she whispers, the words almost choking her. "I can't even imagine the type of suffering she went through. I waited all my life for answers. Please, Merrill."

His face contorts and he struggles with something before slowly nodding. "Stay out of their reach and keep the door open. We want to hear everything they're saying."

"Thank you."

Downstairs, she finds Rita and Sherell standing outside the room where the men are locked up. Both of them have dried tear tracks on their faces and hollow eyes.

"How . . . how?" Sherell asks, unable to finish the question.

"I don't know," Zoey answers. "They must have let her out after induction."

"Why would they do that?" Rita says.

Zoey shrugs. "That's what we're going to find out. Have they been tied up yet?" She nods toward the door.

"Yeah. Eli used some plastic straps to secure their hands," Rita says, sniffling.

"Good. Did Eli give you the keys?"

"Yeah."

"Open the door."

Rita gives her a long look before pulling out the ring and finding the correct key. She twists the knob, letting Zoey step inside.

The seven men sit with their backs to the wall, hands bound behind them to a pipe running the length of the room near the floor. Benny is the closest on the right while Ken sits at the opposite end of the line. Every man looks up and stares as she enters and stands before them. The room stinks of sweat.

"Where did you find the woman upstairs?" she asks.

"Pretty, ain't she, boys?" Ken says. "Gonna tear her apart, aren't we?"

Some of the men rumble their assent, their gazes hungry, unflinching.

"I'll ask you one more time. Where did you find her?"

"The rest of our contingent should be back tonight," Ken says, giving her a smile. "See, we're part of a much larger group. They go out on a scouting trip every few weeks and they should be returning any time now. Ain't that right, boys?"

There is a chorus of "yep" and "that's right."

"You're lying."

"You'll all be gathering flies by the time the sun comes up, and we'll be free."

"Then there's no harm in telling me where she came from."

Ken smiles wider. "No. I guess there isn't." He adjusts himself and tips his head toward the door. "Tell you what. I'm thirsty and I gotta piss. You let me out, I relieve myself, get some water, I tell you everything you want to know."

She glances to the doorway where Merrill has appeared. He shakes his head. "Tell me first, then you can go."

Ken runs his eyes from her feet to her face. "My hands are tied. You gonna hold it for me?" A few men laugh.

She returns his stare for a long moment before turning toward the door. She gets two steps before he calls out to her.

"Calm down, missy, I was just having some fun. I'll tell you where she came from."

Zoey returns to the center of the room. "Start talking."

"You ever heard of the Fae Trade?"

A tremor runs through her. "Yes."

"But do you really know what it is?"

"It's an auction that sells women and any men who try to harbor them."

"Wrong. It's so much more than that. It's a spectacle, darling. It's unlike anything you've ever seen before. You know what a carnival is?"

"I've read about them."

"Well the Fae Trade is the most wonderful carnival in the world. It's been traveling from coast to coast for a couple decades. Comes through once a year. There's games, good food, entertainment, you name it. But you're wrong about the auction part."

"What do you mean?"

"I mean if you want a woman, especially one as young as our girl upstairs, you put up a bid. But it's not only a bid of cash, it's also for your life."

Zoey frowns. "What are you talking about?"

"Let me tell you a little story," Ken says, his grin exposing his yellow teeth. "There once was a couple who had a little girl that they loved beyond anything else in the world. They raised her the best they could, but the girl, she had a rebellious streak in her, a little fire. So she starts getting into drugs and drinking like any kid does when they're seventeen or so. But that really wasn't the problem. Love was. She fell for a guy from the wrong side of the tracks, so to speak. He was charismatic and funny but he also relied on his fists to express some of his innermost feelings."

Ken pauses, licking his lips. "Now he would beat her up a little and she'd run back home to Mommy and Daddy and they'd be angry but glad that she'd come back. They tried calling the cops on the guy, but every time their daughter would vouch for him, tell the authorities that he hadn't hit her at all. Needless to say, this was one of those vicious circles that just went round and round and round. And I'm sure it would've kept going for a while but something came along that upset the cycle."

"What was that?" Zoey asks impatiently.

"The Dearth," Ken says. "See, the lawlessness was just taking hold when the charming boyfriend with the itchy fists went a little too far one night. He beat her to death and left her in his apartment to rot. It was days before her parents found her and by then the guy was long gone. Not that the police did anything about it. They had bigger fish to fry. Riots, fires, civil war. Who had time to look for a guy who killed his girlfriend?"

"What does this have to do with Halie?"

"Halie. Aww, see we never knew her name. She'd never tell us, no matter how persuasive we were. Mmm, Halie. I like that. Slides right off the tongue." Several of the men laugh again.

Zoey draws her gun and points it at Ken's smiling face. "Don't you ever say her name again." She's shaking but her aim is steady. "Finish the story."

Ken clears his throat. "Where was I? Ah yes. The girl's parents, they didn't take their daughter's death well. They were angry, not only at the man that took her from them, but at their daughter as well. She didn't heed their warnings, didn't know what was best for her. This couple, they owned a small, traveling carnival and they went on the road. No one really bothered them, because they provided entertainment and everyone needs entertainment, even at the end of the world.

"But see, here's where things get a little twisted. In each young woman they found, they saw their daughter. Young, rebellious, not smart enough for her own good. So they took each girl in and put her up for bid. I'm guessing they figured any man who would fight to the death for the right to have one of them was a step better than who their daughter had ended up with."

Zoey lowers the handgun, slowly processing what Ken said. "They let men bid for the women, then fight to the death?"

"You got it, missy. That's what the Fae Trade is, and the true spectacles are those battles that sometimes go on for days when the woman's young or pretty enough. You put up the cash, then kill until there's no one left except for the best man."

"That's what you did." Zoey spits the words. "That's where she came from. Then you brought her back here and used her."

"Now, you gotta understand. You caught us at an inopportune time here. See, she wasn't always in that state you found her in. Normally we treated her good. Fed her, clothed her, mostly." Ken stops the grin that tries to crawl onto his face. "She was being punished for a little escape attempt a few weeks back. She got the better of your friend Benny over there and managed to get past the fence. Normally she was treated like a queen."

Zoey spins away, unable to look at Ken anymore. She knows if she stays, she'll kill him. Kill them all.

"Hey! Sweetcheeks! How about our deal? Still gotta piss here," Ken says.

She stops at the door, not looking back. "Normally I treat people better. But you're being punished," she says, and steps out into the hallway.

Merrill, Ian, and Chelsea all stand outside the door along with Rita and Sherell. Zoey sucks in the open air of the hallway, air that doesn't smell of men, their pores, their breath. Rita locks the door, muffling Ken's indignant yells to murmurs.

"You heard what he said?" Zoey asks, scanning the group. They are all solemn eyes, bleached expressions.

"I never thought . . ." Chelsea says. "We always heard stories but nothing like that."

"NOA must give or sell them to the Fae Trade—that's the most logical way Halie ended up there. They're handed over and auctioned off." Zoey glances at each of them. "And I bet the trade notifies NOA if they come upon a woman young enough for their research."

There is a stunned silence as her words sink in. She knows it's the truth even as she considers other scenarios. It's like a fact in one of Ian's encyclopedias.

"Fucking monsters," Rita says quietly. "All of them."

"What are we going to do?" Sherell asks. "Do you think he's telling the truth about a larger group?"

"He's lying," Zoey says. "I could see it. He's arrogant enough to think they're going to get free."

"That's not going to happen," Merrill says. "But it won't hurt to keep a lookout in the tower at all times. Who wants first shift?"

"I'll take it," Ian says. He shoulders his rifle from where it leans against the wall.

"We'll switch every couple hours," Merrill says. "I'll work up a schedule for guarding them too."

"Where's the other one?" Zoey asks. "Lyle. Why isn't he in with the rest of them?"

"He's still claiming he was a prisoner here like Halie. He said they were using him to get that big vehicle in the garage running," Chelsea says.

"Which room is he in?"

"That one," Rita says, pointing at a door across the hall.

"Can I speak to him?"

"If you want. When we talked to him earlier he was scared to death, we didn't get much out of him. But I think he's telling the truth. Maybe he'll open up a little more to you," Merrill says.

Rita moves to the door and opens it. Inside Lyle sits on the floor with his back against the wall, hands bound behind him like the other men. Zoey stops near his splayed feet.

"Hello. My name is Zoey."

He is slow answering. "Hello."

"Who are you, Lyle?"

He swallows dryly, eyes watering behind his glasses. "Nobody. I'm nobody."

"If you're nobody they wouldn't have kept you around. Unless you're lying and you are with the rest of them."

"I'm not." Lyle shakes his head. "You have to believe me."

"Then tell us who you are."

He sighs, looking down at his grease-stained knees. "I'm from Boise. Lived there all my life. I was a computer programmer and technician with a software company, NewScan. Ever heard of them?" His voice is almost hopeful as he gazes up at her. "Course not. You're too young. Everything had gone down by the time you were born, I bet. I lived with my parents. Both of them had diabetes. Had it pretty bad. One day when I went to the pharmacy to get their insulin, it was on fire and there were people shooting one another on the next street over." Lyle stops, his brow furrowing. "My dad went first; he was always worse off than Mom. Couldn't quit the sweets. Mom died two weeks after him. Both of them smelled like fruit from the hypoglycemia." Lyle lets out a small, choked laugh that he stifles by tucking his chin to his chest.

Zoey crouches down so that she's level with him. "I'm sorry."

Lyle jerks his head in response. "It's okay. It happened a long time ago, so . . ." He sniffles once and begins to stare at a corner of the room. "I buried them in the backyard and hid in the house until I ran out of food. Then I roamed for a bit. The president was already dead then, everything was gone. I met up with a small group who was traveling north and we joined a little community south of here. They were dedicated to restarting things. There were a few women who were pregnant. Course they gave birth to boys, but it was something. Everything was okay for quite a while. Then the trade came through."

"The Fae Trade?"

"Yes." Lyle swallows again. "They took the women, killed some who tried to fight back, captured others. I only survived by hiding in a crawl-space under one of the houses. I'm a coward." Lyle finally meets her eyes and his gaze is like shattered glass. "That's the only way I've lived this long." He falls quiet and readjusts himself on the floor. "That's who I am."

Zoey studies him for a moment. "How did you come to be here?"

"Those bastards in the next room captured me and were going to kill me until they found out I was tech savvy. They forced me to work on that military vehicle in the garage. They want to use it when they go out scavenging. They kept me locked up at night."

"How long have you been here?"

"Almost a year. I'm not sure, I've lost track of time."

"And you haven't been able to fix the vehicle?"

A glint of humor enters Lyle's face. "I could have fixed it after the first week. I just never told them that. I don't think I would've been worth much after it was running."

Zoey appraises him before standing. "Did you ever touch the woman they were keeping upstairs?"

"No. God no. Of course not."

"Because they wouldn't let you, or because you think it's wrong?"

"Because it's wrong. Lord, I'm not an animal like them. If I could've done anything to help her . . ." He wrestles with something and falls silent.

"When she's able to speak, she's going to tell me the truth." Zoey lowers her voice. "And if you're lying, you'll answer to me."

"I'm not lying."

"I hope so. One last question. Have you ever heard of the National Obstetric Alliance?"

"Course. Everyone has."

"How about around here? Have they ever said anything about it? Mentioned it in reference to this place?"

"No. But I'm not sure all of them can read."

She frowns. "What do you mean?"

"Because there's a room downstairs with papers everywhere that have NOA written on them."

9

The door is as inconspicuous as any other in the installation.

It sits to the left, third down on the long corridor running underneath the facility. Ahead, the cement hallway is lit by staggered fluorescent panels, several bulbs humming and flickering in their cages like animals. The end of the hall splits, ten ways from what Eli says. Each individual tunnel leads to one of the missiles that are dug into the ground and capped by a hydraulic, steel covering.

But it isn't the missiles Zoey wants to see. She needs what is behind the door.

Her fingers tingle as she reaches out and twists the knob.

Pushes it open to a dark room.

"The switch is on your left," Lyle says from behind her. He stands with his hands bound before him. Merrill and Tia flank the small man.

The first thing she sees when the lights come on are open file cabinets, their interiors toothless mouths. The floor is littered with dozens of sheets of paper. There is a desk in one corner, a large computer screen taking up most of its top. Against the opposite wall is a graveyard of circuit boards, computer screens, jumbled and twisted wires.

"This is where I got some of the replacement parts for the vehicle upstairs. Most of its circuitry was fried. Some kind of high-energy surge got it. Maybe EMP. Not sure. They never left me alone in here, but while I worked I always got a look or two at the stuff on the floor. Most of them have the NOA symbol on them somewhere."

The room smells of still air and time. Zoey bends down and gathers a handful of the papers. Lyle is right. The NOA symbol she knows so well emblazons the top of nearly every document.

Most of the pages are filled with meaningless notations, numbers attached to the bottom of paragraphs whose words look almost out of order. She pores over the sheets, trying to make sense of them, connect one to the next, but there is nothing that jumps off the page. The only thing she latches onto are names, but each one is attached to a military title.

She drops the pages on the floor, letting them scatter before moving to the open file cabinets. She pulls each drawer fully open, the emptiness of each one like a slap to the face. She turns in a slow circle and leans against the desk.

"Are there any other rooms like this? Any others that have NOA documents?"

Lyle shakes his head. "I've never seen any. This is really the only room that has any papers in it. I think most of the others were storage for tools, maintenance supplies, that sort of thing."

Zoey's head drops forward.

Nothing. After coming all this way. The wasted days. The danger. The risk.

All for nothing.

She wheels on the file cabinet and shoves it. It clangs to the floor, handles bending flat, paint scraping. She breathes hard, wanting something else to destroy, to ruin. Anything to keep the pressing knowledge at bay.

You'll never know who your parents were.

Never know your last name.
Never know your heritage.
Never know who you are.

She clenches her jaw. Teeth grinding.

"Zoey. Honey. It's okay," Tia says, standing on the other side of the downed cabinet. Her face is soft. Hand outstretched. Zoey hesitates, the anger widening the void within, trying to swallow reason, calm, anything that fights it. She reaches out, grasps Tia's hand.

"I'm sorry. I'm sorry for bringing us here. I'm sorry for risking everything." Zoey looks over Tia's shoulder at Merrill. "I'm sorry."

"It's okay. We're here because we want to be," Tia says. "You and Rita and Sherell, you're important. Don't be sorry. I'm not." She smiles.

"Thank you." She squeezes the older woman's hand before releasing it. "I thought it would be here. Right out in the open. Stupid. Nothing's ever that easy."

"What were you looking for?" Lyle says, finally stepping into the room.

She looks at him for a long time. "We were trying to find records."

"Of what?"

"Information on women that NOA took into their research systems."

Lyle lets out a small laugh. "Well no, you're not going to find things like that lying around here."

"Thanks. I know that now."

"No, no, that's not what I mean. I'm saying they wouldn't have printed that type of information out. Not unless it was in the most secure place they could keep it."

The ARC surfaces in Zoey's mind. "I can guess where that is."

"Well regardless, they wouldn't have used dead trees to keep track of most of that stuff. I'm sure they wanted it multi-accessible. The information would've been classified, especially after all the shit hit the fan. It's harder to burn a stack of papers than it is to wipe a hard drive."

Zoey frowns. "What are you talking about?"

"Data. Electronic data to be exact. I'm sure NOA had dozens of access points like this one. Probably several staff assigned here along with the missile techs."

Zoey glances at the computer screen sitting atop the desk. "You're saying the information might still be there? It might be stored electronically somewhere."

"Not somewhere. Here," Lyle says, pointing with his bound hands at the floor. "I would wager this is one of the remaining operational missile facilities in the western United States. Power comes from geothermal generators, built to last. That's why we have running water, lights, everything."

"Are you telling me you could find the information we're looking for?"

"I think if I can get access to the installation's mainframe, yes. Yes, I think I could find it if it's there."

She leaps over the downed cabinet and grabs Lyle's upper arms, squeezing them hard. He flinches. "Please," she says. "If you can do it we'll let you go."

"I can do it. I'll need some supplies and a little time, but I don't think it will be a problem."

"Thank you," Zoey says, releasing him.

"You're welcome."

"What do you need?"

◆ ◆ ◆

She spends the next hours helping Lyle, Merrill, and Tia gather the supplies the computer tech needs. Most of the equipment is foreign to her. Terms like processor, RAM, and terabyte, a language she's never heard before. She collects what seems like miles of data cable, stringing it down the lower hallway to another room that is cooler than any other in the installation. Tall black boxes with blinking lights stand behind sealed glass doors and give off a burnt-dust smell. It reminds her faintly of the fire she saw on the plains before encountering Ian and Seamus.

Curiosity gets the better of her as she's returning to the NOA file room, and she takes one of the tunnels leading farther away from the building. The sense of weight above is palpable. Tons and tons of earth pressing down, waiting for its chance to crush through the concrete and bury her.

She comes to a platform ringed by a steel bannister, the light from the hall ending in the space beyond the handrail. Zoey senses the openness, the echo of her footsteps, and stops, hand brushing the wall and finally finding a panel of switches.

She flips one.

A cone of light snaps on somewhere to her right, cutting through the darkness past the bannister. She steps up, placing her hands on the cold steel.

The missile is over twenty feet tall, its top ending in a gleaming tip. It is mostly white with strips of black along certain panels on its rounded sides. Wide fins are barely visible at the bottom of the silo, mere suggestions in the gloom.

"They were mostly for protection from other missiles," Merrill says from behind her, and she nearly jumps. She hadn't heard him approach. He comes up beside her and leans over the railing, gazing down at the weapon's length. "Antiballistic. They'd launch if a bigger, badder missile was coming toward the United States. It was their job to cut down the threat before it took everyone out."

Zoey looks at the smooth lines, the silence in the silo almost deafening. "Kind of like a protector."

"Kind of. But there was talk in the last days that the government was considering using some of these for strikes against the rebels since they weren't nuclear but had enough punch to kill an entire battalion if they locked on a location." They stand side by side for a while in the semidarkness before Merrill glances at her. "I saw the look on your face after you came out from talking to Ken. I know what you're thinking and you have to stop."

"I wasn't thinking anything."

"You were blaming yourself."

She is quiet for a time, fingernail tracing a peeling patch of paint on the railing. "Maybe if I'd tried escaping sooner . . ."

Merrill looks down through the darkness. "You would've died. It was a miracle you made it out when you did. It happened the way it was meant to. As hard as it is for me to accept that, it's the truth. You can't keep bearing all the weight. In the end, if you try to save everyone you'll only lose yourself."

He reaches out and squeezes her shoulder before returning down the hall. Zoey stands at the railing, looking into the silo, tracing the smooth lines of death in the darkness.

10

"Okay. Everyone keep their fingers crossed," Lyle says.

He sits at the desk in the NOA storage room, computer screen dark before him. Two small, white towers rest on the floor beside the desk, a multitude of wires and cords running from their backs, out the door, and down the hall to what Lyle calls "servers."

Zoey stands behind the chair the computer tech sits in. Merrill, Tia, and Eli form a tight semi-circle to her right. When Lyle deemed the setup ready to try, the humming excitement had returned to her, a warmth almost like stepping from shade into the sunlight tingling on her skin. Her stomach turns with nervousness as Lyle reaches down, touching a button on the front of one of the towers.

There is a terrible moment of silence in which her hopes teeter, then the sound of a small fan whirs from the back of the unit and lights appear on its front. The computer screen flashes, going bright, dark, and bright again before an insignia she's never seen before appears in its center.

"We're up and running," Lyle says. "Okay. Let's see what we have here." He bends forward over the keyboard, fingers moving slowly at first, then faster, until the steady tap fills the room like falling rain. "Do you know how long it's been since I've done this? But it's still there. Like riding a bike."

A series of boxes open up on the screen, letters and numbers configured inside each of them. Lyle navigates his way through several before homing in on a single one that he begins typing in.

"How will you find the information?" Zoey asks, squinting at the gibberish filling the screen.

"Oh the trick isn't finding the information. The trick is getting access to the system that has the information. Once we're inside it will be a piece of cake."

"And you know how to get inside?"

"Well, in theory, yes. I did do a little hacking for fun when I was younger. And our firm took on several government contracts, which exposed me to some of their operating systems, but . . ."

"But what?"

"But you have to realize, it's been decades since I've even touched a computer, let alone tried to slip around firewalls and administrator passwords." Lyle's typing slows and tapers off until he's simply staring at the screen.

Zoey steps around the side of his chair and waits until he looks up at her, the screen's glow reflecting in his glasses.

"You used to love doing this, right? You were passionate about it?" she says.

"Yes. It was my life outside of my mother and father."

"Then you've dreamed of it. You've imagined being able to do this again." Lyle blinks. He opens and closes his mouth. "Haven't you?"

"Yes."

"Then let yourself remember."

"I can't promise you anything."

"I'm not asking you to. I'm asking you to try."

Lyle swallows, eyes glancing from her to the screen before he pulls himself toward the desk again, setting his fingers on the keys.

Another set of boxes appears on the display and he discards them. A new menu drops down, the words meaningless to her, but Lyle readjusts himself, his shoulders tightening in his shirt. He types for nearly a minute straight before the screen changes again and the largest box she's seen yet materializes, a string of code layered in descending levels that reminds her of plateaus dropping away toward a river.

"Got it," Lyle says. "This is where I need to be."

"You've got access?" Zoey says.

"No. I just found the correct path. Now I can begin."

"How long do you think this will take?"

"I don't know. A while. I'll need some time."

She glances at Merrill, who nods. "I'll sit with him. We'll relieve each other in shifts."

She observes Lyle to see what his reaction is to still being treated as a prisoner, but the man is lost in his own world, oblivious to all but the screen before him. "Thank you," she says, but he doesn't acknowledge her. His typing speeds up.

Zoey makes her way into the main hall with Tia and Eli. "I'm going up to check on Halie."

"I'll go relieve Ian," Eli says. "Catch you ladies at dinner."

"Guess I'm cooking tonight," Tia says.

"Never mind dinner," Eli calls over his shoulder. "Rather eat dirt."

"That can be arranged!"

Eli's laughter peals back to them as they make their way toward the stairs. At the top, they part ways, Tia toward the entrance, while Zoey continues up the flight of stairs to the next level. She pauses at the second doorway on the left, fighting against the sudden surge of vertigo.

Halie lies on a low mattress in the far corner of the room. A dark blanket is pulled up to her chin, her white skin contrasting so much with the fabric that it nearly hurts Zoey's eyes. Her face, now clean of filth, appears even more gaunt and sunken than before. A clear tube runs out from beneath the blanket, extending up to a fluid-filled baggie attached to the wall above the mattress.

Chelsea sits on the edge of a short table, hands clasped together, head lowered.

For a terrifying second Zoey thinks the worst but then hears the faint whistle of Halie's breathing, and steps into the room. Chelsea sits upright, glancing over one shoulder.

"Hi," Zoey says, approaching the bed.

"Hi."

"Did I wake you?"

"No. I was praying."

"For what?"

Chelsea smiles sadly. "For lots of things, but mostly for her to recover."

"You think it helps?"

"It helps me."

Zoey opens her mouth to ask why she would pray to someone or something that would allow this to happen. What kind of god would accept praise and thanks while letting suffering and injustice continue? Instead she focuses on Halie.

"How is she?"

Chelsea sighs, giving the prone woman a quick glance. "Honestly, not too good. I managed to rig up a rudimentary IV drip. It's working for now. But after giving her a closer examination I found a pretty bad contusion on the back of her head. She was hit with something hard. And . . ."

"And what?"

"She might have bleeding on her brain. Of course I can't know for sure, but if that's the case . . ." Chelsea lets her words trail off.

"Could I have a few minutes with her?" There is a slight tremor to her voice and she clears her throat.

"Of course. I'll be in the hall if you need me."

Chelsea moves past her, shutting the door slightly on her way out. Zoey watches Halie breathe for several minutes, the slow rise and fall of her chest beneath the blanket, before kneeling beside the mattress.

She wants to hold her hand but is afraid of disturbing her, afraid of seeing the bruises again, the cuts, lacerations, all the depictions of what Halie endured. Instead she settles for placing her palm on the other woman's forehead. Her skin is cool and dry.

"I'm here, Halie. You're safe now. I don't know if you can hear me, but no one's going to hurt you anymore." She struggles for a second, trying to control her voice. "Guess you're wondering what I'm doing here. I got out, escaped from the ARC. Rita and Sherell are here too." Zoey swallows, bringing her hand back from Halie's forehead. "I'm sorry," she whispers. "So sorry for everything." She tries to go on but tears clog her voice. There is nothing she can say, nothing that will take back the torment Halie's gone through. So much pain and violence. And why?

The void inside her widens.

Her hand shakes as she places it on the grip of her handgun to steady it.

"You're going to be okay," she manages finally. "Everything will be okay."

◆ ◆ ◆

They eat in what could've only been a lunchroom at one time. Two long tables are shoved together in its center, a row of empty lockers built into one wall. It reminds her of a miniature version of the cafeteria at the ARC. They gather enough chairs so they can all sit around the tables to eat the stew Tia made.

The warmth of the food melts the cold knot in Zoey's chest that's stayed with her since visiting Halie. She listens to the others talk, only giving one- or two-word answers when someone asks her a question. Ian keeps glancing at her, trying to hold eye contact for more than a few seconds, but she looks away, finishing her meal as quickly as she can.

Leaving the others behind, she descends to the lower level again, stopping before the door that's ajar, light spilling out along with the rattle of a keyboard. Newton sits against the closest wall tapping his long fingers on his knees in a complex rhythm, a handgun on the floor beside him. Lyle is in the same position as she left him hours ago: head thrust forward, shoulders drawn back, spine bowed. His hands are in constant movement and she hears him swear under his breath.

She leaves the doorway without saying anything and finds herself walking down the same corridor she explored earlier. She didn't shut the light off, and its glow still drapes against the missile's length. She sits down, dangling her legs over the edge of the platform, and rests her chin on the lowest rung of the safety railing.

It is a noble instrument, she decides. What better purpose than to cut down a terrible threat before it harms anyone? Something inherently deadly and violent that serves a higher purpose.

She taps a fingernail against the steel, the ringing soft and sad in the large space, an echo that fades to silence.

That's all I am. An echo. Something left behind, no way of knowing where I came from.

She straightens, pulling her legs up away from the drop. That isn't true. She has people that care for her, who love her. She has purpose and will.

But what if I find my origins and don't like where I came from? What if there's nothing left of me by the time I realize who I am?

Zoey turns, resting her back against the railing and pulling her jacket tighter around her. She closes her eyes to the questions, shoving them away. Merrill's words come back to her and she studies them for a moment. *You'll only lose yourself.*

"Can't lose what I don't have," she says quietly. She shifts in place, getting more comfortable. The air is fairly warm in the silo, something to do with the missile's care, she's sure. Warm. So warm.

His hands are warm on her skin, cupping her face while his lips find hers. She keeps her eyes closed, opening them only when their mouths part.

Lee holds her closely to him, his body hard and trembling beneath his clothes. His eyes are wide and seeking, a question there. She answers it by guiding his hands beneath her shirt. His palms and fingers so gentle against her back, rubbing, caressing. An inevitable attraction is pulling her toward him, closer and closer, but she needs more. They need to be one. She kisses him again, more insistent this time, urging his hands up and around her front until they're almost . . .

"Zoey," Lee says. And when she looks up at him, she nearly screams.

His eyes are missing, their empty sockets endless, blackened depths.

"You killed him. You killed them all," he says, but she doesn't hear him. His voice is in her mind. "You're death."

She struggles to free herself but his eyes widen into gaping holes that become one mass of swirling darkness. She is going to fall into it. Fall forever. And she knows then that the darkness is familiar. It's been with her all along. It is the void within.

And it swallows her whole as she begins to scream.

"Zoey! Zoey, wake up."

She jerks, lashing out. Her knuckles brush something solid while her opposite hand latches onto her pistol, but there are already fingers there, covering the weapon.

"Stop. You're dreaming," Merrill says, his face slowly coming into focus in the low light. She draws in a deep breath, letting her surroundings solidify.

Warm, dry air.

The silo.

Her body aching from sleeping against the rail.

The dream. Nightmare.

She fights the sickness that swells and recedes until she's able to speak.

"Sorry. I'm sorry. I was . . ."

"Having a bad dream by the looks of it," he says, standing and taking a step back from her. "I heard you moaning from the main corridor."

She's suddenly thankful for the lack of light as her face heats up. There's no way of knowing which part of the dream she was moaning from. In fact, she doesn't want to know.

She stands, legs tingling. "What time is it?"

"Nearly morning. I . . . you need to come to the NOA room."

"Why, what happened?" And it's then that she sees his expression. He's smiling.

"Lyle broke into the system. He found the records."

11

The hallways fly by and then she is in the NOA storage room.

It is nearly full of people. Everyone is there except Ian who, Rita tells her, is watching the room containing the prisoners.

Lyle sits at the desk, haggard but with a sense of giddiness about him. He looks younger than the day before, fewer lines around his eyes and mouth. Everyone turns to Zoey as she makes her way through the room, a taut expectance hanging in the air as if a wire has been drawn to the breaking point above their heads. She stops a pace from the desk and glances from the screen to Lyle.

"You did it," she says.

"I did it. It took almost ten straight hours, but I did it. Their operating system was complex, but nothing I'd never seen before. I used an old trick of overloading the system so that it dumped the memory and gave me a chance to insert a code. The code allowed me to rename a main administrator." Lyle smiles. "Which of course was me."

"I really don't understand most of what you just said, but it sounds like it worked."

He laughs. "It did. I gained access to their information logs a few minutes ago. Their file system is enormous, since it encompassed something like a hundred thousand individuals during the Dearth."

"That's how many women they were testing on?" Rita asks.

"Something like that," Lyle says. "But who knows how many women and families weren't coded or notated."

"So you're saying what we're looking for may not be in here?"

"I can't guarantee it, no. But on the bright side I can narrow our search to pinpoint exactly what we're trying to find. That is, as long as you know your birth dates."

The thought of the numerous calendars in the ARC makes Zoey glance at Rita and Sherell, and all three burst out laughing. "Yeah. We know our birth dates."

Lyle frowns but nods and turns to the computer screen. "Okay. Whenever you're ready."

Zoey motions to Sherell. "You go first. You're the youngest."

"You should go. You're the reason we're all standing here," she replies.

"No. I'll go last."

Sherell studies her for a beat before saying, "December 12, 2021."

Lyle's fingers rattle the keyboard. "Okay. Narrowing it by that date, we have ten. How do you spell your name?" She tells him. "And there we are." He taps a key and a screen comes up layered with information. "Would you like some privacy to read it?"

Sherell steadies herself on the back of Lyle's chair and Zoey sees that she's shaking.

"No. Go ahead."

He clears his throat. "Sherell Ali Davis. Mother: Tanya Alice Davis. Father: Tyson Germaine Davis."

Sherell's eyes shimmer and she brings her hands up to her mouth. Zoey steps forward and puts an arm around the other woman's waist. "That's a beautiful name," she says quietly.

Sherell takes a deep breath in and smiles, tears leaking from both eyes. "Yes. It is."

"Do you want me to keep going?" Lyle asks. "There's a lot of technical jargon, but there's also some background on you and your parents. I can transcribe it on paper for you if you want."

"Yes, that's fine. It's Rita's turn."

Sherell steps aside and Chelsea hugs her tightly, the others smiling and murmuring their congratulations. Rita moves forward, steady and resolved, her expression that of granite.

"October 10, 2021. R-I-T-A."

Lyle taps away. A new screen appears. "Rita Marie Carroll. Mother: Nell Marie Carroll. Father: Unknown."

The room is hushed, a spring-loaded silence.

Rita stares at the screen for a long time, eyes boring into and through it. Zoey reaches out and touches her lightly on the arm and the other woman seems to come back from somewhere distant.

"I remember now," Rita says. "I remember one of my mother's friends saying her name."

Her jaw tightens and she glances at Zoey. It appears as if she's about to say something, but then she lowers her eyes and moves through the throng of people to the door and out into the hallway.

All eyes fall on Zoey.

She's trembling, her hands two twitching things at the ends of her arms. She moves a step closer to Lyle. "March 17, 2021. Z-O-E-Y." Heart booming like gunfire in her chest, she watches him type.

The screen flashes, computer humming.

Everyone stares.

She wavers, suddenly terrified of what will happen next.

This is the moment she's been waiting for, dreading, craving, hating.

A single line of text appears on the screen.

Lyle leans forward, brow furrowing. "What the hell?"

"What is it?" Zoey asks.

"No matches."

"What do you mean, no matches?"

"Your information isn't pulling up anything. No birth dates that correlate with your name."

She's afraid that she'll scream. Terrified that it will simply leak out of her in one long anguished howl. "Are you sure? Check again."

Lyle rattles the keys. Nothing changes. "No entries found." He glances at her, cold light reflecting on his glasses obscuring his eyes. "I don't know what to say. I'm sorry."

She feels her chin quiver. Clenches her jaw.

A hand grasps her arm but she pulls away. The air in the room is too close, stifling to the point that she feels like she's swimming. She strides into the hallway, ignoring calls of her name. Her feet hit the stairs and she climbs quickly, two treads at a time, rushing away from the awful knowledge trying to catch up to her.

Nothing. You're no one. You have no heritage except what you've created for yourself. And that is only death.

She doesn't stop at the main level but turns and rushes up the second flight of stairs. The dark emptiness inside her pulses like a cancerous heartbeat.

Growing, thickening, smothering.

She stops outside Halie's room, panting, out of breath, but not from the exertion of jogging up the stairs. She leans against the wall. The urge to scream rises again and she bites it off, swallows it down. Her head is two sizes too large, ungainly, swarming with thoughts. Why? Why is there nothing for her? It's all she's ever wanted. Dreamed of. And now, just when she's nearing the light at the end of the tunnel, it winks out.

Zoey spins and slams her fist into the wall. It dents, puffs of dust leaking from the cracks. She hits it again.

And again.

And again, until her fist blasts through the drywall, the hole's edges red with blood from her torn knuckles. She lets her aching hand fall to her side.

Her vision is smeared, eyes wet with tears of rage. She swipes at them and the sight of the small, inconsequential hole in the wall angers her so much she winds her arm back to strike it again, but freezes.

Through the open doorway and across the room Halie's eyelids flicker.

All the anger drains from her and she hurries to the bed, dropping down to a crouch.

"Halie? Can you hear me?" The woman's eyelids continue to flutter, only the whites behind them visible. One of her arms twitches and tries to rise beneath the blanket and Zoey peels it back, grasping the clenching hand in her own.

Slowly Halie calms, taut muscles relaxing until she is still once again. Her mouth opens and closes silently.

"Halie? I'm right here. You're okay."

Halie's eyes open halfway. Her left pupil is huge while the right is shrunken to a pinpoint.

"Halie?"

The woman bolts upright to a sitting position, head thrown back, mouth open in a silent scream. Her eyes skitter around the room like a tormented animal searching for a way out. A keening sound, inhuman and chilling, comes from deep in her chest and it raises goose bumps along Zoey's arms.

"Halie, you're okay. Lie back. Lie back." Zoey tries easing her down to the bed but she stays locked in place. A shudder runs through her entire body and her frantic gaze finally finds Zoey.

It is filled with complete terror.

The amount of fear in her eyes is so overwhelming Zoey nearly recoils. It is as if they are two pools of torment, everything Halie's endured collected there, displayed in naked and raw horror.

After a drawn second that lasts an eternity, Halie stiffens and falls to her back, her spine flexing, bowing up from the bed. Zoey still holds her hand, the other woman's fingers like bands of iron over her own. In the distant confines of her mind she knows she has to get Chelsea here, get her to stop what's happening before it's too late. But another part of her, the cold void that tells only truth, is already beginning to speak.

"No," Zoey says.

Halie twitches, mouth opening wide.

"Please."

She shivers, feet drumming beneath the blanket.

"Stop."

The other woman's grip releases, breaking the hold as if all the tendons in her arm have been cut. Halie draws in a long, ragged breath.

And doesn't exhale.

Zoey stares, waiting for something more, some new spasm or violent tremor, but there is nothing.

"No." She leans forward, putting her ear against Halie's mouth.

Stillness. "No. Halie? Halie?" Zoey gets an arm beneath the other woman's shoulders and cradles her. Halie's body is warm and limp, lolling against her.

Body. Because that is all that's left.

Zoey chokes out a sob, holding her friend close. She rocks slowly back and forth, unaware of everything beyond Halie's skin, growing cooler by the second.

After years that are only minutes, she gently lays Halie back down, placing her arms at her sides, and covers her with the blanket. She puts two fingers over Halie's eyelids and draws them closed. When she stands, she rocks back on her heels, sure that she will faint, but her head is clear, crystalline and calm. Halie appears as if she's sleeping and

Zoey studies her for a long moment before turning away and walking out of the room.

She meets Ian on the stairs, his face lighting up when he sees her.

"Good morning. I heard that Lyle had some success."

She nods.

"And what did you find?"

"Everything I needed."

"That's wonderful, Zoey!" He sweeps her into a soft hug. "I always knew you would." He holds her at arm's length, face darkening. "Are you all right?"

She opens her mouth to tell him about Halie, to let the pain spill out, because in that second all she wants is to be held, to have someone make it go away.

A shout from below cuts her words off.

Ian's eyes widen and he turns, hurrying down the stairway. She follows, hand already finding the grip of her pistol.

Eli, Chelsea, and Merrill stand outside the prisoners' door, forms rigid, weapons out.

"What happened?" Ian says.

"One of them got loose somehow," Merrill says. "Rita was on watch. They have her."

"No," Zoey says. "No, no, no." She moves toward the door but Merrill steps in her way.

"Stop. We have to think for a second. I saw them grab her from down the hall. She must have opened the door to check on them. She did manage to toss her gun out but she still had a knife on her, so now they have a weapon."

"Offer to let them go if they give her to us," Chelsea says.

Merrill steps to the side, one hand on his forehead. "We'll ask them what they want."

Zoey waits, vision becoming a red haze around the edges, fingers squeezing her handgun so hard a knuckle cracks.

She sees Halie spasming on the bed, the horror engraved in her features, feels her go limp, the coolness of her skin.

And then she's moving.

In the split second it takes Merrill to register what she's doing, she yanks the door open and steps through.

Two of the men are still seated on the ground, hands bound behind them. Benny kneels beside one of them, working on his restraints. The other four, including Ken, stand at the far end of the room in a half circle around Rita.

All eyes shift to Zoey.

There is a dead beat of silence. Then frenetic movement.

Ken lunges toward Rita, the flash of a knife in his fist.

Zoey fires.

The round clips him in the side and he collapses against the wall. Benny rises and rushes her, a steel receptacle cover in one hand that he must've unscrewed from the wall and sawed through his bonds with.

She shoots him in the forehead, spattering the seated men with a spray of crimson.

When she brings her aim back around, the other three men are there, sprinting forward, snarling.

Zoey fires three times, the reports so close together they nearly coalesce into one sound. The men stumble and fall, one grasping her arm as he careens past. His skull explodes as another shot rings out from the door where Merrill stands.

A hand grasps her pant leg and yanks, the man who Benny was freeing trying to climb to his feet. She fires a round into his throat as he comes level with her, a feeble punch glancing off her temple.

The last seated man is the sniper from the tower. He stares her in the eyes through the gathering smoke and cordite of the room and tries to throw a kick at her legs.

Zoey steps over it and presses the muzzle against his forehead.

She pulls the trigger.

When she looks up, Rita is limping past, eyes wide with terror, but there is utter relief there as well. She falls into Merrill's arms as she reaches the door and he guides her out, throwing a look at Zoey over one shoulder.

She moves through the room, stepping past twitching bodies, avoiding puddles of expanding blood, until she stands before Ken.

He lies half upright against the wall, one hand covering the wound in his side. The knife lies several feet away in the corner.

She trains the pistol on him.

He smiles, suddenly diving toward the knife and slashing it at her legs. She leaps back, letting the strike go wide before pinning him with her gaze over the pistol sights. He scoots back into place, breathing hard.

The air is clouded with acrid gun smoke and the sharp odor of blood.

Shouts come from the corridor, but there is nothing except the man before her, eyes hard and unforgiving.

"Well, I suppose—" Ken rasps.

Zoey shoots him in the stomach. The bullet splashes crimson in a short arc that lands near her feet and Ken screams, tipping sideways. She fires again, hitting him in the upper arm, bone shattering in torn muscle. She pulls the trigger over and over, blowing pieces off his body until the gun clicks empty and then she is standing over him, gripping the pistol by the barrel, bringing the gun down like a hammer to his skull.

She swings five times before rough hands grasp her by the shoulders but she spins away, thrashing, not seeing who she's striking at until she's free and bolting from the room that's heavy with the stench of death.

Zoey runs.

Pushing past obstacles that reach for her, call her name, scream at her. The taste of blood is in her mouth, coating her sinuses, slick on her palms.

She bursts through the outside door, out into the cold morning light, face hot and wet, feet churning in the ground, propelling her forward away from the installation, away from her empty past, away from Halie, away from what she's done.

And the void within her flows outward, consuming everything it touches with a darkness she can't outrun.

12

The fifth floor of the ARC is silent except for the faint whir of computers and the tap of a pen against a table. Vivian sits before her personal workstation reading through the files for at least the three hundredth time.

They are like old, familiar friends now, so old and so familiar they've become enemies. She hates the text on the computer screen but cannot help being immersed in it, even now over twenty-five years after she first compiled the reports. She rubs her brow and scans the screen, knowing almost every word by heart.

The Maclear's rat's (Rattus macleari) *sudden decline and supposed extinction on Christmas Island is thought to have been caused by trypanosome, communicated by the accidental introduction of the common Black rat, or* Rattus rattus. *The last sighting of the species was in 1903.*

Vivian clicks a button and the screen flashes, bringing up the next document.

The Thylacine (Thylacinus cynocephalus), *more commonly known as the Tasmanian tiger, is estimated to have vanished from mainland Australia over 2,000 years ago. Its subsequent demise on the continent is thought to be partially due to lack of food. Extinction from the neighboring island of*

Tasmania occurred much later, with the last known example of the species captured in 1933 and dying in 1936. A number of factors, such as disease, hunting, and competition for food, are theorized to have driven the Thylacine into extinction.

Vivian clicks to the next screen and barely reads one paragraph before looking away.

Neanderthals (Homo neanderthalensis) *are thought to have become extinct from several causes, susceptibility to disease being a prime candidate, but another, widely recognized theory is that extinction was the result of violent conflict with more modern humans. In essence, their extermination is one of the first known examples of genocide.*

She drops the pen and stands, moving away from her workstation in the lab adjacent to the empty operating room and stops at the door. Across the hallway the soft pulse of light comes from the Axiom Monitor. Its ever-fluctuating luminance has always calmed her in ways nothing else can. There is something comforting in its constant motion, a shifting that reminds her of the constellations trading positions in the night sky. But even its serene colors can't stop her from thinking about the endless streams of information she's pored over time after time.

Disease. Genocide. Extinction.

All the terms come down to the same thing. Weakness.

You can't fight nature, Vivian.

She grimaces when her college professor's voice echoes in her ears as if he's standing right behind her. He's been dead for the better part of thirty years, but his haughty authority still haunts her.

Dr. Oren Manning had been an odd fixture at Purdue during her time there. The only head of the biomedical and genetic engineering program who had ever believed that there were limits to science. Natural limits were in place for a reason, he insisted, and the leaps and bounds being made in the field of genetic engineering meant science was evolving faster than human beings were prepared for. He had repeatedly said mankind's egotism would be its undoing in the face of nature.

She leaves Manning's words behind and travels down the hallway to the elevator doors. She turns left and finally stops at the room where Zoey had Tasered her and left her locked inside with Carter's corpse.

Weakness. Maybe the same term applies to them all. But no, weakness wasn't the reason Zoey was able to escape; it was stupidity and arrogance on their part. They'd operated so long under the assurance that no person could ever break out of this place, that it was unthinkable with the safeguards they'd developed, both physical and mental. That all of the women would abide without question and never contemplate escape.

Yet Zoey had done it.

Not only escaped, but had brazenly returned and taken the remaining subjects with her. It was the last thing they imagined she would do.

Vivian glances down the corridor at the row of doors. All of the rooms, at one time, held the parents of the girls who grew up in the levels below. Zoey accused her of lying, and she has to admit she hasn't been fully honest in all her years at the ARC. But at one point the women's parents had been here—that was the truth.

The fact was, they'd been weak.

She recalls the bitter disappointment of conducting test after test in the early days of the ARC. The rigorous screening of both parents. How every woman who had given birth to a girl failed to do so again. Time after time, embryo after embryo, all male, no matter how perfect the conditions their scientists created or the genetic modifications they used.

She had told Zoey they didn't understand why the Dearth had occurred, but that was a lie. They've known the truth for many years now.

A single gene had been the cause, one so innocuous no one would've ever considered it a threat to humankind.

The SRY gene, which is typically encoded on a Y chromosome and helps develop male sexual organs, was the problem.

It took some time after NOA was formed before their research determined that the SRY gene was present on the Y *and* X chromosomes in the sperm samples they'd collected. Not a translocation of the gene, but a duplication. And the largest problem of all was that the duplication was encoded in *every one* of their test subjects.

Vivian remembers the heated early meetings. Scientists and doctors shouting over one another, screaming about the impossibility of it all, while every one of them knew what the repetitive data meant. Without intervention, every child, even those born with two X chromosomes, would be male.

Theories were espoused about the cause of the phenomenon itself. Pollution. Overpopulation. Lack of essential nutrients in the soil and in food. A genetic mutation. The degeneration of the Y chromosome. David Pilcher's theory of genome corruption. But no single source was ever proven. Perhaps it had been a combination of them all. Maybe it was nature's final slap to the face; extinction through complete maleness. A domination ironically fitting when compared to men's conquering of the world. But what did it matter really? The genie was already out of the bottle, as her father used to say. So instead they began working on a solution.

Dr. Raj Chaudhri, the newly appointed lead scientist of NOA, was the first to propose the simplest remedy. Remove the SRY gene from the X chromosomes either before or after conception. And everyone had agreed. It was something a first-year genetics student would've suggested.

But that's where things hit a roadblock.

The gene editing they attempted had been used almost exclusively in mice up until that point. The Chinese had conducted human experiments years before and reported several problems, but the scientists within the National Obstetric Alliance were the absolute best in the world and went forward without hesitation.

The results were catastrophic.

The method commonly used and trusted in non-human experiments cut unintended genes, which resulted in unacceptable consequences. And when they finally managed to successfully delete SRY, replacing functional DNA over the gap along with the other genes that were affected, the strand breaks created frameshift mutations. The mutations in turn caused innumerable developmental problems in the embryos, ranging from sterility to several debilitating syndromes. In short, the children born would have had very brief and painful lives.

She still remembers the stunned silence in the lab after yet another failed attempt, their former gusto and confidence dimmed almost to nothing. Chaudhri had settled slowly onto a stool, his deep brown eyes hazy as he stared at the floor.

"It's like nature decided to flip a switch and shut humankind off," he said quietly.

The next day Chaudhri resigned and Vivian took over as lead scientist. She recalls her disdain of Chaudhri's defeatism, the exhilaration of being in charge, of having unlimited resources at her disposal, the challenge of discovery on the horizon even as reports came in that several nuclear weapons had been launched in the Middle East and Russia. Despite the looming destruction, she held on to hope. But soon thereafter it faded.

Her team went on to attempt more than a thousand trials, but all failed in one way or another. The failures shouldn't have happened. Not any more than the SRY gene should've been duplicated on the X chromosomes. But they did. The best and brightest minds in the world were just as dumbstruck and helpless about their experiments' lack of success as they were when postulating why molecular evolution had become an epidemic. Even the men who had previously fathered healthy baby girls were affected, their once normal sperm now altered with the same duplication as the rest of the population.

By the time Vivian realized that their last hope might be combining preserved sperm and eggs from before the Dearth, the rebels had started assaulting their stronghold adjacent to the president's location outside Washington, D.C.

Days later, the atomic weapon detonated, killing the president and many top cabinet members, not to mention thousands of innocent women and children.

Vivian closes her eyes, still able to feel the shudder and violent pitch of the NOA lab as the building shifted on its foundations. They'd had no choice but to evacuate to the ARC, leaving behind the frozen sperm and embryos along with any prospect of finding an escape from the extinction barreling toward them like a freight train.

It took years after that to locate the girls that used to live in the levels below her now—the last female children born in the Dearth, their eggs still holding reproductive promise. But their inductions became a series of empty hopes just as before. Male embryos, one after the other. After taking as many of their eggs as she could for possible future testing, she discarded the women to the Fae Trade. Because now she had an entirely new take on how to reverse the Dearth, and when aligned with her theory the inducted women weren't of any use to her, their genetics weak and yielding.

And weakness isn't a part of the future. There is no place for it.

One of Manning's speeches comes out of the darkness of memory, one that's surfaced hundreds of times over the years since she came to this place to continue her work.

It may not be today, or tomorrow, ladies and gentlemen, but in time the discovery that you think is a miracle in one moment may become a disaster in the next. Now, it is not to say there will not be forward motion in scientific medicine or that we won't be able to help people with our research. I'm saying I believe, on a cellular level, we cannot ever begin to understand the enigmatic causes and effects of diseases that are older than time. We may think we do, but just when we type the last period on a thesis, some hidden or unexplainable fact will surface that destroys all prior logic and reason. This is why a cause for autism cannot be thoroughly explained. This is why we have not beaten cancer. We are swimming, not in a definable pool, but in an ocean that is greater than our comprehension.

At the worst of times she and many of her classmates considered Manning a defeatist, at the best a smug Pantheist.

But the bottom line is he was right.

She had realized it after rising up through NOA, outworking and outthinking almost every man and woman in the organization.

The keystone.

She'd developed the theory after taking control of the research helm from Chaudhri, after watching the gene deletion fail miserably. It was then that Manning's voice had begun to whisper in her ear, telling her that nature governed itself and that if she was patient and observant enough, she would find the answer.

And now she has.

The elevator doors open at the end of the corridor, shocking her back from the past. Reaper steps out and spots her, stopping several feet away. His shoulders are rounded and there's dust and sand speckling his clothes and hair as well as the mask that covers his injury. He has become more and more withdrawn as of late, his mood dour, their interactions strained as if something unsaid hangs between them.

"So? Did you find the team?" she asks when he says nothing.

He sighs and nods. "Sixty miles south. They were ambushed. Some kind of modified explosive device in the road. Fulton and Arnold were killed first but Garrety managed to get away from the road before they caught him."

"And?"

"Looks like he died from blood loss. Gunshot to the thigh."

"Was it one of them?"

He shifts back and forth as if so weary he can't stand. "I don't know. There were three sets of larger tracks and one smaller."

Vivian chews her lower lip. "I think it's time to send out the scouts."

"Are the arms ready? Have they been tested properly?"

"We can't wait any longer."

"You're sure?"

"I'm sure."

He nods, his eyes holding hard on hers, and she thinks he's about to finally say what she's sensed building in him over the past months, but the sound of the door opening behind her breaks the moment. They face the figure that walks in their direction, giving them each a cold smile.

Vivian tries to return it and fails. "Hello, Director."

13

Wen gazes up at the faultless night sky and drinks in the starlight.

She stands at the eastern border of the camp outside the last ring of tents. The desert beyond is a mixture of basins and plateaus rising up in indistinct shapes like stalking animals beyond the edge of firelight. The land is slowly changing with each day's travel, the flat scrubland growing less prominent, while the scattered mountains in the west become bolder. The trade doesn't so much drive as it trundles. It is a giant, ungainly creature growling down forgotten highways, portions of it lagging and stretching for miles, but always coming back together to form a protective circle around itself by nightfall.

A guard stalks by in the darkness, the scuff of his boots the loudest sound besides the faint hum of the generators. He merely glances at her, continuing on his rounds, another shape of a man moving forty yards behind him, their circling of the camp endless, tireless since there is always another man to replace one that's going off shift.

She glances up into the sky again.

The stars have always captivated her. When she was too young to know better she dreamed of traveling to one, seeing its burning aura up close. This was before she understood that the sun was a star and that traveling to the next closest one would take hundreds of lifetimes. But her father had set her straight on that account.

There's no way you'll ever be an astronaut, he'd told her after taking another long pull from the bottle he held. *You don't have the brains for it, number one. And number two, they'll be shutting that NASA shithole down soon enough anyways. Everyone's got their eyes stuck on shit that's unreachable instead of dealing with the problems right in front of us.*

The line between being practical and being a bastard is thin. And she knows which side her father fell on.

Wen tears her eyes away from the glittering heavens and searches the charcoal land beyond, giving in to practicality herself. The scavenging crew should've returned by now. Robbie, Fitz, and the rest had left before dawn that morning, the quiet rumble of their convoy waking her out of a dead sleep. She hates the days Robbie is gone, and yearns for them at the same time. Maybe he'll find it today. Maybe in three. Maybe never. Maybe she should quit hoping.

A streaking movement above catches her eye and she looks up in time to see the phosphoric trail of a meteor flare across the horizon. The memory of making a wish rises and falls away. There's no time for wishing now. Not in this world. Her father would be proud.

She's about to turn back from the edge of camp when an odor assaults her and she has half a second to process what it is before hands wrap tight around her arms and yank her behind the closest tent. Wen stumbles, regains her balance, and spins toward him.

Vidri is a darker shadow before her like the plateaus and buttes in the distance. Besides his body odor she smells the strong liquor that several of the guards distill in their tents, something between gin and sour wine.

"What are you doing?" she asks, glancing around. They are completely concealed from the guard's rounds between two tents; a low pile of equipment is stacked at one end of the alley. She's not sure she can leap over it if she flees.

"Came to talk to you. Looked everywhere. You're a hard woman to find." This strikes him as funny and he wheezes out a long laugh.

"Yeah, well, I was just heading back to my tent." She tries to shoulder past him but he latches onto her again, shoving her back.

"Hold on, sweets. There's no hurry. No one to cook for at this time of night. Ma and Pa are curled up in their nest and everyone's fed. You got time." Now she can see the shine in his eyes that isn't a reflection of starlight. "Whatcha doing out so far anyways? Waiting for your weird little helper?"

She tries to shove past him again and this time he catches her and brings her in close, pulling her against him so that his face is inches from hers. "Someday that whelp's not going to come back from scavenging, you know that, right? He'll piss off the wrong guy out there and get shot in the head and left for the birds and bugs." She struggles against him, keeping silent, not willing to give him the satisfaction of letting him hear how afraid she is. There is no one close by to yell to and she's sure Vidri wouldn't let her scream go on for more than a second.

He nuzzles her neck, untrimmed whiskers sharp and scratching. "Listen," she says, trying to drink in air that he hasn't contaminated. "You need to let me go. If either of the Prestons hear about this—"

"Oh sweets. They know how much I like you. In fact, that's why I was trying to find you. They finally caved. You'll be bunking with me tomorrow night." His tongue flashes out and slicks the side of her neck with saliva. Her skin crawls. A weapon, she needs something to hit him with. She'd still be in her right if she defended herself now. God, why didn't she think to bring the crochet hook? She leans away from him, shuffling her feet to see if she can feel anything beneath her shoes she can use, but there's nothing but the scratch of dirt and pebbles.

Vidri's breath plumes out in the cool air. He's breathing faster and the scent of booze nearly burns her nose. "Come on, honey, just a little taste before we get to the whole shebang tomorrow." He forces her hand down below his belt to the bulge in his pants. "Oh. What did you find there?" She tries to squirm away but he holds her fast, making her stroke him. "I'm gonna treat you so good. You won't even know why you held out this long." His voice is airy, strained by lust.

Wen's gorge rises and she searches again with her foot behind her. Nothing.

"Oh, I'm gonna take you so hard. Make you say my name." His breathing quickens and he rubs her hand faster.

She's screaming inside, wishing for something, anything, to kill him with. Because she would. If she had any type of instrument there would be no hesitating. She's about to recede within herself until it is over, until he's gotten what he came for, when she realizes she can still see the shine of his eyes.

Wen reaches up and gouges her thumbnail deep into Vidri's right eye socket.

The effect is instantaneous.

He shoves her away, a short mewl coming from him as he stumbles in the dark. She doesn't falter, uses the motion he put her in to run and jump as high as she can over the pile of equipment.

Her feet graze something and she tumbles forward, losing all sense of direction.

Her hand strikes something hard, shoulder bashing against the ground. Then her face.

Dirt grinds into her mouth, coats her tongue as she rolls over and sees the sky again. Her lungs are locked shut, air smashed out of them from the impact. She pushes up from her back, gets a leg beneath her as something hits her in the side of the head.

The world cartwheels.

Her vision spins and the stars blur as she tumbles across the ground. When she raises her head Vidri is there, coming closer, blocking out the glimmering sky.

"You dumb bitch! I'll fucking kill you."

She scrambles backward, trying to gain her bearings. A hundred yards to the nest. Twenty yards to get between tents she can hide behind. Where are the guards doing their rounds? Why isn't anyone coming? But maybe Vidri's planned this well. Being the captain of the guards has its perks.

She gets her feet under her as he looms closer, one arm cocked back. She knows she won't see the blow coming, and part of her is thankful.

A band of light illuminates the top of Vidri's head and he pauses, fist clenched beside his ear. He glances toward the light's source and Wen follows suit.

Four sets of headlights are approaching from the east, the rumble of engines becoming clearer. Several guards appear out of the shadows surrounding the tents and take up positions near the drive that cuts through the center of camp.

"Scavenge returning!"

"Let 'em through!"

Vidri turns his attention back to her and for the first time she can see the damage she's done to him.

His right eye is a mass of blood, the corner seeping crimson tears onto his cheek. The eye is still there, still tracking her as she begins backing away, but he keeps blinking more and more blood onto his face and doesn't move to pursue her.

The convoy rattles closer and she hurries away, one hand cupping the side of her head where Vidri struck her. There are several more calls announcing the return of the scavenger group, a few lights flickering between tents, some of the men eager to see if there's anything they can trade for before inventory takes over the collected goods.

Wen jogs between two temporary shacks and finds the modified mess hall in the next section of camp. It is only the kitchen and the serving window, but it looks like a sanctuary to her. She pushes through the door into the faint light thrown by the single lamp over the stove and collapses against the farthest cabinet, sliding down to the ground. She holds herself, mind racing, nausea roiling inside her.

How could they? How could the Prestons give in to that monster?

But of course she knows how.

It is plain as day. Plain to anyone who has ever come into contact with the trade.

The Prestons are insane. And this is how they "care" for women.

Her thoughts are a whirlwind that won't slow down no matter how hard she tries. Vidri will have his way with her tomorrow. There will be no stopping him. She just sealed her fate by fighting back. Tomorrow she'll pay for it.

Or maybe she'll pay tonight.

Wen freezes, halting the forward-and-back rocking she didn't realize she was doing. What if Vidri comes looking for her now? Would he go outside of the Prestons' orders? Would he risk it? It's only one day. Perhaps they would forgive him for being anxious.

She forces herself up enough to reach the knife block on the counter beside her, fingers scrambling across handles until she finds the right one. She sits back on the floor, butcher knife clasped in one hand, and waits, listening for sounds outside the mess building. There are the distant yells of men, exclamations and curses carrying on the air. Then something else. Something that cools her blood.

Footsteps. Close, and coming closer.

Adrenaline jets into her system, tensing muscles, prickling the hair on the back of her neck. She stands, making her decision.

She will fight and kill or die right here.

She regrips the knife, steadying her stance, listening to the footsteps come nearer and nearer.

They stop outside the kitchen door.

The hinges squeak and a shadow steps inside.

Wen raises the knife and is about to rush forward and bury the blade up to the hilt in Vidri's chest when she notices the shadow is too thin, too tall.

Robbie stands inside the doorway holding a thick canvas bag by a strap over one shoulder. His face is smudged with road dust, but he's grinning and he doesn't seem to register that she's pointing a knife at him.

"I found it," he says, swinging the bag off his shoulder. "I finally found it."

14

It takes several seconds for Wen to process what he means.

"You what?"

"I found the ten-eighty," Robbie says, and truly sees her for the first time. "Oh my God, what happened to you?" He drops the bag and comes forward, placing a hand on her face where it's tightening with a bruise.

"They finally gave in to Vidri."

"What? How could they?"

"He wore them down. It doesn't matter. He found me tonight while I was waiting for you to get back. Tried to get a head start on tomorrow's festivities but I got away."

Robbie touches her ear, which feels like something inanimate glued to the side of her head. "Doesn't look like you got away clean."

She tries to smile and turns back to the counter, dropping the knife into its place in the butcher block. "I thought you were him. I was going to . . ." She tries to continue but her throat cinches shut and all the strength goes from her spine. She bends forward and places her forehead on her hands atop the counter. Robbie is there, arm around her, supporting her so she won't crumble to the floor. Because that's what she wants to do. She doesn't want to be a comet anymore. She could fall down, break apart, and become the rubble that she feels like inside, everything held together simply by necessity.

"It's going to be okay," he whispers. "Everything's going to work out now that we've got it."

Wen fights the instability, the sensation of disintegrating, and gathers herself, slowly straightening. She looks at the bag on the floor and swallows. "You're sure it's the right stuff?"

"Positive." He hurries to the bag and opens it, pulling out multiple canned goods, a faded package of flour, a large bucket marked "vegetable oil," and finally a small silver canister with a blue cap on its top. "I found it in the back of a barn that was falling down. The container it was in was buried under a pile of old hay that was turning to dust. Most of the label was rusted away, but I could still make out the numbers on the side." He hands her the small canister. "You said we didn't need very much, right?"

Wen twists the cap off and holds the bottle beneath the light so she can see its contents.

The white crystals shine up at her, some of them discolored from time and moisture. She shakes the container and the poison shifts inside. It looks exactly like salt.

"You did it, Robbie."

"We did it. I wouldn't have known that stuff from table salt."

"Well, that's the point, isn't it?" She spins the cap back on and sets the canister down on the counter between them. They both stare at it.

"How much will you put in their food?"

"I'm not exactly sure. It depends on how much they weigh. But I'm guessing it'll take less than an ounce between the two of them."

"Shit," Robbie breathes, wiping his hands on his pants. "I touched some of it. Do you think—"

"No. But wash them just in case." He hurries to the sink and scrubs his palms for several minutes before returning to the counter.

"How fast do you think it will work?"

"Fast. We'll only have ten minutes or so before they notice something's wrong. Maybe twenty until they come looking for us. Will Fitz be ready?"

"He damn well better be. The man's not the smartest I've ever been with, but his heart's in the right place and he wants to leave as much as you and I do. I'm not going to tell him how it's going to go down though. I don't think he wants to know."

"As long as he's got the vehicle ready outside the gate, we'll be fine."

"When can we . . ." He gestures at the poison and motions to the rest of the kitchen.

Wen sighs. "We have to wait until setup and opening night. Which at the rate we're going will be within the next week or so. The Oregon border's not too far off."

"Another week. Are you sure we can't—"

"Yes. Like I said, we have to wait until there's enough distraction. Opening night's perfect for that."

Silence grows in the kitchen. Outside the yells and excitement of the returning supply run have died down. The trade is quiet once again. She's about to hide the ten-eighty away when Robbie clears his throat and glances around the room, looking everywhere but at her. He's done this so many times she doesn't even need to ask what he's thinking.

"I'll be fine, Robbie."

"They're going to make you test their food, just like you do every day."

"Yes. They will."

"And you'll have to eat it."

"Yes."

"You'll get sick."

"Most likely, yes, I'll get sick. But it will be a much smaller amount since I only take a bite of their meals."

"You might die."

"I'm pretty sure I won't."

"But you don't know."

"No."

"But what if—"

"I don't know!" she yells, and Robbie recoils as if she slapped him. "This is the best I could come up with and it's all we've got." He looks down at the floor, mouth working soundlessly. Wen puts a hand to her temple, which aches from where Vidri struck her. "Look, I'm sorry. I know it's not perfect, but I'm willing to go through with it. I have to. We don't have any other choice."

Robbie shifts from foot to foot and runs a hand through his hair. "I know. The only reason I said anything is that I don't know what I'd do without you. I would've put a gun to my head years ago and pulled the trigger if it hadn't been for you and Fitz. What I'm trying to say is I love you and don't want to lose you."

She looks at him, emotion tightening her throat again, and crosses the distance between them. Wen embraces him and he squeezes her tightly, the two of them not moving for a long time in the center of the dingy kitchen. Finally she draws away, seeing the tracks his tears have carved on his dirty face. He rolls his eyes.

"Damn you. Smeared my mascara." They both laugh and he clears his throat. "I should get to my tent. If a guard happens to step in here . . ."

"Yes, go."

"Do you want me to hang around outside your tent tonight in case Vidri tries something?"

"No. I'll stay here. There's an old blanket under the sink to catch leaks. I'll be fine."

"Are you sure?"

"Yes. I'll feel better here. At least I can brace the door and have weapons if he does come poking around."

He surveys her for a long moment before nodding. "Okay. I'll see you in the morning."

"Bright and early."

"God I miss sleeping in, lounging around my apartment in the mornings. You think we'll ever get that back? Pieces of our old life?"

She hears a baby's tinkling laughter somewhere in the wings of her mind that she's almost completely boarded shut. "Let's get some sleep, okay?"

He grimaces and heads for the door, stopping outside in the night coated in milky starlight. "You're the strongest person I've ever known," he says, then is gone, disappearing amongst the layered shadows.

His words keep her rooted in place for nearly a minute before she shuts the door, using the handle of a pan to wedge it closed. The blanket from under the sink is damp but she barely notices it as she lies down, all of her adrenaline depleted, strength drained from the fight. She tucks her arm beneath her head, keeping her opposite hand wrapped around the handle of a butcher knife.

Tomorrow night I'll be sleeping in an entirely different place, she thinks. *And there will be no one to help me.* But no one's really ever helped her before, not counting Robbie. All her life she's had to fight for the things she's wanted. And this is no different.

I'll do the only thing I know how to.

She closes her eyes and begins to drift away from the pain and into the promise of sleep.

I'll help myself.

15

It is not yet dawn when Wen rises from her makeshift bed, unrested, sore, joints throbbing, with a spinning sense of vertigo so strong she rushes to the sink and vomits.

She wipes her mouth with her arm and rinses the sick down the drain, splashing her face several times with icy water fed by a tank attached to the roof outside. She steadies herself against the counter and breathes.

Concussion. Has to be.

The room pivots around her and she fights the nausea. Her ear is a crooked piece of meat that brings tears to her eyes when she touches it, and when she finds her reflection in the bottom of one of the baking pans, there is a purplish bruise growing out of her hairline and down below her eye. She looks like hell.

"I'm getting too old for this," she says. But her joke falls flat in the empty kitchen. She moves to the door, pulling the pan's handle from where she wedged it the night before, infinitely glad it wasn't needed.

The camp is still quiet, a distant bird's call the only thing breaking the solitude. Slowly the queasiness passes, and she is able to start working.

She opens cans, tears sealed packets apart, smelling odors from another time, preserved by the miracle of plastic and aluminum. She mixes, fills a huge pot full of water that will be the base for a new soup, one of the easiest things to make while on the road. Her large fridge is on one of the trucks, so her supply of fresh ingredients is limited to what she can keep in the more mobile and compact cooler in the corner of the room.

After working for nearly an hour, she hears the beginnings of movement outside, the trade shaking loose its slumber to continue the never-ending trek down the highway to the next town or settlement filled with men who will pay for what Elliot Preston calls "the last, greatest show on Earth."

Her hatred for him and his wife is so strong, so potent, she imagines for a moment she can taste it. But it is only the acidic remnants of bile in the back of her throat.

She spits into the sink and is about to begin cleaning a dirty mixing bowl when the door to the kitchen creaks open. She doesn't need to turn around to see who it is. She can smell him already.

"Good morning," Vidri says. She dries her hands and turns to face him, forcing away the swaying in her vision.

The captain of the guards is dressed in his usual attire: dusty boots, stained jeans, a ratty work shirt, but his face is what catches her gaze and holds it.

His eye is swollen nearly shut and what of it she can see is red as a desert sunrise. The blackness of his pupil stares out at her and there is a long scratch leading up to his temple that she assumes came from her thumbnail.

"Did quite a number on me last night," he says, coming closer. She says nothing. "Could've blinded me, you know."

"I'm sorry."

Vidri's eyebrows rise. "Are you?"

"I didn't mean to hurt you that bad. I was still trying to process what you told me."

He smiles, revealing teeth in serious need of brushing. "Don't think you can go butter up Ma and Pa with some fancy cooking and a sob story if that's what you're trying to do. I already have permission. You're mine now."

"I know that. I'm coming to terms with it."

Vidri studies her. "You're not going to fight me again?"

"Would it do any good?"

"No."

"Exactly. I know there's no changing what's going to happen. I'm trying to adjust myself, that's all."

Vidri's smile widens and he steps closer, only an arm's length away. "I can be nice, you know. I can be real gentle. If you're good to me, I'll make your life easy." He reaches out and traces her undamaged cheek with one finger, trailing it down past her chin and onto her chest, where it lazily makes a circle. "Real easy."

It takes every ounce of will to stand still, to not scream, lash out, and stab him with the knife on the counter behind her. Vidri comes closer, reaching around her back to pull her to him.

She places her hands against his chest as he dips his face down to hers. "You need to wait. At least until tonight. Give me today to get ready. This evening I'll have all my things moved to your tent and you'll be able to do what you want. I won't stop you."

He doesn't move, and for a horrible beat she thinks he's going to kiss her anyway, keep his hands on her, tear her clothes open. But then he steps back, the rank miasma retreating somewhat with him.

"You got yourself a deal. I've been waiting for this day for a long time. I can wait a few hours longer. See you tonight." He begins to move toward the door but she steps toward the small fridge, opening it quickly.

"I made you something this morning," she says. "As an apology for hurting your eye. If we're going to be living together we should start off on the right foot."

She sets the small paper bowl of chocolate pudding down on the counter and retrieves a plastic spoon, sliding it into the dessert.

Vidri eyes the bowl before glancing up at her. "You made it for me?"

She nods. Heart picking up speed.

"Well, that was pretty thoughtful. You did do a job on my eye, had to drink a full glass of gut rot just to go to sleep." He spins the bowl around several times before stirring the spoon through its middle. "Looks great."

"I know it's your favorite. Just don't let anyone else see you eating it or I'll have everyone trying to get some."

Vidri licks his upper lip and dips an index finger into the chocolate, holding it out to her. "Little taste?"

"No. It's for you."

"C'mon. Pretty please? Something to tide me over until tonight?" His finger comes closer to her lips, brushes them.

She opens her mouth and he slides it in.

"Mmmm, see? Now that wasn't so bad." He works his finger against her tongue, and she wonders if he can feel her pulse hammering through every inch of her body.

Slowly he draws his finger from between her lips and smiles, picking up the bowl. "I'll be seeing you soon."

Vidri saunters across the kitchen and out the door, giving her another lingering look before closing it behind him.

Wen spins and spits into the sink, trying not to vomit again. Or maybe that would be better? No, just rinse it out. She didn't swallow; it was just in her mouth. She swishes several mouthfuls of water around until her saliva runs clear and she can't taste chocolate anymore. Her heart continues its furious pace and she wonders if that's from the fear or the ten-eighty taking effect.

She breathes deeply, focusing on calming herself. The poison wouldn't be working that fast, not with the small amount she might've absorbed. After drying her mouth with a towel she drinks several glasses of water and stands against the counter. The sound of work outside the kitchen is louder, the soup beginning to waft up from the pot, filling the room with the delicious scent of onions, potatoes, and cooking venison.

Everything normal. An average day on the road. Nothing suspicious.

She holds her hand out, watching it tremble until it finally steadies.

She's fine. Everything's going to be fine.

Five minutes later the Prestons' omelets are nearly done and she's feeling somewhat steadier on her feet when the door to the kitchen opens and a young, blond-haired man steps inside looking nervous, hat twisting in his hands.

"Um, Mr. and Mrs. Preston would like to see you as soon as possible."

Her pulse skyrockets again. "Why? What's the matter?"

"Don't know. They just said to tell you to come to the nest."

He fidgets with his hat for another beat and does a quick nod that is almost a bow before retreating from the doorway.

The room begins its slow rotation around her again.

How? How did they find out so fast? Had the poison killed Vidri quicker than she'd estimated? She'd only used just enough. Did someone see Robbie transferring the container off the truck? Did Fitz say something he shouldn't have?

She bends down, searching in the lowest cupboard behind a stack of worn hot pads until she finds the lipped ledge at the very back. Her fingers graze the cold steel of the canister. Should she hide it somewhere else? Take it with her? No, they'll search her at the nest. No choice but to leave it.

She swallows the solid lump of fear forming in her throat and finishes preparing the omelets before striding to the door, all the while calculating if there's any chance of escape. Outside she surveys the landscape in the early morning light. The bluffs that would provide a hiding place are too far to sprint to; the milling guards would overtake her at once. And besides, there's no way she could leave Robbie behind.

She moves in the direction of the nest, looming above every other structure in the camp since the coliseum isn't erected each evening like the Prestons' home. She stops before the entrance and endures the groping search of the guard there.

"Guess I'll have to quit doing this after tonight," he says in her ear. "Property of Captain Vidri."

She ignores him and enters the building, climbing the stairs before being let into the living area, vertigo hounding her the entire way.

Hemming stands near the windows, his shoulder touching the drapery as if he's considering concealing himself behind it. His gaze finds her and holds. He shifts in place, interlacing his fingers over and over.

Elliot and Sasha sit in their customary places at the low table. Elliot wears a dark, silk shirt above pressed slacks, looking comfortable and dapper even at this early hour. Sasha on the other hand wears only a red velvet bathrobe tied at the waist. Her feet are bare and rest on a heating pad beneath her chair.

"Good morning, dear," Elliot says. "My goodness, what happened to your face?"

She sets the tray down and brushes the blooming bruise with her fingertips. "A pan dropped from a cupboard last night and caught me in the side of the head. It's nothing."

"Would you like Gerald to have a look at you?"

"Gerald died in his sleep a month ago, Elliot," Sasha says, not taking her eyes from Wen.

"That's right. We must attain a new physician at the next town. Hemming, make a note of that." Elliot gestures to an empty chair across the table. "Have a seat, won't you?"

She sits down, senses still heightened. Would they invite her in like this if they knew?

As if reading her mind Elliot says, "I suppose you're wondering why we summoned you here so early."

"I am curious," she says, thankful that her voice doesn't waver.

"We wanted to discuss something, something that I know might not please you."

"Okay."

"We and Vidri have come to an accord. We've decided to grant his request of your transfer to his quarters."

She lets the appropriate amount of displeasure seep into her features. "What if I don't approve?"

Sasha shifts her feet on the pad. "There was a reason Elliot said *we* and Vidri came to a decision. Your viewpoint isn't wanted or needed."

"Now Sasha, let's be civil about this. You see, dear, there is a certain symmetry between Vidri and yourself, whether or not you can see it. You have both been with us for many years, dedicated yourselves to service, and if I have my math correct you are both within a year of one another as far as age."

"We are," Wen says after a pause.

"Well then, there you have it. Vidri is one of our most trusted men. Outstanding service, impeccable character, always willing to help and command. You'll be very happy together, I'm sure."

Wen scoffs before she can stop herself.

"What was that?" Sasha says, sitting forward slightly. "Did you just snort at our decision?"

"No."

"I believe you did."

"I need some time to adjust to this. Can we please wait another week, at least until we're done with setup?"

"No," Elliot says, face hardening. "What we said is final and we won't be questioned. You see? That's the problem with so many young women. You can't tell the forest from the trees." His eyes narrow, losing any warmth they had moments ago. "No matter the warnings, you do what you think is right, or simply what you want, even if it is wrong. Too stupid to know what's best." He spits the last sentence as if it is a dart that might pierce her.

She remains silent, dropping her gaze to the floor, away from the insanity that comes off the couple like heat. After a long time, Elliot clears his throat and glances out the window.

"Regardless, it is done. You will live with Captain Vidri from now on or suffer consequences that Sasha and I would rather you not incur." She waits, eyes averted and penitent until Elliot motions to the tray holding their breakfast.

Wen leans forward to take the customary bites, silently sending thanks out into the universe that her fears concerning the poison were unfounded. She's swallowing the two bites of egg when footsteps pound up the stairs and the door bursts open.

A wild-eyed guard stands there, flanked by the doorman. "It's Vidri! Something's wrong with him. I think he's dying."

16

"What do you mean, 'dying'?" Elliot asks, rising.

"He threw up outside and he's shaking. Keeps grabbing his chest. We got him downstairs on one of the tables. Didn't know what else to do."

Wen glances around the room. Sasha has a disgusted look on her face, whether from the description of Vidri's ailments or the idea that he's lying on her polished table downstairs, Wen doesn't know. Elliot looks stricken, while Hemming takes a step back toward the wall, a sharp glint of steel disappearing into a sheath beneath his arm.

"Get Geral—" Elliot begins, but stops himself. "Damn it. Doesn't anyone else have any medical training?"

"Not that I know of, sir," the guard says.

"One of the guys in the container we picked up a month or so ago," the doorman offers. "I heard two of them talking one night and he said he was a doctor."

"Which one?" Elliot asks, already moving toward the door.

"The guy with the longer dark hair. The one that was with the youngest we have now."

"Fetch him," Elliot says, continuing toward the stairs. Hemming leaves his post by the window and falls into step behind the ringmaster. Wen looks from the doorway to Sasha, who continues to glare at her.

"Get out," Sasha says, standing.

Wen rises and makes her way down the stairs, legs shaking beneath her.

A doctor.

One of the men in the shipping container is a doctor.

He'll know Vidri's been poisoned.

And she is the one in charge of the food.

She steadies herself against the wall, the concussion wreaking havoc on her balance again. There is nothing to do but move forward. Whatever happens now is in motion; she made that choice this morning when she dosed Vidri's pudding with enough poison to kill a horse.

She steps off the last stair into the lower dwelling of the nest.

A group of men huddle around the center table and she can see scuffed boots sticking off the end. They jitter and twitch as if Vidri's having a bad dream. Despite herself she moves closer, a morbid sense of curiosity drawing her along with the responsibility to see what she's done. One of the men moves aside, leaving a clear view of the table.

Vidri lies on his back, neck and head twisted away. His body shakes, tremors running its length. Two men hold down each knee while two more secure his shoulders. One of his arms snaps out and Elliot himself latches onto it, stilling its movement.

"Someone get some water!"

"Something to tie him down!"

"He's going to swallow his tongue."

"Heart attack for sure."

"Stroke."

Murder, Wen thinks, and takes another step forward. The realization that it was her own hand that caused this isn't tangible. It floats away each time she tries to grasp it.

Vidri turns his head so that he faces the ceiling. His eyes are open, bulging in their sockets. The one she damaged is a bright red marble of pain. Foam gathers at the corners of his mouth, and his lips are drawn back, revealing clenched teeth.

He turns his head again.

Eyes locking onto hers.

Something moves in his gaze. A shifting of recognition, fear, rage.

She stares back. Doesn't blink.

The arm Elliot holds straightens, shaking, rising up into a straight line. His fist clenches and slowly his index finger extends.

Directly at her.

Another powerful spasm wracks Vidri's body, his back arching up off the table. His knees flex so hard neither man holding him can keep their grip and his legs flail wildly.

"Grab him, damn you!" Elliot yells.

A gurgling scream warbles up out of Vidri's throat and for an instant she feels a tug of sympathy. But then it is gone with the memory of star shine and blossoming pain in her skull from the night before. His hand forcing hers to touch him, fondle him.

Vidri vibrates in time with his cry, muscles jumping beneath flesh like struck chords of an instrument. He seizes, going very still, shudders, and seizes again.

Then like a balloon losing air, he deflates back to the table, tendons going slack, jaw limp and mouth open, eyelids fluttering, fluttering, closing, closed.

All is still.

The outside door bangs open and everyone flinches as two guards rush inside, a middle-aged man between them. He is sallow skinned with very dark hair that hangs down to his shoulders in stringy clumps. His features are sunken but she can see that if he were twenty pounds heavier he would be handsome.

Elliot spots him and motions to Vidri's body. "You! Do something. Now!"

"I told them, I'm not a doctor," the man says.

"My men heard you say otherwise."

"They heard wrong. I was a med student and that was twenty years ago."

"Then you did have medical training."

"Some, yes."

"Then get over here and save him," Elliot hisses, jabbing a finger at the table.

The man from the container moves to Vidri's side, the guards that brought him following close behind. He puts a hand beneath Vidri's jaw and holds it there for ten seconds before facing Elliot.

"He's dead. There's nothing I can do."

"CPR! Do something!"

"He's already getting cool. It's beyond me. I have nothing to save him with."

Elliot's anger fills the room and Wen backs toward the door, but one of the guards stands in her path. It's then she notices Hemming watching her intently. She glances away, clasping her hands together to keep them from trembling.

"Who saw what happened?" Elliot asks.

One guard raises his hand. "I found him behind the big top truck throwing up. He could barely stand, and when I asked him what was wrong he couldn't speak. So I brought him here, and when he laid down he started shaking. That's when I came for you."

Elliot's breath hisses out between gray teeth. "Did anybody else see anything? Did he mention he felt sick yesterday or the day before?" No one says anything. The ringmaster turns back to the corpse, raising Vidri's limp arm up from where it hangs off the table, and places it by his side. After a long pause he says, "What is your name?"

"James," the man says. "James Horner."

"James, you said you were a med student."

"Yes. But I never got my license, I was still studying."

"In your studies, did you perform autopsies?"

Wen blinks, eyes jerking from Elliot to James.

"Yes. It was part of the requirements."

"I'd like you to perform one on this man."

James shakes his head. "That was twenty years ago, like I said. I wouldn't know the first—"

"Let me rephrase that," Elliot says, iron gaze falling on him. "You *will* perform an autopsy on this man."

James swallows. "What if I say no?"

"Then you'll die much sooner than planned."

James dips his head forward. "If I do, what will you give me?"

"What do you want?"

"Let me and my wife go."

The room erupts in laughter and Elliot lets it go on and slowly die down before smiling. "Shoot a little lower, son. We both know that's not going to happen."

A streak of anger creases James's face and Wen thinks he's going to strike Elliot, which will be the last thing he ever does. Instead he licks his lips and says, "Double the women's rations and I'll do it."

"The women already get all the food they want. Their container is padded, insulated. They have a toilet and plenty of clothing. They are safe and protected. They don't need anything."

"Then double the men's rations, we're starving."

Elliot's smile widens. "Done."

Wen's heart sinks.

"What will you need?" Elliot says. And as James begins listing off several instruments, his voice flattens, fades, until she can only hear her pulse drumming in her ears.

"Hey, the boss is talking to you." The guard beside her nudges her shoulder and she comes back to the room, every eye upon her.

"I'm sorry. What?"

"I said, please make James a plate of food while the supplies are gathered," Elliot says, looking at her strangely, prying into her.

"Of course."

Elliot watches her for another drawn moment before focusing on the rest of the group. "Notify the camp of Vidri's death. We won't be moving today, so everyone can suspend their work. Tell them to remain in their tents in case this is some kind of communicable disease. By the end of today we will know what happened to our captain."

They file out of the nest in a funeral procession. Wen leads the way toward the mess building with James and two guards steps behind. The thought of putting a dose of ten-eighty in James's food dances fleetingly through her mind. But that would be the same as an admission to both murders. One death could be overlooked, but two?

She runs through her options as she enters the kitchen, pushing up the overhead serving door to reveal the exterior counter, but there is nothing viable beyond killing the innocent man outside. If she and Robbie were to go ahead with their plan, their chances of escape would drop to almost zero. It is daylight and the entire trade is milling about now, news of Vidri's death spreading like wildfire. No, she would only be killing herself, Robbie, and Fitz if they tried. She might as well put a gun to their heads and pull the trigger.

James sits on the opposite side of the serving area, head down, hair obscuring his features. The two guards move away from the window to light up hand-rolled cigarettes, voices low and steady in conversation.

"What would you like?" she asks, mind still whirring through possibilities.

"To know why you poisoned him," James says, bringing his eyes up to meet hers.

17

It's like she's fallen off a cliff, spinning out of control toward a rapidly approaching ground.

"What are you talking about?" Wen manages.

"Don't. I'm not an idiot," James says. "I saw enough poisonings when I was in med school. You don't forget things like that. And since you're the one that serves the food . . ."

Wen holds his gaze for a moment before turning toward the kitchen. She begins taking out the makings of a cold sandwich, her back to the window.

"Regardless of what you say, I have to do the autopsy. But the outcome can be up to you," James says. She continues to work. "If you do something for me I'll say he had a cerebral hemorrhage. That has a lot of symptoms similar to poisoning. But if you choose not to, I'll tell them that you did it. And when they search this place or your tent, or you, they'll find the poison."

She returns to the counter with his plate and sets it before him along with a tall glass of water. "I don't know anything about any poison."

"Sure you do. I saw the look on your face in the nest, just like now when I called you out on it. You did it. I want to know why."

Wen glances past James to the guards. They are still smoking, facing away, voices barely audible. "He tried to rape me last night and he got permission from the Prestons to move me in with him this evening."

"I figured it was something like that. But my question is, if you have a poison that's untraceable except by autopsy, would you really be keeping it only for Vidri?"

"Are you going to eat that?"

"You're going to kill the Prestons, aren't you?"

"I have work to do."

"It sounds like you've already been busy."

"What do you really want?"

James picks up his sandwich, inhales the scent of the bread. "You've been the one giving us the cakes every week. It's really the only thing we look forward to. Knowing someone cares makes all the difference sometimes. A couple of us ration the cakes out to last until the next ones come, but the others eat theirs right away. They say they're not going to draw out the inevitable if there's no more. I want you to know how much we appreciate your kindness."

"Then tell Elliot that it was a natural death and we'll be even."

James takes a bite, chewing slowly, carefully. "In another life I would. But my wife is in the other container. She's forty-three, the youngest. She'll be next to . . ." His voice fails him and he sets down the sandwich, taking a long drink of water. "So you see, I can't do that. I can't call it square."

"I know what you're going to ask but the answer is no."

"You have to take us with you."

"I can't."

"When are you going to try?"

"James, I'm sorry, but I've worked this every way in my head already. Don't you think I would set you all free if I thought I could? What do you think I see when I lie awake at night?"

"What's important to you. What you truly hope for outside of this place."

Distantly she hears the ghostly echo of a baby's laughter.

"I'm sorry."

"No, I am. I'm sorry I'll have to tell Elliot exactly what happened to Vidri if you won't take us with you. Because I will. I'll tell them if you don't promise me right now you'll free us."

She feels as if she's being pulled apart inside, her organs stretched and strained until she fears they'll tear. "You can't ask that of me. There's other people involved, I'd be risking their lives as well."

"I care about one person, the only person I've ever loved in the whole world," James says, his voice a whispered scream, eyes aflame. "She's been locked in a steel container, abused, threatened, and soon she'll be auctioned off like livestock. Her name is Amanda. Don't talk to me about risking lives."

The guards drop the butts of their cigarettes and smash them out on the ground before glancing toward the kitchen.

"They're coming back," Wen says.

"Then you'd better make your decision."

The guards walk toward the serving window, still talking in low voices.

She looks from them to James who merely stares back.

"Okay. I'll get you out."

"Promise me."

"I promise."

"Here." He shoves his plate across to her, the single bite missing from the sandwich. "Get that to my wife and tell her I love her."

James stands up and meets the guards, who shove him roughly in the direction of the nest. He glances back at her once before they're out of sight and then she is alone in the kitchen, fingers gripping the plate so hard her hands ache.

◆　◆　◆

On the edge of dusk Wen sneaks to the side of the women's container, its hole much higher since it is now on the top of a flatbed truck. She climbs up the two steel steps mounted to the trailer, leaning out to make sure the guards at the rear haven't noticed her.

When she is almost even with the hole she whispers in a low voice, "Amanda?" A quiet shuffling meets her ears, a murmur of conversation, then a patch of white skin with a blue eye centered in it appears.

"Who are you?" Amanda says.

"No one. You're husband sent you this." Wen holds the sandwich wrapped in a plain piece of brown paper up to the hole. After a second it is taken. "And he says he loves you."

Quiet crying issues from the hole and Wen grimaces, climbing down quickly.

"Tell him I love him. Tell him, please!"

She walks away into the shadows of a large tent, the raucous laughter from inside drowning out the woman's pleading voice behind her.

When she enters the kitchen, the light is almost gone from the sky and Robbie is leaning on the counter, a glass of alcohol in one hand. He waits until she's secured the door before setting his drink down to embrace her.

For a long time he holds her and she lets the day drain from her as if it's a noxious chemical in her bloodstream. When she steps back from him his eyes are shining.

"I'm sorry I couldn't get here until now. They had me mending fences all day. Are you okay?" he says.

"I'm fine."

"I can't believe it. I can't believe you did it."

"That makes two of us." She takes his glass from the counter and slugs half of it. Her throat screams from the alcohol but then it erupts in nulling warmth in her stomach and she sighs.

"That was so risky."

"Are you saying I shouldn't have? Because right now we wouldn't be having this conversation. I'd be in Vidri's tent and—"

"Of course not. The sonofabitch deserved everything he got." Robbie studies her. "I heard you were there when it happened. When he . . . you know . . ."

"Yeah. I was."

"And?"

"It was the worst thing I've ever seen and I'm ashamed to say there was a part of me that enjoyed it."

"I don't blame you a bit. In fact, you should get a medal." He mimes opening a box and pinning something to her shirt. "I hereby christen you with the national medal of bastard slaying. It is the highest honor you can receive."

She smiles tiredly. "Thanks. But we're not out of the woods yet."

"See, that's just it. The guy they brought out of the container to do the autopsy, he totally fucked up. He told them it was a cerebral something or other, I can't remember. Everyone's talking about it—how it's not a surprise Vidri's brain fried since he was such an asshole." Robbie stops mid-gesticulation and lowers his hands. "What's wrong?"

"That's what I need to talk to you about."

"Ah shit."

He listens intently, narrow features growing paler by the minute, until she's finished.

"Ah shit," he says, with less force, and drains the last of the booze. "It won't work. There's always three or four guards hanging out at the container doors and there's no way to cut through the sides; we'd need about half an hour to do that. Fuck! That asshole."

"He's not an asshole. He's a man who loves his wife and wants to be free. If that's being an asshole I guess I'm one too."

Robbie visibly deflates, sinking down to the floor of the kitchen to rest against one of the cabinets. "God. I just told Fitz today that we'd be going really soon. He's got the truck primed and everything. It's ruined. It's all ruined. What the hell are we going to do?"

She turns and rests her hands on the sink, looking out the window into the darkness that smothers the camp's grounds, her own battered and exhausted reflection staring back at her.

"The only thing we can do. We're going to leave them behind."

18

Zoey watches the bleeding sunrise, not looking away even as the light grows painful.

She sits on a heating unit mounted to the roof of the main building, legs dangling over the side, shoulders slumped, fingers and toes numb from the cold. Her vision blurs from looking at the growing dawn but she refuses to blink. The red of the sun churns the longer she stares, swirling, burning brighter and brighter until she can't stand it anymore and drops her gaze, squeezing her eyes shut.

In the darkness she sees the last few days play out in a half-remembered dream haze, all details softened, images muddied and broken. She watches Halie twitch and jerk on the bed, feels the life leave her body, sees the gun sights come even with Ken's face.

Feels the gun's recoil.

Again.

And again.

And again.

Then only the openness of the plains after sliding through a narrow gap in the installation's fence, a crushing avalanche of darkness behind her. After that, nothing for a long time.

Ian found her huddled beneath an outcropping of rock behind a layer of dead sage. She had run over a mile from the facility with no memory of it. He had talked in a soft, soothing voice that gradually coaxed her out from the fugue she'd barricaded herself behind. After a time he'd guided her back to the installation, dirty, bloody, barely aware of her surroundings. She hadn't spoken a word to anyone since; she'd met everyone's attempts to talk to her with simple nods or shakes of her head. Chelsea had gotten her to shower and dress in fresh clothes, but after eating a meager amount of food she'd come to the roof, staying through the night into the morning embracing the biting cold.

And now the reality of what she's done is as real and bright as the light in the east.

Killed them. Killed them all. Just like Lee had said in the dream.

Maybe that's truly why he left. Perhaps he could see inside her, see what she was becoming even before she realized it herself. Saw her for what she is.

A murderer.

But each time remorse begins to invade her, break her will to hold herself together, the rage returns, almost as strong as the moment she opened the door to the prisoners' room. It overshadows the guilt.

And the void grows.

Zoey swallows. Her throat is dry. She should've brought water up here. Then she could stay longer. Away from the others.

She glances around the facility grounds. All is serene in the gray dawn, morning shadows that will soon be eaten by the day, vague outlines on the soil. She shivers. The nights are getting colder. It won't be long until the mountaintops are capped with snow and the days will be only brief interludes between darkness.

A sound draws her attention to the left as the roof's access door opens and Tia appears. She is wearing her heavier coat and her typical direct demeanor is absent.

Tia looks at her before glancing away. "We're going to bury Halie this morning. The others wanted you to know."

"Thanks."

"So you'll be down?"

"Yes."

Tia begins to turn but stops. "I know how it feels when you think no one understands what you're going through. I know what it's like to be truly alone. If you want to talk, I'm around."

Zoey tries to respond but when the words won't come she nods and Tia disappears down the stairway.

The wind picks up and swirls shrunken tornados across the plain and tugs at her hair. There is nothing left but to go forward. She can't stay on the roof for the rest of her life, no matter how much she wants to.

She finds Chelsea, Merrill, Rita, and Sherell in the front entryway on the ground level. As she approaches Merrill stiffens though his eyes don't leave hers and the same softness is still there. The door to the prisoners' room is partially open. Someone has tried to clean it, though the wall is stained and the smell of blood is still a suggestion in the air. Chelsea spots her looking at it and shuts the door. A sense of claustrophobia grips her and it feels like the walls are closing in. Or maybe it's simply being around more of the group again, wondering what they're thinking, if they're judging her.

Merrill nods before saying, "Okay. We put Halie in the back of the Suburban. The ground looks soft at the far north corner of the compound—"

"We're not burying her inside the fence," Zoey says.

"No," Sherell says.

"I'm sorry. Of course not," Merrill says. "I'll drive everyone out and we'll find a different place."

"We'll do it," Rita says. "We knew her."

Merrill frowns but finally holds out the keys, letting Zoey take them from him. "Be careful. If you're not back before noon, we'll come looking."

The three of them file out of the front entrance and climb into the waiting vehicle. Halie's body lies in the very back, wrapped tightly in a white sheet. Several shovels and a pickax rest on the second-to-last seat. Zoey starts the vehicle. Eli leans out from the guard tower and waves. Rita and Sherell wave back as she drives past and heads out the gate, which rumbles open with their approach.

They travel across the small bridge and wind down the dry dirt road toward the main highway, the facility fading in the rearview mirror until it is swallowed completely by a hill that they turn at and leave the drive.

Zoey follows an opening in the scrub and heads up a wide washout studded with boulders half buried like enormous bones from some forgotten race. None of them speak over the sound of the engine. The washout crests at the shoulder of the hill and she turns left out of instinct, the ground leveling before rising again to a plateau that looks out over the sprawling landscape below. She stops the Suburban and shuts the engine off.

"This is perfect," Sherell says.

They climb out, bringing the tools with them to the edge of the natural lookout. Without saying anything else they begin to dig. Rita uses the pickax, wielding it with an ease that surprises Zoey even though she knows the other girl is strong. She and Sherell shovel the loose dirt free and soon the hole takes shape as the sun moves above them in the sky.

The work is mindless, repetitive, therapeutic. Zoey loses herself in it, imagines the hole is for the last several days and that she will leave them here when they go.

Finally the grave looks deep enough and they stand beside it for a moment before returning to the vehicle. Halie's body looks much too small and it's this more than anything that wrenches at Zoey's insides.

They gather her gently and carry her between them to the grave, lowering the body into the earth. The sheet is very white against the dark clay and sand. Together they begin to fill in the hole and Zoey tries not to listen to the sound the dirt makes as it lands.

When it's done they collect as many stones as they can find and cover the loose earth with them. Sherell finds a large, flat rock that takes all three of them to carry and they set it in the center of the grave, flecks of quartz catching the sun's rays in its edges.

Zoey begins to say something. Something about Halie and how kind she always was to the younger women at the ARC. But the words are sharp edged and lodge in her throat. She feels the tears rise and recede, turning the quartz shine of the gravestone into a thousand diamond points.

"I never thanked you for getting us out," Rita says. Zoey glances at the other woman, who is staring out across the valley. "Since that night I've been trying to find the right things to say but couldn't ever come up with them. I was even going to put it down on paper, but I wasn't ever very good at writing, you both know that. But seeing what happened to Halie put everything in a whole new perspective. And when they grabbed me . . ." She shudders and turns to Zoey, her face red, eyes shimmering. "That could be me in the ground, or Sherell. We were cruel to you and Meeka and Lily, and you didn't have to come back for us, and you didn't have to go into that room after me, but you did, and I don't know how to ever thank you."

Zoey shakes her head, completely speechless. Rita has treated her warmly ever since the escape, but never have they broached the topic of their relationship before that.

"Yeah, we were real bitches," Sherell says, beginning to tear up too. "It was that place. What they did to us. What they were going to do to us. Everything. I've told you I was sorry before, but Rita's right. What happened to Halie was worse than death. I would've slit my own throat before going through it." Zoey can only nod and gaze down at the grave.

"And now you've given us what we never thought we'd have: our names, the names of our parents, knowing what little life we had before the ARC," Rita says.

Sherell nods. "I used to lie awake at night imagining what it would be like to see my parents again after induction. How they would look, what I would say, how it would feel to hug them and have them hug me. But as I got older it started to fade and I made up stories about where I came from and the life we would've had if the Dearth had never happened. Now I have something real, something I can hold on to because of you."

Rita smiles. "I did the same thing—imagined a past without the ARC and NOA. I think I knew deep down it was only my mother and me. I never remembered my father, so he must've . . ." She clears her throat. "I'm just sorry that you didn't get the same."

"It's okay," Zoey says, voice hoarse.

"It's not fair."

"The world isn't built to be fair. I've learned that much already."

"Look, no one blames you for what happened the other day."

"There's no one else to blame. I pulled the trigger."

"And you saved me. I'd be dead or worse right now if it weren't for you."

She tries to say something but the warring emotions inside her null the words.

The silence is broken only by the gusting wind that carries specks of sand across the plateau and creaks the Suburban on its springs. After a beat she feels something brush her fingers and looks down to see Sherell's hand holding her own. A moment later Rita grips her opposite hand so they stand in a half circle around the grave.

"Halie was beautiful and kind and she didn't deserve to die so young," Sherell says. "No one deserves to go through what she did. I don't know what's after this life, but I hope Halie is somewhere peaceful and free, and that she's finally found her family after all."

Zoey feels the void waver, flex as if it will break and everything inside her will come spilling out. But then Ken's face appears in her mind and she knows if he were here right now, she would only do one thing differently.

She would kill him slower.

She squeezes her friends' hands and finally releases them to keep the other women from feeling the tremor that runs through her.

"We should get back," she says, walking toward the vehicle. They follow and after one last look at the resting place, she wheels them around and heads down the side of the embankment.

The ride back is quiet and uneventful. Sherell and Rita make light conversation and Zoey knows they're trying to engage her, draw her out, return her to the group. But she is lost in her own thoughts, the words Sherell said over Halie's grave repeating themselves in an endless echo.

No one deserves to go through what she did.

No one deserves to go through.

No one deserves.

No one.

No one.

No one else.

♦ ♦ ♦

The lunchroom is stuffy, the space narrower than before, or maybe it's the others' eyes on her that's creating the feeling of being trapped. Seamus lies at her feet, nudging her leg from time to time with his nose, but she doesn't reach down to pet him. She picks at the meal Eli made for everyone, eyes unfocused, not truly seeing anything until Merrill's voice brings her back to the present.

"We need to talk about what's next," he says, looking at them individually, gaze lingering longest on Zoey. "First off we need to decide what to do with Lyle. He's been compliant and helpful, and what he says makes sense about being held against his will. I'm sure he'd like to come with us when we leave, but we need to vote on it. All in favor of giving him the option, raise your hands."

Every hand in the room goes up, Zoey lifting hers last. "Okay. That's decided then. Secondly, Ian and I have gathered as many useful supplies as we can haul. There's a large fuel depot at the rear of the property, enough gas to fill all our cans and then some. In about three weeks the passes we came through are going to be in pretty rough shape. In six they'll be impassable if we get a decent amount of snow. We'll make it no problem, but there's always a chance of an early storm sliding in over the mountains so I think it's a good—"

"I'm not going back," Zoey says.

Merrill's voice dies and every head turns toward her.

"What did you say?" Tia asks.

"I'm not going back."

Merrill squints at her and leans forward, resting his elbows on the table. "What are you talking about, Zoey?"

"The Fae Trade. I'm going after it."

There's a shocked silence that breaks as almost everyone starts talking to her at once. She glances at each of them, sees the looks in their eyes.

Pity, concern, confusion, love.

Ian's voice carries to her across the room. "I know you're upset, but it would be suicide."

"It's not about me," she says, and the group quiets. "I know you think that. Maybe you think I'm going there because it's the best chance of finding something about my parents since there was nothing for me here. But it's not. I'm going because of Halie. Because of Grace, and Annie, and Natalie, and all the others that were inducted before us. Growing up, we never knew what happened to the women who disappeared. Now we do. And it's worse than dying. The spy from NOA said they're still searching, still trying to find girls. If they find one, she'll be raised to the right age and then sold to the trade if she can't produce a female. I won't let that happen."

"But the director of NOA is dead. They're leaderless," Tia says.

"That won't stop them." She pauses, smiling painfully. "That *didn't* stop them. They're still doing what they've always done. Someone else is in charge, maybe Reaper since his body wasn't in the helicopter that crashed. Us escaping only slowed them down. They'll never quit. And the Fae Trade is just one more gear in the machine."

"Zoey, it won't bring her back," Merrill says softly. "It won't bring any of them back."

"I know that!" she yells, jumping to her feet without meaning to. She pounds a fist on the table and several glasses tip over, spilling water. She breathes hard, as if she's been fighting, and realizes she has. "But I won't go and hide away while something like the trade exists. There's a good chance they have women right now, locked up and waiting to be fought over and purchased and brought back to a place like this." She gestures at the walls. "If I can stop it, I have to try. I'm not asking anyone to go with me. In fact I don't want you to." She feels the tension slacken in her shoulders and she's suddenly very tired. "Sherell, you said nobody deserves to go through what Halie did. I'm going to make sure no one else does."

She turns from the group and moves through the open doorway, not knowing where her feet are taking her until she's on the lower level, standing in the feeble light beside the missile.

She traces its outline in the near dark. Smooth, solid contours. Seamless construction. And above it all the sense of waiting, of restraint and concealed power. When the sound of footsteps comes from behind her much later, she's already made the decision.

Ian stops beside her and gazes down into the darkness of the silo. "I suspected I'd find you here." She says nothing. "I know you think that we hate you for what you did. It was terrible, but necessary. Rita is safe." She waits, reeling in the anger that's building exponentially. "No one hates you. There's nothing you have to prove to us."

"I'm not going to the trade to cleanse my conscience."

"I know that." He sighs. "Some of the most charismatic people in history were leaders. They knew how to speak to people, how to ignite passion and reverence in a crowd with only words. But many of them weren't good leaders. They used their talents for the pursuit of power and vengeance, and when they fell, they fell far."

She looks at him. "Why are you telling me this?"

"Because whether you know it or not, or even want it, the group is looking to you now to lead them."

"What? Merrill's in charge, he's always been in charge."

"I'm sure he told you before that he never meant to be, but he's done the best he can. He's made mistakes and decisions that he's regretted."

"Like trusting me?"

Ian shakes his head and reaches out to her. She lets his hand hang there between them for a long moment before grasping it. "Absolutely not. You are part of us now, part of our family. We love you, Zoey. When I knew my children were gone, truly gone forever, I nearly lost it. I wanted to end it all the first night Helen and I found out. But we continued on because we had one another, and sometimes that is enough. The day you awoke I saw something in you. I saw hope and determination and strength unlike anything I'd ever encountered before. You gave all of us purpose again." Ian's eyes shine wetly. "And even though I miss my wife and my children every day and will until my heart stops beating, I have something to live for. We all do. That's why we're coming with you."

Her chest tries to hitch and she stops it. "You can't. I won't let you."

He smiles and squeezes her hand. "See, that's the thing about this group, they're stubborn bastards, every last one of them, myself included. Once you put an idea in our heads, we won't let it go."

Unable to resist the urge that comes over her, Zoey laughs. She steps forward and hugs him fiercely. "Thank you."

"There's nothing to thank us for," he says, stroking her hair.

"I'm sorry. For everything."

"I know. It's okay. But promise me you won't lose control like that again. You can't. You'll get yourself or someone else killed. Promise me."

The smothering darkness within her pulses with a life of its own. "I promise."

He holds her for another beat before letting her go. "We've got another problem on our hands."

"What's that?"

"Actually finding the Fae Trade. It travels all over the country. There's no way of knowing where it is, and none of us have actually seen it."

She glances toward the main tunnel. "No. But there's someone here who has."

19

Lyle looks up from the computer screen when Zoey enters the room.

His eyes are bloodshot from lack of sleep and there are dark circles beneath them, but the vitality she noticed before, while pulling up Rita's and Sherell's information, hasn't diminished.

"Hello," he says as she shuts the door to the tunnel.

"Hi."

"What can I do for you, Zoey?"

"You told us that the Fae Trade came through your community and took the women. Killed anyone who fought back, right?"

"That's right."

"Where was this?"

Lyle licks his lips. "It was near a little town called Brigeton in northern Nevada."

"And you saw the trade itself?"

"In the distance, yes. We didn't know what it was until it was too late."

"What did it look like?"

"Like an enormous carnival. You're probably too young to know what that is."

"I've read about them." She walks to the file cabinet she overturned the day they'd arrived and runs her fingers along the drawer's handle. "Ken said that it travels all over the country."

"That's right."

"Do they go to the same places or do they take a new route every time?"

"I'm not sure exactly."

"How long ago did you see it?"

"I can't say for sure. It was years ago. But like I told you, I've lost track of time."

"Did they already have Halie when they brought you here?" It takes a second for her to recognize the confusion on his face. "Halie was the woman's name."

"Oh. Yes, yes she was already here."

Zoey walks back to the door and leans against it. "Do you know which direction the trade was headed?"

Lyle squints, eyes narrowing to slits behind his glasses. "They came from the southeast, so I would wager they were moving northwest toward Seattle."

"Did the men ever leave the installation to go to it again since you've been here?"

"No. They'd go on scavenging missions, but they were never gone more than a couple days. I think they liked the comforts of this place." Lyle stares at her for a long moment. "Is it true? Are they all dead?"

"Yes," she hears herself say.

"You killed them."

"Yes."

"Are you going to kill me?"

"No." She surveys him for a moment. "But there is one thing I need your help with."

◆　◆　◆

Twenty minutes later she leaves Lyle sitting in the same place she found him. When she explained what she wanted, he'd gone pale.

I wouldn't know where to begin.

You'll have time.

But even then, I'm just a computer tech who's had zero practice in the last twenty years.

If you can gain access, could you do it?

In theory, yes.

Then that's all I'm asking.

Zoey climbs the last few stairs to the main floor and finds Merrill talking to the rest of the group. He falls silent when she appears.

She gazes at all of them, a spike of warmth shooting through her chest each time she meets someone's eyes and they are steady and unflinching. "Thank you," she says. "I don't know what else to say."

"Then shut up with this mushy shit and tell us what the plan is," Tia says. A rumble of laughter runs through the group and Zoey smiles.

"From what Lyle told me, I'm guessing the trade follows the same path each year and ends in Seattle. Which seems logical since they'd continue to hit the largest communities."

"How do we know where they're at now?" Eli asks.

"We don't. But Ken said it comes through once a year, and Lyle's been here close to a year. I asked him if Ken and his men had ever left to go to it since they'd captured him, and he said no. So if the trade follows the same route and it hasn't been close by in nearly a year . . ."

"Then it's a good chance they're going to be near here soon," Ian finishes. "It's a brilliant deduction, my girl, but how do you intend on pinpointing their location?"

"Our only option is asking people who we come across on the road. I'm sure it's a common question, and it won't raise any suspicion if one of the men inquire about it."

"That's all fine and dandy but the country you're talking about traveling through is rough, honey," Tia says. "And I'm not just talking about the landscape. There's going to be highwaymen, rapists, murderers, and that's before we ever get to the damn trade."

"I know," she says, walking down the hallway. She hears the shuffle of feet following her as she nears the garage door and opens it. With a flick of her fingers the lights come on. "That's why we're taking that."

20

They spend the next day and a half equipping the armored vehicle with weapons, ammo, food, and water.

The inside has been stripped, leaving empty bolt holes everywhere in the walls and floor. Only two padded benches remain behind the driver and passenger seats in the front. The interior smells of oiled steel and grease.

Zoey turns in a slow circle between the benches, back bent slightly to keep her head from hitting the roof. A steel box is mounted in the upper-right corner of the space, and when she unhooks it from the wall and peers inside she finds a large flare gun, flares, and a first aid kit that's been looted of everything but two rolls of gauze.

"Not sure we're all going to fit in here," Rita says, climbing up into the vehicle. Sherell appears behind her, and both women set down an armload of ammunition.

Zoey reattaches the steel box to the wall. "We'll make do," she says, sitting beside Sherell.

"Yeah, we're good at that," Rita says.

They are quiet for a time, the sounds of the group moving something heavy at the far end of the garage muffled by the thick walls of the vehicle.

"I didn't mean to put this idea in your head," Sherell says, gesturing to the supplies accumulating in one corner. "By saying what I did at Halie's grave."

"You didn't. I was thinking about it way before that," Zoey says.

"You're not responsible, you know. For everyone else."

"I know."

"We could go back to the mountains, keep working on Ian's house. Forget about everything. We're safe there."

"We could. But it's like you said about knowing where you came from, the bruise that won't heal. I'd always wonder if there was someone like us in a cage somewhere."

Sherell nods and smiles sadly. "I always knew you were different. Better than us. Even back in the ARC. Maybe that's why I picked on you."

"I'm not better than you. I'm not better than anyone."

"Yes you are," Rita says. "And saying that you're not proves it."

"I'm doing what I need to. I'm sorry everyone's getting dragged along."

"No one's dragging us. We volunteered, remember."

Silence falls again except for the soft tread of feet near the open door and a moment later Newton appears carrying a large plastic water jug. He glances to each of them before Sherell moves to take the container from his hand. She smiles at him and Newton blushes, dropping his eyes and hurrying away across the garage.

"You can't help yourself, can you?" Rita says as Sherell places the water with the other supplies.

Sherell shrugs, smiling again. "Why should I?"

"You've been spending quite a bit of time with him."

"I think he's interesting. He says things with his eyes if you're watching."

"Um-hmm."

"And it doesn't hurt that he's gorgeous to look at, either." Rita and Sherell laugh and Zoey smiles. "Never know. Someday maybe we'll have a little place of our own in the mountains. Maybe even a baby. Do either of you ever think about that kind of thing?"

"Babies?" Rita asks. "I'd have to find a guy who could stand me first. But yeah, from time to time." Her eyes grow distant and when she realizes they are both watching her, her face becomes as deeply red as Newton's and she glances away.

"How about you, Zoey?" Sherell says. "Maybe Lee will come back and . . ." Her face falls and she closes her eyes.

"I'd never bring a child into this world," Zoey says with such vehemence it surprises even her. She swallows and shakes her head.

"I'm sorry," Sherell says.

"It's fine."

"But—"

"I'm actually glad you both came in here," Zoey says, cutting the other woman off. "There's something I need you to do."

"Okay. What is it?" Rita says.

"I need you to stay behind with Lyle."

Rita and Sherell look at her, stricken. They both begin speaking at once, their refusals overlapping and intermingling with one another.

Zoey holds up her hand to quiet them. "Let me tell you why."

She does. When she's finished the other two women simply stare at her as if she is a complete stranger that's wandered into their midst. She supposes on some levels she is.

"Why?" Rita finally asks, her voice husky.

"Because it needs to be done. They'll never stop. Never. You both know that. I've gone over every other option and I don't see another way."

"You know, Merrill was right the other day," Sherell says quietly. "Nothing we do will bring back the women who died before us."

"No, it won't," Zoey says, stanching the flow of faces that cascade through her thoughts. She closes her eyes. "But it will stop NOA. Forever."

They sit motionless for several minutes, the air within the vehicle beginning to thicken with their combined breathing.

Finally Rita glances at Sherell. "She's right."

"I know."

"You'll stay then?" Zoey asks.

"We'll stay," Rita says.

"Thank you."

Zoey clears her throat, standing from the bench. "There's still a lot to be done, so we should probably get moving." She's stepping out the door when Rita's voice stops her.

"Zoey?"

"Yeah?"

"Be careful not to become them."

She tries to answer but can't. Instead she turns away and leaves them sitting on the benches.

Out in the hangar the air feels close and oppressive, like she's still inside the vehicle, but she knows it's only her imagination. The uneasiness in her center from hearing Lee's name hasn't dissipated. Why did Sherell have to mention him? Especially in a context like that? Because now the image won't go away. She sees Lee standing before a small cabin gathering firewood. His back is to her but he turns, his face lighting up, and she can't help the warm and comfortable sensation that runs through her—a rightness. And there is someone else there, she can feel it. Someone behind the cabin door that opens. A tiny hand and face peering out with a smile that is not Lee's nor her own, but a combination of the two.

The clang of a wrench against concrete snaps her free of the daydream, and she blinks, reality coming back so harshly beneath the fluorescents that her heart aches. Zoey shakes her head, willing the fantasy away. There's no reason to think of things that won't ever be.

At the front of the vehicle she finds Lyle tightening an armor plate. He torques the last bolt and steps back.

"Is it ready?" she asks.

"As far as I can tell. Really there were just a couple relays burned out. Other than that, everything seems fine. I may be wrong though since the electronics are the only parts that I have any knowledge of. Tia did a rough check on the engine though and says it looks okay. We can test start it in any case."

Zoey glances past his shoulder and sees the others approaching from across the garage. "Rita and Sherell are staying behind to oversee your progress. You try and run or do anything stupid, they have instructions to kill you." Color drains from Lyle's face. "Remember, you can't tell anyone until the time is right. Okay?"

"Okay."

Merrill reaches them first. "Are we ready for a test drive?"

"Should be," she says. "But first I wanted to tell you, Lyle is staying behind and I encouraged Rita and Sherell to stay too. I don't want any more of us in harm's way than is necessary."

Merrill's brow wrinkles and he looks from her to Lyle. "Okay, but what brought this on?"

"There's additional information I've already tapped into and more I think I can glean from the database about the National Obstetric Alliance. Besides, I'd be more of a hindrance than a help where you're going."

Merrill studies the older man for a long moment. Zoey watches Lyle, the bead of sweat that's forming at his temple. "Okay. If that's what you want. You've been a big help to us so far. But there should be a contingency plan in case anyone else shows up here while we're gone."

"I think it would be a good idea for Newton to stay behind too," Zoey says.

Merrill grimaces, glancing over at the young man who stands quietly watching Sherell. "I hate to leave him."

"I know. But they'll all be safer here."

After a long moment he nods. "Okay."

"Also, if it gives you more peace of mind, there's a tunnel running the length of the compound on the lower level that comes up behind the storage shed beside the northern fence. If someone tries to get in we can take it and cut through the fence and be gone before they know where we went," Lyle says.

"All right." Merrill looks at Zoey. "Rita and Sherell staying back wasn't your idea, was it?"

"They offered."

He watches her and she worries that he'll see through the façade she's putting up, know that there's something more. And what will he say when he realizes what it is?

Eli slaps Merrill on the shoulder and the moment is broken. "We gonna fire this bad bitch up or stand around and look at it?"

"Yeah, let's try it."

Lyle tries to hand the keys to Merrill, but he pushes them back. "You're the one that fixed it. You have the honors."

Lyle smiles and climbs into the cab with some effort. The heavy silence throughout the garage is finally broken by a loud click, followed by the explosive growl of the machine's engine. It idles roughly, blue smoke pouring from its rear end. The engine revs and howls, making the large room reverberate with sound. After another few seconds the vehicle falls silent and Lyle appears in the hatch once again. The group breaks out in applause and he takes a little bow, the smile still on his face.

"That is the sexiest sound I've ever heard," Tia says, running her hand appreciatively over the vehicle's side.

"Damnit, girl, if I growl like that, will you touch me?" Eli says, sidling up to her.

"You do growl like that. The problem is it typically comes out of the wrong end."

Zoey smiles as the rest of the group laughs. Eli hangs his head and shakes it. She looks from person to person, each of their personalities shining through, the subtlety of who they are so clear to her.

And she knows when the time comes she will miss them all very much.

21

They leave the installation at dawn, the first lancing rays of light deflecting off the hills in the east, creating a half halo in the ashen sky.

Merrill drives the armored security vehicle, or ASV, as Lyle told them it is called. Chelsea sits beside him in the passenger seat while Zoey rests on one of the benches behind them along with Ian, Tia, and Eli. The rough road crackles beneath the heavy machine, the sound almost lost beneath the constant hum of the engine. Through the thick, tinted windows Zoey watches the land glide past, the rise and plateau where Halie rests appearing in the view pane and then gone.

She readjusts her position on the bench and silently wishes that the rear of the ASV had a window. Then she could look back, watch the installation grow smaller and fainter until it was swallowed up by the distance and curve in the road. She imagines Rita and Sherell and Newton standing there with Seamus by their side, watching them fade away down the drive, and feels an apology on her lips for the weight she's burdened them with.

"Penny for your thoughts," Eli says, nudging her in the ribs.

"What?"

"It's an old saying. Kinda means you want to know what someone's thinking so bad, you'll pay them."

"Did some people actually make money that way?"

Eli chuckles. "I guess you could say that."

"I wasn't thinking anything."

"Now you're straight-up lying. Everyone's always thinking something. Even if it's bullshit."

She sighs and glances at Ian and Tia. They are talking quietly to one another. "Do you regret anything you've done?" she asks.

Eli sits back, one of his hands going to his arm with the tattoo before settling onto his thigh. "Regret is like air: can't be alive without it." He seems to be lost in a memory for a second before coming back. "But I'll tell you what—regret's made out of lead. It'll drag you under if you let it." He glances down at the name tattooed on his arm and looks away. "If I could go back to do some things over, I would in a heartbeat. But that ain't reality. It ain't life. You got to forgive yourself before you can move on. When you forgive yourself the regret gets lighter and lighter and you manage to keep going."

"Have you forgiven yourself?"

Eli's face darkens and he leans back against the side of the ASV. He tries to smile and fails. "No. Not yet."

◆　◆　◆

They drive for most of the day, stopping several times to gain their bearings and relieve themselves. Zoey watches the landscape recede into itself, the highest buttes gradually leveling off, ravines rising into wider plains. The sky expands so that it becomes half of everything she sees. The scope of it stuns her to the point she can do nothing but look out the window, marveling at the immensity of it all. Just when she's sure she's got a grip on the world, it unfolds again, revealing another side of itself.

"Pretty vast, isn't it?" Merrill calls from the front seat in the midafternoon. "We're on the edge of the Great Basin Desert. This whole area burned flat about fifteen years ago. Doesn't look like much grew back since then."

Zoey gazes out the window at the rolling desolation. The scrub is shorter than any she's seen before, the land pocked and cracked like burnt skin. As she watches, an area far left of the road drops and opens into a wide hole. Something flashes there, bright and gone in an instant.

"What is that?" she asks, pointing toward the depression.

"Not sure. Maybe a sinkhole?" Merrill says.

"I saw something."

"What was it?"

"I don't know. A flash of metal maybe." She turns from the window. "Can we check it out?"

"Sure. No sign of life yet." Merrill slows, turning off the highway onto a rocky decline the ASV handles with ease.

Zoey leans up between the two front seats, staring at the drop in the land. It is more defined than she thought before, its edges somewhat squared rather than round. Beyond the depression the horizon is smudged with the smoky outlines of a mountain range.

Merrill stops thirty yards from the hole and shuts the vehicle off. He stares out the windshield, and after a moment Chelsea glances at him.

"What?" she asks.

"This looks manmade."

Zoey frowns. "What could make something this big?"

"Backhoes, dredges, a bomb, I don't know. It's washed some but the shape is still here."

Zoey grasps a pair of binoculars from the center console and opens the side door, dry wind buffeting her face and hair. She jumps down and walks around the front of the ASV, stopping a dozen steps away from the drop's edge.

Merrill was right. The hole is square shaped, its far border at least a hundred and fifty yards away. Some of its sides have crumbled and fallen down, but for the most part the work of men is recognizable. Its middle is strewn with dried tumbleweed and bramble, the twisted remains leached of any color by the unrelenting sun.

She walks along the edge's perimeter, the others joining her. There, the flash again. It's partially up the opposite wall, glinting when she moves a certain way. Zoey brings up the binoculars.

The shining comes from a rounded dial, small and rimmed with silver. Bleached sage roots twist into the parched soil above and below it. She squints at the small disc adjusting the binoculars so that it comes into tight focus.

It's a wristwatch, burnished from the weather, its face broken and clouded. Several of the guards at the ARC wore them on the arm opposite their bracelets. She always wondered why they bothered with them since you couldn't turn a corner in the compound without seeing a calendar.

What is a wristwatch doing in a hole in the middle of a desert?

"Zoey," Merrill says, somewhere beside her. She can't see him since her eyes are still glued to the binoculars, but his voice is odd, light and airy. The sage roots are weird under the magnification, straighter and whiter than they ought to be.

"Zoey."

And they seem to run through the watch's band.

Something locks into place in her mind and her breath catches.

Not roots.

Bones.

The wristwatch is still attached to an arm, clean and dry of any flesh. The binoculars waver and she catches sight of more bones protruding from the thin layer of dirt to the right of the watch. Her arms lose some of their strength and the binoculars drop away from her eyes, allowing her to see the entire hole at once.

It is full of bodies.

Most are covered by soil that's eroded or blown into the depression, but the details emerge as she stares. A row of skulls here, a frayed and blanched patch of clothing there. What she first mistook for dried sage that had tumbled down into the hole becomes clear. Bones, so many bones interlaced and partially buried.

Thousands.

"Zoey." Merrill's hand touches her shoulder and she nearly screams. She looks up into his eyes and sees a reflection of the horror she's feeling.

"What is this?" she breathes.

"A mass grave. These are rebels. I heard about things like this but never saw one."

She swallows bile and glances again at the pit. It draws her gaze like a magnet, unbearable to look at but impossible not to. "So many."

"Come on." He tries to guide her away but she stays where she is. Entranced by the overwhelming weight of death.

"NOA did this."

"Yes, or the military. At the end it was basically the same thing."

"How. How did they . . ." She falters, the sheer mechanics of the genocide numbing her mind.

"Come on. There's nothing here for us. We have to go."

She lets herself be led away, the hole an engraved picture behind her eyes. *How?* she asks herself. *How could they do it? How could they let it happen?*

But already she knows. She's felt the rage, the hatred, the absolute and utter need to destroy. She's partaken in it, drank the bitter draft of murder and did it unblinkingly. That is how all travesties occur. Because of people like her.

When they begin to drive again, she curls up at the far end of the bench, tucking her legs in close to her chest, becoming as small as she can be. A hurricane of emotions rises inside her, pummeling her mind with accusations and vindications at the same time.

You're a monster.

They deserve it. Every last one of them.

Monster.

No one else. Never again.

Murderer.

She clenches her eyes shut and wishes Meeka's voice would return and speak to her like it did when she was traveling alone and feverish in the wilderness.

But Meeka is silent. And she knows she'll remain that way.

Because she's on her own again, as solitary as she was when she escaped.

22

Zoey wakes, arm asleep beneath her, neck brimming with pain from the awkward angle she's lying at on the bench.

She sits up, groggy, eyes crusted with sleep, and blinks at Tia who's watching her.

"Nice nap?" Tia says.

"Didn't realize I fell asleep. How long was I out?"

"Maybe two hours. We figured you could use it."

"Thank you." Zoey cracks her neck and stretches her tingling arm, the feeling slowly returning. "Where are we?"

"Passed into the great state of Oregon a while back," Merrill says from the front. "Thinking about stopping pretty soon for the night."

Zoey nods, swiping at her eyes before feeling an indentation in the side of her face. Her fingertips run over it and she glances at Ian and Tia who are grinning at her.

"You've got quite the imprint from the seam in the seat there, my girl," Ian says, beginning to laugh.

"Looks like someone put a zipper in your face," Eli chimes in.

She smiles, trying to rub the mark away, only then recalling what happened before she fell asleep.

The pit.

The bones.

The death.

I still have a choice.

"Zoey?"

She looks at Eli whose brow is furrowed. "What?"

"Didn't you hear Tia?"

"No, sorry. What did you say?"

Tia shakes her head, all the mirth gone from her now. "Nothing. Never mind."

Zoey meets Ian's eyes and looks away, unable to withstand the concern within them.

The ASV shudders as Merrill slows their speed, glancing around the deserted highway. "Well, there's a drive headed off to the left and a draw to the right we could hide the vehicle in overnight. Wouldn't be visible from the road. What do you guys thi—"

"Holy shit!" Tia says, standing suddenly. "There's a kid over there."

Zoey spins, nearly knocking her forehead against the window behind her. It takes a split second for her to see the small figure standing in the center of the small drive on the left. The light is still good enough to make out delicate features, blond hair that hangs down over his ears. Gauging from his height she guesses he's anywhere from twelve to fourteen years old.

The boy stands his ground for a long second, then bolts away from the highway, feet kicking up puffs of dust.

They watch him run until he vanishes over a small rise in the road.

"Should we follow him?" Chelsea asks.

"Yes," Zoey says at once. Without another comment, Merrill turns the wheel of the machine and guides it slowly down the drive. They come over the rise where they lost sight of the boy and drop down into a narrow gully with steep sides. Far ahead the path rises again before opening up into a vast field populated by a low stand of brush, dying grass, and a solitary tree holding on to its last few leaves. Beside the tree is a small stone house and garage.

The boy stands on the front porch and as soon as he sees them, ducks inside the building.

"The hell is going on?" Eli says.

"Don't know if I like this," Tia says, holding on to the back of Chelsea's seat.

Zoey looks for cover that could conceal someone on either side of the drive but it is an open expanse of nothing but wilting grass, barely knee-high. Beyond the house is a twisting stream that flows out of sight into a larger brace of trees.

"Think it's a trap?" Eli asks, already picking up his rifle from the seat beside him.

"No. It doesn't feel like one," Merrill says. "I think he's scared."

They idle up to an overgrown turnaround, white rocks set in a circle that have gone mossy with time. "I'm keeping this running until it's clear," Merrill says. "Eli and I will check it out."

"I want to——"

"Zoey. No. Let us at least make sure it's safe. This was your plan, remember?"

"Yes," she says begrudgingly.

"We'll be quick." He slaps Eli on the shoulder and hoists a rifle sling over his head.

"Be careful," Chelsea says.

"Always. And if anyone comes out of that house besides us, you drive away and don't look back."

With that, he and Eli open the ASV's door and step into the evening light. Their boots puff dust up just as the boy's had while he ran. Tia yanks the door shut behind them and Zoey stands, peering through the windshield, watching their progress.

Merrill and Eli move well together, one leapfrogging while the other covers him. After they gain the porch they stand to either side of the door. Merrill reaches out and knocks with one fist. Zoey waits, the anticipation of gunfire as an answer bringing her heart rate up. After several seconds Merrill nods and Eli swings in, opening the door before going inside low. Merrill follows, standing high, rifle pivoting back and forth. They move out of sight leaving the door wide open.

Minutes tick by.

The interior of the vehicle is quiet save for everyone's shallow breathing and the idling of the machine itself. Just as Zoey is about to insist that they go in after the men, Merrill reappears with Eli behind him and trailing them is the boy they followed to the house. He steps out onto the porch and stares at the ASV with a look of wonder. Zoey is about to reach for the door handle when another child appears. He is several years younger but has the same characteristic blond hair as what can only be his brother.

"Two kids?" Tia says.

But then two more boys step into the light, the youngest no older than five. Behind them two taller figures appear. One is a slender man with dark, shaggy hair and a goatee who walks with a slight hunch, while the other is a heavyset woman with long, reddish-blonde hair. In her arms is another boy, much smaller than the rest, who wears only a long-sleeved shirt and a diaper. He has a mop of hair matching the man's.

"My God," Ian says.

Merrill waves toward the vehicle and nods. Tia shuts the ASV off and the others climb out. Zoey hears the man say something in an awed voice, words that are lost to her but whose meaning is clear. He is as surprised to see them as they are to see his family.

The dark-haired man blinks, mouth opening and closing several times before taking a step forward, his hand reaching out toward Zoey. Tia steps in front of him, pulling her handgun free of its holster.

"It's okay, Tia. We checked them. They're clean," Merrill says. Tia reholsters her weapon and lets the man step past her. All the while his gaze hasn't left Zoey's face. He continues to blink and stops several feet away, both hands now palms up in supplication.

"Thanks be to God," he says, smiling widely. "Unless I'm dreaming."

Zoey shifts her gaze from the man to the rest of the group, uncertain of what to do. "Hello," she finally says, holding out her hand. "My name is Zoey."

The man takes her hand and squeezes it. "I'm Travis. And we are so glad to see you."

◆　◆　◆

Firelight dances across the gray stone hearth. Shadows, from the simple furniture in the room, elongate on the close-set walls. Zoey sits in the closest chair to the fire, chewing the last piece of bread slathered with rich butter. She savors the taste, similar to the flavor of butter she had at the ARC, but wholly different as well. It is richer, saltier, more . . . real. She drinks cold water from a chipped glass painted with flowers on one side, their yellow petals delicate and outlined in black.

"It was part of my mother's set." Zoey turns to see Travis's wife, Anniel, standing in the doorway that leads to the small kitchen beyond. "There's only two glasses, three plates, and one bowl left. Everything else has been broken or lost over the years."

Zoey turns the cup around in her hands. "It's beautiful."

Anniel smiles. "Would you like more food? There's still some soup left."

"No. Thank you. It was delicious."

Footsteps approach from outside and a second later Travis enters the room followed by Merrill, Chelsea, and Ian.

"The ASV is pretty well hidden behind a stand of trees to the east. Should be fine overnight," Merrill says.

"Are Eli and Tia still outside?" Zoey asks.

"Yeah. They're entertaining the young ones." Merrill smiles at Travis who shakes his head.

"I'm sorry, they're probably bothering them."

"No. I'm pretty sure they're enjoying the attention."

"They've led pretty sheltered lives up until now," Travis says. "None of them have ever met a black man before. That's probably part of the fascination."

The baby, whose name Zoey learned is Isaac, squeals somewhere in the kitchen and Anniel leaves to tend to him while the others all find a place to sit in the cramped living room.

"On that note," Ian says, "tell us how it is you came to live here with your family."

Travis smiles and gazes at the fire. "Anniel and I met through our church years before the Dearth. It was a nice little congregation maybe a hundred miles west of here. I was studying to become a pastor and she worked as a consultant for a railroad. When the Dearth came we went to stay with my parents on their farm but it soon became clear it wasn't safe. Anniel and I were terrified of what was happening, so we decided to go into hiding."

"Smart choice," Chelsea says.

"It turned out to be, yes. We searched for a remote area along with several other families from our church, thinking there was strength in numbers. We settled here along with our pastor at the time. There's around forty of us, counting the kids, scattered in the area. We have a regular commune every Sunday after service, each household taking turns hosting it. We try to keep traditions close even though it's hard to do in these times."

"Staying alive is hard, let alone traditions," Merrill says, glancing out a window.

"Amen to that," Travis says. "When John, our oldest, was born, we knew God had blessed us and that we would be safe in this place. And for the last fourteen years, we have been. We have worship, community, plenty of food from the river and surrounding land, and, of course, the children, which are the most important."

Travis's eyes grow distant and Zoey studies him. "You said earlier that you were so glad to see me," she says. "What did you mean by that?"

"Forgive me if I'm wrong, but are you not by far the youngest of your group?"

"Yes," she says, still hesitant to mention Rita and Sherell.

"Well, we are of the Quiverfull belief."

"What's that?"

"We believe that each child is a gift directly from God and that it is our duty as Christians to multiply, to fill the Earth with mankind. These last decades have proven to us how important our mission is. The world is growing sparser and sparser of man, and we will vanish without the effort to fulfill God's will."

"I still don't understand what that has to do with me."

"My wife is forty-four now, and I am nearly fifty years old. You are by far the youngest woman we've seen in over twenty years." Travis leans forward, the firelight splashing against his features. "You are a symbol of hope, Zoey. A living, breathing testament of God's plan. Just sitting here with you fills me with a divine wonder and renewed vigor of spirit." Tears shine in his eyes. "When I look at you, I know that everything will be all right."

Zoey shifts in her chair, the weight of Travis's stare and reverent smile pressing upon her. "Thank you, but I'm not sure I'm who you think I am."

"It doesn't matter if you believe or not."

"Okay. Well, we did have a couple questions for you if you don't mind?"

"By all means."

"Have you ever heard of the Fae Trade?"

Travis's face instantly darkens, eyes flicking toward the floor. "I suppose that's what they call themselves."

Zoey sits forward. "Who?"

"The men that pass through every so often. It's usually a little later in the season than this. We haven't seen them in nearly three years now, thank God. They're scouts, I believe, for the main body of the group. They come in vehicles looking for women. That's why all of us have hidden root cellars outside our homes. We hide there the minute trouble appears, like today when you fine folks came up our drive. That's where Merrill and Eli found us."

"I thought you said the cellars are hidden."

Travis looks somewhat sheepish. "Isaac wasn't able to keep quiet like the rest of us. He's only a year and a half. Merrill heard him. I didn't see any other choice than to open the doors and accept our fate. You could've burned us out. That's what happened to the Starks."

"Who are they?" Zoey asks.

Travis sighs. "They were the oldest of our community. Got caught unawares six or seven years ago. There were four of them. Two sons, eighteen and twenty. All of them burnt up in their home by those you mentioned. I'm assuming Glenda wasn't taken because of her age. She was past childbearing, you see."

Zoey traces the flowers on her glass with a fingertip. "You said they haven't come through here in several years. Do you know their route?"

Travis shakes his head. "No. But I heard rumor that they stop at the largest towns to draw in crowds of men. I can only imagine the unholy things that go on there."

"Where's the next largest town?"

"I suppose that would be Southland. It's about a hundred miles to the west. Used to be a little ski resort town at the base of Scrimshaw Mountain."

"Tia's been there before. She told me about it years ago. She'll know the way," Merrill says.

Zoey shares a look with the others before returning her gaze to Travis. "Thank you. That helps a lot."

"You're very welcome, but you're not thinking of seeking this trade out, are you?"

"Curious. That's all."

"Well, be forewarned, they are brutal men. If you come across them your only hope is to run the other way." A strained silence falls over them before Travis says, "In any case, please, by all means, consider staying with us as long as you'd like. We don't have a lot of room, but the house is warm at night and there's plenty of food."

"We appreciate your and your wife's hospitality," Merrill says.

The fire crackles and spits a small ember out onto the tile that Travis moves back into the flames. "Do not neglect to show hospitality to strangers, for thereby some have entertained angels unawares. Hebrews 13:2." He smiles again at Zoey and she tries to return it.

"I'll bring these in to Anniel," she says, standing with the dishes. She moves past Ian, giving him a wide-eyed look, and sees the corner of his mouth quirk.

In the kitchen she finds Anniel at a deep sink filled with steaming water. A woodstove in the corner throws waves of heat across the room, and Isaac holds a small, wooden hammer, banging it on the floor where he sits. Zoey places the dishes on the counter beside the sink.

"You didn't have to trouble yourself," Anniel says. "I could've come got them."

"It's fine." Zoey stares at Isaac who begins inspecting a knot in the hardwood floor with acute interest. "Can I ask you something?"

The older woman pauses in her washing. "Of course."

"Do you ever worry about bringing children into the world?"

Anniel smiles broadly, her wide face lighting up. "No. I don't."

"How can you not? Today you hid from us because you were afraid we were here to take you away and do something terrible to your family. How do you live in fear like that and ever in good conscience subject another life to the same thing?" She realizes she's shaking now, voice sharp, rising in volume. Anniel stands placidly beside the sink, eyes soft and knowing. "I'm sorry, I didn't mean—"

"It's okay, dear. I can understand what you're saying. But our faith is something beyond the fears of life. God's will transcends barriers we put around ourselves as well as those in the outside world. In the face of belief, all fear pales."

Zoey feels something brush her leg and she nearly reaches for her handgun before seeing it is only Isaac balancing with one hand against her thigh. The little boy looks up at her, eyes very blue and clear, studying her with innocent curiosity.

Abruptly he holds up his arms.

"He wants you to hold him," Anniel says.

"What?"

"He's only been walking a few months and he gets tired. That's his sign for wanting to be held."

"No, that's okay, I really shouldn't—"

But Anniel cuts her off by picking Isaac up and placing him in her arms.

The boy looks at her for another long second before flopping against her shoulder. One of his hands winds in her hair, tugging gently. He is warm, and soft, and there is no reservation about how he embraces her. His trust is complete.

She feels a growing warmth in her chest that has nothing to do with Isaac's body heat. Zoey places one hand against his back and he makes a sound that is between a giggle and a sigh.

All at once the image of the mass grave returns to her.

The stark whiteness of the bones.

Scraps of withered clothing.

The wristwatch still attached to the man who died trying to climb free of the pit.

She sees him clambering over dead bodies and she knows each and every one of them. There are her best friends, Meeka and Lily, and those who were kind to her, like Simon and Crispin. Merrill and Chelsea lie intertwined, the backs of their heads broken and ruined. The man climbs over Ian's lifeless body, paws past Tia and Sherell and Rita, who lie faceup, mouths open in breathless screams. He steps on Eli's and Newton's limp bodies, reaching the edge of the huge grave, and there is a concussive blast, a gunshot that takes him in his back. He falls, twisting over, blood spraying from his torn chest, and it is Lee who looks up at her then, Lee who is dying, the wristwatch shining with his blood.

And she can feel the gun in her hand.

Zoey presses Isaac into Anniel's arms. She tries to say something but her tongue is a useless lump, too large behind her teeth. She stumbles out of the kitchen, through the living room past surprised faces, and into the open evening air.

Eli and Tia glance up at her as she rushes past them and three of the boys, who are cartwheeling in the driveway. She makes it to a skeletal thicket of bushes before vomiting. Bracing her hands against her knees, she tries to force away the image of Lee's bloody face and torn body, but can't and is sick again. Her hands shake and she rubs them against her pants, unable to rid the feeling of the gun in her palm. Slowly she straightens, head pounding, stomach still clenching like a fist.

Footsteps sound behind her and she turns to see Ian approaching. He stops at her side, looking out over the darkening field behind the house that merges with the river and trees.

"Are you all right?" he finally asks.

She wipes her mouth, acid thick on her tongue, in her nostrils. "Yes."

"Whatever it is you're carrying, the weight is too much, Zoey. You can tell me, no matter what."

"I'm fine."

"No. No you're not. Some things are too heavy to manage on your own. Certain burdens will break a person if they insist on bearing them alone."

The wind begins a gentle caress of the long grass, undulations of a great, unseen hand. The light fades further to a purple hue that blankets the east, sliding closer and closer toward them.

She almost tells him then. Almost spews out the words as she did her dinner minutes ago. But she can't. It is like the truth is locked solidly inside her. She is a prison of secrets.

"I'm okay," she says finally. Ian's face is half-shrouded in shadow and she gives him only a quick smile before starting back toward the house. The three young boys round the house's corner as she nears it, Eli in close pursuit behind them, playfully growling. The littlest trips and falls and Eli tickles his sides before standing the child upright once again.

"Can we play tag again, Mr. Eli?"

Eli winks at Zoey, his chest heaving. "I don't know. You boys are wearing me out!"

"Aww, you're too big to get wore out," the next oldest boy says. Zoey thinks his name is Michael. "Maybe when John gets back we'll play more! He's really fast. The fastest of us all."

Zoey is about to reach the front of the house when she stops and turns back to the children. "What did you say about John?"

"He's the fastest," Michael says earnestly.

"No, you said when he gets back. Where is he?"

"At Pastor Rogers's house. He lives a few miles, uh, that way," Michael says, pointing in the direction of the highway.

"What's he doing there?" she asks, an icy tingling beginning to grow in the base of her stomach.

"Telling Pastor Rogers and the rest of our church about you so they can celebrate. He'll be back soon."

Zoey locks eyes with Eli, who is already moving. "I'll get the others," he says, hurrying around the building.

Ian stops beside the youngest boy. "What's the matter?"

"Travis's oldest son went to tell their pastor about us."

"Oh no."

They hurry to the front porch, where Eli and Tia are talking with Merrill and Chelsea. Travis is in the doorway, hands held out in a placating gesture.

"You have nothing to fear," he is saying. "Nothing at all. John is very obedient. He'll return soon with our pastor and you'll see. This is a blessed night."

"You sent him?" Zoey asks. "You sent your son to tell others about us? About me?"

Travis smiles. "Yes. But there's no need for alarm. Our community is close knit. They will relish your presence and it will sustain their hope for years to come simply by seeing a woman as young as you are."

She is about to swear at him when a sound rises above the slight wind.

Engines.

Several of them.

When she looks again at Travis, a frown has creased his brow. He stares past them down the long drive and steps close to the porch railing.

"That's not right," he says. "The pastor doesn't have a vehicle."

Zoey's head spins, thoughts whirring past faster than she can reckon them. "We have to go. Now!" she yells. She begins to run around the side of the building, Merrill catching up with her at once. "Where's the ASV?"

"Behind that farthest stand of trees by the river."

"Go. I'll be right there." He yells something at her but she's already gone, around the back of the house. She sprints to the small wooden door set there and almost bowls Anniel over as she pushes it open from the inside. Isaac is in her arms, eyes wide and shining in the near dark.

"Come on," Zoey says, grasping the other woman's arm. "You have to come with us. The boys too, everyone."

"Travis said to get in the cellar."

"They'll find you. You need to come with us." She tries to yank Anniel with her but the woman moves in the opposite direction. Three small shadows race out of the house, running ahead of their mother as Isaac looks back in Zoey's direction, whimpering quietly.

"They're going to kill you," Zoey hisses, an almost irresistible force dragging her in the direction of the ASV.

An engine revs somewhere beyond the house and a powerful light slices across the tops of the nearest trees.

Anniel pauses at a rough rectangle of darkness that's opened in the ground before her, then vanishes inside it as if swallowed whole.

Zoey turns and runs.

Her feet slip in the heavy dew that's becoming frost with the falling night and the lower part of her spine sends a lightning bolt of pain down her left leg as she catches herself and continues. Numbness floods her thighs.

No. Not now. Not now. Can't fall. They'll find me. Can't fall.

The engines are nearer, loud against the field's broken tranquility. She glances left as she enters the long grass and gains sight of the house's front yard.

Three vehicles are parked there, vivid orbs of light blazing from their grilles and cabs. Travis is walking toward them, hands out as they were before, his thin body outlined like ink on a white page.

"I'm alone except for my son! Where is my son?"

A gunshot rings out and Travis's head rocks back, knees folding as he pitches forward and falls to his stomach on the driveway.

Zoey cuts off the moan that tries to come from her chest and plunges into the long grass, its touch wetting her pant legs instantly.

The ASV. It's their only hope. Inside they have a chance of breaking through, of outrunning or at least buying some time since the armored vehicle will protect them from gunfire.

The strong light begins to sweep toward her across the field, igniting the trees and bushes to her left.

She pitches forward, falling hard on her side as the light passes over, tingeing the dead grass white. She breathes hard, breath pluming above her until she realizes that anyone watching will see it highlighted there, and covers her mouth and nose with her shirt collar.

The seconds tick by.

Her left leg is numb to the knee, the crawling deadness seeping down into her calf.

Men's voices float across the night. One yells a high, piercing shriek followed by stuttering laughter. Another gunshot rings out and it is then she hears something that shrivels her heart in on itself.

Isaac's short, wailing cry.

It warbles to her, slightly muffled, but unmistakable. There are several whoops and more gunshots before a man's voice cries out to cease fire.

They're going to find them. She has to do something.

Zoey yanks her handgun free, flicking the safety off as she sits up. A large truck is parked to the closest side of the house, a spotlight mounted in its bed. The light points to the ground in front of the bumper and a man stands near the tailgate, a rifle propped against one hip. She searches the night for any figures nearby and sees nothing. Two men appear from the back of the house and begin sweeping flashlights across the lawn.

She can do it. She can save them if she goes now.

Zoey pushes herself up to a crouch, another bolt of pain flashing through the leg that isn't numb. She's about to launch herself up and sprint for the shrub nearest the house when two hands grasp her arms and yank her back into the grass.

A scream wells up inside her and she brings the handgun around, but a rough palm covers her mouth, another grasping her wrist.

"Stop, Zoey, it's me," Merrill whispers in her ear. The fight goes out of her and he takes his hand from her mouth.

"They're going to find them."

"Come on, crawl after me. It's only another hundred yards."

"No. We have to stop them."

"There's nothing we can do. There's at least twenty of them, heavily armed. They'd kill us all."

Isaac's cries continue to drift to them and tears film her vision. "Please, Merrill."

There is a single pop and a man's strangled cry, followed by a chatter of automatic rifle fire.

Then complete silence.

Zoey curls onto her side, soundless sobs strangling her. Merrill places a hand on her shoulder and squeezes. A series of yells come from near the house, followed by a hoarse exclamation of pain. But everything is muted background noise, her hearing deadened like her entire left leg. She lies there, crying silently into the rough, dying grass and cold ground as Merrill holds her.

After an unknowable amount of time, the spotlight dances across their hiding place, turning her vision into a thousand fractured jewels. Zoey wipes at her eyes even as Merrill whispers into her ear.

"They're coming. Be ready to shoot. Ready to run."

Footsteps, crackling closer and closer. A pause. Then voices.

"The fuck I gotta look out here for, man? I'm the wounded one. I should be in the truck."

"You messed up, Brad. You killed the woman. The only thing we came here for."

"The hell was I supposed to do. Bitch shot me in the fuckin' hand. Blew off two fingers. Hurts like a bastard. Besides, there's no one else here. Fuckin' kid was full of shit. Ain't no girl. Ain't no military truck."

"What am I supposed to tell the Prestons?"

A long quiet filled only by the breeze. "You tell 'em we didn't find nothin'. Buncha guys and that's it."

"See, there's where we run into the problem, Brad. Everyone else saw what happened same as I did. And someone will tell the Prestons when we get back to the trade, and if it's not me, then I'm the one in a shit heap."

"We'll think of somethin'. Come on, man, my fuckin' hand is killin' me."

"Here, let me help you."

The click of a hammer being drawn back is loud and the injured man's shocked cry is drowned out by the gunshot. Zoey flinches and Merrill's fingers dig into her shoulder. She gazes through the grass surrounding them but can't see the remaining man, though she can hear him clearly. He hawks and spits.

The minutes pass with agonizing slowness.

Finally the grass rasps with his departure, footsteps growing fainter each second.

"Burn it!" the executioner yells in the distance. An engine rumbles to life and after another span there is a woof of yellow light that grows exponentially, gradually gilding the tips of the wilting grass gold.

Engines howl. Gravel crunches and sprays, rattling off stone. The mechanical rumble decreases, flowing away as if the volume of the entire world is being turned down, leaving only the static hiss of flames.

Zoey slowly sits up, Merrill rising beside her.

The stone house's roof is ablaze.

The few windows that line the sides are broken, flames licking out and upward like orange tongues. She can feel the heat from where she sits.

"Come on, Zoey. Let's go in case they come back."

She doesn't move, only stares at the growing inferno, fire leaping twenty or more feet into the sky.

"Zoey. We have to go." Merrill lifts her from the ground, holding on to her arm. He tries to guide her away but she yanks free of his grip, forcing her traitorous leg to hold her.

"We should've done something," she says, not looking away from the flames.

"We were outnumbered, outgunned. They would have killed us."

"It was them, wasn't it? It was the trade."

A long pause. "Yes."

"They're close."

"Yes."

Zoey turns away from the burning house, tears evaporated by the heat. "Then let's go find them."

23

Wen stares at the meat sizzling in the small frying pan, eyes unfocused, hands hanging by her sides.

"You're going to burn those," Robbie says from the other side of the trailer.

She comes out of her stupor and stabs the steaks with a two-pronged fork, flipping them. The smell that wafts up from the pan is enough to make her salivate. She hasn't eaten beef in months.

"You mind your own," she says, not looking at him.

Robbie finishes chopping the last potatoes, dropping them into a stainless steel pot, and brandishes his knife. "I've killed for less."

She smiles wanly. "You've never hurt a fly."

"No. Not a fly I guess. But some big damn spiders that I used to find in my apartment. And don't get me started on cockroaches."

Wen removes the pan from the heat, covering it to let the steak rest for a minute. She moves the two plates onto the gas cookstove's stand, the sides of the Prestons' meals already in place. She lets her gaze become fuzzy again, everything fading into a blur. She could live this way, all things out of focus. Nothing substantial enough to recognize. But maybe she already is.

"Hey, are you listening to me?" Robbie asks.

"I'm sorry, no, I wasn't."

He finishes wiping down the narrow work counter mounted to the trailer's wall and moves to her. Bending down a little so their eyes meet, he grasps her hand. "Don't beat yourself up over this. We haven't got a choice. In all the time we've been planning this, we always knew we wouldn't be able to take anyone from the containers with us."

"I know that."

"Then nothing's changed."

"I promised him. I looked him right in the eyes and promised that I would get him and his wife out."

"And I promised Luke from marketing that I'd call him after our first date twenty-five years ago. Sometimes things don't work out."

"Robbie . . ."

"I'm sorry, trying to lighten the mood." He sighs and squeezes her hand. "I know how much this kills you; it's one of the reasons I love you, but no new angles have presented themselves to us in the last few days. Nothing's changed. Our only option is the one that you came up with originally, and it will be a miracle if we're able to pull that off."

"Yeah."

"Look, maybe when the king and queen are dead, things will change. Maybe the trade will die with them and the women and men in the containers will be set free."

"You know as well as I do that will never happen. Someone else will step into their place and continue their work."

She turns from him and transfers the steaming steaks from the pan to the plates. Covering them, she starts for the open doorway at the opposite end of the trailer.

"Nothing is ever perfect. You know that," Robbie calls after her.

The air outside is cooler now, even in the bright sunshine of mid-day. The highway the trade sits on is partially hemmed in on the north by an encroaching forest of pines. To the west the land drops away into rolling hills dotted with bunches of homes, all quiet and empty, their occupants long dead or moved on.

She walks up the line of vehicles and trailers similar to the mobile kitchen she cooks out of during the day while on the road. Second in line behind an armored semitruck and trailer is a large recreational vehicle, its paint a dusty brown highlighted with worn gold swirls that have lost their sparkle. Two guards stand outside, rifles hanging from slings. One of them pats her down, his hands surprisingly gentle. He touches her only where he needs to before ushering her inside. *One of the decent ones*, she thinks, climbing the few stairs into the vehicle.

Sasha sits in the nearest seat beside one of the long windows, what looks like a tall glass of water beside her. But Wen knows if she were to take a sip from the woman's drink she would taste pure vodka. Sasha flicks her eyes to the plates then away, one long finger running around and around the lip of her glass.

Hemming stands at the far back of the RV, cadaverous eyes watching her come down the aisle. Elliot sits at the largest table across from a man with long, dark hair tied back now in a ponytail. James Horner glances at her as she approaches and she has to stifle the shock that tries to crease her features into a grimace.

"Ah, lunch. Thank you, dear," Elliot says, motioning for Wen to set the plates on the table. He draws off the covers and immediately the scent of cooked steak fills the air. "My goodness. You've outdone yourself this time." Elliot inhales the steam coming off his plate and smiles at her. "What a fortunate occurrence it was to meet that man with the heads of beef."

"Not for him it wasn't," Wen says.

The smile slides from Elliot's face. "Sasha, darling, lunch is served."

"I'm not hungry," Sasha says from the front.

"But dear, you have—"

"I don't *have* to do anything, darling." Sasha takes a long drink of liquor and looks away out the window.

"Traveling always affects her appetite," Elliot says. "My dear, if you please?" He motions at both plates and Wen comes forward, cutting off a slight chunk of each steak. She puts them both in her mouth and chews, taking samples of the roasted potatoes and black beans as well. James watches her intently the entire time.

"I was just telling James here how much of an asset you are to the entire troupe. Without you I'm sure most of us would have died of malnutrition or simply killed ourselves from the lack of culinary variety."

"I do my best."

"And we are thankful. Just as we're thankful for our new doctor."

Wen blinks, eyes moving from Elliot to James and back again. "What do you mean?"

"Without James here we never would have known what killed our captain, would we? A terrible thing, not knowing. Afterward I invited James to stay on as our resident doctor since we were in great need of one, and he embraced the position gladly."

"I'm not really a doctor," James says, smiling up at Wen.

"Nonsense. In this new world we are all what is needed of us. Entertainment is in Sasha's and my blood. None of us could exist without purpose. It would simply be chaos. Don't you agree, James?"

"Oh yes. Most definitely."

"Choice is sometimes a very dangerous thing. Logic and common sense will always be the true north of humankind's compass. It is those that fly in the face of rational decisions that suffer." His expression changes as if he's tasted something sour. "Those that never listen or heed competent warnings. They are life's greatest folly." He sits silently for a moment, staring through his meal, through the table. At last he comes back to the present and nods. "Yes, I believe deep down we were all meant for something, and to deny our calling is to deny what truly makes us human." Elliot slides his plate closer and picks up a knife and fork. "Since Sasha isn't feeling up to it, would you like to partake, James?"

"Oh, no thank you, sir. I actually should look in on one of the guards who is down with the stomach flu before we continue," James says, rising from his seat. "Out of curiosity, when will we be arriving at the next community?"

Elliot places a large chunk of steak in his mouth and chews before answering. "It depends on when our latest reconnaissance party returns, but we should make Southland by tomorrow evening and be set up by midnight at the latest."

"When will, um, the contests begin?"

"The following day. I trust you've made your peace with this?"

James draws in a deep breath and finally nods. "Yes."

"Good. You'll see, James. Your life will have so much more meaning doing what you've been made for."

"Yes sir."

Elliot gestures at the door and Wen files down the aisle, past Sasha, who has downed most of her drink, and out into the open air. She moves by the two guards, walking fast toward the kitchen trailer. When she's a dozen steps from the door, a hand grasps the inside of her elbow, slowing her. She stops and turns, using every ounce of willpower not to strike James in the face.

"Now you know where you stand," he says quietly. "I'm sure you thought you'd be able to slip away with me locked in the container, but now things are a little different."

"We were going to take you with us."

"You're lying, but I can't expect anything else. From now on you'll include me in any deviation or new step in the plan. Or I swear to God I'll tell Elliot, and I don't think he'll be impressed with your skills anymore once he knows what was going to be in his and his wife's food."

"Okay. Okay, keep your voice down," Wen says, glancing past him up the highway. Three guards are meandering toward them.

"When are we going?"

"Tomorrow night after I serve them dinner."

"And how are we going to get my wife out of the container?"

"I don't know yet."

His fingers tighten on her arm. "We don't have much time."

"I'll figure something out."

One of the guards glances at them and says something to the other two.

"Let me go or they're going to shoot you." James releases her. "I'll let you know soon."

"I'll be waiting outside the nest tomorrow night after it's done. And if anything isn't kosher, I will scream at the top of my lungs what you did."

She steps away from him as the guards come even with them and lowers her head, ignoring the muttered comments from the three men. Her mind rings with James's words as she hurries to the kitchen trailer and climbs inside. Robbie is putting supplies away in the cupboards mounted to the floor and looks up at her when she enters.

"They made James the doctor," she says, barely able to get herself to utter the sentence.

"What?"

"They made him the doctor and now he says he'll be waiting tomorrow night when setup begins, and if we don't break his wife out, he'll tell everyone what we did."

Robbie looks shell-shocked, face paler than usual. "Now what? It's over. When we thought he'd be locked up it wasn't going to be an issue, but now . . ."

"I know. Let me think." She paces through the tight space.

"I have to go," Robbie says, moving to the door. "We're heading out soon."

"Can you get us a gun?"

He stops dead with his hand on the doorknob. "You know I'm not allowed to have a gun."

"Can you get us one?"

Robbie's head tips back and he exhales loudly. "Maybe. Fitz might be able to sneak me one. But a single handgun isn't going to get us past all the guards at the containers. Especially with everyone milling around during setup."

"I know."

"Then what do you want one for?"

"Because. I'm going to have to kill him." She meets Robbie's wide-eyed gaze. "I'm going to have to kill James."

24

I am a comet.

The thought has gone through her head so many times in the last twenty-four hours it is nearly meaningless. The trailer hits another bump, making things rattle in the cupboards and drawers. Wen takes another drink of the moonshine, wincing as it plummets with a fiery trail down to her stomach.

She's not drunk, but she isn't entirely sober either. She's been in a semi-fog since the prior day, when Robbie left the trailer and the caravan began its lumbering trek once again, slow at first but picking up speed until the entire trade howled down the desolate highway like a runaway freight train off its tracks.

She recalls reading about one of the only comets to come into contact with the Earth when she was a girl still dreaming of going to space. Millions of years ago it had detonated above what would become Egypt, the explosion so hot it had melted the sand into glass for thousands of square miles.

Such destruction, nothing could stand against it.

Wen sets down the mostly empty glass and picks up the other item on the table. The small leather sack still has the name of the whiskey distillery etched into its side, letters worn but legible. She turns the bag over in her hands, feeling the texture slide across her fingertips. It looks as though it should be heavy, its sides full and bulging as if it still contains a bottle. But it is light, nearly weightless.

She opens the mouth of the sack and peers inside. The bag is stuffed full of cotton she extracted from the lining of a winter coat she found the night before in one of the supply trucks. The fluffy interior begins to expand, trying to escape the confines of the bag, and she cinches it shut again, imagining how she'll have to jam the gun's barrel into the opening.

It isn't a perfect silencer, but it will have to do.

The trailer hitches, sending her rocking back on her chair as the truck pulling it slows. The engine's growl drops in pitch and she stands up, moving to the window.

They're here.

The town of Southland sprawls to the west in the center of a wide valley. Before the Dearth it had been a quaint community based mostly on tourism and a fluctuating timber industry. She had driven through the streets as a teenager several times on her way to the coast, the luxuries of meandering past candy shops, catching the earthy aroma of fresh-brewed coffee drifting from an open door, and watching a flock of geese paddle soundlessly across a central pond not yet lost.

Now she looks at possible escape routes. Where will they hide after everything goes down?

She scans the streets, the hills beside the looming mountain range in the distance. There is a large lake to the south and what looks like a narrow county road twisting west around it. Beyond that the beginnings of a tree line rise up, a spattering of pines and deciduous alike. Maybe there. If they are able to slip away without being seen immediately, they could get to the other side of the lake and into the trees. After that the trade would be hard-pressed to track them. But where will they go once they're free?

"It doesn't matter," she says quietly. *Anywhere but here.*

The trade flows down a gentle grade leading to the town's main street like a swarm of locusts descending upon a ripened crop. The only thing the Prestons love as much as magic and entertainment is an entrance.

She gazes out at the first buildings, their slumped shapes only suggestions of what they once were. Slowly the town straightens and inhabited storefronts appear, their signs obscured by time but with the occasional face appearing at a grimy window, eyes wide and full of wonder as the trade passes by. Some of the drivers honk their horns and men start to emerge from houses along the street, hands held aloft, mouths open in yells, some of them clapping.

At the end of the main street the trade turns left and cruises through another neighborhood that has fallen into disrepair though there is life here as well. A dog barks from a canted porch where a man sits drinking something out of a tall tin can. A figure waves from the far end of a small garden, the last of the harvest stacked in a wheelbarrow beside the road. A man urinates on a street corner, barely looking up as the vehicles blast by him, ruffling his dingy jacket and hat.

They turn once more and come out of the shade of a dilapidated timber mill and pass into the greater shadow of Scrimshaw Mountain.

It rises above the western edge of the town like a giant shark's tooth, its very top dusted with snow. She can make out the main ski run that cuts straight down its side and empties out a half mile away. The white paint of the chairlift towers has partially flaked and peeled giving the steel T's studding the mountain a mottled look against the browning grass. A broken lift chair halfway up dangles like a hanged man fifty feet above the ground.

The trade swings wide into a large clearing at the end of the street; trucks holding the components of the nest and the coliseum taking up positions in the very center while flatbeds carrying rolls of chain-link fencing spread out around them in a loose perimeter.

The trailer shudders to a stop and Wen moves to the door, stepping outside.

Already the work has begun. Guards move outward, creating a perimeter. Men from Southland approach the camp, steps fast and eager. The nest's walls rise from the back of a flatbed, thirty or more workers racing around the structure. All at once, the movement and noise is too much for her. It assaults her senses, boring into her eyes, ears, even her skin.

Pounding.

Yelling.

Colorful flags snapping in the wind.

The leather bag full of cotton inside the trailer.

A hand grasps her shoulder and she spins, bringing up a fist.

James stands there, eyelids fluttering as he holds his hands up.

"Calm down. I didn't mean to startle you," he says.

She exhales, shooting a look around the immediate area. "What do you want?"

"We need to talk."

"We talked enough yesterday."

"No, I mean, I want to apologize."

She studies him, watching his eyes to see if they say anything different. "This way," she says, leading him to the opposite side of the kitchen trailer. Several workers stream past them carrying lengths of rope and electrical cables. Wen moves to one of the large tractor-trailers that hauls the tents for the midway, and ducks behind it.

"We'll only have a couple minutes," she says.

"I know. I'm sorry for how I've acted, how I've treated you in the past several days. But I'm desperate. If I don't find a way out of this for Amanda and me . . ." He falters, looking at the ground. "I want to thank you for helping us."

Her stomach churns. "I haven't done anything."

"You kept us fed when our rations were low. And you've given me hope. For that I can't thank you enough."

Her mind flits to the leather bag. The drawstrings pulling tight. "It's okay," she finally manages.

"So what time are you doing this?"

"The Prestons normally eat at seven sharp."

He gestures toward the looming peak. "It'll be mostly dark by then with the mountain in the way. There's normally four guards stationed outside the containers, sometimes only three." He pulls out a small, wooden-handled knife from the inside of his coat and quickly puts it away again. "If I climb onto the women's container and drop down on them, you could come around the corner at the same time, and with a little luck we can take them out, especially if everyone's distracted by what's going to be happening in the nest."

It's an insane plan. One that is almost completely hopeless, but the look in his eyes tells her everything she needs to know. He won't be talked out of it. She has no choice.

"That might work," she says.

"Can you sneak a knife from the kitchen?"

"Yes."

"Where should I meet you?"

Hating herself, she licks her lips and drops her gaze. "The back of the sideshow tent. There's usually no one behind it."

"I'll be waiting there." His eyes narrow slightly. "But you taste their food. I saw you do it yesterday. How—"

"Let me worry about that."

"But—"

"Hey, cook!" a voice yells.

They both spin in the direction of the truck's front end. Three guards are striding toward them, gazes feral, hands gripping rifles.

Oh God, they heard us. They heard us talking. This is it. Years and years of planning and all for nothing.

Wen tries to keep her features placid, tries not to let the terror leak through the mask she's built over time.

The men stop several paces away and the lead guard gestures with his rifle. "You making that beef stew again tonight?"

For a moment she's completely lost, the cogs of her thoughts free-wheeling. But then they catch hold and she nods. "Yeah. That's what's for dinner."

The guard grins. "Good deal. Can taste it already. Come on, guys, let's go." They stride past and disappear around the back of the truck, and Wen feels herself physically deflate, the drop in tension leaving her weak.

"Seven," James says, sidling away, almost as visibly shaken as she feels. "I'll be there." He rounds the truck out of sight and she sags against the trailer, the coldness of the steel soaking through her jacket. She stays that way for several minutes before feeling steady enough to head across the field that is quickly taking shape into what will be the midway.

The nest is already erected, its generator humming, guards standing before the entrance. She gazes up at the second-floor windows, a tremor of fear going through her as she sees Hemming staring back down at her. She looks away, moving in the direction of where the mess area is customarily situated. When she arrives the workers have assembled the low building and are partially done setting up the seating out front. She weaves her way between them and enters the kitchen, shutting the door behind her.

Everything is in its place, the cabinets where she always has them, the stove somewhat off center from its customary spot, but all else seems organized. Wen moves to the lowest cupboard and drops to her knees. She pulls open the door, reaching back past a stack of hot pads, fingers finding the lipped ledge.

The canister isn't there.

Her heart does a funny half beat before double-timing.

She drops lower, reaching from one end of the ledge to the other. It must've slid while the men were reassembling the kitchen. But it isn't on the ledge at all. The lip is empty.

The first inklings of panic start growing in her like seeds freshly watered.

Someone found it thinking it was something valuable and took it. They're going to open it and see what's inside and tell the Prestons. Maybe they already know. She sits up straight, listening past the sounds of the workers finishing the seating outside. She sinks back to her hands and knees, lungs heaving now with a constricting sensation that's getting stronger with each second.

So stupid! It wasn't safe here, wasn't safe to leave but wasn't safe to take either. The hot sting of tears fills her eyes at the same moment she catches a glint of silver behind one of the pans.

She shoves the heavy pots out of the way. There it is. The little canister with the blue top. She snatches it up, gripping it so tight she's sure she'll dent it. It fell down in transit, that's all. Fell down off the ledge. Why hadn't she thought of that? But it's plain to her now.

She's losing her hold on everything.

Losing the grip she's always kept, even when the trade found her originally. Found them. And . . . and . . .

Wen squeezes her eyes shut, blocking out what comes next in the memory.

The door to the kitchen opens and she nearly screams.

With a swift movement she slips the poison into her jacket pocket and slams the cupboard door shut even as a shadow falls across her, pinning her to the floor.

"What the hell are you doing down there?" Robbie asks.

"You asshole. You scared the hell out of me," she says, reaching out to him. He grabs her hand and hauls her to her feet.

"Wow, it's great to see you, Robbie. How's it going risking your life trying to get a gun?" he says, mimicking her voice.

"I'm sorry. A little on edge today."

"Welcome to the club. So everything's a go?"

She turns and starts gathering ingredients for the beef stew she'll be serving that evening. "Yes. It's a go."

"Even the . . . ah . . . thing with James?"

She pauses in her movements and glances at him. "Yes. Even that." Robbie begins helping her, pulling out and arranging spices that have fallen over during setup. They are quiet for a long time, moving around each other in the way they do. Finally she breaks the silence and says, "Did you get it?"

"Not yet. Fitz says he'll have it ready tonight when I bring him the last of the supplies for the truck. Where do you want me to meet you at after you leave the nest?"

"Next to the main water tank. You can give it to me then."

"And after that?"

"James will be waiting behind the sideshow tent."

He nods. "Lots of noise coming from there."

"Yeah. It'll help cover the . . ." She lets her words trail off and loses herself in the food preparation. But after a time a niggling memory surfaces and she freezes, her hand nearly losing its hold on the long wooden spoon she's stirring the stew with.

Robbie notices her expression and touches her arm. "What?"

"Sasha didn't eat her lunch or dinner yesterday."

"What? Did she eat today?"

"She just picked at it while I was there."

"Well, what are we going to do? Sometimes I think she's the worse of the two." Robbie lowers his voice to less than a whisper. "If she's not dead when we run, she'll never stop looking for us."

Wen moves past him to the far side of the kitchen, fumbling open one of the two small barrels in the corner. She frowns, putting the lid back on before opening the one beside it. She reaches inside and brings out a handful of ripened apples, their skin beginning to soften.

"I'll have to make something she can't refuse," she says.

25

"That's unbelievable."

Tia hands the binoculars to Zoey, who lifts them to her eyes. They lie side by side on a low rise a half mile from the mass of structures that's slowly growing out of nothing on the outskirts of Southland. Zoey gazes through the magnification, panning across the expanse of the trade.

Tia's right. It is unbelievable.

They arrived at the small town late that afternoon, circling in far from the north after having caught sight earlier in the day of the string of vehicles on the horizon that never seemed to end. They had parked the ASV behind a small bluff stitched with pine trees that concealed its sand color well and hiked close enough to the trade to get their first real look at it.

Zoey watches dozens of workers erecting a chain-link fence that begins to completely encircle the camp. A two-story building rises above a mass of tents and support poles. Beside it is a circular enclosure that's taking shape in the form of tiered scaffolding. Spaced out evenly around the trade's border, armed guards pace, eyes searching constantly outward, seeking anything out of place. Already there is a line of men milling about at a rough entrance that faces the town, a long booth beside it. Everywhere there is movement, an excitement to the men's steps, exuberance in their expressions.

Zoey yearns for Ian's rifle to be in her hands. The men wouldn't have a clue where the shot came from. She shakes her head. The thought equally frightens and thrills her.

Murderer.

Merrill crawls up the bank, snapping her back to reality. He stops beside her and she hands the binoculars to him.

"Do you see the two shipping containers being unloaded from the back of those trucks?" she asks.

"Yes," he says after a pause. "The ones with the three guards around each of them?"

"Yeah. I think that's where they're keeping the women."

Merrill looks through the binoculars for a long time before lowering them. "It's massive."

"How many do you think?" Tia asks.

"Rough guess? Maybe a hundred guards, hundred workers, who knows how many performers or whatever the hell they are." He glances sideways at Zoey, who continues to watch the perimeter fence rise in sporadic glints of steel in the evening sun. She feels his eyes on her like a physical weight but doesn't return his gaze.

They've all been watching her over the last few days since leaving Travis and Anniel's burning home, but none of them have said a word about it, not even Ian, who has only looked at her with a soft pity that's only infuriated her more. She's barely spoken to anyone, the sound of Isaac's wailing suddenly cut off in a rattle of gunfire loud in her ears, even during the complete silence of night. She recalls how the little boy snuggled against her, all the while trying to force away the memory and failing.

She swallows and looks toward the foothills below the looming mountain that is still dotted with bright flares of colorful leaves. The trust Isaac had exuded, the faith the entire family had displayed, is a toxic thing. More dangerous than anything else, she decides. There is no room for it in the world that exists now. Maybe years ago it was something good, precious even, but that time is long gone.

"Seeing the trade now, it's hard to imagine people coming here to ski down the mountain," Merrill says, motioning at Scrimshaw's peak. "Probably was a nice town once."

"I skied here before," Tia says. They both glance at her. "What? A lesbian can't ski?"

"I didn't say anything," Merrill says.

"Um-hmm. Anyways, you're right, it was a nice town. Used to be a beautiful bed-and-breakfast over on the south side. Can't believe I rode one of the chairs on that lift. Seems like a lifetime ago."

Zoey gazes at the decrepit benches dangling from the cable attached to the steel towers running up the side of the mountain like an artery. Again she's able to glimpse the life of the world that once was beneath the scarring that's here now. How would it have been to travel here simply to enjoy nature and the landscape instead of looking at it as a tactical vantage point? Instead of jumping at every sound not made by their group, she might have welcomed a stranger with a smile and a wave.

She lets herself envision it for another moment before putting the fantasy away in the corner of her mind.

Zoey shimmies backward, careful to not rise until she's completely hidden by the swell of the hill. Tia and Merrill follow, their footsteps crackling in dry leaves that have coasted from the nearest trees on the wind. They make their way into the deeper cover of the pines, winding past low-hanging branches and around trunks, all the while the darkness grows like mold. In the dusk they spot the shape of the bluff, the ASV coming into view a few seconds later. The rest of the group stands beside it, all of them armed and wary. When they are within speaking distance, Eli nods in the direction of the trade.

"So? Is it doable?"

"I don't know," Merrill answers, leaning his rifle up against one of the ASV's tires. "It's unlike anything I've ever seen before. Everyone's working in succession, like a bunch of ants. The whole thing will be up and running in another hour or two."

"Did you see any women?" Chelsea asks.

"No, but they're there," Zoey says. "There's two big steel containers that are being closely guarded. I can't think of anything else they'd be that worried about."

"She's probably right," Merrill says.

"So what's the plan?" Chelsea asks.

No one says a word, the breeze whispering overhead through the thick branches of needles.

"We have to get a closer look," Zoey says finally. "There's no other way to plan anything."

"And by 'we' I'm sure you mean those of us of the male persuasion," Eli says. "Cuz girl, you can't be going any closer than you just did."

"I have to. This was my idea, my decision."

"Zoey . . ." Ian says.

"No. You don't understand, do you? It's my responsibility to see this through. I didn't ask you to come, but now that you're here I definitely can't ask you to take all the risk. I won't." She stares around at them, the vehemence in her voice making most of them look to the ground or over her shoulder. "I don't want anyone else to die because of me."

"What happened the other night wasn't your fault," Tia says. "Travis made a stupid decision."

"But if we hadn't been there . . ."

"You don't know that."

"Neither do you." She feels the prickling heat of tears forming behind her eyes.

"This is something none of us have ever encountered before. We don't—" Merrill says.

"I'm going. There's nothing—"

"No!" Merrill bellows. His eyes are ablaze in the near dark. "No, you're not going. It's stupid and reckless." He blinks before fixing her with his gaze once again, voice much lower. "I already lost Meeka. I won't lose you too."

With that he turns and stalks to the ASV. Eli gives her a last look before following. Ian begins to approach her but she backs away into the embrace of the pines below the bluff. She stops a dozen yards in where the darkness is nearly complete and looks back, barely able to make out the shape of the group near the vehicle.

She wants to scream, to destroy something with her bare hands. The impotency of her rage only infuriates her more. How could Merrill say something like that? Control her and keep her from what she has to do? But each time she replays his words they dig deeper into her, boring until they are at her center.

I already lost Meeka. I won't lose you too.

She leans back against the trunk of a pine and slides to the ground, hugging herself against the cool air, listening to the low voices until they're silent. A spark of fire ignites beside the ASV, so small it barely illuminates Ian's face. She watches him tend to the flames, artfully building the blaze until it is the perfect size.

She rises and moves toward the light, stopping only when the illumination touches the ground at her feet. Tia and Chelsea stand a short distance from the ASV looking out into the forest, their shapes darker shades in the night.

"He loves you, Zoey. That's the only reason he made you stay," Ian says, not looking up from the fire.

"I know."

"Sometimes the smartest decision is the last one you want to make." When she doesn't reply, he says, "We will find a way to rescue the women within the trade. I promise you. As soon as Merrill and Eli return we'll know more about what we're dealing with." He finally glances up at her. "Are you hungry?"

"Not really."

"Well, some of the best cooks are those who don't covet food." He gives her a smile. "In other words, you can still help me make dinner. Inside the vehicle in the back are a few cans of beans and the last of the bread. Could you get them?"

Zoey hesitates but then walks away from the fire to the ASV, pulling open its heavy door. She finds the food tucked beside Merrill's duffel bag, some of his clothes spilling from between the long zipper. She begins shoving them back inside when she spots a wad of money, rolled tightly and held by an elastic band, lying next to one of his hooded jackets. She picks up the faded paper, feeling its texture, and glances at the heavy coat before looking over her shoulder.

Ian is still beside the small fire, his hands out, warming over the flames.

She peels off several of the bills and snatches the jacket before stepping out of the ASV, pausing only a second before heading into the forest, away from the light.

26

The tray is warm in Wen's hands, the chill air biting her face as she walks past several dozen men eating the stew she prepared that afternoon.

Some of them mutter obscene things as she passes, others say what they're thinking through looks that make her feel like stripping down and scrubbing her skin raw beneath scalding water. Even after all these years, it doesn't get any easier.

But everything is slightly muted as she moves; the ground strange and unsteady under her feet, sounds of the trade's final setup muffled and indistinct, the bright lights dulled and soft around their edges. There's only one thing that is clear and real.

What she holds before her.

She weaves between two of the large tents, the nest coming into view ahead. Heart thundering in her chest, she approaches the guards at the door. Hands pat her down, linger on her chest, buttocks, then she's through, moving up the stairway, legs trembling so badly she has to stop for a beat and take several deep breaths before continuing. When she comes into view of the door, the second-floor guard opens it unto the brightly lit interior.

She staggers drunkenly, only then aware of the floating sensation that's enveloped her head. Wen catches herself, the covered plates on the tray sliding dangerously toward the edge.

"Are you all right, dear?" Elliot asks. He lounges on a settee, dressed in a suit of silver thread, a matching vest and tie, and a dark shirt beneath everything. He squints at her as she regains her balance, nausea slopping in her stomach.

"I'm fine. Stumbled a little there."

A glass clinks across the room and Sasha turns her frigid stare first at the tray, then out the window at the lights that blaze above the trade. She sips the amber liquid in the glass she holds and saunters toward the closest chair; the gown she wears is the same color as her husband's jacket and slacks. Hemming loiters in the farthest corner of the room, face blank, bleached skin sickly beneath the artificial light.

"I'm sure it's the excitement," Elliot says. "Nothing like opening night, is there?"

"No. Definitely not."

"We were afraid it would be too late to open the midway tonight, but the crew seems to be nearly ready. By chance, did you see how many are waiting outside the gates?"

Wen moves to the table centered in the room, setting the tray down as if it holds a house of cards. "No. I haven't been out that way yet."

"No matter. We always draw a great crowd here. It's nothing like Seattle, but it keeps the money and supplies flowing, isn't that right, darling?"

Sasha nods into her drink. "Of course."

"I still get the jitters. Isn't that odd after all these years?" Elliot rubs his palms together and grins, teeth glinting wetly. "You would think it would wear off, but it never does. That's a sure sign you've picked the right career for yourself. It never gets old and it doesn't seem like work."

Wen's legs shake from a mixture of fury and dread. She shifts slightly, trying to calm the muscles holding her upright that feel as if they're hooked to high voltage.

Elliot smiles for another moment before sniffing the air. "Ah, what have you brought us tonight? It smells delicious."

Wen reaches out, drawing the covers off two of the three plates. "I made fresh pasta with cheese sauce over the last bits of beef." Her eyes shoot from Elliot's delighted face to Sasha, who hasn't looked at the food.

"That's marvelous! It smells heavenly, doesn't it, dear?"

"Why did you go to all the trouble?" Sasha asks. Her voice is layers of ice. She gazes at Wen and it feels as if she's staring straight through her, seeing the secret that sits on the table. Knowing.

"I . . . I thought you would appreciate a change. I haven't made pasta in months and I know it's one of your favorites."

Sasha studies her and she swallows the acidic taste of fear on her tongue. It's all come down to this moment.

Years and years kept inside the walls and fences.

Being groped, leered at, told when and where she must be.

Nearly losing her mind when she was first brought here. The cold steel of the container around her for what seemed like eternity until they learned she could cook.

All of it compounding in her mind starting from the moment the men from the trade had come. How they ripped away what she held so tightly to her chest; the scream of her soul tearing as they dragged her in the opposite direction.

And then it was these two people standing above her, both of them towering like gods with their cold features and dead eyes.

It all has led them to this moment.

"I'm not hungry," Sasha says, flicking her fingers as if to shoo an insect away.

Wen nearly staggers again, the room losing its solidity. "What?"

Sasha glares at her. "I said, I'm not hungry. Besides, your pasta was never that palatable."

She feels her lips go numb, chin quivering. "I apologize. I didn't know."

"You do now."

She nods, eyes flitting to Hemming who watches the exchange with vague interest. "Okay. Well perhaps you'll prefer the other dish I brought." Wen grasps the last lid and lifts it, releasing a warm, tart aroma that floods her mouth with saliva despite everything.

The apple pie is golden brown, steam drifting lazily from the slits in its top.

Elliot stares, transfixed. "Is that . . . apple?"

"Yes. There were only a few left so I thought I'd put them to the best use." She glances at Sasha, who is also looking at the steaming pie, something like a candle flame wavering behind her eyes.

"Do you remember?" Elliot says quietly.

"Yes." Sasha breathes the word.

"Sometimes our whole house would smell like this. And Sondra would have flour on her cheek or in her hair from you both baking all afternoon. And we'd have the first piece together," Elliot says, voice going hoarse.

"Stop," Sasha says. She sets her drink down as if it weighs too much for her to hold.

Elliot's mouth works and he grimaces before glancing up at Wen where she stands, still holding the lid. "Thank you," he says. "Thank you for this."

"You're welcome. Would you like me to cut it?"

"No. No, I'll do it." His hand shakes as he picks up the silverware and begins slicing the pie into slivers. Wen watches the blade slide in and out of the crust, syrupy apple sticking to it in places. Without asking if she wants any, he places a piece of the warm pie on a plate and hands it to Sasha, who accepts it without comment. Elliot lifts another large slice onto his own plate before pausing. With a quick motion he cuts a third piece, setting it on a drink saucer, its tip sticking over the edge, a single drop of sweet filling hanging there like amber.

He holds it out to Wen, eyes still swimming with emotion. "Please. Sit and eat with us."

27

Zoey peers out from behind the dilapidated shed to the street beyond.

She is completely enclosed in shadow, the large hood of Merrill's jacket like a tunnel around her face. The hat she pulled on to secure her hair beneath sits low on her forehead.

A hundred yards away the line of men shifts like a snake eager to slither forward.

There are perhaps two hundred of them beside the brightly lit ticket counter waiting for the gate to open. They mill about, some gesticulating to the night sky, the air punctuated by the steady hum of generators and wild laughter. And beneath it all a strange, fluting music that causes her to shiver.

About three quarters to the end of the line, she spots a tall figure standing absolutely still, another shorter man with very dark skin beside him. Merrill leans over, seemingly listening to something Eli is saying, and as if he feels her eyes on him, turns and looks directly at her hiding place.

She resists the urge to duck behind the shed. There's no way he can see her here, lost in the darkness. But nonetheless she can't help but wonder if he knows she's close, if he suspects she's disobeyed him and followed. It is something Meeka would have done without thought.

Zoey glances down the length of fencing that seems to go on for miles. Two armed guards are in sight, separated by sixty yards or more, steps matched and even as they pace the circumference of the trade. There is a continuous succession of guards, as well as several walking the inside of the chain link. Even as she watches, one of the trade's sentries approaches a man who has left the line and sways drunkenly toward the fence. The guard shoves him hard and he goes down, one arm holding a bottle while the other flails uselessly in the dirt.

She lets out a long, shaky breath. So many men. All of them here for one thing.

Movement behind the gate causes a roar from the line. A door opens in the rear of the booth and a man appears there, a tall hat perched upon his head, lank hair covering his ears.

"Welcome, gentlemen!" he calls out, his voice smooth and inviting. "Welcome to the last, greatest show on Earth!"

The roar is deafening. Arms are thrown into the air, fingers splayed, reaching toward the heavens.

"Step inside these gates to another world! See spectacles that you've never dreamed of! Eat! Drink! Be merry! And of course, feast your eyes on beauty rare and most delicate. Come! Enter! But before you do, I issue one warning. There is a woman here employed by the owners of all you see. She is off limits. And anyone who lays a single finger on her will be burned alive. Remember, you are guests within Presto Preston's dominion! Take heed to never forget your manners and all will be well!"

With a flourish, the man in the tall hat flings his arm out and the gate rumbles aside. The men surge forward, hands outstretched to drop crumpled bills on the ticket man's counter along with aluminum cans that gleam beneath the lights before being swept away inside the booth.

Zoey watches the line move, feet shuffling, yells and yips piercing the night. She tugs at the large hood, assuring herself that her face is covered, and inhales deeply before stepping out of the shadows.

She walks, head down, seeing only the rough ground at her feet as she approaches the entrance. Her vision vibrates with each heartbeat.

This could be it. She could be discovered in the next few minutes and there would be no escaping. The urge to turn around and flee into the safety of the darkness is almost overpowering. How much money should she pay for entrance? She couldn't see the numbers on the cash itself that the men paid before her but it appeared as if they were laying at least three bills down. She'll have to take a chance. Her legs nearly betray her a dozen steps from the gate and she stumbles slightly.

"Whoa, old man! Too much to drink already tonight?" a voice says from her left. Zoey lifts her head enough to see one of the guards gesturing in her direction. "Gotta pace yourself! Too much excitement and you'll be a puddle in an hour we'll have to mop up!" A chorus of laughter rebounds around her and she digs in her pocket, drawing out several crumpled bills with the number fifty on them, so thankful she had enough wits to bring a pair of ratty gloves to hide her hands. She places the money on the counter when it comes into view and waits, almost able to feel the entrance man's stare burning holes in the side of the hood. After a pregnant pause a hand snatches the cash away.

"I'll just keep the extra as a tip," the man with the tall hat says. "Probably can't count anyways. Get on with ya!" She moves forward, trying not to run. Instead she shambles in what she hopes appears to be a drunken stupor. Zoey steps to the right out of the way of a throng of men passing a large bottle back and forth between them. The smell of their unwashed bodies is powerful even in the open air and she turns her head away.

She's beside a low building, its front open, hundreds of necklaces hanging from hooks driven into the lean-to's ceiling. Shining stones adorn some of the necklaces while others are silver and dagger-like. A hunched man calls to the passersby, yelling something about good luck. His voice is one of hundreds, a babble of incoherence and chaos. Zoey touches the hard shape of the handgun in her pocket and peers out into the main area of the trade.

Hundreds of tents are situated on the far left side of the grounds in what she can only assume is the living space for the members of the trade. Beside them are dozens of vehicles of all makes. Most are battered trucks but she spots several cars and a few semis untethered to their trailers, which are parked out of the way near the closest fence. A few spires of taller tents rise above the many low buildings like the one she hides behind, and farther away is the two-story structure she spotted earlier along with the circular configuration of scaffolding. Many men are already standing at its very top, arms propped over the side, their attention toward the center of the circle. She searches for the shapes of the steel containers but her vantage is much lower than it was on the hill, and the layout seems to be different now that she's here. She has to move closer.

Tentatively she steps behind the building and hobbles along the backs of two more just like it before coming to a wide and straight clearing in the grounds. Dozens of the little open-fronted structures line either side of the expanse, the busiest area she's seen so far.

A man rides a one-wheeled bicycle down the center, tossing colorful balls into the air and catching them in a graceful motion.

A blast of flame erupts from another man's mouth and she flinches as someone's hat catches fire, an anthem of laughter ringing out amidst cries of fear.

A figure dressed completely in black pedals a boxy cart topped with gleaming pipes that emit the unnerving music she heard before. At the very far end of the lane the chain-link fence separates the trade from the wilderness and rising mountain beyond.

And at the entrance to it all a tall steel arch rises up into the night with letters ignited in electric lights.

MIDWAY.

Zoey searches for another route around the bustling area of the trade, but guards stand next to some of the little buildings, shoving back into the midway anyone that tries to circumvent the aisle.

She steadies herself, fear bubbling in her center. She starts to step out below the arch just as two men round the nearest building. Zoey ducks back as Merrill and Eli pass by, their steps even and unhurried. She watches them move up the rows of shops, the men inside hawking their wares as they pass. Unable to stand still any longer, she moves, walking along the opposite side of the midway as Merrill and Eli. She catches glimpses inside some of the stands.

Here there is the potent scent of alcohol, a line of men waiting to be served tall, dark bottles.

There a well-lit alcove emits a delicious smell that causes her stomach to jerk with hunger as a man pushes bags of roasted nuts across the pitted countertop.

To the right a large tent has the sign FREAKS scrawled across its front, a man no more than three feet tall waving a carved wooden stick and calling out to the crowd to step inside.

Farther along, the busiest stand sells faded magazines to a swarm of men, their covers indistinct but she catches the pale glow of nude flesh within the pages.

Zoey moves past them all, the cacophony and intermingling scents and colors coalescing until the air shakes with it. The tempest that is the trade thrums around her and she steps into a shadow beside the last stand, bracing herself on the rough wood. When she's sure she can move again she hurries past a man spinning two swords around in dazzling flashes of steel and sidesteps a crowd gathering at the base of the circular structure. She spots an entrance that the men are filing through, two armed guards keeping the crowd moving. The rounded and open design of the structure triggers a memory that comes to her fully formed. In the NOA textbook she had seen something like it in the history section;

ancient Greece or Rome, she isn't sure which, had a similar building. A coliseum. That's what it was called. Some type of arena where both plays and bloody combat took place as entertainment.

She shivers.

This is where men fight to the death for the right to own a woman. This is where Ken won Halie and took her away to be raped and tortured for months on end. Everything and everyone around her is a part of the monstrous machine.

She doesn't realize she's drawn her weapon until she feels the safety click off.

Zoey glances around, making sure no one has seen, and conceals the pistol again, rage simmering in her blood. It would do no good to lose composure now. She would only die because of it, or worse, become an attraction in this place.

As she's about to move in the opposite direction her eyes snag on something partially hidden by the rounded structure's bulk.

The front end of a shipping container.

She waits for a group of yammering men to pass, throwing looks in every direction before hurrying across the open space beside the coliseum to the shadow of a small, humming shack. The wood buzzes beneath her hands and she smells heavy exhaust. There must be large generators inside the building. She traces the thick electrical cords running out from her position through the base of the coliseum as well as to a set of tall lights that illuminate the immediate area. As she leans closer to the shack, she hears raised voices coming from the opposite side, one of which she recognizes instantly. She peeks around the corner.

Merrill and Eli are backing away from the closest container, their hands held up as a guard advances toward them, rifle pointed in their direction.

"Just trying to get a look," Merrill says.

"You'll get your chance when we bring her out. Now wait your fucking turn like everyone else," the guard growls, snapping off the rifle's safety.

"No need to get jumpy, man. Our first time here," Eli says.

"No one's allowed in this area. Great way to get yourself killed. Now beat it!"

Merrill and Eli turn their backs on the guard, heading her way as Zoey ducks behind the shack.

Just as she's weighing her options on where to move next, gunfire erupts nearby, the sound of the shots splitting the night and rising above all the other noise of the trade.

28

"What?" Wen says, sure her ears betrayed her.

"Join us," Elliot says again, motioning to the empty chair across from him. "You've always been compliant, appreciative of the things we've given you. You test our food for contaminants at risk to your life. You deserve at least to partake in some of your own hard work."

She lets out a slow breath, wondering if they can see her pulse through her shirt, see it beating at her temple like a base drum. She licks her lips. "I couldn't. It's not my place."

"We're inviting you."

She jerks her eyes to Sasha, certain the woman will object as she has throughout the years whenever leniency or compassion has been shown. But she is silent, staring down at the plate in her lap.

"Please, sit with us. We have time. We're not due for the commencement of events for another hour." He gestures to the seat again and when she doesn't move his face contorts. "Sit down, Sondra!"

Wen watches his expression change from furious to stricken in a second. Elliot fumbles with his fork, nearly dropping it to the floor. "I'm . . . I'm sorry. I don't know why I called you that." The fork hovers over the pie, touches the crust before he draws it away. "Please. Sit."

She feels herself glide toward the chair, not walking, unable to feel her feet.

Her mouth is full of dust, all the saliva from smelling the pie sapped by the knowledge that she will have to eat it. There is no other choice.

Wen sinks into the chair, reaching out with trembling fingers to take the plate Elliot hands her. "No need to be nervous, dear. There's no reason we can't be civil and enjoy a meal together, isn't that right, darling?"

Sasha glances up from the dessert as if she's waking from a dream. "Of course not."

"Go ahead, dear," Elliot urges.

Wen tries to swallow but her throat is locked shut. She slowly cuts a chunk of the warm pie with her fork. "I'm . . . I'm really not that hungry," she says, staring at the dessert. "Setup always does a number on my stomach."

"Come now, the way this smells I don't know anyone that could turn it down."

The room pulses around her, her vision going hazy at the edges as she lifts the fork up, bringing it close to her mouth. Robbie. What will he do without her? Could he still get out? And James. When she doesn't show up at their meeting place, he'll come looking. And when he knows their arrangement is off, he'll tell the Prestons everything.

But really how much is her life worth when compared to ending the two people across from her? How many will she save in the aftermath?

Wen slides the fork and pie into her mouth and begins to chew.

Elliot smiles widely, bringing the first bite to his lips as Sasha cuts her dessert and does the same.

Gunshots ring out above the sound of the trade outside.

Wen's jaws lock together, the pie filling crawling across her tongue.

"What was that?" Elliot says, letting the fork and the uneaten pie drop to his plate. He glances at Hemming, who is already moving across the room to the windows. "It sounded like gunfire."

"One of the locals most likely," Hemming says, staring outside. His voice is ragged and thick from disuse. It is only the second time Wen has ever heard him speak.

The pie in her mouth is dissolving into mush, gradually making its way to the back of her tongue. The urge to swallow is nearly unbearable.

Another gun blast, followed by two more. Now cries of alarm drown out the calliope music, drawing Elliot to his feet.

She has to swallow. She can't take it anymore.

Wen shoots a glance at Sasha, who is looking at her, but then a high-pitched yell rises to a crescendo and the older woman's eyes flit to the window.

Wen smoothly reaches up, pulling her shirt collar close to her mouth, and spits the gelatinous bite of pie onto her chest. She tries to clean every trace of it from her tongue and teeth but Sasha sets her plate down, giving her another look. Wen drops the collar of her shirt, praying the moisture from the pie won't soak through.

"Something's wrong," Elliot says from beside Hemming. "There's a disturbance on the west end of the coliseum. See the crowd there? Get someone to check it out."

The taste of apples curls her tongue on itself and she's sure then that she's going to vomit. All the while she forces herself not to swallow the clotted spit and remains of pie that's gathered in the space between her cheek and gums.

Hemming strides toward the door and opens it, murmuring something Wen can't hear to the guard outside. Elliot returns to the table but doesn't sit, while Sasha remains stoic in her chair.

"Always an inconvenience," Elliot says. "But that's show business for you. How is the pie, dear?"

"Delicious," Wen manages between gritted teeth.

Elliot begins to respond, but at that moment a commotion from the stairway outside draws his attention away. There is a yelled curse then a grunt of pain from somewhere downstairs and a vague sense of disbelief washes over her.

Because she knows that voice.

Several seconds later three guards appear in the doorway, a thin man draped between them, legs limp, feet dragging as they carry him into the room, throwing him to the floor in a heap.

Slowly Robbie raises his head and looks at her.

A cut extends from his eyebrow to his temple, leaking blood, but there are also crimson droplets on the opposite side of his face as if he's been sprayed with gore as well. Tears run from both his eyes, telling her everything she needs to know.

They're both going to die.

"What's this all about?" Elliot says, voice frigid.

One of the guards nudges Robbie hard with the toe of his boot. "Saw this piece of shit *kissing* a western gate guard and when I yelled at them this one's lover tried to shoot me. But we got him first." The guard grins and draws a pistol out of his coat, dangling it before him. "He's on a scavenger team but had this on him, and they were smuggling supplies to a truck outside the fence. Looks like they were going to make a run for it." He kicks Robbie again in the ribs, harder this time, and it's all Wen can do not to leap from her seat and attack him. Robbie groans and blood drools from his mouth to the floor.

"Get him on his feet before he ruins the carpet!" Sasha yells.

They yank Robbie upright, but the guards have to support him because his legs keep unhinging. Wen blinks away the tears welling in her eyes as Robbie meets her gaze and shakes his head almost imperceptibly.

Elliot rounds the chairs and stops a pace from Robbie, looking him up and down. "So you have a touch of the lavender, do you, son?"

Robbie licks his bloodied lips. "Fuck you."

Elliot frowns. "I understand. You and your friend thought you could steal from us and the rest of the troupe. Run off to be footloose and fancy free on the outside. Live in your sinful ways. It's been tried before, my boy, and it's always failed. No one takes from us who hasn't earned it. Everyone has a place and a purpose in the show, and if one is greedy or unfit as yourself, it poisons the rest."

Robbie sways in the guards' grip and they steady him. "You're a monster. Both of you," he says, looking from Elliot to Sasha.

"Hmm, that's ironic because that's what I see before me now. A monster. A sinful, lying, stealing creature that I thought the world had mostly taken care of." Elliot squints at Robbie for a moment before turning his head toward Wen. "My dear, am I mistaken, or doesn't this man assist you in the kitchen when he's not scavenging?"

She lets out a shaky breath. "Yes."

"Did you know anything about this?"

She searches for a way out, eyes flashing to the windows, the door blockaded by guards, back to Robbie's battered face, the pleading there. She knows what he wants and gives it to him, hating herself even as she does so.

"No. I had no idea he was planning this." Her heart fractures a little at the gratitude that is there and gone in Robbie's gaze. "He's always been an excellent worker." She can't stand to look at him anymore so she addresses the guard behind him. "Are you sure he was trying to escape? Maybe you're mistaken about what you saw."

The guard sneers. "I have two fucking eyes just like you. I can tell if one guy's kissing another. Damn queer." He shakes Robbie whose head jostles from side to side.

"Yes, well. This is most unfortunate," Elliot says. "To mar opening night this way is definitely a sign of bad luck. But the show must go on, no matter what hiccups arise."

Robbie purses his lips and, before Elliot can react, spits a mouthful of bloody saliva into his face.

Elliot's arm swings up, the derringer pistol snapping into his hand. He lunges forward, pressing the barrel hard into Robbie's forehead, a maniacal grimace tearing his face in two. "You piece of filth! I should end you right now," the old man growls, pushing the gun hard enough into Robbie's skin that Wen sees fresh blood pool around the steel. Elliot breathes hard, shoulders heaving, and she knows any second she'll hear the gunshot, see Robbie, her only true friend in the world, crumple lifelessly to the ground, and then it will all be over. She will try to kill both of the Prestons with her bare hands, and she will die alongside her friend.

But instead of firing, Elliot drops his hand to his side, the gun retreating into his sleeve. He tips his head back, accepting a towel proffered by Hemming, who has moved to his side. After wiping his face clean of Robbie's blood, Elliot smiles, flashing his small, gray teeth.

"You know, I do believe you can serve one last purpose for the show."

29

Zoey hears the roar of the crowd and feels the drumming of feet through the coliseum's framework before she ever sees the procession.

When the gunshots rang out she had dropped to the ground in the shadow behind the generator shack, pistol coming out automatically. In a span of a few seconds she pinpointed the direction of the firefight, seeing only the last two muzzle blasts a significant distance down the fence line. After that the yells and ensuing chaos had been too much to contend with, and she'd scuttled to the coliseum's bracing, sliding between two steel beams into the hollow space below the structure. Through the interweaving joists she spotted several guards dragging a slender man in the direction of the two-story building. The crowd had gradually calmed, the spectacle gone from their direct observation.

She had watched Merrill and Eli move through the milling men, trying to get a look at what was happening, before she lost sight of them among the many bodies. For a long time the center of the coliseum had remained empty while the stands above her began to fill up. Dozens of feet and legs passed by her position, most climbing higher while some remained, partially blocking her view until she was forced to move to another, clearer section on the left. But just when she had convinced herself that she might be able to sneak from her hiding place and get a closer inspection of the containers, several men appeared in the center of the ring, a tall apparatus on wheels concealed beneath a heavy tarp between them. This had elicited a rumble from the crowd above her.

But the clamor now is tenfold in comparison.

The midway is mostly clear of men, so the movement in the direction of the taller building catches her eye almost immediately. A procession walks steadily toward the main entrance to the coliseum, led by an older man and woman, both of them dressed extravagantly. They move with the unmistakable air of leadership, walking almost exactly in the same way the Director used to across the stage at inductions. Behind them is a man dressed entirely in black, his skin whiter than any Zoey has ever seen before. Behind him, the same man she saw being dragged away earlier walks between two armed guards, head drooped low, shoulders rounded.

And following them is a woman.

Zoey scoots forward, and against her better judgment, draws her hood back to get a better look. The woman walks with her gaze focused on the ground. Every so often her eyes lift to look at the skinny man being escorted ahead of her before dropping again. There is an uncanny despair about her, as if she is enshrouded by suffering but still hasn't fully succumbed to it.

But there is also something else that captures Zoey's full attention, locking her vision on the woman that comes closer with each step.

It is an undeniable notion of familiarity.

She has seen her before.

Her concentration breaks as a large man dressed in a filthy coat steps before the group, halting their progress. He holds a clear bottle half full of a brown-tinged liquid Zoey had seen being sold from a booth in the midway.

"Hey, Presto! How 'boutcha share the wealth? Gimme a shot at that one back there; she's too old for the tournament anyway."

The man in the suit turns his head slightly and the white-skinned man behind him smiles, moving toward the drunk staggering before them.

"Hey whitey, whatchu think you're—"

But his words are cut off as the man in black draws something out of his coat, and in a movement so quick Zoey can barely track it, swings his arm past the drunk's throat.

Crimson beads catch the light, their cascade a red rainfall on the ground beside the man.

He drops the bottle, clutching his neck, and totters to the side. He turns enough for Zoey to see the deep stain below his chin growing by the second, the flesh split there from ear to ear. He takes two more steps, blood misting from parted arteries, before falling to his side on the ground where he lies still.

The man in black wipes the shining blade he holds on a dark cloth he draws from a pocket and disappears the knife back beneath his coat as the procession continues toward the coliseum.

Zoey watches the woman trail behind them through the entrance and into the center of the arena, where the line of people stops beside the shrouded apparatus. The man in the silver suit holds one hand up to silence the crowd, and begins to speak.

30

"Gentlemen of Southland! Welcome to the last, greatest show on Earth!"

The men's cheers reverberate in the air around Wen, but she barely hears them. She stares at the shape beneath the stained tarp, sure that at any second her will or her mind will snap and she'll be oblivious to this all. And she prays for the release.

Her gaze trails to Robbie, who's looking back at her through the crusted blood around his eyes. He gives her a quirked smile, the small expression saying everything that he can't. *Well, isn't this a shit show.*

"I am Presto Preston, the ringmaster and your humble host. We've traveled thousands of miles to be here with you tonight!" Elliot continues, his voice deep and rich in timbre, carrying over the last of the crowd's cries. "To bring you marvels of the fantastic." He draws a white handkerchief from the breast pocket of his suit. "And to let you experience the magic still alive in the world."

Elliot does a small flip of his hand, tenting the handkerchief with his fingers. He holds it steady for a beat before ripping it away in an exaggerated motion.

A small songbird rests in his palm.

Elliot gives it a toss and the bird flits up into the night over the heads of the men, disappearing past one of the powerful lights.

The men cheer once again, applause rippling through the crowd, which draws a wide smile on Elliot's face. Sasha stands behind him beaming.

Wen's fingers ache from being clenched into fists. She releases them, imagining encircling Elliot's neck with both hands and *squeezing*.

"I know why you've all come. The pinnacle of our show. The paramount of entertainment." Elliot pauses before throwing his hands up into the air. "The Tournament!" Once again the men in the stands seethe with sound, feet stamping, fists raised, mouths open in bellows. "And you will get what you came for," Elliot says. "But tonight we have a special event, an added bonus, if you will, preceding the beginning of the Tournament tomorrow." There is some unrest and rumbles of dissent and Wen glances hopefully around the coliseum. Maybe if the masses get unruly enough, she might have a chance to stop this.

"Please, please, hear me out," Elliot says. "The man you see being held here now was caught earlier tonight stealing goods, hiding weapons, and worst of all, fornicating with another man!" The prior mumbling of discord turns to boos and shouted slurs. Wen watches the row of men closest to the arena's floor spit in Robbie's direction, one after the other. "This man! Is not only a thief, but also goes against the very fabric of humankind! In a time such as this when humanity needs and hungers for salvation in the form of procreation, this man flies in the face of all we hold dear! And that, my friends, cannot be tolerated."

With the same flourish he used to reveal the bird in his palm, Elliot grabs the corner of the tarp and yanks it free, exposing what lies beneath it.

The night resounds with the crowd's roar and Wen bites back a sob, looking away from Elliot, from Robbie, and from the guillotine and its shining, angled blade hanging high in the air.

31

Zoey inhales sharply as the tarp is lifted.

She takes in the tall, twin wooden columns, the vise-like base with a hole carved into it above two wheels, the rope leading to its top, two buckled straps at the bottom, and worst of all, the enormous blade hovering between the supports like a shining grin.

Her face creases as the mechanics of it all creates a picture in her mind.

The men's cries of delight are deafening, the world brimming with so much sound it makes her eyes water. She watches, unable to look away, as the two guards guide the slender man to the machine, forcing him down on his knees while fitting his neck into the base. Once his hands are secure in the straps, they step back, giving room for the older woman dressed in the silver gown. She glides to the side of the apparatus, the broad smile on her face looking more like a demonic grimace beneath the light's glare.

The woman's hand reaches out and grasps the rope.

32

Wen stifles a sob and looks down into Robbie's face as Sasha takes her position.

A tear falls to the dusty ground from his chin. He gives her his smile again and mouths something, winking even as his eyes fill with tangible fear.

I love you.

She doesn't hesitate or check to see who might be looking. She doesn't care anymore. *I love you too.*

And even as every atom in her body revolts and tries to turn her away, tries to shield her from what is to come, she keeps her gaze locked on Robbie, pours every kind thought and prayer she can into him. She will watch until the end. It is the least she can give him.

The crowd screams.

Elliot capers in a circle.

Robbie smiles.

Sasha pulls the rope.

33

The blade falls and Zoey closes her eyes.

The men's voices reach an ear-shattering crescendo that consumes all thought. She rises from her hiding place, drawing the hood back up as she picks her way through the scaffolding until she's in the open air again. She starts in the direction of the containers but spots three guards near the generator shack looking toward her, hands on their rifles.

She moves away from them, not having to force the drunken stagger as much, legs weakened from what she witnessed.

Evil. Pure, undiluted evil.

The brutality of the spectacle is overshadowed in her mind only by the men's enthusiasm. The cruelty and bloodlust is beyond anything she's ever encountered.

Is this what is left? Is this all there is?

She moves numbly past the stands where voices shout, trying to gain her attention, draw her to their wares, but she strides without stopping, oblivious to all except the disbelief and despair that roils within her.

"Leaving so soon, old boy?" the man in the tall hat calls as she passes through the entrance. She doesn't acknowledge him, only walks away into the dark embrace of Southland.

The trek to the ASV is a blur, the image of the huge blade plummeting toward the man's neck all she can see, the collective voice of the crowd howling approval the only sound, the smell of sweat and fear hanging thick in her nostrils. The man they killed, he was put to death for being like Tia, for being different. Where does the hatred come from? How can cruelty be dealt out so casually and with such cemented conviction?

But she knows how. She lived in the company of people who believed they knew better than those they held captive nearly all her life. She saw what they would sacrifice in the name of the greater good.

And the Fae Trade is the epitome of all she despises.

Zoey doesn't realize she's arrived at their campsite until she sees the glow of the fire. When she steps into its light Ian is there, a pistol in one hand. She pushes back her hood and they stare at one another for a long second.

"Come get warm by the fire, I'm sure you're cold from the walk," he finally says, sitting down. The fire feels good on her outstretched hands, the air cold enough for her breath to plume out before her. Neither of them moves for several minutes, the dancing flames the only motion in the dark. Ian glances at her and sighs deeply. "Do you have a death wish, Zoey?"

"What? No, of course not."

"I ask in all seriousness because your decisions say otherwise."

"It was my choice to come here. I know everyone wants to keep me safe, but I'm not their responsibility."

He drops his gaze to the fire. "No. No I suppose you aren't. But you misunderstand me. As much concern as I have about outside forces, I worry more about your very worst enemy."

"Who?"

"Yourself."

Zoey opens her mouth to reply but no words will come. She remembers the looks on Lyle's, Rita's, and Sherell's faces when she told them what she planned. They had been afraid, but she'd been wrong about what it was they feared. It wasn't what she was suggesting.

It was her.

The sound of someone approaching cuts her thoughts off abruptly. She brings up her weapon, stepping closer to Ian as Merrill and Eli enter the ring of light.

"Just us," Eli says, striding to the fire. "Damn, it's cold out here. After this is through, I for one nominate Arizona as our next destination. This Pacific Northwest bullshit has run its course."

Zoey smiles but feels it fade when she sees Merrill looking at her, examining how she's dressed. He closes his eyes and swears under his breath. "You went anyway, didn't you?"

"I had to."

"No. You didn't." He moves around the perimeter of the fire, stopping directly across from her. "That was stupid." She says nothing, only nods. "You're lucky no one noticed how much smaller you were than everyone else and happened to pull that hood off of your head."

"Merrill, she's safe. No one's hurt. Please," Ian says.

Merrill looks as if he's going to launch into another tirade but instead sits down, looking toward the ASV. "Where's Chelsea and Tia?"

"When we realized Zoey was missing they went out to see if they could find her and left me here in case she returned."

"And they're not back yet?"

"No, not yet."

Merrill stands, gazing out into the darkness beyond the bluff. He frowns and turns his attention to Zoey. "You saw everything?"

"Yes."

"Where were you?"

"Beneath the seating of the coliseum."

He shakes his head. "How close did you get to the containers?"

"Not very. But I saw both of you did."

"We were able to make it most of the way around them before the guards ran us off."

"And? Could you tell how many women they have?"

"No, we couldn't get close enough for that."

"How about getting them out?"

"There might be a way." Merrill gives the darkness another long look before sitting once more. "They set up the fence line partially inside the city limits. The last residential street ends within the trade's boundaries. Eli was the one that actually spotted it."

"Spotted what?" Ian asks.

"A manhole cover," Eli says. "About ten yards behind the second shipping container is the edge of a street and there's a manhole set just inside the fence."

"What's a manhole?" Zoey asks.

"It's an access point for the city sewer system," Merrill says. "We can enter somewhere well away from the trade and make our way to that specific manhole. If we time it right we can climb up, incapacitate the guards around the containers, and get the women out and through the pipe before anyone knows they're gone."

"The only problem is the sewer system will probably be like a maze. We need a map," Eli says.

"A map? Where would we get that?" Zoey asks, shifting her feet closer to the fire.

"At the public utilities building, although we don't know where that is," Merrill says.

"But we can find it?"

"Yes, I think so. Since Tia was here before, maybe she has an idea where it is. But there's also the problem of the lights. There's too damn much light around the containers. If we had a little darkness it would be easier to pull off, but as soon as the lights go out, they're going to know something's up."

"Just like the ARC."

"Yep. But we can't wait around for a thunderstorm, especially since the next thing that's going to fall out of the sky will probably be snow."

Zoey picks up a small stick and begins drawing an outline of the trade in the ground. "We should take two of the guards with us when we bring the women out."

"What? Why?" Eli says.

"Because it will throw off whoever comes looking for us when they realize the women are missing. If they think two of their own men took the women it might lead them in the wrong direction."

"But what are we going to do with the guards once we're out?" Merrill says. Zoey gazes at him across the fire and she sees his jaw tighten. "The answer isn't always killing."

"Did you see what happened tonight? Did you see what that place is?"

"Yes. And I see you right now." He stands up. "I'm going to look for Tia and Chelsea. They should be back by now."

She starts to say something, to call him back and apologize, but they all freeze as footsteps crackle through leaves on the fringe of the light. A moment later Tia appears out of the darkness, eyes tracing each of them before addressing Zoey. "The hell did you get off to, girly?"

"She went to the trade," Merrill says.

"Well that was brilliant. Were you born dumb or did you have to work at it?"

"I'm sorry," Zoey says, looking at all of them. "I am."

"Being sorry means you won't do it ever again," Merrill replies before looking at Tia. "Where's Chelsea?"

"Isn't she here? We split off about a half hour ago. She was heading west and was going to swing down through the trees to meet here," Tia says, pointing into the woods.

"Damn it," Merrill says, and runs in the direction Tia motioned to. There are a few yells for him to wait or stop, but in less than a second he's gone, swallowed up by the gloom.

Zoey rises and goes after him, hearing the others follow behind her. Ahead she can barely make out the dense population of tree trunks, the sound of Merrill's passage drifting back to her over her own footfalls. A shriveling sensation invades her chest, a cold constriction around her heart.

No. Chelsea is simply late. Or maybe she got turned around heading back to camp.

She follows Merrill as he rushes onward through the trees, Chelsea's whispered name coming from him every few seconds. Zoey silently wishes for an answer from somewhere nearby, but the forest remains silent.

Someone curses behind her. A branch snaps.

Ahead Merrill's outline disappears and she slides to a stop, bracing herself against a tree, trying to listen for the direction he's gone.

There, to the left. The crunch of several footsteps.

And something else.

The low throttle of an engine.

A gunshot.

Her stomach folds in on itself as she sprints away from the tree, down a small grade, and out into the clearing lit with a sickly orange by the trade's glow from below.

She skids to a halt near a low growth of sage, heart skipping every other beat as her mind processes what she's seeing.

Several vehicles are parked in the lowland below the rise, their headlights facing each other. Outside the ring of illumination, four figures walk together. Three of them carry weapons, and the other is stooped over as if in pain.

Zoey hears the rest of the group approaching from behind her and she wants to scream at them not to look, because she doesn't want to see, to believe what she already knows.

The figures below step into the wash of headlights. They are only visible for a split second, but it is long enough to see Chelsea's red hair and her hands bound behind her back before the men shove her into the closest vehicle and tear away in a spray of dust toward the Fae Trade.

34

"I wonder how they're doing," Sherell says.

She and Rita sit across from one another in the lunchroom, remnants of their dinner between them. The room is warmer than the rest of the installation, so they've taken to spending most of their time there when not outside on watch or idly scanning the radio frequencies on the transistor they found in the garage.

"As well as they can, I'm sure," Rita says, nudging a bite of gristle off the table, which Seamus snaps out of the air before it can hit the floor.

"What would you have done?" Sherell asks after a time.

"You mean if I were Zoey?"

"Yeah."

Rita flicks another crumb to Seamus. "I don't know. Maybe nothing."

"You'd be okay with the Fae Trade continuing what they do?"

"I didn't say that. But there's a lot of things in the world that aren't right. Someday she'll figure out she can't fix it all."

"What if she would've kept going after she got out of the ARC?"

Rita pauses in feeding Seamus. "Then we'd still be there, wouldn't we?" They fall silent for a time, the dog's eating the only sound in the room. "One thing I know," Rita says finally. "With what she's got Lyle working on right now downstairs, I don't ever want Zoey angry with me." She spins her plate in a circle. "At least not again."

Sherell smiles. "Speaking of Lyle, I forgot to bring him supper." She stands and moves to the corner where they've taken to storing most of their food.

"Not like it matters. He's eaten about four bites since he started working."

"Yeah. And he's always in that chair. I haven't even seen him go to the bathroom yet."

"Maybe he's wearing a big old diaper."

Sherell glances over her shoulder and meets Rita's honest gaze. They both burst out laughing at the same time. After two more bouts of giggles, Sherell manages to fix a small plate of food for Lyle and leaves Rita, who continues feeding Seamus.

She moves down the hallway, glancing in each room as she goes, searching for signs of Newton, but he is nowhere to be seen. He's taken to working most days in the garage, and spends his nights sleeping on a cot in the entrance to the facility. The fact that he takes his job of protecting them so seriously never fails to send a warm rush across her skin. The day before, he let her cut his hair, a task that should've taken at the most twenty minutes, but she had stretched it out over an hour, the memory of his soft hair in her hands and his body heat keeping her awake long after Rita's snores had commenced for the night.

Downstairs she stops at Lyle's door and knocks. They call it his room now since none of them have seen him leave the area since the rest of the group departed. Thankfully all the chambers in the facility have excellent ventilation, otherwise she'd be sliding his food in beneath the door.

"Come in," Lyle says.

She enters and sets the plate of food beside the one she brought him for lunch earlier that day. There are several bites missing from the canned potatoes as well as the apple, but other than that it is untouched.

"You know, you really need to eat more," she says, picking up the lunch plate. Lyle hasn't looked away from the glowing computer screen since she entered. He does now, but only for a second before returning his bloodshot gaze to the monitor.

"Can't say I'm burning many calories here."

"Doesn't matter. You're going to get sick if you don't eat."

"I'll be fine." He stops his typing for a moment. "But thank you for your concern. And thank you for bringing me food. I can definitely do it myself."

"Well, I'm not burning that many calories myself. Does me good to move up and down the stairs." When he doesn't respond she inches closer behind him, studying the lit display. "Do you really understand all that?"

"Code? Yes. More each day in fact. Like riding a bike."

"What's that mean?"

"There's some things that never leave you no matter how long you're away from them."

She is quiet for a long time before she says, "So do you think my parents would recognize me if they saw me now?"

Lyle pauses, turning slowly toward her. "Yes. I'm sure they would."

She nods and gives him a quick smile before stepping into the hallway. After a few seconds, she hears Lyle resume his typing.

Sherell climbs the stairs and carries the old plate to the lunchroom, setting it on the floor for Seamus to find. She's about to go looking for Newton when Rita steps into the doorway holding an oblong object. Its body is a curved, hollow box with a hole in it while its opposite end narrows to an oddly shaped head, thin brass wires strung down its length.

"What the hell is this thing?" Rita says, holding it out.

"I don't know. Where'd you get it?"

"In one of the storage lockers upstairs. I've been cutting the locks and going through the last few we didn't search right away. There hasn't been anything really useful besides clothes so far. This was leaning in the corner of the last one." She turns the thing in her hands and runs her fingers across the strings. A discordant thrum issues from it and she glances up at the sound.

"It's an instrument," Sherell says, reaching out to take it from her. "Remember Chelsea telling us about, oh, what were they called? Bands? Remember? People would go and listen to them play music." She strums the wires and the same ugly hum comes from the wooden box.

"That sounds like shit," Rita says, and Sherell shoots her a look. "Well it does. That one disc Ian calls Elvis, now that's music."

Sherell laughs but quiets at the sight of Newton standing in the hallway outside the room, watching them.

Except he's not watching them, he's watching what she holds in her hands. He stares at it, an unreadable emotion running beneath his features. Sherell looks from him down to the instrument and back before holding it out.

He blinks and steps into the room, hands coming out to take it from her. He holds it so lightly and gently she's sure he's going to drop it, but he doesn't. Instead he goes to the nearest chair and sits, fingers moving to the end of the instrument where he turns the windings the strings are attached to, flicking at them all the while. Each note bends, rising and lowering in pitch as he works. Sherell watches, transfixed, until Rita's voice pulls her out of her daze.

"That thing's broken, Newton. Sounds like a dying animal. Maybe we could use it for firewoo—"

But her words are cut off as Newton strums out a chord so soft and clear, Sherell feels her mouth open slightly.

His fingers begin to work down the instrument's neck, pressing and sliding across the strings, first slow, then faster until a melody begins to build upon itself and fill the room. Sherell moves to the closest chair and sits, watching his hands, his graceful hands, create the sound that is something she could never put into words.

The song tilts between beauty and sadness, and she imagines if she knew its name it would give her hope and make her want to cry at the same time.

And even as she wishes he would never stop playing, his fingers fall still and the last note fades into nothing.

Newton tilts his head and reaches up, turning one of the windings slightly, then simply looks at the instrument before holding it out to Sherell.

"God, don't give it back to her. Not after that," Rita says.

Sherell smiles as Newton glances between them. "You keep it, it's yours," she says.

His lips begin to move and for a moment she thinks he's going to cry. But then she sees his tongue working behind his teeth along with the concentration on his brow.

He's trying to talk, she realizes.

His lower lip shakes and a wheeze comes from his throat. Then he is on his feet, shoving the instrument into her hands, and is out the door before she can reach for him, try to hold him like she wants to even if Rita's watching.

But he's already gone. Not only from the room but receded into himself the way he is the rest of the time, between the small glimpses of who he truly is.

Rita looks after him before glancing at Sherell. "Where did he learn to do that?"

Sherell sets the instrument on the table, the haunting melody still echoing in her mind. "I don't know, but I think he was trying to tell us."

◆　◆　◆

Newton wakes, the dead of night surrounding him in the entryway to the facility. He brings the handgun he keeps beside his pillow out, unsure of what woke him. He listens, hearing only wind outside the secure door, then below it, the soft shush of footsteps.

Instantly he is fully awake, sitting up and sliding into a crouch, eyes seeking out the sound. But it isn't coming from the exterior of the building, it is to his right, up the corridor leading to the stairway. He catches a glimpse of Sherell ascending the stairs in the faint light at the far end of the hall, then she is gone.

Newton relaxes, rising to sit on the edge of his cot as he replaces the pistol, but something is different in the entry, and he freezes.

The guitar leans against the wall across from him and a sheet of paper is woven between three of the strings. He moves to the instrument, drawing the paper free before flicking on the small flashlight he keeps beside his cot.

His breath catches.

The drawing is charcoal, made in sweeping shades that cover almost the entire page. He recognizes himself in the center holding the guitar, head down in concentration. The detail of the drawing is remarkable and he takes it all in, noting the skill and reflection that went into it.

Newton looks at the drawing for a long time before turning off the light. And in the darkness he lets himself smile.

◆　◆　◆

Lyle finishes the sequencing command and waits, eyes itching from lack of sleep. He glances at the mattress he moved into the corner of the room and wonders if he'll be able to drift off tonight. The insomnia hasn't been this bad since those first months after everything went to hell. When he was afraid to close his eyes for fear of opening them to the sight of a gun barrel inches from his face.

But the last weeks since Zoey's group arrived have been a Godsend. Truth be told, he doesn't care how Ken and his despicable crew went out. In fact, what Zoey did was probably too good for them.

No, the insomnia hasn't been due to fear but to excitement.

Hacking was never something he truly pursued or endorsed while he was employed, but he realizes now it was simply because he'd never seriously delved into the act before. Now after days and days of work, each breakthrough is like a dose of a powerful drug, leaving him craving more in the aftermath.

Even if the ultimate endgame is something that sends chills through him each time he contemplates it.

He shakes the thought from his mind and focuses on the percentage of correct binary series that he's already determined. He'd broken through the military's firewalls within thirty-six hours, but to do what Zoey tasked him with meant he would have to dismantle the very fabric of the system's security before he could gain full access.

And he's close. Very close.

The computer pings and brings him back from his musings. He opens the file he's been running on the side, associated with the last information NOA stored in the database. Lyle clicks on a series of icons, the pages opening various memoranda concerning medical supplies, stage settings for operations in different parts of the country, as well as personnel listings for departments within the organization itself.

He scans the files and slowly shuts them down one at a time and is about to return to the progress of the sequencing application when another NOA pathway link appears in the search parameter he set earlier.

Lyle leans closer to the screen, rubbing his eyes and readjusting his glasses. "What the hell?" he says quietly seeing the volume of contents. He frowns, clicking on the link.

The entire screen lights up with rows of downloads. It takes a second for him to realize what they are.

E-mails.

Thousands and thousands of e-mails.

After nearly five minutes the list finishes populating. He hesitates before opening the message at the top of the section. It is scrambled, half of the words missing in a jargon of nonsensical code. He sends several commands through the server, searching for the matching message header but turns up nothing. With trembling fingers he searches for the recipient e-mail and waits, breathing shallowly as the computer hums.

Just as he hoped, the original message appears in its entirety, attached to the recipient's response.

Lyle reads slowly at first then faster as more and more words that chime memories in his mind appear. Soon his eyes are leaping down the page, the inquiries and responses forming a picture that finally makes him sit back in his chair, his hand slowly coming up to cover his mouth.

"Oh my God," he whispers to the empty room.

35

Zoey watches the sun dash itself on the side of the mountain, dead grass below it shifting from brown to gold in the morning light.

She's cold and hungry but can't get herself to move from the tree she leans against. The trade is quiet now in the early hours, the music having spiraled into silence before dawn. The valley is crystalline with a coating of frost that came down in the night, and she feels like it not only covers everything she sees, but has penetrated her skin as well, chilling her to her core.

Her fault. Meeka, Crispin, Simon, Lily, and now Chelsea. All of them gone because of her.

When Merrill realized what happened the night before, he'd raced after the receding taillights, stopping only when they blended into the glow of the trade itself. He didn't say a word to her as he passed back by in the direction of the ASV and she hasn't been able to return to camp and face any of the others either.

Zoey looks down at her hands. How has it come to this? From where she started to where she is now, at what point did everything fall apart?

But I'm asking the wrong question, aren't I? It's not how this happened, it's why. And I know why. It's because of who I've become. I'm what's changed, and the problem is, I never really knew who I was to begin with.

She feels the urge to cry. To lie down in the frosted undergrowth of the forest and simply let it all flow out of her. She's sure if she did that she wouldn't ever get back up. *And the others would be better off for it.*

When the sun begins to melt the frost around her, she rises, moving through the trees until she can see the tan shape of the ASV beside the bluff. Ian, Tia, and Eli all sit around the cold fire ring, glancing up as she enters the clearing.

No one says anything for a time. Finally Ian motions to a rock beside him where an open jar of fruit waits. She goes to it and sits, using a plastic spoon to eat while the others avoid looking at her. When she finishes she clears her throat and struggles to find the right words.

"I'm sorry," she says, meeting each of their gazes. "It's my fault that Chelsea was taken. It's my fault we're here at all. I never wanted . . ." She shakes her head, her voice failing her.

Ian appears as if he's going to respond but then looks at the ground. A raven flies overhead, letting out a mournful call before coasting off in the direction of the trade.

"Where's Merrill?" she asks after a time.

"In the ASV," Tia says. "He hasn't come out all morning." Zoey rises and turns toward the vehicle. "I'm not sure he wants to speak to you."

She hesitates but muscles past the impulse to simply run into the woods and never look back, run until her lungs burn and her legs fail her, run until she can't remember. Instead she knocks softly on the ASV's door.

"Merrill, it's me." She pauses, tongue growing numb. "I can't say anything that will make you forgive me. I know that. But please let me help you get her back. We can, I know we can. Please, let me help." She rests her forehead against the cold steel of the door, listening for a reply but there is none. Gathering all her courage she slides the door open and climbs inside.

The interior is dim and it takes a second for her eyes to adjust, to search the benches for Merrill's form, but even as her mind is processing the emptiness of the vehicle, she already knows he's gone.

"No," she whispers, seeing his pack is missing as well. Zoey steps down out of the ASV and returns to the fire ring. "He's gone," she says.

"What do you mean, gone?" Tia asks, coming to her feet. She hurries past Zoey as Ian and Eli both stand as well. Tia's muffled curse is clearly audible and a moment later she comes striding back to them.

She stops in front of Zoey and without blinking, slaps her hard across the face.

Zoey's head snaps to the side, the corner of her mouth on fire as she tastes blood.

"Tia," Ian says.

"No! She did this. She disobeyed him and now they're both gone." Zoey looks up into the older woman's face, her normally placid features rigid with anger. Tia brings a finger within an inch of Zoey's eyes, her hand trembling with rage. "You know what he did, don't you? He entered himself in the fucking competition to get her back."

"You're right," she says, her vision blurring. "It's my fault."

"Tia, we don't know exactly where Merrill went," Ian says, stepping up beside both of them. "Perhaps he's doing reconnaissance. Maybe he's even gathering the schematics for the city sewer as we'd planned before."

Tia continues to stare, undaunted by Ian's words, and Zoey drops her eyes, unable to withstand her glare. She feels a tear slide down her stinging cheek.

"There's only one way to know for sure," Eli says, moving to the ASV. He grabs a small pack, hoisting it over his shoulders. "I'll go check things out. Be back as soon as I can."

"Eli," Ian says as the other man starts out of the clearing. "Be careful." Eli nods and is gone among the trees. Tia stares at Zoey for another drawn moment before stalking off around the side of the ASV.

Zoey stands with her head down, blinking away hot tears. Ian's hand touches her shoulder, trying to draw her into a hug, but she pushes him away.

"You should give me to the trade in exchange for Chelsea. They'd do it, I'm younger than her."

"You didn't mean for her to get taken, and you couldn't prevent Merrill from going after her, just as he couldn't stop you from witnessing the trade firsthand."

"But Tia . . ."

"Tia will calm down and see that we will have to work together to get them both back. She will forgive you."

"I can't forgive myself," Zoey says, turning away from him. She paces to the edge of the forest and finds a small hollow at the base of a crooked pine that she nestles herself into, curling into as small a shape as possible. She wishes she could keep folding in on herself until she disappears, become only an empty place in the world where she once was.

Because that is what she feels like now.

She closes her eyes, but the image of Chelsea being dragged away is there waiting for her in the dark, and when it fades she sees new and horrible visions of what will be done to her as soon as she's fought over and sold.

Her thoughts become elongated and spastic as they meld into a nightmare where Chelsea is hauled away again and again, but this time she can see the faces of her captors. She recognizes Ken's yellow grin, and the Director's cool gaze, and when the last figure turns she wakes herself with a scream, because it is her own face she sees floating there in the darkness.

Zoey pants, sucking in breaths of air that do nothing to calm her as she comes fully awake. She unclenches her aching fists and sees bloody half moons where her fingernails gouged her palms.

The sun has moved past the center of the sky and is angling toward the mountain in the west, its glittering peak barely visible above the trees. She manages to stand and is about to head back in the direction of their camp when Ian appears from around the nearest pine.

"Ah good, we were beginning to worry," he says.

"I'm fine."

"Eli's returned."

They hurry back to the ASV and find Eli and Tia leaning against its side. Eli gives her a tired smile as they approach and she can't help the quaver in her voice when she speaks.

"Did you see them? Is Merrill there?"

"Yes. He's there." Eli sighs. "He was one of four men who had enough money and entered into the competition for Chelsea. Looks like they auction the women off according to age. They must've got her to tell them how old she is because she's the youngest at thirty-nine."

The forest begins a lazy spin around her, nausea squirming in her stomach. "When?"

"Tonight."

She sinks down to the nearest rock. "Is there any way to get Merrill out? If he comes back, we can find the map of the sewer and get Chelsea—"

Eli shakes his head. "All the men who entered are locked up in separate cells in the center of the trade. It's like they're on display. Guys were taking bets on who would win, some were yelling at Merrill because he's obviously not from Southland and the others are. There's guards all around the cells, no way I could see to get him out. Besides, I'm pretty sure he wouldn't want us to."

Tia winds up and kicks a small rock off into the underbrush and paces away then back, hands on her hips. "Then we hit them before the competition. Right now. We go in through the sewer and take our chances."

"That would be suicide, Tia, and you know it," Ian says.

"Do you have a better idea?"

"No. But getting killed will not help Chelsea or Merrill."

"I'm not just going to stand by and watch!" Tia yells, her fiery gaze falling on Zoey. "I won't."

"Maybe that's all we can do," Eli says.

"What are you talking about?" Tia asks.

"Merrill's trained in hand to hand. He's strong, a good fighter, and with Chelsea being what he's there for, it wouldn't surprise me if he won."

"Yeah and he's missing a fucking leg too. Did you forget about that?"

"Both of you, calm down," Ian says, holding his hands out. "This is not a time to quarrel." He glances between the two of them. "But Eli may have a point. If Merrill were to be victorious, he could simply walk away with Chelsea, no worse for wear."

"What if he doesn't?" Tia says. "What if he slips or the guy he goes up against is better than he is?"

Ian rubs his grizzled chin. "Eli, how is the competition set up?"

"From what I heard, they lead Chelsea out to watch from the stands in the center of that ring along with everyone else and then put two of the men in with each other. They get to choose what kind of weapon they fight with, but it's all blades or axes, no guns."

Zoey cringes. Of course they would promote the most brutal and bloody death. Judging by the reaction of the crowd the night before at the execution, the competition would have to be as ruthless as possible to please the masses.

"And do they limit the competition to one fight an evening?" Ian asks.

Eli shakes his head. "No. All of them draw straws. The two with the shortest straws fight. Whoever wins faces the next guy chosen until there's only one left."

"But if Merrill's first and wins he'll be worn down by the second fight, and what if he gets injured?" Zoey asks. "That's not fair."

"This isn't something built on fairness," Ian says. "It appears a lot is left up to fate."

Zoey rises to her feet. "We have to do something. We can't just let him fight and hope he wins."

"Yeah? And what's your plan, girly?" Tia says. "You have some brilliant idea you've been keeping to yourself?"

"No. But there was a woman at the execution and I . . . I recognized her."

They all stare at her. Eli licks his lips. "What do you mean? You know her from the ARC?"

"No. Not from the ARC. She looked familiar, like I saw her in a picture once or something."

"Regardless, what difference does it make?" Tia says.

"Last night, she was right beside the man who was killed, and her face—I could tell she was dying inside. For some reason she's not locked up. Maybe she can help us."

"And what, you want to go back in there? Forget it."

Zoey moves past the others to the ASV and climbs inside. Merrill's coat, the one she wore the night before, lies in the far corner of the bench and she picks it up as Tia climbs into the vehicle behind her.

"You don't listen very well," Tia says, her voice softer than it has been all day.

"No."

"But I guess that's the one thing that got you out of the ARC in the first place." Zoey traces a frayed patch on one shoulder of the coat. "And it's why you're walking again." Tia steps closer and cups Zoey's chin in her hand, bringing her gaze up so they are eye to eye. "I'm sorry for hitting you."

"I deserved it."

"No. You didn't. The bastards that took Chelsea deserve it, not you."

"They deserve worse than that."

Tia studies her for a long moment. "Are you sure you want to go in?"

"Yes. I owe them both that much. And if we don't try tonight, tomorrow might be too late."

Tia releases her chin and draws her into a rough embrace, which she's never done before. Zoey hugs her back, emotion rising in her so suddenly she almost bursts into tears. When Tia lets her go she's surprised to see the older woman's eyes glistening.

"What do you need?"

She thinks, briefly running over a list in her mind. But it's all guesswork right now; she won't know exactly how anything is going to go down until she's spoken to the woman from the execution. "Money," she says finally. "And another couple magazines for my pistol."

"I'll get what cash Ian has on him."

Tia is partially out the door when Zoey stops her. "We're going to get them back," she says. Tia gives her a brief smile and a quick nod before disappearing outside, and Zoey wonders if Tia believes her any more than she believes herself.

36

Wen shudders, dry heaving over a pail in the corner of the kitchen.

Her stomach unlocks itself from the solid constriction it's become in her middle and she slumps to the floor, sweaty hair hanging in her face.

She wants to die.

Maybe she should do it. There are enough knives at hand to finish the job the poison started. She gazes at the handles sticking out of the butcher block. It would be so easy to slide one of the razor-sharp blades up the length of her forearm and just go to sleep.

Another tremor runs through her and she holds her hand out before her eyes. It shakes slightly, but nothing like it did the night before.

She's not sure how much of the ten-eighty got into her system, but she wishes now she would have swallowed the bite of pie. She wouldn't be sick and weak now, and she wouldn't keep catching herself looking for Robbie to walk through the kitchen door at any second. Routine is a cruel thing, especially when the years of unchanging repetition make you temporarily forget your best friend is dead, only to suddenly remember and kick-start the grief all over again.

Wen wipes at her face, hand coming away slick with sweat. The only good thing is she's been basically healthy all the years she's been in the trade and this morning's sickness was accepted without question by the Prestons when she sent word to them that she wouldn't be able to cook today.

She fingers the bulge inside the pocket of her pants, the little canister empty now, useless and hollow. Just like she is. Why did she use the entire amount?

But she knows why. She didn't want to take any chances. She wanted both of them dead. And even more so now. She wishes James could understand how destroyed she is, how much she wanted the plan to work as well, but he is carrying his own burden now.

He came to her earlier that morning, furious and unwilling to listen. And she was so weak there was nothing she could say or do to appease him. She even considered telling him what fate he would've met if Robbie and Fitz hadn't been discovered, but the anger she felt at his selfish indignation wasn't enough to fuel the blistering words.

So she weathered the storm of his fury and told him to leave her alone. And he had. But being alone was almost as bad as absorbing his rage. Between periods of vomiting she had dreamed of ways to finish what she and Robbie started. But short of sneaking a gun into the nest and trying to cut the Prestons down before Hemming kills her, there are no options. Her one chance was thrown out with the trash last night.

Before she'd gotten sick, after enduring the coliseum, she'd checked the waste bin behind the nest, hoping against hope that the Prestons would keep at least the pie to eat the next day. But her heart sank at the sight of the poisoned food splattered across its bottom, the slices of apple unmistakable even in the dim glow of her flashlight. Their vanity and wastefulness, two things she utterly despised about them, were what saved their lives.

Wen gazes at the window, the darkness growing thicker by the minute. The intermingling yells and music outside sets her teeth on edge and she has to breathe deeply to keep her stomach from clenching once again. This is what hell sounds like. She's sure of it.

And soon the terrible noise will rise to another level as the competitors enter the dance floor, where the dark stain of Robbie's lifeblood isn't wholly dry yet. They will fight and die for yet another nameless woman, this one found, unbelievably, wandering less than a mile away from the trade.

It seems luck wasn't on anyone's side last night. Except the Prestons'.

"So close," she whispers, and the husky rasp of her voice is like the sound of an animal trying to speak.

The smell of vomit is oppressive in the kitchen, making her tortured stomach turn even more. She stands, hobbling to the bucket, and without looking at its contents, moves to the door and outside.

The trade is in full swing, men moving in droves through the grounds, up and down the midway, their calls and fits of laughter like the constant buzz of a hornet's hive. She glances around to make sure no one is in the vicinity of the mess area before walking to the side of the building and dumping her sick onto the ground. She returns to the door and closes it behind her.

Alone again, she pulls the single chair over to the sink and sits, leaning her head against the counter.

She sees Robbie smile, the terrified sadness on his face as the guillotine falls. Wen moans, clamping her eyes shut, but he is there too, and she knows then that she'll never forget or be free of the night before.

Shaking, she reaches out and grasps the handle of the largest butcher knife, holding it so that it catches the feeble light thrown by the overhead fixture. She turns it several times before bringing it down to her wrist, pressing the tip there not quite hard enough to break the skin.

Goodbye Robbie, goodbye Prestons and trade, and goodbye . . . but she can't get herself to utter the name, even in the silence of her own mind.

Wen draws in a breath, realizing it will be one of the few she has left, and focuses on the blade and the final cut she'll ever make with it.

The muscles tense in her arm as she begins to bear down, a cry coming from her. The pain is so much sharper than she thought it would be.

And as she commits herself fully to what she's started, there is a hard rap on the door and the knife slips from her grasp.

37

Zoey throws a glance over one shoulder, making sure the area in front of the little building is still clear.

The woman hasn't been inside for more than a minute, so she's fairly confident she hasn't left out the back, especially since the dim light is still burning inside. She raises her fist to knock again, but the door swings inward and then she is looking at the woman's pale face. The woman opens her mouth to say something but stops, eyes widening as Zoey tilts her head back enough for the light to fall on her features inside the hood.

They stare at one another.

And the recognition heightens to a point where Zoey nearly says a name that slips away almost as quickly as it comes.

Zoey pushes past her and shuts the door, the woman still dumbstruck. She looks around the room, confirming they're alone before drawing the hood back.

The woman's hand comes up to her mouth and it's only then that Zoey notices the steady stream of blood running from her left wrist, crimson soaking through the fabric of her shirtsleeve.

"You're bleeding," Zoey says, nodding toward her arm. The woman looks down dazedly, and wipes at the flow coming from a slit above her wrist. Zoey spots a long towel hanging from a hook and grabs it, wrapping it around the woman's forearm. She watches the blood seep through the towel and cinches it tightly, aware of the woman's eyes boring into her.

When the bleeding slows enough that she's sure the woman won't faint, Zoey finally meets her gaze.

There is a feral quality to the woman that she recognized in her own features after escaping from the ARC, a lean wildness that speaks of horrors survived. As she studies her, the familiarity washes over Zoey once again, and this time her eyes catch on something that takes her breath away, the realization powerful enough to weaken her legs.

Above the woman's right eyebrow is a white line of scar in the shape of an L tipped on its side.

"Rita," Zoey manages to say, and the effect on the woman is immediate. Her lower lip trembles and she takes a step back.

"What did you say?" she whispers.

Zoey swallows. "You're Rita's mother. You're Nell."

The other woman blinks and begins to shake her head. "You're not real. I'm dead. I'm dead on the floor." She looks down at her arm to the towel tied there. "I'm dead."

"No you're not. I'm here. And you're Rita's mother."

"She's dead."

"She's alive."

Nell closes her eyes, tears escaping from their corners as she leans against the nearest wall and slowly slides down it. Zoey kneels beside her. "She has red hair and green eyes and she looks just like you."

"Stop. Stop it," Nell moans. "Don't say that. I don't have a daughter, she was taken. She's dead."

"She's alive. She's my friend," Zoey says, putting a hand on Nell's shoulder. "And she remembers you."

Nell tips forward, quietly sobbing into her hands. Slowly she brings her tear-stained face up to look at Zoey. "You're real."

"Yes."

"You're telling the truth."

"Yes."

"Because I'll kill you if you aren't."

"I believe you."

Nell watches her for another long moment. "Who are you?"

"My name is Zoey. I was kept in the same place Rita was. But we're free now. And I need your help."

"My help." Nell gazes down at the floor between her splayed legs. "Help."

"Yes and I don't have much time. Two people are being held here. The woman that was brought in yesterday and one of the men who's going to fight for her tonight. I have to find a way to get them out."

Nell issues a muffled laugh and tugs at the towel around her wrist. "Get them out. It's impossible."

"There has to be a way. You know this place, how it works. Please." The men's voices outside rise in volume and a short cheer erupts before the din returns to normal.

"They took her. Took her from me and brought me here. And I tried." Nell brings her glassy eyes up to Zoey's. "Tried to escape but they always caught me. And then Robbie came and we planned for years. Robbie's dead now. He's gone."

Zoey leans in closer and puts a hand gently on the older woman's face. "But your daughter isn't. Help me save my friends and I'll bring you to her."

Nell's eyelids flutter and Zoey thinks she's going to pass out, either from blood loss or shock. But the other woman steadies after a second and licks her lips. "When they're bringing them all to the coliseum. That's the only chance. They lead the men in first, then the Prestons take their seats with the youngest woman."

Zoey's mind whirs. *Such a short span of time. The distance between the cells and the coliseum is less than a minute's walk. How? How to get Merrill and Chelsea free at the same time and then make it outside the fences?*

"There has to be another way. How long until the competition starts?"

A deep sound, unlike anything Zoey's ever heard before, begins to build somewhere to the east. It climbs in volume until she can feel it in her chest, vibrating her heart against her rib cage. The call ends as abruptly as it started, its vacancy filled by hundreds of men's voices screaming at the top of their lungs.

"Now," Nell says.

38

Zoey leaps to her feet and whips the hood up, glancing at the darkened windows.

The bass sound comes again but it can't override the fevered howls. She moves to the closest window and peers out, careful to keep her face hidden in shadow.

The crowd floats past the mess area in the direction of the coliseum, and in the center an open space is cordoned off by a dozen guards. Four men walk single file there, a thick chain binding them to one another.

Merrill is the third in line, hands tied together before him. The two men in front of him are shorter and leaner, and compared to him they look scrawny. But then her eyes are drawn to the man behind Merrill and the slight hope building inside her crumbles.

The last man is a giant.

He stands at least a foot taller than Merrill and his shoulders protrude from a sleeveless jacket in two round balls of muscle. Even from the distance she can see the massive thickness of his legs as well as the size of his hands, which flex into fists almost as large as her head. A cheer erupts from the crowd as the giant hoists his arms above his head and grins a mostly toothless smile.

"Oh no."

"There's nothing you can do now," Nell says, rising to her feet. "They'll be inside the coliseum in a few seconds and there won't be any way to get them out once it's begun." Zoey steps away from the window and draws her pistol. "What are you doing?"

"I'm going to shoot the owners of the trade when they walk past me. Maybe I can cause a big enough disturbance so Merrill and Chelsea can get away."

"The men. They'll tear you apart. And your friends won't escape."

Zoey wavers, part of her already out the door, pushing through the crowd and finding the perfect position. But the other part is there in the dim room with Rita's mother, logic overriding the building panic and rage at her helplessness.

She lowers the gun and tucks it away.

"If he wins they'll be free," Nell says. Zoey puts her hand on the doorknob and hesitates, looking back over one shoulder.

"If that happens we'll come back for you. We'll get you to Rita."

"And if not?"

But she barely hears Nell's question as she pushes through the door and into the night air.

The throngs of men are rapidly disappearing into the coliseum when she reaches the entrance. Merrill is already inside, swallowed by the structure's walls. To her right a convoy of guards surrounds the two people who beheaded the man the night before. They walk with the same gloating dignity of the powerful, and behind them, hands shackled together and wearing a flowing dress of red, is Chelsea.

Despite the horror that rises within Zoey, she can't help but notice how beautiful Chelsea looks. Her hair has been washed and styled, her lips glow crimson, and her pale skin seems to shine in the harsh overhead light.

A foul-smelling man passes within inches of Zoey and she shifts slightly to avoid brushing against him. When she turns back, she catches only a glimpse of Chelsea's dress disappearing into the coliseum. An earsplitting cheer comes from inside the walls a moment later and she curses, hurrying into the nearest blanket of shadow. She makes her way around the side of the coliseum until she reaches the place she witnessed the execution from and slides between the support beams. Above, hundreds of feet stomp and pound, filtering a thin haze of dust down on her. She shimmies forward as far as she can and peers out through a shifting sea of legs.

Merrill and the other three men stand in the center of the open ring. A table rests to their right, its top littered with weapons of every shape and size. Zoey spots the sharpened bits of axes, glittering swords, and heavy hammers. Directly across the coliseum is a long, enclosed wooden box raised halfway up the rows of seats. Inside sit the Prestons and below them Chelsea in plain view of the entire crowd. Even with the distance Zoey can see the shining tear tracks that streak Chelsea's face as she stares at Merrill below.

Zoey draws her pistol.

She will wait, and if it appears that Merrill isn't going to win a fight, she'll shoot the other man. There is no way she's going to sit by and watch him die. Consequences be damned.

Presto Preston stands and raises both hands. Gradually the rumble of voices falls into a low undercurrent. "Gentlemen and the two ladies who are present!" he yells, gesturing at his wife as well as Chelsea. "Thank you for coming! Tonight we have entertainment of epic proportions. The four brave men you see before you have paid their dues and stepped forward for the right to claim the hand of the beauty you are witness to now." Preston motions to Chelsea again and the crowd's voices rise as one. Several lewd statements are screamed within the cacophony and Zoey grits her teeth. Preston makes his calming gesture and the calls quiet. "Each of the combatants have put their life on the line, have come to terms with death for the chance to claim this woman.

Their sacrifice amazes me to no end. Anyone willing to die for her has our blessing when he walks out with his prize."

Preston falls silent and gazes around the coliseum. "Within the right of the Tournament, the winner will not be followed nor harassed once it is over. He will be allowed safe passage and this woman will be rightfully his until their dying day." Preston presses his palms together before yanking them apart again. A flash of light and a loud boom erupts from between his hands, resounding throughout the coliseum. "Let the Tournament begin!"

The entire structure shudders with the mass's yells. Two guards approach the four men and one holds a fist out. The first man draws something away from the guard's hand. He smiles and holds it up as the crowd cheers. The next man follows suit, shaking his head in disgust as the guard continues on to Merrill.

Merrill reaches out and retrieves what the guard offers. He nods once and raises his arm in the air to combined screams of approval and bellowed curses.

Zoey's breath hitches in her chest. The hope of at least one of the men being eliminated before Merrill had to fight evaporates. She watches as the second man and the giant are led to the edge of the arena and placed inside a smaller version of the box the Prestons and Chelsea occupy. The remaining guard motions to the table full of weapons and the first man steps forward, hefting a huge hammer into the air to a round of cheering. Merrill approaches the table and examines it, eyes tracing from one end to the next. She fights down the urge to crawl through one of the gaps and run to him. They could fight, side by side, and die together at the very least. But she knows that isn't what he would want.

After a pause of deliberation Merrill grasps a long-bladed knife from the table, studying its edge for a beat before stepping away. The weapon looks insignificant when compared with the other man's hammer, and raucous laughter explodes in the coliseum as the table is hauled outside the large ring and Merrill and the other man are left standing in its center.

"Gentlemen!" Preston says from the box. "There are no rules. May the best man win!"

Merrill's opponent grins, hefting the large hammer, and begins to circle. Merrill remains where he is, pivoting slowly to keep the other man in front of him. A chant of "Billson" rises from the stands.

Zoey adjusts her position, steadying the handgun, tracking Billson with the sights. He feints toward Merrill suddenly, jabbing at him with the hammer, and Merrill flinches. More laughter erupts from the stands. Chelsea leans against the box's rim, hands clasped before her in the shackles, mouth open in a soundless sob.

Billson circles.

Merrill follows him.

Zoey aims, finger tightening on the trigger.

Billson feints again to Merrill's right before charging straight at him, hammer raised over one shoulder.

He swings the heavy steel in a bone-crushing arc aimed directly at Merrill's skull.

Merrill moves.

He shifts hard to the left, tipping his head and shoulders away from the hammer as it whistles past him, throwing Billson off balance.

In one motion Merrill steps behind the other man and brings the arm holding the knife up and back.

The long blade sinks deep into the base of Billson's skull.

Merrill yanks the knife free and the hammer drops from Billson's hands as blood spews from his open mouth. He tries to take a step but drops to the ground in a heap and doesn't move again.

Utter silence floods the coliseum.

Elation flows through Zoey in a warm wave and it's all she can do not to cry out Merrill's name. She watches as Chelsea covers her mouth with both hands and sinks back into her chair with relief.

Slowly a grumble of voices returns to the arena, the men's boots scratching and clunking overhead. Two guards enter the coliseum and drag Billson's limp body away while a third approaches the holding area containing the remaining combatants. Zoey stares as the giant reaches out and plucks a straw from the guard's proffered fist. Anger creases his face and he sits back in his seat as the smaller man stands and enters the arena to renewed cheers.

Merrill steps well out of the other man's path as he makes his way to the table of weapons. Zoey can't be sure but she thinks she catches a look of trepidation in his eyes as he selects an axe and turns it over once before facing Merrill. The crowd's volume rises again, the smell of fresh blood now permeating the air, fueling the lust for carnage that is almost a physical presence. Zoey moves to the left around a supporting column to get a better view and glances over her shoulder.

Two guards stand a dozen yards behind her, their shadows thrown by the overhead lights almost reaching to where she crouches. They are talking loudly to be heard over the sound of the arena, a cigarette passing from one to the other and back again. They stand with their backs partially to her, but if they were to turn and look down, they would surely see her.

Preston begins yelling something again but she doesn't hear what he says, her focus completely on the guards. Smoke plumes out of their mouths and one of them laughs, slapping the other on the shoulder. Zoey sinks in on herself, wedging back farther beneath the coliseum's struts.

The crowd roars and now it is impossible to keep her eyes on the guards. She turns her head.

The man with the axe circles Merrill much like Billson did, but there is a careful calculation in his movements. He steps forward and back, testing the distance while keeping the wicked bit of the axe before him. Merrill bends his knees, knife-arm held out to the side, blade dripping crimson onto the ground.

Something hits Zoey's back and she freezes, sure the next sound she'll hear will be the gunshot that propelled the bullet into her.

But there is only the sweet smell of tobacco. She glances at the guards, who are ambling away, still deep in conversation. At her feet the stub of cigarette they flicked toward her glows briefly before winking out.

She faces the arena again just as the man with the axe lunges forward, swinging the weapon at Merrill's waist.

Merrill leaps back as the blade whistles past and resets himself, his knife slashing out with a quick glint of steel.

A long gash opens up in the other man's coat across his chest, a hint of red seeping through immediately. He backpedals, catching himself before he falls, and begins to circle Merrill again, one hand pressed to the wound.

Merrill's eyes shine with concentration as he follows the man's movements, waiting several seconds before springing forward. The knife flashes as he stabs downward at the man's chest, but it is blocked as the axe handle comes up and cracks hard across his jaw.

Zoey's heart stops as the knife pinwheels away through the air.

Merrill staggers back and shakes his head, the other man walking forward. Zoey raises the gun, sighting down the barrel, finger tightening on the trigger, but Merrill steps in front of her, blocking the shot.

The axe rises and comes down, missing Merrill by inches. He counters with an elbow to the man's head and tries to wrench the weapon from his grasp but loses his balance as the other man shoves him hard in the chest.

Merrill trips and falls, his back kicking up dust as he rolls to his side.

The man is instantly upon him, raising the axe over his head, and Zoey aims, knowing everything will come to an end within seconds.

But Merrill's leg lashes out, catching the other man in the knee. He falls to the ground, axe flipping away, but in less than a second is atop Merrill, raining down punches.

Merrill blocks them and grasps him by the coat, digging his fingers into the wound across his chest. The man screams and the crowd's cries intensify.

With a quick movement, Merrill pivots his hips and tosses the man to his side, scrambling toward the knife lying several feet away.

His opponent latches onto the axe.

Zoey leans forward, one hand gripping the rail in front of her, willing Merrill to move faster, to get to the blade and end his opponent before he can rise.

Merrill snags the knife and rolls over just as the man swivels on his knees and brings the axe up and then down in a brutal, sweeping blow.

The weapon buries itself in Merrill's leg, biting through his pants and into the ground.

Zoey's scream is lost in the men's thunderous exclamation. Her stomach clenches painfully as tears cloud her vision. She fires at the man, the gun's report nearly soundless beneath the noise.

The shot goes wide, kicking up dust in the center of the circle.

The arena is all movement, sound beyond reckoning.

The man, still on his knees, yanks the axe free, yelling his triumph as he rears back for a killing blow.

Zoey aims again, willing her arms to remain steady.

Squeezes the trigger.

But in the split-second pause that stretches into infinity, Merrill raises his injured leg off the ground and drives it toward the man's face, metal glimmering through his pant leg as he thrusts the ragged shaft of his artificial limb through the man's left eye.

Zoey stares, dumbstruck, while he jitters, pinned in the air by the jagged aluminum jutting from the end of Merrill's leg.

The axe slips from his hands and falls harmlessly in the dirt.

Merrill kicks out with his good leg, shoving the dead man off the broken prosthetic.

The coliseum is quiet again, a murmur weaving through the men as Merrill rolls to his stomach and onto his knees. The flare of relief Zoey felt moments ago is doused as she watches Merrill try to stand and fall immediately back into the dirt. The lower half of his artificial leg and foot lie in the folds of his severed pant leg, useless and irreparable. When he tries to stand again and falls, laughter courses through the crowd.

"Silence!" Preston says, rising from his seat. He stares down until Merrill turns and faces him, still on his knees. "This is a most unfortunate turn of events. I was unaware of your disability. But I suppose it became an advantage, didn't it?" Merrill watches the ringmaster, unmoving, and Zoey can see the slight tremble in the muscles of his back. "You are a valiant warrior, and normally I would recommence the Tournament immediately. But given your predicament, you've earned yourself a day's rest. We will resume tomorrow evening and finish what was started."

Preston's words are met with an outcry of anger. Several pieces of thrown trash land in the center of the arena as two guards enter and hoist Merrill upright. The Prestons begin to turn away, another set of guards pulling Chelsea from her place in the box, but a voice rises above the collective clamor.

"Wait!" Merrill yells, and the Prestons pause, the commotion dying down. "How will I fight with only one leg?"

Presto moves to the edge of the box, and in that moment Zoey sees the flicker of insanity in his eyes.

"You did admirably today. I'm sure you'll figure something out." Preston smiles and turns away, following his wife down the stands with Chelsea close behind.

Zoey shifts her gaze from Merrill's limping form across the arena to the toothless giant's grin. An overwhelming dread encases her, freezing her solid where she crouches.

The coliseum gradually empties, heavy footfalls trailing off and giving way to the horrid music that begins again in the distance. She could lie down and become part of the dirt, sink into the soil and leave it all behind. Maybe she could forget everything, everyone who's ever meant anything to her. It would be so much easier not to care.

She waits until the grounds begin to thin of wandering men before climbing out of her hiding place.

The night is deep, stars muted beyond the cold lights of the trade. Bellows and laughter hang in the air along with the smell of roasting food. She moves through shadow to the kitchen building, rapping once on the door. It opens, and Nell stands there looking more solid, coherency rather than shock in her eyes.

She searches Zoey's face for a second before saying, "He didn't win."

"No. But he's not dead yet. Tomorrow he fights again." Zoey gazes to the side, past the tents and low buildings to where the fence begins. "I need you to get him a message. Can you do that?"

"Yes. I think so."

"Tell him to be ready." And with that she turns and moves away, weaving through shadows and leaving the wretched music and din of the trade in her wake.

39

When Zoey returns to the ASV, Eli is already there talking in a low voice to Tia and Ian.

They turn as one at the sound of her footsteps, Eli raising his handgun in her direction.

"It's okay. It's me," she says, stepping into the soft glow of Tia's flashlight.

"You have any trouble?" Eli asks, holstering his weapon.

"No. Did you see . . ."

"Yeah. I was just filling them both in."

Zoey moves to the steps of the vehicle and sits down. Her scalp itches. She needs a shower or a bath. Her hair is a tangled mass that she unclips and combs through with her fingers.

"He won't be able to fight," she says, glancing at the others. "There's no way he can fix his leg by tomorrow night. Besides, they wouldn't let him."

"It's all anticipation. Part of the show. Merrill getting killed by the big bastard will bring the crowd in for another night," Eli says. "I got some information out of a drunk guy while I was there. Merrill's opponent didn't enter on his own."

She glances up. "What? What do you mean?"

"From what this guy told me he was backed by six or seven other men because of his size and ability. They paid his way into the tournament in exchange for sharing Chelsea if he wins."

"Motherfuckers," Tia says. "We have to kill him. Kill the remaining guy."

"That won't work," Zoey says.

"Why not?"

"Because they'll find someone else for Merrill to fight. Or they'll kill him and start the competition for Chelsea all over again. We couldn't get close enough to do it anyway."

Tia curses quietly and begins to pace. Ian strokes the side of his face and gazes off into the darkness of the surrounding forest.

"So what, we do nothing? We let Merrill die and watch Chelsea get taken by a group just like the one we found at Riverbend? No. No way that's happening," Eli says. "We have to find a way. How about the woman you went to see? Can she help somehow?"

The realization that she hasn't told them who Nell is hits Zoey like a punch to the stomach. "I don't think there's anything she can do. But I know why I recognized her. I know who she is now." Tia pauses in her pacing and Ian and Eli stare at her. "She's Rita's mother."

Their stunned silence is broken as Ian takes a step closer to her and says, "Are you certain?"

"Yes. That's why she looked familiar, and when I told her that Rita was still alive she completely broke down."

"Holy shit," Tia says. "I can't believe it."

"I couldn't either, but even though it's absolutely wonderful, it doesn't help us get Merrill and Chelsea back."

Zoey gazes down at her feet and continues to comb her hair in slow, deliberate strokes, the repetitive motion soothing. For a split second she imagines it is Lee's hand, not her own stroking her hair. If he were here he would have a solution for the situation; he would know what to do.

The longing to have him near, to embrace him and feel his skin against hers, his safety and comfort flowing through her, is so overpowering that her throat closes up with emotion. She can't remember ever missing him this much.

But Lee is gone. Probably forever, and no one is going to help them.

She blinks away the gathering tears, lowering her face so as not to let the others see, and refocuses on the present. There has to be an answer, some weakness in the Fae Trade's defenses that they've overlooked. Zoey runs her fingers through her hair again, working slowly on a stubborn knot. She gazes past the tops of the trees at the brilliant pinpoints of starlight, the distant peak of Scrimshaw Mountain a blunt shadow jutting into the sky. When the knot comes undone she winds her hair up and is about to tie it tight when it slips free and falls to her shoulders.

She freezes, eyes glazing over, staring at the mountaintop.

Weakness.

I'm their weakness.

"I have an idea," she says, fingers gripping her hair in a solid fist.

♦ ♦ ♦

They leave an hour before morning light in the ASV, its engine at a low idle until they are more than two miles away from the trade's border. It is dawn by the time they find the small access road that splits from the main highway and meanders through a parched gully before winding into the forested foothills at the base of the mountain from the north. The road narrows until it is only a path, the scraping of overgrown tree limbs loud against the sides of the heavy vehicle.

Ahead there is the bumper of a car nearly overtaken by nature, a twinkle of dusty chrome only a suggestion in the sooty light. Past the car, the path opens up into a clearing of cracked concrete, dozens of trucks and cars parked between faded lines painted on the ground. A stainless steel tanker truck that looks much newer and cleaner than the other vehicles leans dangerously close to a hollow depression at the far corner of the lot, the words *Westward Pacific Petroleum* ghosts across its side. A log building stands before them straight ahead, windows broken, doors flung wide.

"That's the ski chalet," Tia says. "The main run starts on the opposite side. We should stop here." Eli guides the ASV to the left, tucking it close to the forest edge, and parks. They climb out into the crisp morning air.

Zoey gazes down past the chalet, breath pluming before her. The slope drops quickly away and beyond it the western side of Southland is visible. She moves closer to the building until she can see the trade, quiet now after the night's revelry, small dots of guards patrolling the perimeter the only movement.

"Zoey, I can't make a shot from this distance," Ian says, coming to stand beside her.

"I know."

"Then why did you want us to come here?"

"I'm not sure yet." She glances at Tia. "How does the chairlift work?"

"It runs off a diesel engine most likely. See that shack below the first pole? That's where it's housed."

"Do you think it will run?"

"How the hell should I know?"

"Could you make it work?"

"I can make anything work, girly, but I don't see what you're getting at."

"Me neither," Eli says. "What do you have in mind?"

Zoey surveys the structure Tia pointed out before running her gaze up the cables supporting the dangling chairlifts, looking for breaks or frays. A dozen yards up the main run of the mountain a rounded nozzle points at an angle into the air. A large hose leads from its opposite end, running down and into the depression behind the fuel truck. As she studies the mountainside she sees more and more of the hoses and nozzles positioned on either side of the slope.

"What are those?" she asks, pointing upward.

"Snowmaking guns," Tia says.

"How do they work?"

"Usually they siphon water from a source, like that dried-up reservoir there, and spray it under high pressure across the ski run. The mist freezes in the air and becomes snow."

Zoey's heart starts to pick up speed. "How are they powered?"

"With a pump. Probably another engine or generator. Why?"

"Yeah, girl, what's going on in that head of yours?" Eli asks, coming closer.

Her eyes flick up the steep grade, to the chairlifts, down to the trade, back to the snow guns. Her mind buzzes with frenzied thought, the panorama that takes shape creating a sinking hole in the base of her stomach.

Can we do it?

But that's not the question, is it?

The question is, can we live with it?

She stumbles over the enormity of it. No. What she's having Lyle create is one thing, but the thought of what will happen if the plan works, what she and the others will see, is unforgivable.

But then the image of Merrill lying on the ground, one leg missing as the giant towers over him, blooms to life in her mind. She sees Chelsea being taken, carried away by a half dozen men, her screams of anguish so heart-achingly real Zoey shivers.

There's no other choice. We have to.

"Zoey?" Ian asks. There is something in his tone, a cautiousness that borders on fear.

She looks at him, at all of them. "I'm their weakness."

"What are you talking about?" Tia asks.

"I've gone over every terrible situation I've been in since escaping the ARC. In each one the only reason I've survived is because of weakness." She ticks off her fingers. "NOA underestimated the women's ability to escape and they never thought we could infiltrate the facility when we broke the others out. Overconfidence was their weakness. At Riverbend Ken thought he could force his way out, dominate us, that we would never meet him head-on. That was his. And the trade's weakness is auctioning off the youngest woman they can find." She steels herself for what she knows will come. "In other words, me."

Ian shakes his head. "No. That's not going to happen."

"It's our only option. There's no other way to save Merrill and Chelsea."

"So you're going to sacrifice yourself?" Tia says, huffing a laugh. "Maybe I'm wrong about you. Maybe you are dumb as a stump."

"No, not sacrifice."

"Then what?" Eli asks. He puts a hand on her shoulder when she doesn't answer. "Then what?"

She tells them.

When she's finished they stare at her. Tia's mouth is partially open and Eli keeps shaking his head in small movements as if tormented by an insect. But Ian's eyes are the worst. The sadness in them nearly crushes her resolve and she almost tells them to forget what she said, discard the horror of the proposal and search for another avenue.

But she knows there is none.

They stand beside the chalet in the cool air, Ian, Eli, and Tia on one side, Zoey on the other. And at that moment she's sure this is how it will be from now on. She is outside, separate and getting further away even though she's standing still.

"We won't let you," Ian says. "It's too . . ." But his voice fails and he swallows, glancing away.

"It's my plan. I own it. I'll take responsibility for it."

"If we were to go through with it, the burden lies on all of us. You know we wouldn't let you shoulder it alone."

She feels a spark of gratitude that's instantly snuffed out by the knowledge that he's right. If it works they'll all share the weight, and that hurts her more than anything. "What we need to do is figure out if it's even possible."

Zoey stares at Tia until the older woman finally sighs. "If the fuel was stored decently and will still ignite in the diesels, yes, it should."

"I won't do it," Eli says. "You can't go through with this, girl. It's suicide."

"Not if it works."

"If it doesn't work, you die." He taps his chest. "And if it does, you die here." He rolls up his sleeve, exposing the tattoo on his arm and points to the ink. "She was my fiancée. And she's dead because of me, of the decisions that I made." The fierceness in his eyes fades and he swallows. "Please. There's some things you can't take back."

Her jaw trembles. "I know, but it's the only way."

"I don't think you understand what you're saying," Ian says.

"Yes I do!" Her voice rings off the building, drifting away in the forest. Ian frowns, looking down at the broken concrete beneath their feet. "I do," she says more quietly, voice cracking.

She gives each of them a long, pleading look. "It's my fault they're going to die, and I know I couldn't live with that. So please. Please help me."

40

Merrill watches the guards bring the starving man out from the shipping container and lead him to the high wire strung above the row of spikes.

He is emaciated, bones poking at his pale skin so harshly that he reminds Merrill of a house stripped of its siding revealing the structure beneath. The guards shove and prod him forward through a mob of jeering men, most of whom, up until only minutes ago, were calling out epithets at Merrill through the bars of his cage. They had assured him he would die tonight in the arena, die on the ground like a crippled dog being put out of its misery.

Merrill rubs the smooth stump of his right leg, touches the scarring like a blind man reading a story. He tried fitting a twisted length of wood that he'd found outside his cell into the remnants of his prosthetic, but the branch was weathered and dry and snapped as soon as he put any weight on it.

No, there will be no fixing his leg by nightfall. He will face his final opponent from the ground.

Or there is the other option that he won't let himself think about.

The guards guide the scrawny man to the ladder leading to the makeshift platform, twenty-five feet above the ground where the high wire is attached. The man eyes the eight-inch spikes driven into the soil below the wire and tries to flee back toward the container, but the guards catch him by the thinness of his upper arms and sling him hard into the ladder.

Merrill grimaces at the howls of the crowd. Animals. Nothing more. And the idea rises again like a nightmare.

When they give you the knife tonight, throw it to Chelsea. She'll be able to slit her wrists before they stop her and you'll die knowing she won't suffer like Halie did.

He lets out a shaky breath. Could he do it? Could he give her the means to kill herself? Watch her die? When compared with the alternative that awaits her, he's sure he can.

The man mounts the ladder and barely has the energy to climb, but one of the guards produces a knife and pokes him in the buttock hard enough to make him bleed. A bright ribbon of blood runs down the man's leg from beneath the torn shorts he wears and he climbs to the platform. At the top a balance pole waits and he grasps it before edging to the wire.

"That's it! And if you make it all the way across, you're free!" one of the guards yells before turning his head to grin at the crowd. They erupt in laughter, and taunts are thrown like javelins as the man puts one foot on the wire.

He steadies himself, bare sole wobbling, before swinging his other foot out.

The balance pole tips and he leans almost inhumanly far to the right before coming back to center.

The men below boo and hiss.

He takes another step, and another.

The spikes below wait like hungry teeth.

Merrill slides to the bars and hoists himself upright, eyes following the man's progress. Even though he knows there is no freedom at the other end of the wire, hope still rises within him and quiet words of encouragement come from his lips with each successful step.

The man sways, correcting his footing, sweat shining on his wrinkled brow, eyes looking straight ahead.

He is twelve steps from the end.

"Come on," Merrill whispers.

Eleven.

Ten.

Nine.

When he is less than fifteen feet from the platform, Merrill hears it.

A low whistling coming across the valley, the brown grass and sage stirring. The midday sun peers through the overcast sky for a brief second under the wind's insistence, its light snagging on the points of the spikes.

Then it recedes again, turning the world to ash beneath the scudding clouds.

The wind shoves the man to the left.

The pole tips, tips, tips, and drops from his hands.

His arms pinwheel.

He finally looks down to the waiting points beneath.

And falls.

Merrill looks away but he can't block out the wet crunching sound or the deafening roar of approval.

He hops away from the bars and slides down the rear of the cage. The last time he knew this kind of sorrow, this much hopelessness, was when he buried his wife beside her rose garden in their backyard. The despair fills him up and overflows as tears cloud his vision and he weeps into one hand.

After a time the mass of men disperses, the spectacle over for now, and his tears dry in the cold, arid wind that continues to blow. Footsteps bring his head up along with a smell that drowns out the scent of blood.

The woman who attended the beheading stands outside his cage, a steaming bowl in her hands. She is medium height and has the shrunken look of someone whose frame is used to carrying more weight than it holds. Her hair is reddish brown and when his gaze lands on her face he realizes he knows her.

She kneels, tipping the bowl slightly to the side to slide it through the bars. She sets it on the ground and meets his eyes.

"Careful, the bottom's hot," she says, and then is gone, moving past the guard that stands before his cage.

Merrill watches her until she disappears around the side of a tall tent then scoots forward, grabbing the bowl from the ground. A plastic spoon is lodged in the steaming stew and he uses it to dig down, sliding it until a small corner of plastic appears on the surface. He quickly pinches the plastic free of the food and puts it in his mouth, cleaning it with his tongue before carefully spitting it into one hand. Glancing at the closest guard, he unseals the tiny bag and draws out a folded piece of paper no larger than his thumbnail.

The writing is miniscule and rough and it takes him the better part of a minute to discern what it says before his head jerks up, eyes frantically searching the grounds.

I'm a friend. Your daughter says to be ready.

"Zoey," Merrill whispers.

41

Chelsea stands before the man and woman seated in their chairs like royalty and swallows the saliva she wants to spit at them.

They watch her with cold, reptilian eyes and she knows before the man they call Presto speaks that they won't grant her what she asked.

"No. Absolutely out of the question," he says, leaning forward in his chair, a glass of wine in his hand. "If I gave you permission to see him before the tournament, how would that look to the rest of the troupe? If you were given a favor from us, why not every guard in our employ? Why not every performer? Where would it stop?"

"Please," Chelsea says, barely able to form the word for all the hatred that's coursing through her. "Just a moment. That's all I'm asking for."

The wife, she thinks her name is Sasha, tips her head to the side. "So he is your husband?"

She hesitates. "Yes."

"Where did you come from?"

"I already told you, we were traveling south from Seattle and got separated in the mountains."

"And he was able to follow you here?"

"Yes."

Presto rises, gliding over to a small table, behind which stands the unnerving albino dressed in black. The bodyguard refills Presto's drink, strange eyes flitting to her and away.

"I think you're lying," Presto says. "Who else were you traveling with?"

"No one. We were alone and I hadn't seen him in well over a day."

"If you tell us the truth, we will allow you to see your husband before the tournament, which starts in . . ." Presto glances at the ceiling. ". . . about an hour." Chelsea says nothing, trying to swallow the dryness away in her throat while keeping herself from shivering. "Hmm. As old world as it sounds, I'm inclined to believe that most women never gain intelligence past the age of fifteen." He comes closer to her and she can smell his cologne, stale and without the spice it once carried, along with the wine. "Do you understand your husband is going to die tonight? He is defenseless and outmatched. Wouldn't you prefer to speak to him one last time before you part forever?"

Chelsea wonders if she could kill him before the albino brought her down. Snatch the wineglass from his hand, snap the base off, jam the stem into his throat. But then she would never see Merrill again, never be able to tell him what she needs to, and that's something she's not willing to give up.

Presto sighs, returning to his chair. "There's no one coming for you. You might think so but there isn't. We know you weren't traveling alone. Several of our men found heavy tire tracks this morning while scouring the area where you were located. Do you know where they lead?"

Chelsea tries to swallow again but her mouth is completely parched, heart slamming so hard in her chest she's sure they can see it.

"They lead away to the main highway running north. They left you. Left you and your husband to your fates and moved on. And if you only would have told me you could have said goodbye." He smiles, lips peeling back from gray teeth. "But now you'll have to do it from across the coliseum. Guard! Get her out of here."

The door opens behind her even as she starts to move forward, unaware that her hands are clenched into fists until she's being dragged away, heels thudding against the stairs as the room and the couple inside rises out of her line of sight. The anguish that builds inside her is a tsunami, washing away any hope she'd harbored for a rescue.

The others ran. Maybe they'd been flushed out or decided it was too risky to try to free them, but the end result is the same.

She and Merrill are alone.

42

The night drifts down from the hills like dark water seeping into a basin.

The forest fills up with it and the already clouded sky thickens, deepening in bruised folds until the world seems as if it has said goodnight for the last time.

Gerald walks the silver dollar across his knuckles and back, watching the coin flip like magic. He's getting good. Hopefully by the end of the month all his tricks will be as smooth and the Prestons will grant him his own show in the big tent. Watching the gate and taking cash and canned food from the bumpkins is getting older than old.

He readjusts his top hat, wanting to throw the idiotic thing into the wind and watch it tumble away. But his chances of his own show would fly away with it. Costume, misdirection, and dedication. These are the things Presto says are most important for a magician. If he were to defy the old man now, all the effort and time to learn his secrets would be wasted and he'd be stuck at the gate for yet another season.

One thing is sure, he thinks, walking the coin again across his fingers, *when I'm finally a magician I'm getting a way better hat.*

He pauses his musing as a figure emerges out of the dark, the large hooded jacket triggering his memory.

"Hey old-timer, you're almost late. Tournament's starting in a few minutes." The old man shuffles up to the counter, dropping a crumpled wad of bills there. Once more it is too much payment but Gerald isn't one to complain. "Thanks for the tip again. Hey, if you have cash to burn maybe you should've put your name in to fight for that woman. She's a looker, bet she'd ruin your old ass in bed." He laughs, making the silver dollar dance again. "If you could get it up that . . ."

Gerald's voice dies as the hood turns toward him and the glint of an eye fixes on his own. There is a deep, burning hatred there, a profound fury within the fleeting look that steals his words away.

Then the man is gone, moving amongst the tents toward the midway, walking taller, straighter than he remembered from the nights before.

Gerald grabs the money from the counter and shoves it in his pocket, gazing into the night that's full upon the land.

And he shivers, but not from the cold.

43

Zoey steps onto the midway.

It is in full swing, bustling activity everywhere. Men line the booths and tents to either side, and a queue is beginning to form before the coliseum at the far end.

The music floats to her, loud and obnoxious as ever, the competing delicious and revolting smells coat the breeze, and the ground trodden flat by hundreds of feet over the last days is solid below her.

But everything is muted.

Flattened and simplified in her senses.

She starts forward, slowly unzipping Merrill's jacket before pushing the hood off.

She slides her arms out, and the coat falls to the ground behind her.

She raises her hand and grasps the heavy wool hat, tugging it free from her head as she passes a booth where several men turn and stare.

She drops the hat and feels her hair fall free to the middle of her back.

More men pivot to look as she walks by and she sees jaws begin to slacken, mouths opening in *O*'s of disbelief.

Zoey keeps her attention forward, eyes locked on the fence at the far end of the midway, coming closer with each step she takes.

Shouts rise behind her like a large wave cresting out of an already churning sea, their sound meaningless in the din that is the trade. More men turn from the booths and she begins walking faster.

A guard steps into view from between two tents ahead, searching for the source of the disturbance, and locks eyes with her.

His widen. Hers narrow.

He sprints toward her, arms outstretched, body lowering to prepare the tackle he's going to employ.

Without breaking stride, Zoey grasps her pistol from the holster at the small of her back and whips it up.

She fires.

The gunshot booms down the midway, fire leaping a foot from the end of her barrel.

The guard's head snaps back, gray matter flying from his ruined skull. He crumples in a lifeless pile at her feet.

Zoey runs.

The screams of men become a ringing dissonance. She can feel the sound tingling against her skin. Feet thunder behind her and another man steps into her path. She shoots again and he clutches at his stomach as she sprints past.

She chances a look over her shoulder.

The entire midway is alive with movement behind her, the shine of the men's eyes manic in the overhead lights. Arms pump at sides, feet trample the man she shot as well as another who trips over him.

It is a tide.

Ahead the mass before the coliseum is torn with confusion. Three guards raise their rifles at her but she doesn't slow and no shots come. She catches a glimpse of them lowering their weapons, absolute disbelief in their features.

Now there are shouts she can define.

It's a girl! A young one!

She's running toward the fence!

Don't shoot! Don't shoot! Hold your fire!

Where the fuck did she come from!

Get her! Get her! Gethergethergether!

The fence line looms closer, rising high, much higher than she anticipated it would be. A dull ache spreads like cool water across her lower back and she has a split second to pray it doesn't get worse before a guard outside the fence steps into view and raises his rifle.

She fires two shots as a blast comes from his barrel.

The bullet's passage is hot and reverberates in her teeth. She feels a tug in her hair and tries to aim again at the guard but he's already falling, a blossom of red spreading across his chest.

Then the fence is there and all thought turns to static above the yells behind her and the movement closing in from either side.

Her eyes search the fence.

She takes two more strides, back beginning to pulse with pain, and dives forward, arms covering her head.

◆ ◆ ◆

The guard stops before Merrill's cage and eyes his missing leg.

"Have to say, I've never seen a one-legged man fight before."

Merrill pulls himself up the bars and hops forward. "You will tonight." He glances down the row of cages to where another guard is letting the giant free of his cell. The huge man stretches, flexing muscles that ripple like knotted rope below his skin. He sees Merrill watching and grins toothlessly.

"We're gonna see something. That's for sure. You ever heard that saying about a one-legged man in an ass-kicking competition?" the guard says. He inserts a key into the padlock on the outside of the door and is about to open it when a chorus of yells comes from the midway, climbing in volume until it sounds as if every man in the trade is screaming at the top of his lungs.

Merrill leans to the side as the guard turns around, eyeing his compatriot. "The hell is that?"

Zoey. It has to be.

A gunshot booms from the direction of the commotion, and the guard down the row of cells begins to run toward the sounds. Merrill's guard takes a step as well but is yanked backward as Merrill snags his collar through the bars.

"The fuck are you—"

Merrill slams him against the cage hard enough to rattle the door, then slides his forearm across the man's throat. The guard squawks and one hand scrambles down to his sidearm, but Merrill grabs it, yanking his arm through the bars, pinning him there.

He flails, trying to break the hold, but Merrill cinches it deeper, the man's ears going from red to purple.

The fight suddenly goes out of the guard. Merrill feels muscles slacken and he tightens the choke for another second before releasing him. He drops to the ground in a heap, an autonomic wheeze squealing in through his swelling windpipe.

Merrill waits, searching for movement in the vicinity, but all the action is on the opposite side of the tents and buildings before him. As he twists the key in the lock and steps out of the cage, several more shots punctuate the crowd's cries. He begins looking for something to use as a crutch but the sound of rusted steel shrieking draws his attention to the giant's cell, where the huge man steps free.

He grins at Merrill and clenches both fists before starting in his direction.

◆　◆　◆

Chelsea sits on the bench in the lower level of the nest and stares out the window at the bustling midway. It's the largest crowd she's seen yet. The element of death that's drawn the men for entertainment still escapes her. Why in a world already so full of suffering would a person crave more?

She tucks the dress tighter around her legs. She's been cold ever since they forced her into this outfit and all she wants is to be somewhere safe in her own clothes, with a hot cup of Ian's tea, and Merrill's arms around her.

Merrill.

Chelsea closes her eyes. She's not going to think about anything anymore. She's done with the endless circle of useless thoughts. All the sorrow and tears have been wrung out of her. Now there is only what will come. And she doesn't want to think of that either.

She places a hand over her stomach and grimaces. She should have said something before they left Riverbend, but now it is too late.

Too late to tell him he's going to be a father again.

She jerks with the sound of footsteps on the stairs and a moment later the Prestons appear accompanied by the albino. They are dressed up again like they're attending some type of gala instead of going to watch a man be murdered.

"It's time, my dear," Presto says. The guard at the door turns to open it as several shouts come from the midway outside.

"Hold on, sir," the guard says, putting his hand out. "Something's happening."

"What is it?"

"Not sure. Disturbance on the midway. I'll check." He slips out the door as the voices increase in volume, getting nearer, more frenzied.

"These small towns. I don't know why we even stop in them anymore," Sasha says, adjusting the velvet scarf she wears over her shoulders.

"Now darling, we're entertainers and they're in need of entertainment."

"They're animals. Listen to them."

A gun blast comes from outside, and both Prestons duck while the albino moves to the door, his hand going to the knife beneath his coat.

"What the hell is happening out there?" Sasha asks, one foot on the stairs again. Chelsea stands and moves to the window, the sound of screaming so loud now she can't hear anything else.

Then she spots movement. A blur of dark clothing and darker hair flowing back.

Muzzle flash and a crumpling body.

And she is gone.

Chelsea's heart sings, hope reigniting inside her. "Zoey," she breathes.

A guard bursts through the door, nearly tearing it from its hinges as the seething mass of men stream by like a river of flesh.

"A woman!" he yells, eyes wide. "Really young."

"What? Here?" Presto says, straining to see past the running men. More gunfire erupts outside and both Prestons duck. "Go! Go get her before the rabble does! They'll tear her apart!"

The guard nods and rushes out again. Chelsea sees him sprint through the last of the crowd and motion to three other guards standing dumbstruck across the midway.

"It seems the surprises aren't over yet," Presto says, dusting the front of his suit off.

"No," Chelsea says, still staring in the direction Zoey went. "I don't think they are."

44

Zoey's arms and head strike the fence and she flies through the place where Eli had casually cut it hours ago with a wire snipper between the guard's rounds.

She hits the ground hard, grit biting into her shoulder and hip as she rolls to her feet. A chunk of her hair hangs from the jagged flap of fence and her scalp burns on the right side. The herd of men try to stop as they reach the fence but the momentum is too much and the ones at the front who saw how she got through fall beneath the stampede as the entire mass hits the fence.

Steel screeches and gives.

The fence bows and topples toward her.

Zoey runs.

The overhead lights only reach several dozen yards past the trade's confines before darkness takes over. She leaps a shadowed boulder and nearly stumbles on a dry piece of sage that gives under her feet. Ahead, the solemn shadow of the mountain rises into the night, its peak blending with the roiling clouds above.

Less than half a mile.

Twenty-six hundred feet.

She pours on speed, leaning into the slight breeze that comes down from the main ski run, the smell reminding her of Ian's home in the Cascades. The wind whistles in her ears, partially drowning out the guttural calls chasing her. With one hand she reaches back, feeling in her belt for the object, but finds only empty air.

Her heart sinks. *No. No, it has to be there. It won't work without it.* She must've dropped it when she dove through the fence. Her fingers scrabble at her back and they touch hard plastic, ready to slip free. It only shifted beneath her holster. The relief is enormous. She shoves the object down, locking it under her belt once more. Immediately she checks the heavy nylon strap around her wrist. It is secure, the two chunks of hooked steel attached to it pointing toward her elbow. A glance backward sends a jolt through her nerves.

At least two hundred men, maybe more, run full speed thirty paces behind her.

And behind them are headlights.

Many sets of them.

They're all coming.

Zoey fires two shots back, both going wide but they have the effect she wants. The lead man stumbles and falls hard, tripping up a half dozen others.

When she looks forward again the ground is gone.

She flies across the six-foot drainage ditch and hits the other side hard enough to send spangles of light dancing through her vision.

Her breath is gone, torn away by the impact.

And worst of all her thighs are growing numb.

She claws up the bank and yanks her legs free as the first men leap into the dry canal. They are ready for the drop and land on their feet, scrambling toward her, shadows with wild eyes and open mouths. She shoots the closest one in the chest, hobbling away as the others climb over his body as if it is part of the landscape.

The lead man, wearing a torn sweater and pants that end at his shins, pours on speed as he tears free of the ditch, and she's suddenly aware he will catch her. He's close enough to see pale light reflected in his eyes.

There's a quick whining, like an insect buzzing past, and the man's head rocks to the side, pieces of skull showering the ground.

He falls in a heap and she sends up thanks to Ian as two more men slump lifelessly behind her, the gunshots from the mountain where he rests lost in the din of the pursuit.

Slowly the numbness seeps lower toward her kneecaps, the familiar cold-water sensation, but she pushes on, fighting the growing realization that soon she won't be able to use her legs.

A quarter mile. Maybe less.

She runs.

To her right the vehicles circle to a wider area of the ditch that isn't as steep, their headlights igniting the dying grass and sage into skeletal creatures.

The land rises and falls twice before leveling out to the field below the ski run. A broken, waist-high fence materializes before her and she seeks the collapsed section she scouted that morning through the binoculars.

It is there to her left. She changes direction, not slowing, and hurdles the downed partition. Ahead the field climbs and empties out at the base of the wide run. She reaches down, drawing the small flashlight from her pocket and aims it at the dark shape of the shack below the first chairlift pole.

She flashes the light on and off.

The same signal comes back to her from the shack, and she drops the flashlight, tucking away her pistol.

The numbness is past her knees now, pain shooting down through it from her lower back and rebounding in her feet, keeping her aware that she's still alive, still moving.

Engines roar to the right, yellow light illuminating the ground before her, throwing her shadow against the steep grade. She rushes on, a limp forming in her right leg, slowing her as she adjusts the strap on her wrist again.

Almost there. Almost. Please let me make it. Please . . .

◆　◆　◆

"Listen, I've got no quarrel with you," Merrill says, leaning against the cage. The huge man rolls his shoulders and continues a steady pace toward him, unhurried and confident. Merrill glances down at the guard near his feet and reaches for the handgun holstered on his side, but the giant hits him first.

The blow lands on the side of his head and it's like getting hit by a car.

His foot leaves the ground and he is airborne for a full second before landing at the base of the nearest tent.

The world spins, ground tottering beneath him.

He plants a hand beneath his chest and pushes upright as the man latches onto his shoulders and tosses him down the row of cages. Merrill hits the ground, skidding and rolling once before coming to a stop. He's never felt this kind of physical power from someone before. It is beyond human.

"Stay still and it'll be over quick," the man says, his voice as deep as Merrill expected it would be. He towers over him, reaching down to grasp Merrill by the shirt.

Merrill jabs upward in a quick strike, two fingers to the man's left eye.

The giant staggers backward, grunting in pain, and Merrill crawls to the base of the nearest cage, pulling himself upright, vision slewing slightly before shifting back into focus. There is a high-pitched ringing in his ears and he opens and closes his jaw as the big man wipes at his bleeding eye.

"Gonna hurtcha for that," he says, stalking forward.

Merrill hops to the side, nearly losing his balance as he sees he's bracing himself on the man's cage door, which swings open freely. Merrill opens it farther, one hand on its edge.

He holds still, watching the man come, trying to calm his breathing, and raises his chin.

The giant swings his huge fist in a looping haymaker that actually whistles as it comes at his face.

Merrill ducks, letting the blow fly over the top of his head.

The man stumbles, off balance. His fist clips the doorframe and he falls, one arm in the doorway, the other catching his weight on the bars.

Merrill drops to his back and kicks the door as hard as he can with his good leg.

The heavy steel shrieks and slams shut on the giant's forearm.

Skin shreds. Bones snap.

The man bellows and tries to yank his arm free, but Merrill kicks the door again, wedging his flesh tighter as the latch engages with a solid clack.

The giant whimpers, fumbling with his free hand, but the latch is set too far away for him to reach. Blood leaks from his ruined arm down the doorframe, and he tries again, undiluted agony flashing through his features before he drops to his knees with a yelp.

Merrill scoots to the bars and drags himself upright, hopping closer to the man, who's breathing in short gasps. He turns his bloodied face up to Merrill as he approaches.

"Please."

Merrill brings his elbow down hard, smashing the giant's nose to the side in a crunch of cartilage.

The huge man sags, unconscious against the cage, his pinned arm the only thing holding him upright.

Merrill glances down the row of cells and hops slowly past the man, stooping to pick up the guard's handgun before turning back. He aims at the giant's wide back, finger tightening on the trigger.

After a long second, he releases the pressure. With a final look around he hops to the nearest tent and yanks a pole from its side. Using it as a makeshift cane, Merrill moves through the narrow alley in the direction of the midway, gun sweeping the space before him.

◆　◆　◆

Nell steps onto the midway and listens. The distant banshee echoes are eerie and she watches as the cavalcade of trucks and vehicles rumble toward the mountain, headlights jostling over the uneven ground.

She glances at her surroundings, struck for a second that something is very wrong. But after a second she realizes what it is.

The trade is mostly quiet.

Several vendors and performers stand in the tent openings and doorways, their eyes searching past the end of the midway and the destroyed fence. A single soldier sprints past in the direction of the shipping containers and a muffled gunshot comes a minute later. The rest of the grounds are empty.

She did it.

A surge of warmth rushes through her. If Zoey is telling the truth then maybe, maybe there's a chance that she'll see . . .

But she still can't get herself to think her daughter's name. She's trained herself too long to shut the thoughts and memories down. But perhaps now things will change. She won't let herself hope quite yet, but maybe . . .

Nell swallows the lump in her throat, gazing across the midway at the nest. It is lit as always, and through the lower-story windows she sees the woman Zoey came here to save seated on a chair.

Taking a deep breath she moves to the unguarded door and opens it.

The woman looks up at the sound of her entry, eyes instantly tracking to the left and back. Nell tries to turn but Hemming is already there, hands gripping her upper arms like steel clamps.

"What are you doing?" he says, face inches from hers, the gun oil smell coming off him in layers.

"I . . . I came to check on the Prestons. I didn't know what was happening."

"They're fine."

"Are they upstairs?"

"None of your business." Hemming shoves her toward the door. "Now get out."

"I will," Nell says. "But I have something for them."

"Come back later."

"I'll just give it to you."

Nell draws the carving knife out of her pocket and thrusts it at Hemming's stomach.

He twists to the side and catches her wrist easily, the blade falling to the floor. He kicks it away and grins, the white skin of his face wrinkling monstrously.

"Now, now. After all the years we've known one another." Hemming flings her to the floor and kneels in the middle of her stomach. All the air rushes from her and it feels as if a hot coal has been placed in her center. "You know I've had fantasies about you. Not the ones you're probably thinking of. Sex is so dissatisfying. No, I've dreamt of removing your skin an inch at a time. And the things I'd do with it, oh, you'd be amazed. You have beautiful skin."

Nell jerks, trying to shimmy out from beneath his weight, but Hemming balances on her expertly. He leans closer, his irises the color of clotted blood. "Maybe now they'll let me have you. You were planning on killing them after all." He puts more pressure on her midsection and she opens her mouth in a soundless cry. "Usually I'm allowed one of the male prisoners. But in this case I think they'll make an exception."

Her vision grows smoky, the corners of the room filling with shadow. But behind Hemming a flash of red moves. The woman is there, arms over her head, carving knife clutched in her hands.

She stabs downward.

Hemming turns, lazily snagging her wrists, stopping the knife a few inches from his face. He pries the blade free of her hands and shoves her, hard, across the room. She stumbles, feet tangling, and falls to the floor.

Nell brings her arms up, the momentary lapse in pressure making the darkness in her gaze flee. She reaches, straining for what she knows is there as Hemming turns back to her, the horrid grin stitched on his face.

"I'm going to make you a work of art. My masterpiece," he says, putting his full weight on her again.

And then he is close enough for her fingers to find what they're looking for.

Nell draws the long knife out of the sheath beneath Hemming's jacket and plunges it into his open mouth.

His eyes flare wide, tears flooding them as blood fills his mouth, running over his lower lip in a waterfall of red. It splashes on Nell's shirt and she pushes the knife deeper.

Hemming loses his balance, falling to his ass, hands scrabbling the air before finding the hilt of the knife jutting from his mouth. He touches it, gently. With a feeble motion he tries to pull it free before his eyes roll up into his skull and he sags to his back, a long, gurgling cough coming from him that spatters the wall with crimson.

Nell rises to her feet, entranced at the sight. Her stomach roils and she swallows bile. Hemming's eyes reappear and find her but the life in them is already fading, dark blood puddling around his head. She breaks the trance and moves to the woman in the red dress.

"Are you okay?"

"Yes, I think so."

She helps the other woman to her feet, steadying her. "Can you stand?"

"Yes. I'm all right. Thank you."

When Nell glances at Hemming again he is still, eyes staring sightlessly at where she was standing. She's about to retrieve the carving knife from the floor when she catches movement outside the windows.

"Get down," she whispers, and the woman obeys.

The doorknob turns.

Nell eyes the knife lying six feet away. She has to try for it. Without it they'll be completely defenseless.

The door opens.

She springs forward, snatching the blade from the floor, and turns, arm up, ready to stab, slash, kill, whatever it takes to finally be free of this place.

Merrill stands in the doorway, framed by the lights outside.

He leans against a tent pole while his other hand holds a pistol.

He registers her and the knife as she lowers it, but then his gaze shifts, face slackening with relief.

"Chelsea," he says, hobbling past Nell. Chelsea rushes forward, crashing into him in a fierce embrace. Nell leaves them to their reunion and moves to the stairway, looking up.

It's empty.

She regrips the knife, wondering if she has the ability to do what she was planning. Merrill and Chelsea come to her side and follow her gaze.

"We have to go," Merrill says.

"I can't."

"Why?"

"Because it ends now. They're up there and I'm not going to let them get away."

"We need to leave. I don't know what Zoey planned but it's only going to buy us so much time. The guards could be back any second."

But she barely registers what he's saying. She's already taking the stairs two at a time, turning on the landing and up the last set. There's no guard outside the door; he's gone with the rest of them. But she's not sure even an armed guard could stop her at that moment. She is single-minded, unwilling to retreat now. It bolsters her to know Hemming was their last line of defense, and now he's dead.

Without slowing Nell flings a kick at the door and it bursts open.

She comes in low, knife ready in case the Prestons have heard her approach. The lounge area is empty, a chair on its side by the table, broken plate on the floor. There is movement behind her and she spins, sure that somehow they flanked her or that Hemming reanimated and will be there, knife protruding from his mouth, eyes dead, arms out, reaching for her.

But it is only Chelsea, Merrill's pistol in her hand. She nods once to Nell and they both move to the opposite door, pausing a heartbeat before Nell kicks it in like the first.

Chelsea sweeps the dimly lit bedroom with the gun before stepping inside, Nell close behind.

A plush, king-size bed takes up the majority of the space. An ornate desk and dresser are mounted against the wall, drawers out, contents jumbled. Nell drops to her hands and knees, looking beneath the bed, already knowing the Prestons won't be there. They'd never hide like some kind of vermin, even though it would be fitting.

As she rises, a brief flicker of movement comes from the far side of the room and she nearly calls out a warning to Chelsea, but she is already there, drawing back the curtain that Nell mistook as part of the wall, revealing the open window beyond.

45

Zoey stumbles, rights herself, another blast of pain running down her legs like a lightning strike before the sensation of paralysis returns.

A puff of dirt explodes to her left and she zigs the opposite way. They're trying to scare her, make her stop and give up. She's sure the guards from the trade are terrified of the other men reaching her first. They're racing one another. Good.

Come and get me.

The ground rises in another slight grade as she passes the shack housing the drive engines, but then she's at the first chairlift, its seat broken and canted.

She turns, facing the horde speeding toward her.

More than a dozen trucks from the trade, all of them carrying guards in their beds, lead the pack, but behind them is a sea of men on foot. Some of them are already fighting, striking at one another with clubs, slashing with knives, but most are simply running, trying to outdistance the rest and get to the prize first.

The trucks rumble closer, headlights pinning her where she stands.

She waits.

The men's yells rebound off the trees and sprawling ski run above.

She waits.

A flash comes from the shack again. Blinks fast, insistent. She can almost hear Tia screaming at her to move.

So she does.

Zoey reaches up and latches the two steel hooks attached to her wrist on the chairlift bar over her head.

There is a coughing bang followed by a low chugging that is barely audible above the sound of engines and screams.

The chairlift jerks into motion.

She's yanked off her feet, the cable overhead twanging in the cool air as it whisks her up the ski run and away from the masses.

The trucks were slowing as they neared her but now their engines gun again, leaping forward up the steep incline.

The strap digs into her wrist but holds, her feet brushing the ground before being lifted free again. She barely feels it; her legs are like two dead pieces of meat. Her back twinges in pain with each jolt of the lift.

One of the trucks' wheels spins as it loses traction on a particularly sheer section, and the trailing vehicle slams into its tailgate.

A man tries to leap onto a chair at the base of the run as it rounds the corner from the shack, but it's going much too fast and hurls him in the opposite direction, his body bowling over five others.

Zoey sends up silent thanks for Tia's mechanical brilliance. Without her the lift wouldn't be running at all, and it definitely wouldn't be traveling this fast.

The ground speeds by, forested sides gliding past as if the earth is slipping away from her, a cloth pulled from a table dragging everything with it. Wind whips at her hair, trying to spin her around, but she grasps the freezing steel harder. Glancing to the side, eyes watering, she spots a snow gun. Which number is that? Six? Seven?

She strains to see in the wan light and glimpses a small red glow atop another of the hosed apparatus farther up the mountain.

The last one.

Headlights jounce on the uneven ground that's become strangled with natural decay. The lead truck accelerates, its grille within forty yards of her now, and Zoey reaches back with her free hand, stiff fingers fumbling for her belt and what it holds.

Don't drop it, can't drop it.

As she jerks it free, the lift carries her higher above the ground, boots dangling over thirty feet from the rock and soil.

The red light passes by.

And at that moment, every snow gun on the mountain jerks with pressure and exhales a blast of air before a fine mist explodes from their nozzles.

The scent of gasoline fills the night.

It rains down on the trucks, covering their windshields and hoods.

It soaks the men on foot, their voices shifting from frenzied cries of conquest to yells of confusion. The fuel splatters everything, covering them with its stinging touch. She imagines the tanker truck near the reservoir below slowly draining dry from the pumps they hooked to it that afternoon.

Zoey aims the flare gun she took from the ASV's first aid kit.

Time halts.

The pain in her wrist fades, taking with it the aching in her back. She is unfeeling now. As deadened as the nerves in her legs.

She sights down the short barrel, remembering Chelsea dressed in the gown of red and put on display.

Sees Merrill being led into the coliseum, hands shackled before him.

Watches the huge blade falling and beheading the man on his knees.

And she feels Halie going limp in her arms, the last breath she never exhaled coming from Zoey now as she squeezes the trigger.

The flare gun's hammer falls and the pistol kicks.

A sizzling corona of red launches from the barrel, a thick smoking tail extending behind it.

The trucks have stopped. Several reverse. The men howl, rubbing at their eyes as they stumble and roll back down the side of the mountain.

And the flare screams toward them.

The light is the first thing her eyes register. It is beyond anything she's ever witnessed before. The air itself ignites into a glow so bright it flashes her entire vision white.

Next is the heat.

It rushes past her in a furnace blast that tightens every inch of exposed skin. Her hair crackles. She bats at it, feeling it burning, choking on the fumes and smoke.

And still the heat climbs.

Fire encompasses the entire ski run. Even the trees to either side are alight, the snow guns spewing fountains of flame. It is a roiling inferno of orange and yellow that cascades like an avalanche to the base of the mountain.

And in the center of it all, the men shriek.

They are walking pyres, lurching, falling to the scorched earth. The vehicles amble sideways or roll backward, balls of fire that crush the dying. A gas tank explodes, showering more waves of flame outward before melding with the rest of the blaze.

The lift carries her up and away from it, high enough to see everything, every last square foot of the destruction that is her doing.

She owns it. All of it.

She can't look away, can't break her seared vision from the spectacle, the burning men, the carnage. The smell of charred flesh reaches her and she retches even as her feet clip the ground, heels dragging roughly on dirt.

She's at the top of the mountain, the lift bringing her to a cleared area beside another building that's crumbled in on itself. Zoey tries to unhook herself, forcing her legs to function, her feet to steady on the ground that's still speeding by.

Then she's rounding a bend, a huge pulley creaking above, cable popping in its groove, and her feet leave earth again. The light and heat that was lessening at the top of the run ramps up once more.

She's being dragged back into the flames.

Zoey struggles, trying to break her wrist free of the strap, but it holds fast. She reaches up, realizing she's still clutching the flare gun and drops it, gripping the steel bar she hangs from.

The heat magnifies, as do the tortured screams of those still alive, so unearthly and warbling they make her stomach clench. She pulls, lifting herself, and tries to release the hooks, but loses her grip and falls, hanging from her wrist again. That hand is senseless now, discolored and unmoving. She grasps the steel again and glances down.

The ground is falling away, more and more with each second.

With a final heave she drags herself up, hooking her chin over the bar before pulling her latched wrist free.

She has a split second to realize she's going to die, and falls.

In the weightlessness she wishes she could've apologized to Chelsea and Merrill and all the rest. Told them how sorry she is for tainting their lives with her presence.

Told Lee how much she misses him and how she would gladly take his last name now.

The impact is tremendous.

It knocks her breath away as if she's never had it before. It feels as if she swallowed a glass jar and it shattered inside her. Her eyelids flutter, making the burning world strobe in a succession of hellish images.

Trees on fire.

Vehicles smoldering.

Bodies so burnt they are unrecognizable.

Her lungs inflate with agony. She sucks in scorched air, the black spots dancing on the edges of her vision receding. The ground is tangled beneath her, dried brambles and angles of rock jabbing through her clothes. She tries to sit up and manages it after a horrifying moment of complete paralysis. There is a thudding pain in the wrist without the hooked strap, but when she examines it there are no bones poking free of skin as she feared. Slowly the glass shards in her center dissolve.

Below, the mountain has gone silent except for the crackling of fire. The nozzles of the snow guns flicker but are done spewing flame.

Fuel must've run out. Or Eli shut it off. She glances around. The chairlift continues to run, all of the chairs circling overhead on fire now. They shrink and elongate her shadow into something monstrous, but maybe that's her true shape now.

Maybe it always was.

"Zoey!" Her name drifts across the smoke-laden run, Ian's voice strong and full.

"Over here!" She wants to yell it but it comes out a murmur. She tries again, louder this time, and in the haze three shadows approach through the gloom.

Zoey cradles her injured arm tight to her body, gazing down at what she's wrought.

And the void within her becomes a desolation so thick and dark, all the fire on the mountain can't penetrate it.

46

She fades in and out of reality, consciousness as insubstantial as gas shadows.

Eli and Tia are carrying her through a smoldering portion of forest. Darkness.

The inside of the ASV, something soft beneath her and Ian's face above, kind, smiling, rough hand against her cheek.

"Rest now."

She does.

The rumble of the engine and a series of bumps. A glow filling the cab of the vehicle.

Lee's fingers intertwined with her own. His lips pressing against hers, the repressed longing coming back full force.

You're safe. Sleep.

It is only minutes and years later that the sound of the doors opening wakes her, achingly familiar voices close by. She opens her eyes to Merrill and Chelsea climbing in beside where she lies on the bench. They kneel, Merrill's hand grasping hers. Chelsea placing a cool palm on her forehead, brushing her singed hair back before checking her pulse.

"Hey," Merrill says, voice thick.

"Hey."

"How do you feel?"

"Great." She smiles.

"How . . ." His mouth works but nothing comes out.

"You're both okay?" she asks, reality returning by degrees.

"We're fine," Chelsea says. "It's you we're worried about. Ian says you can't walk."

"No, but—" And she doesn't realize it until that second that her feet hurt.

She can feel them.

"Can you sit me up?"

They bring her to a sitting position while Chelsea moves to her legs. With an effort that breaks sweat out on her brow, she twists her feet around in small circles, one of the rehab exercises she's done countless times. Relief nearly makes her sag back to the bench again but she's terrified if she falls asleep now the feeling will be gone when she wakes.

"You inflamed your injury. That's why you can't walk," Chelsea says, checking several cuts on her legs before returning to her side. "Let me see that wrist you're holding like it's going to fall off." She extends her arm and Chelsea gently examines it. "Sprained. We'll wrap it as soon as we get back on the road." Chelsea gazes down at her before tears well up and stream down her face. Then Chelsea's hugging her, hard enough that it causes pain, but she doesn't care. Zoey squeezes her back, her throat closing. Merrill's arms encircle them and she leans her head against his chest while Chelsea strokes her hair.

"I thought we were going to lose you both," she whispers. "That's why . . . why . . ."

"Shhh, we know. It's okay."

A sudden thought draws her back from their embrace.

"Is Rita's mother okay?"

"She's fine," Merrill says. "Safe."

"And the women in the container?"

"Eli and Ian are getting them out right now. When you . . . when the fire started on the mountain, the remaining guards ran. There were only a handful left. Most of the performers are gone too."

"I want to see."

"No. You need to rest."

"Please. I need to see."

Merrill and Chelsea share a look before he sighs. "You'll have to help her since I'm not the man I once was."

"I'd give you a hand, but you need a foot, brother," Eli says from the doorway, wide smile lighting up.

"And if I had it I'd give you two guesses where I'd shove it."

"Don't be flirtin', your lady's right there."

Zoey can't help but laugh, and it feels good even though her bruised ribs make her pay.

They help her to the ground, easing her to her feet. For a second the feeling that's been growing from her ankles upward vanishes and she bites down hard on her lower lip, fixing her concentration to a pinpoint.

With one arm around Eli's shoulders, she takes a tentative step. Then another. They move slowly through the trade, between tents that are half disassembled, flaps open like ragged wounds. When the shipping containers come into view, Zoey spots Nell beside a long-haired man holding a frail woman dressed in stained clothing. There are two other women huddled together, blankets around their shoulders. Nell asks them something and both of them nod before she turns and sees Zoey.

Nell comes to her and they simply stare one another in the eyes for a long moment before the older woman hugs her.

"Thank you," she whispers in Zoey's ear. "You don't know what you've done."

Zoey sees the smoldering things on the mountainside that were once men and nausea churns in her stomach. "I do." Nell draws away from her, a strange look on her face that's both confusion and pity.

"We're going to take you to Rita," she continues, fighting down the bile that threatens the back of her throat.

Nell absorbs this, lower lip trembling before she gives a quick nod. Zoey is about to tell her something else about the daughter she hasn't seen in over fifteen years, but the scream of an engine cuts through the night to their left and they all turn as one.

A large truck with armored plating attached to its sides races between the nearest two rows of tents in the direction of the midway. In the brief flash that it's there and gone, Zoey sees the maniacal grimace of Presto Preston's face in the driver's window, the shape of his wife beside him.

"It's them!" she says even as Nell's cry of rage overshadows her voice. She begins to turn to Ian, but he's already on the move, rifle coming off his shoulder from where it was slung in a fluid motion. He runs around the side of the coliseum in the direction the Prestons headed as the truck's engine roars louder, followed by the crash of steel rending.

The truck shoots out into the open field beyond the trade in a shower of sparks, a section of fence hanging from its bed. The entire group shifts as one to get a better view of the vehicle as it bumps over a deep rut and begins to accelerate into the night.

A gunshot booms from the other side of the arena. Zoey would know the sound of Ian's rifle anywhere.

The shrinking shape of the truck slews to the side, brake lights flaring, flayed tire tread flying. Then it is on two wheels, the undercarriage appearing and disappearing twice as the vehicle rolls and comes to a stop on its side.

Deep quiet rushes back in.

Eli helps Zoey to a nearby crate and eases her down onto it before running in the direction that Ian went. Nell starts to follow them but Chelsea grasps her arm.

"Wait. They'll bring them back if they're alive."

Zoey watches the edge of the arena, the Prestons' overturned truck out of her line of sight. After several agonizing minutes Ian appears, rifle ready in his hands, and behind him are the Prestons, Eli training his weapon on their backs.

Elliot, wearing a mask of disdain, glances at each of them in turn. Sasha stares past them into the night, chin up, a line of blood trickling from her hairline.

"Looks like she hit her head and his right hand's banged up," Eli says. "Otherwise they're full of piss and vinegar."

Nell walks forward, stopping a pace in front of Elliot.

"You," he says, voice dripping with venom. "You did this. You ruined our troupe. Killed all those innocent men."

"They weren't innocent," Nell says. "The innocent ones left years ago."

"You miserable, ungrateful bitch. We took you in, fed you, clothed you, and this is how you repay us?"

"You kidnapped me and sold my child!" Nell screams into his face. "Kept me here for fifteen years and used me, just like you use everyone, to hide how you failed your own daughter."

It's like she's struck both of them. Elliot blinks, jaw slackening, while Sasha lets out a small gasp.

"We were good to her," Elliot says, voice weak. "We were good parents."

"You don't even know the meaning of the word."

Elliot's face contorts, and in the split second before he raises his arm, Zoey sees what he's about to do. She yells a warning and tries to stand, but her legs refuse to hold her and she falls.

Elliot's right hand opens, and it isn't injured at all, only camouflaged with blood. There is a clicking within his sleeve as he brings his arm level with Nell's head and a small pistol shoots into the palm of his hand.

Nell slaps the gun to the side as he fires, the round pinging off the shipping container, and steps hard into the punch she throws.

The blow catches Elliot in the mouth and he stumbles back, feet tangling before he goes down, sitting stunned at her feet.

Sasha makes a mewling sound and drops to the ground beside him, cradling his head as Elliot spits a tooth onto the ground.

"Give me a gun," Nell says. No one moves. She looks around at them. "Give me a gun with two bullets."

Zoey catches Merrill's eye and waits, watching his reaction. After a long pause he nods. "Eli?"

Eli steps forward, drawing his pistol. With a deft motion he ejects the magazine and thumbs out all of the shells but one before snapping it back in place and handing it to Nell. "There's one in the chamber already," he says quietly.

Nell gazes at the gun, turning it over slowly before extending it toward the couple sitting on the ground.

"You stole years of my life. You killed Robbie. You took my daughter from me." Her voice trembles and Zoey sees the gun's barrel wobble. "You deserve much worse than what I'm going to give you. Now get up."

Everyone looks surprised, but none more so than the Prestons. They hesitate before rising to their feet. "Over there. Move," Nell says, gesturing toward the women's shipping container. She walks them to the open doors of the steel box and they stop before it, turning back to her. "Get in."

"What are you doing?" Elliot says.

"Get in."

The old man stares at her for a drawn second and Zoey's sure he's going to rush her and that Nell will kill him, but then she realizes her initial impression was right. He is only an old man now, hollow and alone but for his wife who stands beside him, both of them looking pitiful and small in their suit and gown. A king and queen without crown or court.

Slowly they turn and shuffle into the container. Nell closes the doors with a resounding clang and locks them in. She begins to turn away but stops, emotion warring in her features, and in that moment she reminds Zoey so much of Rita it's as if her friend is standing before her.

Nell turns and strides to the side of the container, pushing the pistol through a hole cut at head height. The weapon thumps the padded floor inside.

"There's a bullet for each of you. Like I said, it's much better than you deserve." Nell walks away, coming to Zoey's side and helping her to her feet.

The group moves as one through the abandoned midway, silent as a grave now, no pervading smells other than the faint scent of smoke coasting through on a cool wind. Rain begins to fall, flecked with ice. It patters a machine-gun drumbeat on all of the tents and roofs.

And Zoey can't be sure if it's her imagination or not, but as they're loading up the vehicle and preparing to depart, she thinks she hears the faint sound of a single gunshot followed by another.

47

Riverbend comes into view in the late afternoon of the third day.

They took their time traveling back, stopping often and setting up camp well before dark each night. They paused in the area of the Quiverfull community, taking half a day to locate one of the families Travis and Anniel had mentioned. After some deliberation, the women from the shipping container, along with two of the men, decided to stay. One of the young boys of the host family had fallen ill two days prior, cementing the decision for James, who began tending to him immediately.

When the time came to say goodbye, Zoey walked down the long drive to the highway, leaving behind the thanks she knew would be uttered to her, the embraces of the grateful women and men. Instead she gazed across the brown and gray hills to the south where a bank of clouds dropped snow in wide columns of white until the ASV had rumbled to a halt beside her.

Now she sits next to Merrill in the front passenger seat, the rattle of his makeshift prosthetic a constant background noise. Tia had cobbled it together for him using the tools they'd brought and a broken leaf spring they'd found in a desolate gas station garage on the side of the highway the first day. His first attempt at walking on it had drawn giggles from everyone in the group along with a few colorful insults tossed in by Eli. When Merrill had attempted to chase him down, the leg partially folded, leaving him in a heap to even more raucous laughter. Even Zoey had smiled.

She reaches up and rubs the short wisps of hair covering her scalp, her hands creeping there whenever she's not paying attention. It was too badly scorched to simply trim. The first time they'd stopped on the road she'd borrowed scissors from Chelsea and cut off the tangled and singed locks, the scent of the burning mountain coming from the hair almost making her sick.

The road bends before them, the missile installation coming into view, and the sight both thrills and frightens her. A cold anticipation begins to grow as they roll through the open gate and the rest of their group bursts from the entrance, Seamus barking wildly and jumping among them. Zoey glances back to where Nell perches on the edge of the bench, body rigid, eyes wide as she watches the people outside the ASV wave and yell.

Merrill pulls to a stop and Ian opens the doors, nearly getting floored by Seamus as he leaps into his arms.

"I missed you too, old boy!" He laughs, turning his face away from the dog's energetic tongue.

They file out of the ASV, Zoey second to last as she passes Nell, who still sits on the bench, gazing at her hands, which she rubs continuously.

"Are you okay?" she asks the other woman.

Nell glances up at her, then out the door, where the group is reuniting with hugs and loud exclamations. "My hands are shaking." A smile pulls at her lips and is gone instantly. "I dreamed of this for years, every hour of every day. But then I made myself stop because it was going to kill me." She fingers the bandage around her wrist. "Now I'm here and I'm absolutely terrified."

Zoey crouches beside her, back screaming its protest but she ignores it. "It's going to be all right. Follow me."

"Zoey! Get out here!" Sherell calls. "You hate us that much you gotta hide?"

She turns, stepping down out of the vehicle. Seamus is the first to greet her, his big paws slapping into her hands and causing her to stagger.

"Seamus! Down!" Ian says, and the dog drops, nuzzling her leg instead. She pets him and looks up as Sherell approaches her.

"What happened to your hair?"

Zoey smiles. "I needed a change."

"Well, you got it. Now we just have to change it back." The group laughs and Sherell sobers. "You made it."

"We did."

"We've missed you," Sherell says, hugging her.

Next is Newton, who leans in awkwardly but doesn't move to embrace her. She grins and hugs him. "Thank you for keeping them safe," she says in his ear. He smiles, blushing slightly before moving away.

Rita steps past Newton. She looks Zoey up and down, eyebrows furrowing. "You look like utter hell."

"Thank you."

"Was it worth it?"

The question makes her throat tighten and she can't reply. Rita frowns and hugs her quickly before stepping away. "Come inside, I was just making a soup that didn't smell too bad."

"It smells terrible," Sherell says.

"Then you can starve for all I care."

"It would be preferable compared with eating your cooking." Sherell smiles evilly and Rita shakes her head as she starts to turn away.

"Rita," Zoey says. The other woman stops. "There's someone else here we'd like to meet." She steps aside and nods to Nell, who comes slowly down the steps. She gazes at Rita, mouth partially open, jaw trembling. Rita stares at her for a moment before frowning at Zoey. She takes a stride toward Nell, her hand coming up as if to shake, but freezes, eyes locking on the scar above Nell's eyebrow.

Already Nell's crying. She takes a tentative step forward, as if the ground might collapse beneath her, and reaches out a hand, gently grazing Rita's hair.

"You're real," she whispers. "And so beautiful."

Rita's face is flushed, her green eyes flickering all over her mother's face. She shakes her head. "You're dead."

"I thought I was."

Rita brings her hand up to Nell's brow, fingers tracing the scar there. Then it's as if an invisible barrier breaks. Rita crashes into her mother and Nell sobs, pressing her face into her daughter's shoulder.

Zoey swallows the solid lump in her throat. The two women rock from side to side before Nell finally holds Rita at arm's length before embracing her again, a burst of happy laughter coming from her.

"Do you want to try my soup?" Rita says in a tear-choked voice.

Nell laughs again. "I'd love to."

They walk, arm in arm, toward the installation, and the rest of the group follows, a buoyancy carrying them toward the doors. Zoey stands for a moment by herself, letting the cold air flow around her before joining the others inside.

♦ ♦ ♦

The soup isn't nearly as bad as Sherell let on, and they all eat like they've been without food for days. Zoey watches them around the table, their voices intermingling in a steady buzz of conversation. There are smiles, jokes, passing of food and drink. Seamus barks at Ian's plate, begging for a scrap as Ian glances in mock disapproval at Sherell and Rita, who look away, both grinning at one another.

Family.

It's the only word for them.

But she's not part of it. Not anymore.

Zoey pushes several chunks of canned meat around in her soup as Merrill and Chelsea both rise to their feet. Merrill taps his spoon on the table, and when the room quiets, he wraps an arm around Chelsea.

"We have some news," he says, beaming. "Chelsea and I are going to be parents."

There is a beat of silence before the entire room erupts in cheers, everyone popping out of their seats to rush to the couple. Zoey rises as well, slower, and studies Merrill's and Chelsea's faces.

They are ecstatic.

Floating.

Chelsea glows with an internal light she noticed on the road along with how close and protectively Merrill hovered near her the entire trip. Now it makes sense.

But it's only another reason why she'll have to leave them all.

Eli puts an arm around Tia's shoulders. "Thrilled to say we're expecting too." Everyone laughs. Tia shoves him away and he nearly trips over a chair, which only makes them all laugh harder.

"You can expect an ass kicking if you touch me again," Tia says, but she's smiling.

Zoey makes her way to Merrill and Chelsea who gaze at her, both of them already registering something wrong in her expression. She's about to tell them congratulations when there's a quiet knock at the door.

Lyle stands in the hallway, sheepish eyes glancing up from the floor to the group. "I'm sorry to interrupt."

"What do you mean?" Merrill says. "You're not interrupting. Come in, eat."

Lyle rubs his hands together. "Um, no. I guess I'm not hungry." His gaze locks on Zoey and he swallows. "I did it. It's ready."

There is a part of her that was hoping the programmer wouldn't be able to accomplish the task. Maybe it's the sane part of her, the part that's still soft, that contains sympathy. That's human.

But the darkness surges at his words, a cold, seething brutality without a shred of empathy. It is the same thing that forced her onward to the ski run, that thought of the plan to burn the men alive in the first place, that pulled the flare gun's trigger.

Zoey nods. "Okay."

She moves past everyone toward the hall, feeling their eyes on her, and it's only when she's at the door that Merrill's voice stops her.

"Zoey. What's he talking about? What's ready?"

She sighs, looking down the hallway. "Come with me and I'll show you."

48

Lyle's workroom smells like the man hasn't left it since they departed.

She supposes that might be a very accurate assumption, given the rumpled look of his clothes and bloodshot eyes.

Lyle seems to become self-aware as he sits at the desk, the group pouring in behind Zoey. "Sorry it's a bit stuffy in here. Haven't gotten out much lately." He licks his lips, hesitating, and Zoey is about to address everyone, tell those who have no idea what's going on the truth, when Lyle continues. "Before you explain, there's something else you all should know. While I was working down here, gathering information on NOA, I happened upon several dormant e-mail accounts. Most were unimportant, fledgling researchers or understaff to the board of directors, but there was one account that caught my eye." He shifts in his seat as if uncomfortable. "It was registered to 'Shepherd,' no other identification, but it was protected well. Whoever created it didn't want someone stumbling on to it."

"What did it say?"

Lyle swallows. "I'm sure you're all familiar with the atomic device that was detonated near Washington, D.C.? The one that killed the president and all those people?"

"Of course," Tia says.

"This Shepherd was the one that planned it."

"Wait, you said you were accessing NOA's files, right?" Eli says.

"Yes."

"But the bomb was used by the rebels."

"That's correct. But it was never explained how the rebels knew the exact location of the president or how the bomb was brought in close enough to kill him."

A dawning horror makes the hairs on the back of Zoey's neck straighten. "You're saying someone inside NOA told the rebels where and how to get through the government's defenses? How to kill all those people?"

"That's exactly what I'm saying."

The stunned silence is dense within the room, like all the air has been sucked from it.

"There are dozens of e-mails from Shepherd to an account that I can only guess was a rebel leader at the time," Lyle continues. "It's all here."

"Those bastards," Tia says. "Why the hell would they do it?"

"Maybe it was a spy?" Rita says. "Someone from the rebels' side who worked for NOA."

Lyle shakes his head. "I don't think so. The account was too well hidden and protected for someone with lower clearance within the organization, and the information was definitely classified. This was top level for sure. Someone who had power."

Zoey turns and slowly looks from Sherell to Rita, seeing the same answer in their eyes. "The Director." They both nod after a moment. "It was him."

"But what purpose would it serve? Why would the Director want to destroy NOA? Without the government's protection, they would've been sitting ducks," Merrill says.

They are all quiet again, no answers to his question.

"What were you talking about before? What's ready?" Chelsea asks after a time.

Lyle turns his head to Zoey and she takes a breath.

Here it is. The moment when I show them who I really am.

"Before we left I asked Lyle if he could hack into the installation's mainframe and gain access to the missile guidance systems. He said he'd try, and he succeeded."

"Okay. So what?" Eli says.

"I want to fire a missile at the ARC to destroy it."

It's like she's slapped them all. Everyone besides Rita and Sherell look shell-shocked.

"Zoey. No," Merrill finally says. "You can't. That's . . ."

"It's what? Barbaric? Horrible? Murder?" She nods. "I know. But if we don't do something, they're going to keep coming. You remember what the spy said who told us about this place; they were searching for us, for other girls. As long as they're able to, they'll keep coming. The three of us will never be able to live without looking over our shoulders, wondering when the Redeyes will show up in the middle of the night to bring us back there. I don't want to spend the rest of my life in fear."

She trembles, with dread or rage, she doesn't know. She gazes at each of them in turn, looking for support or admonishment. But what she sees is worse.

Sadness.

Disappointment.

Disgust.

"I know what you're thinking. That I'm a monster. And you're right. Someone who was anything else wouldn't have done the things I have. So that's why after the missile is launched I'm going to leave."

There are several quick inhalations and glances among them.

"Zoey, let's think about this for a while," Ian says. "This isn't something to be decided rashly."

"I have thought about it. And this is the only way we'll ever be safe from them."

"You can't," Merrill says. His eyes are needlepoints of sorrow, as if he's lost her already. Maybe he has. "Don't. Please."

She can only meet his gaze for a second before looking away. If she were to hold it any longer she knows she wouldn't proceed. Knows the rearing void would lose its grip and wither away like ash in the wind.

She turns to Lyle. "Is it ready?"

"Yes. I used the dam's location to pinpoint the ARC." He punches in several keys and the screen before him changes, a complex series of numbers and letters filling columns. At the bottom the cursor blinks beside a single word.

Execute.

"All you have to do is hit the return key," he says quietly, and rises from his chair before retreating to the farthest wall.

Zoey reaches out a shaking hand, index finger extending toward the key. Its letters spell all kinds of words as her eyes become unfocused.

Monster.

Heartless.

Soulless.

Murderer.

She remembers Terra's broken eyes, a despair so deep it seemed bottomless.

Her finger hovers over the key.

Touches it.

The air in the room thickens. It chokes her. Can she do this? Kill all those people? Kill them like a god from above without preamble or explanation?

Her finger puts pressure on the key.

She closes her eyes.

And steps away from the computer, drawing her hand back and wiping it on her pant leg as if she's touched something filthy.

Without looking up she pushes through the group, noticing Merrill isn't among them. They let her pass and then she is out in the hall, picking up speed. Up the stairs and running down the corridor toward the last blaze of sunlight on the western horizon. She needs fresh air, needs to be away from the confining walls, away from what she almost did.

Zoey bursts through the doors outside, drawing in great lungfuls of air. She stands bent over, hands on her knees, but the earth begins to spin under her feet and she straightens, spine throwing a lance of pain outward in all directions. It's enough to clear away the floating black dots in her vision.

And she sees the sunset.

Sees it for what feels like the very first time.

It is a half crown of radiance that's eclipsing behind the hills to the west, the colors so honest and pure she can't look away from it. Cool air caresses the top of her head but she can't move, not even to shiver. The sun fades slowly into a deeper shade of red, arms of purple stretching up as if it only wishes to hold on to the twilight, to keep the dark at bay for another minute.

The scuff of a boot brings her attention up to the lookout tower where Merrill leans against a support, attention on the sunset as well. She moves to the structure and climbs the ladder, hoisting herself onto the covered platform.

He glances at her as she steps up beside him but doesn't say anything. They watch the sun's glow bruise the skyline until the entire land beyond the installation is gilded in the strange half-light hue.

"I couldn't do it," she says finally.

"Why?"

"Because then I would've been just like them. Taking or sparing life as they see fit. Never giving us a choice. And I don't want to be them. But I'm afraid I already am."

Merrill turns to her, face in half shadow. "You're not a monster."

"I am."

"You're not."

"Did you see . . . did you see the mountain? The bodies?" She can barely get herself to form the words over the raging inside her. Half savagely reveling in the blood-soaked justice, the other half weeping for who she's become. "Did you see them burn? I can still s-smell them . . . hear them screaming." Her voice rises, getting thinner, weaker. "The missiles, when you told me about them, I thought I was the one down there, the one that stopped the other, worse missiles from coming to destroy everything. But I'm not. I'm the worse one. I killed all those men . . ."

And her voice fails her in the sob that escapes in a choked panic. But then Merrill is there, wrapping his arms around her, voice low and soothing as the dam within her finally splits wide.

It is a rush of toxicity in the form of tears and wordless sounds, animalistic and filled with anguish so thick she thinks she'll drown in it. She cries into Merrill's coat, grasping at him, terrified that if she loses her grip she'll fall into the void that's finally opened and will never be able to find herself again.

It is an eternity before the hurricane of her emotion becomes a slowing tide. Her tears begin to dry in salty rivers on her face, the wind cooling them.

She's weak, empty, nothing left inside to give. She's bled it all out.

Merrill holds her at arm's length, only a faint outline in the closing dark.

"You saved us. You saved the women and men who would've been tortured and killed. And by not pushing that button, you saved yourself."

She wants to cry again, to fold up and be carried away into sleep. Sleep for a thousand years.

"Thank you," she whispers. He squeezes her shoulders. And she leans into him again. "I love you."

There is a brief silence before she feels his chest hitch against her. "Love you too."

For the first time in many weeks she feels safe. Not only from the threats they face, but from herself. And now she knows which one is the more dangerous of the two.

"I didn't get to tell you congratulations," she says, finally stepping back from him to wipe her eyes.

"Thank you."

"You both look so happy."

"We are. We're terrified, but we are."

"You don't have to worry. Chelsea's going to be a great mother. And you're already a great father."

He laughs but it is strangled with emotion.

She's about to tell him something, some memory of Meeka that never fails to make her laugh, but stops.

A sound comes from the road outside the gate. Footsteps.

Close and coming closer. A figure appears out of the gloom.

"Eli, Tia, Ian. We have company at the gate," Merrill whispers into the small radio resting on the railing. The response is a double click, a signal that they're coming.

Zoey draws her handgun, checks the safety.

The figure pauses at the gate before crossing the boundary. As the person draws even with the tower, three spears of light cut through the dark.

Zoey moves at the same time Merrill does, both of them aiming down at the man that stands frozen in the others' flashlight beams.

"Stop right there!" Eli yells, approaching. Ian and Tia flank him, shining their lights across the surrounding compound. Eli stops before the man and presses his gun barrel into his chest. "Who are you?"

"My name's Jefferson," he croaks, his voice sounding rusty from disuse. "I'm so glad I found you people."

"Get down on the ground," Eli says. Jefferson complies, taking off the small satchel that's strung over one shoulder. In the glare of Eli's flashlight Zoey sees that the man's right arm ends in a blunted hook.

When Jefferson is on the ground, Eli searches him, kicking his bag out of reach. Stepping back, he opens the bag, dumping its contents free.

A fork and knife fall out along with a few scraps of dried meat.

A yellowed bottle of water.

Two shirts and a pair of worn pants.

Eli glances up at Merrill. "He's clean."

Zoey moves to the ladder and descends with Merrill close behind. When they reach the ground Jefferson is sitting up, slowly gathering his things.

"Who are you traveling with?" Merrill asks, rifle still pointed at the man's head.

"Nobody. I'm alone. I'm from Wyoming, traveling west. Trying to get to Seattle."

"What's your business there?"

"Work. Food. There's nothing in my town anymore. People are starving. Getting desperate."

Tia walks past them to the gate, rolling it shut and locking it. She shines her light across the sage and blanketing dark beyond the fence before returning.

Zoey watches Jefferson pack his things into the bag, coat sleeve riding up over his missing arm. The hook is set in the center of a carved chunk of wood that extends out of sight into his jacket. He uses the hook clumsily to drag the bottle of water to him before placing it inside the satchel.

Jefferson glances around them, eyes hovering on Zoey the longest.

"I'll ask you again," Merrill says, stepping closer, putting the muzzle of his rifle against Jefferson's head. "Are you alone?"

"Y-y-yes. I'm alone. I'm starving. Please. I've been rationing my water. All I want is some food if you can spare it."

Merrill glances at Eli who shrugs.

"Get up."

Jefferson rises slowly, dragging his bag up with him. "Thank you. You have no idea how grateful I am."

Eli, Ian, and Tia begin walking toward the installation, lights still sweeping the fences to either side as Jefferson falls in behind them. Merrill and Zoey follow.

"I've been walking for God knows how long," Jefferson says. "Found some food a few days ago in a house but it was spoiled. Only had the venison left from when I took off three weeks ago." He laughs and it is high and out of sorts. A madman's cackle. "I'm getting pretty sick of venison."

Zoey's hand tightens on her pistol and throws a look at Merrill who frowns. "What town did you say you were from?"

Jefferson continues to walk toward the installation, his good hand ferreting nervously at his hook. "Missoula. Hated to leave, but didn't really have a choice."

Merrill stops, eyes shining in the flashlight's glow. "Jefferson?"

The man pauses, turning back, hand still touching the hook.

"Missoula is in Montana, not Wyoming."

Jefferson's face flattens, the smile he's worn since standing up gone. His hand works at the hook and in the second before his grin returns, Zoey's breath catches in her lungs.

"You're right. I never was very good at geography."

Everything slows.

Jefferson yanks on the hook and it pops free, leaving a dark hole in the wood.

Eli yells something, already bringing his rifle up, but Jefferson is faster.

He aims his stump at Eli and a blast of fire comes from the end.

Eli crumples, a burst from his rifle kicking up a line of dirt.

Even as Zoey raises her pistol, Jefferson trains the prosthetic that isn't a prosthetic on her.

There's a flash and something leaps from the hole, flying toward her.

Merrill steps in its path, jerking as the object hits him.

He stumbles and falls, yanking out the six-inch dart that protrudes from his shoulder.

Zoey fires and Jefferson crumples to his knees, his good hand clutching his abdomen.

Tia steps up behind him as he tries to rise and brings the butt of her rifle down on his skull.

He folds over, blood leaking from a hole above his navel.

"What the fuck!" Tia yells. "What the fuck!"

Zoey kneels beside Merrill as he pushes himself up. "Are you okay?"

"Yeah. It's a tranquilizer of some kind. Powerful. Can already feel it."

She reaches to his front pocket, yanking the radio free. "Chelsea, come outside quick. Bring your bag." Tia's enraged scream cuts her off from saying anything more and Zoey stands, hurrying to where the older woman crouches beside Ian over Eli.

A dark stain spreads across Eli's right side. His face is covered in sweat, breaths coming quickly between teeth locked tight.

"Oh no," she says, eyes meeting his.

"S'all right," he says. "Just a scratch."

Zoey feels her legs threaten to give out, back thudding with pain. She returns to where Jefferson lies.

She raises her foot and smashes her heel down on the fake arm resting in the dirt.

Wood splinters.

Inside is some kind of steel carousel with hollowed-out chambers. Several contain darts like the one that struck Merrill, while others hold the shine of live rounds.

She kicks the smashed arm and it detaches, flying several feet away.

Zoey nudges Jefferson over onto his back and presses her gun to his chin as his eyes flutter open.

"Who are you?"

He smiles. "Hello Zoey." Weakness floods her body. "Almost didn't recognize you without your hair." He coughs, a bead of blood appearing at the corner of his mouth. "Had to get close and be sure."

"How do you know who I am?"

"Have a message for you. About the keystone."

Her heart freezes, then double-times its already frantic pace. "What did you say?"

"The keystone," Jefferson wheezes, more blood dribbling through his fingers to the ground.

Memories of the night she escaped from the ARC batter her.

Running through the corridors.

Finding Terra.

Terra's drug-induced words.

They need the keystone. They're looking for it. They need it.

"What is it?" She grasps Jefferson's collar and shakes the glazed look from his eyes. "What's the keystone?"

His bloodied grin widens. "You are."

The night spins around her.

All sense of direction vanishes.

There is no up or down, left or right. Only Jefferson's bleeding smile.

"What are you talking about?"

"You're the one they've been looking for. You can bring back the human race."

"No."

Jefferson nods, head scraping the dirt. "Yes."

"You're lying." She shakes him again.

"I'm not. And—" His voice chokes into a cough that speckles the front of his coat with blood. "—they wanted me to tell you . . ."

"What?"

"Tell you . . . you have a daughter."

She sits back from him, the hand holding her pistol loosening.

She can't breathe, can't make sense of anything she's hearing or seeing.

Tia crying, leaning over Eli as Chelsea drops to his side.

Sherell and Rita framed in the light of the doorway, unmoving as if in stasis.

Merrill trying to sit up but sinking down into the dirt again.

And the words that keep rebounding in her mind.

A daughter.

You have a daughter.

She finally manages to shake her head. "No. It's not possible."

"You saw the lab, the tanks," he hisses. "You know it is."

"How? When?"

"Your last visit to the infirmary. After you were Tasered."

She has a sudden recollection of the pain she'd felt after waking in the infirmary bed, down deep inside her, almost like menstruation cramps, but different.

"They took an egg. Fertilized it. She's almost nine months old." Jefferson coughs again, and this time it is filled with wetness. He blinks rapidly as if something is in his eyes.

"Who?" she hears herself say. "Who's the father?" But she already knows. And as Jefferson's lips form the name, she feels something break inside her.

"Lee."

She shakes her head, jaw trembling, and points the gun at his face. "You're lying."

"I'm not. P-proof in the arm." He nods toward the broken prosthetic. "They wanted me to tell you s-something else too . . ."

She waits, still aiming at him, the entire world having quieted to a dull hush of static around her.

"They said to come home." Jefferson laughs and grimaces, his chuckle becoming a choking strangle that spurts more blood over his chin. His back flexes, lifting off the ground before dropping, and with a final wheeze, he falls still.

Sporadic patches of sound come to Zoey and fade.

Yells.

Sobs.

Her erratic heartbeat.

She kneels by the disembodied arm, rolling it over.

Opposite the cylinders is a small transparent vial, double-walled glass or plastic of some kind. It's cold to the touch. She pries it from an attachment, bringing it up into the light.

The inside is crimson.

Blood.

When she looks back down she sees a black square set in behind the vial's attachment. She touches it and the square unclips and falls into her hand. She turns it over numbly, faintly registering that it looks like some of the things strewn across the desk in Lyle's room.

As she's about to stand something inside the arm catches her eye. It's there and gone in an instant and she's not sure she saw it at all until it repeats itself.

A flash of red.

Again.

Again.

Faster now.

She picks up the arm and turns it enough to peer inside its length.

A red dot set into the interior blinks at an increasing speed until it's fluttering so quickly it appears constant.

And then it is constant.

She feels her brow crinkle, an instinct sliding snakelike through her mind, beginning as a whisper but gradually rising to a shout.

Run.

Run.

Run.

Runrunrunrunrunrunrun.

She stands, legs revolting, back crying out, every sense igniting as a sound comes across the hills from the north. Distant at first but growing more powerful by the second.

And she would know it anywhere because she's heard it both in real life and countless times in her nightmares.

The chop of helicopter rotors.

Zoey spins toward the group, fear nearly strangling her mute.

"They're coming."

ACKNOWLEDGMENTS

With each book I write it seems I have more and more people to thank. And really, I think that's a very good thing.

Thanks so much to my wife, Jade. You keep me on track more than any other person. I would've lost my way a long time ago without you. Huge thanks to my editors Kjersti Egerdahl and Jacque Ben-Zekry for helping me carve the book into its true shape. Many thanks to Sarah Shaw, Dennelle Catlett, Jeff Belle, Mikyla Bruder, and the rest of the team at Thomas & Mercer; you are all appreciated more than you know. Thanks to Caitlin Alexander for the phenomenal developmental edit. Big thanks to David Zarkower at the University of Minnesota who helped me with the science that I built the fiction upon. And thank you to all the readers who have followed Zoey this far. I truly hope you accompany her all the way to the end.

ABOUT THE AUTHOR

 Joe Hart was born and raised in northern Minnesota. Having dedicated himself to writing horror and thriller fiction since the age of nine, he is now the author of eight novels that include *The River Is Dark*, *Lineage*, and *EverFall*. *The Final Trade* is book two in the highly acclaimed Dominion Trilogy, which once again showcases Hart's knack for creating breathtaking, futuristic thrillers.

When not writing, he enjoys reading, exercising, exploring the great outdoors, and watching movies with his family. For more information on his upcoming novels and access to his blog, visit www.joehartbooks.com.